BLUE INTO THE RIP

HOME IS 400 YEARS AWAY

K.J.HERITAGE

SYGASM

Copyright © K.J.Heritage 2017

Blue Into The Rip

Published 2017 by Sygasm

All rights reserved.

Cover design: *K.J.Heritage*

No parts of this publication may be reproduced, stored in retrieval system, beamed via Black Hole to other dimensions, copied in any form or by any means, electronic, mechanical, photocopying, recording or otherwise transmitted without written permission from the publisher except for the use of brief quotations in a book review. You must not circulate this book in any format.

Travelling back in time to publish this book before its official publication date is strictly prohibited.

All characters in this publication are fictitious and any resemblance to persons, living, dead, undead, existing in parallel dimensions or those having reached a higher plane to exist as intelligent corporeal gases, smells or colours, is purely coincidental.

ISBN-13: 978-1548108625
ISBN-10: 1548108626

http://kjheritage.com

For Suzanne and all the fish

"Fast paced, intriguing, thought provoking, character driven science fiction"
The Written Universe

"It captivated me from the beginning and held me prisoner to the end!"
The Author Alliance

"Hands-down one of the most creative YA books I've read in a long time"
Reading For Pleasure

"An amazing read and K.J.Heritage's writing is superb and unique"
Girl In The Woods

CONTENTS

Prologue 7
RIPPED 9
SATURN 49
ACADEMY 99
STORMS 185
SPACE 233
NUB 281
Epilogue: *The Drop* 339

A Note from the Author 341
About *K.J.Heritage* 341
Acknowledgements 342
Also by *K.J.Heritage* 343
Contact the author 344

Blue Into The Rip

PROLOGUE

BLUE, the colour of the sky, of the ocean, of certain stars and planets and the hue of the bluest eyes you have ever seen.

The lanky teenager, nicknamed *Blue* after those same eyes, ran headlong through the trees. He criss-crossed the rising ground, creating a perfect search pattern in the near total blackness. Dim light from a thin crescent moon was nothing more than flecks of ghostly white poking through the packed canopy. Gloomy, mysterious and dangerous, the crag upon which sat Dooleys Wood dominated the local landscape like the giant head of an old grizzled ape.

Blue rushed closer to the steep ridge, studying every bush, every tree and every broken twig for any sign of Annie, his missing young sister. Far below, muffled by the trees, Eddi and Newt, his hippy parents, shouted for the lost toddler.

A tiny footprint on the ground, glowing through the thin foliage. He crouched, knees cracking.

When he was about thirteen, Blue had discovered this ability to see in the dark, to see heat as others would see colour. He'd kept quiet about it of course, like he'd kept quiet about most things in his life. Night vision wasn't normal, that much was true; but what was normal about the freak boy?

The print shimmered, fading before his eyes.

Annie?

At its side—an adult footprint. Both led along the trail to the cliff edge.

If these are Annie's footprints, then who do the other footprints belong to?

He shuddered.

The annoying ankle-biter is missing, I'm her brother, I lost her and I'm the weird-looking lanky loser who's gonna find her.

He followed the fading tracks, running beside the steep, rocky path. He stopped at a sharp precipice, a frown creasing his smooth, brown, oddly shaped face. A tiny figure lay on the path, legs and arms twisted as if broken.

Jonesy. Annie's raggedy doll. She would never leave the miserable, moth-eaten plaything behind, unless—

"Boo-Boo, I'm scared!" His sister's voice coming from the bushes.

"Annie," he croaked from a hoarse throat. He turned towards that delightful sound, but his world exploded into white and all became blackness.

RIPPED

Blue Into The Rip

2454

Two huge unmistakable eyes opened in the forest dimness. A sore head and aching muscles—as if he'd been dragged behind a car while unconscious. His long thin legs twisted underneath him; his face covered in dust and his blonde-brown afro full of leaves and dirt. Blue wondered if the same car had ran him over a few times to make sure of the job.

He raised himself onto unsteady feet.

Ouch. A sizable and sore lump on the side of his head.

Jonesy lay on the ground. Thoughts stabbed at him: his young sister, lost on the forested hill of Dooleys Wood, the frantic search for her with his parents, Eddi and Newt, her voice calling to him.

"Annie!" Blue picked up the doll, clutching the toy to his chest. "Eddi! Newt!"

Perhaps they found Annie while I was unconscious and took her home. They wouldn't leave me behind—would they? And who or what hit me on the head?

A loud crack somewhere behind him. Blue wheeled around—

A shadow melting into the dark?

"Eddi?" Still no answer. "Newt?" He reached into his jeans pocket for the Cat, his lethal slingshot.

Ack. I must have dropped it somewhere or someone stole it.

Blue jogged downhill, stumbling through dense thickets and overgrown bushes.

I'll go back home. Eddi and Newt will be waiting for me with Annie. Sure.

A peculiar quiet surrounded him, only broken by the buzz and whine of insects and the far off lapping of water. *What's happened to the noise of the town? Cars, buses and lorries? The shouts and shrieks of drunken nutters out on a typical Friday night? The trees of Dooleys Wood seemed different. Thicker. More leaves and stuff. The air hot and humid. Sticky.*

The clogging vegetation ended and he fell, slipping, into heavy mud and water.

"What the—?"

Wet and confused, Blue tried to fathom the inky blackness.

No lights anywhere. Zilch.

He grabbed a handful of sludge and threw it as far as he could. A deep plop.

A shoreline? That makes no sense. The nearest lake is miles away. And besides, I'm half-way up a hill.

Splash! Something heavy slithering into water. A half-submerged log floated towards him. He took a nervous step backwards and fell over, feet trapped by more mud. The watery log-thing reached the shore and, like a dim shadow taking terrifying form from the blackest dreams, raised itself on to stubby legs.

No log, but a bloody crocodile!

"What the hell!" he shouted as sudden crocodile facts popped into his mind.

Upper and lower jaw the same width. Teeth exposed in an interlocking pattern even when closed. Prefers brackish water. Long narrow jaws suitable for eating fish and mammals. More aggressive, bigger and faster than the alligator.

Blue shook his head to stop the never-ending stream of crocodile information—

Has salt secreting glands in its mouth.

—and wrenched a leg free, managing to crab-walk backwards.

The glistening croc' snapped efficient jaws at him. "Get lost!" A stink of foul rotting filled his nostrils.

Lays around eighty eggs in clutches buried in underground caverns.

Reptile teeth caught the fabric of his jeans, ripping them.

A lighter olive colour than its American cousin, the alligator.

Blue threw himself backwards, kicking the crocodile on the snout.

"In your scaly face!"

He found his feet and ran, thrashing at the tangled undergrowth. A gnarled tree blocked his way, its lowest limbs high above, a greasy trunk offering no obvious foot or handholds. Something lumbered with purpose behind him.

Can attack at lightning speed.

He flung himself outstretched to grab at the lowermost branches, swinging to perch below the wood's canopy. Eyes darting, searching for his pursuer, Blue was surprised at how high he jumped. Of the many facts flooding his brain, one dominated all others—

Cannot climb trees.

—but he clambered on, climbing as far as the thinning branches would allow, shouting at the black impassive night.

None of this makes any sense. I'm still in Dooleys Wood, but it's changed. The thick undergrowth, the maddening insects, the waters and their well-dangerous inhabitants.

He glanced at the stars, relieved to spot the same constellations. Orion the Hunter, Ursa Major, Taurus and the others.

There must be a rational reason for all this. A flood then, some disaster? Perhaps some zoo animals escaped?

Implausible, but what other explanation was there? Blue's thoughts stopped dead in their tracks.

The Pole Star.

What should've been a single point of light used for centuries by mariners and explorers to find north and passage home was now part of a cluster of multi-coloured stars moving in slow rhythm.

Where did they come from?

A wave of exhaustion washed over him, a deep body shudder rattling his teeth.

An age later, a mechanical whir broke the endless silence.

A helicopter?

Blue followed the sound and found a light growing in the distance. The helicopter came closer, illuminating Dooleys Wood. An island surrounded by water. Gone was the town and its suburbs.

They are somehow drowned, including, he guessed with a swallow, my own dumb-looking house.

Electricity pylons poked from the murky waters like the masts of sunken ships.

The helicopter flew closer, coming for him. The light meant one thing and one thing only.

Rescue.

He cast his mind back to this morning at the abandoned playground where this weird stuff started.

the past...
YESTERDAY

BLUE took the Cat from his pocket and smiled. The smooth metal fitted his hand with the ease of regular use. The Catapult was a toy for kids in the 50s and *Dennis the Menace* but nothing was old-fashioned about its effectiveness. The slingshot was deadly.

Apart from a cute black and white dog, the long-abandoned playground was empty. The summer sun, low in the azure vault of the sky, warmed even at this early hour.

Far better to be here than slumming at the Gruesome Institution.

School and Blue did not get on; he'd given up on the place about the same time the teachers gave up on him.

The playground, wildlife and weeds taking over from the rusted iron, was a haven from the horrors of education. All the dents and chipped concrete from hours of practice with the Cat made this place a home from home.

Smashing stuff up did that.

Other than the occasional car roaring along the A-Road on the far side of a towering weed-infested wall, the playground was tranquil.

Bunking off school meant a whole heap of trouble.

So what?

Here, everything made sense. No nagging, paranoid parents, no exasperated teachers and, best of all, no kids glaring at the freak boy.

Only Annie accepts me for who I am, but she's two years old.

Blue was peeved at his sister's arrival and how his parents doted on her whilst giving him the elbow. She turned into a shy, but adorable and loving child. The complete opposite of Blue. He had been a loud, confident, brash youngster convinced of his own importance due to his remarkable appearance.

My big blue eyes of da-da-doom.

His eyes had been the feature he was the most proud of—crashingly blue and awesome, framed by his golden brown skin and shaggy blonde afro. In the last few years, they had changed horribly. By age fifteen, the sapphire circle of his iris became gigantic. The one cool thing about him, his nickname, *Blue*, now haunted him like a sick joke.

Typical.

With his changing looks, his youthful confidence deserted him. School became a trial. He preferred zonking off to his inner-world rather than listening to boring lessons. Teachers hated him for his intelligence; they gave him detention, forced him to complete schoolwork he knew backwards and made snide comments about his eyes.

I'm a mega-brain and teachers: 'etymologically-challenged amoebas'. They'd have to look that one up, sure.

The ragged dog scratched itself and yawned, wagging a hopeful tail at him. Blue waved and the mongrel bounded over weeds, concrete and abandoned oil drums to arrive in a flustered over-excited ball of fur.

"You feeling the lonesome, huh? You and me bo—"

The screech of tyres, an almighty bang and a car exploded through the playground wall like a high-velocity bullet through a watermelon. Blue dived, masonry flying everywhere. The out-of-control hatchback flew past him to land on its roof in a smashed, smoking heap. A *whoosh*, and the vehicle caught fire. Unharmed,

Blue crawled onto to shaky legs.

The dog was similarly lucky, running away with a yelp.

Blue hurried over to find an unconscious woman and a boy of Annie's age trapped inside the car. Doors crushed, jammed into the bent chassis. Flames licked, growing in strength. A burning, terrifying, life-and-death spectacle playing out right in front of him.

I've gotta get them out.

He grabbed an old pole, using it as a lever. The rusted metal bent like a straw. He smashed it against the windows, but the toughened glass did not break. The fire found a pool of petrol and exploded, the heat pushing Blue back. Inside the overturned vehicle, the child screamed, a repeated shriek scything into his mind.

They're going to die and I can't help them…

BLACKOUT.

…The sound of sobbing brought Blue back to his senses. He was holding the crying boy, tiny arms linked around his neck, legs locked on to his chest. The young woman lay on the ground, her eyes flickering as if in a daze. She was eighteen, maybe nineteen. Too young to be a mum. Too young to be driving that fast. Apart from a cut to her forehead, she appeared uninjured. The car was a ruin of smashed smoking metal. The chassis lay in two pieces, the doors missing. Totally mashed.

An Australian accent with an air of incredulity, "You okay, fella?" A young man with long bleached hair and 'Oh Crap!' printed on his T-Shirt stood at Blue's side. His eyes danced in shock. "What a wreck. I thought you'd all kicked it for sure. Debris everywhere. Crikey!"

"You got… you got them out?"

"Me? No, I was passing in my truck and saw the smoke and the wall all massacred. Must have been one humdinger of an impact. There's a door lying in the road about half a click away. God knows how it got there."

"Then who rescued them? The doors were jammed, not ripped off." Blue put the boy down next to his mother. "I'd better go,"

"I dunno about that, you could be hurt. I called the emergency services. They'll be here any minute." He held up a mobile phone.

Blue stared at the destroyed car and pushed him aside. "No way."

"Dude, wait for the police."

"I gotta get home."

THE GOTE

The flying machine hovered over the island of Dooleys Wood, a single blade whining in the balmy air.

Various memorised schematics of helicopters popped into Blue's mind (he remembered everything). The aircraft was like no other helicopter. A hybrid. Directional jet engines slung on either side of the fuselage. A traditional helicopter was heavy, noisy and mechanical, challenging gravity for a place in the sky. This machine had no such contest. A bronze-coloured, flitting hummingbird.

The crack of breaking branches and a substantial brass-like ladder crashed through the canopy.

"Hey, Gote." A youthful voice over a tinny speaker. "Get on board."

Blue stared open-mouthed.

"Do you want rescuing or not?"

Rescue.

The word jarred him into action and Blue grabbed hold of the ladder. The whine of the helicopter increased in volume. A few seconds later, Blue dangled hundreds of feet above an inland sea of never-ending water. A plain white logo of the Earth within a ring adorned the fuselage. The artist had done a sloppy job on the continents; the outlines were unrecognisable. Underneath, three words, *OUR VERY EARTH*. Undaunted by the height, Blue pulled himself into the golden-skinned craft.

The ladder retracted and the door slid shut with a hiss.

"Ready for the ride of your life, Gote?" came a boyish voice over the speaker. "Time to light the fuse. *Wahoo!*"

With a deafening roar of engines and prop, quick acceleration flung Blue against the back wall of the compartment.

A second voice, "Way to go, Singh."

Blue found a seat by the window and tried to control his shaking.

Who are these guys? They are enjoying this too much. Don't they realise I'm freaking out here? Something way-out has happened to Dooleys Wood, to perhaps the Earth. Either that or I've gone mental-lentil.

A short flight, maybe ten minutes.

"We're coming in to land, folks. Everyone brace."

The copter descended with frightening speed, the circled *H* of a helipad flew towards them.

We're going to crash!

Powerful jets kicked in and the aircraft touched down with a gentle thud.

"Another top-notch landing from Second-Lieutenant Singh."

"Not too bad for an *old man.*"

"You don't forget Basic Training, that's a fact."

"I'd never pass on an opportunity to pilot one of these crates again."

"Hey, if they need some top-notch trainers to teach those green-assed cadets how to fly, I think we should put in for it."

"I'm cool with that, Buddy."

A draught of hot, salty, decaying seaweed and the door whirred open. A rough hand yanked Blue down to the landing pad. It belonged to a boy of seventeen or eighteen with bright youthful features, greenish-blue eyes and a reddened complexion. He was as tall as Blue and thickset, with a curly-blonde head too big even for his huge physique. A lopsided grin leered at him.

The flying machine sat in an enclosed, imposing courtyard.

Impressive architecture on every side. The far buildings had partly collapsed, algae-covered masonry strewn haphazardly. Exposed rooms, stone stairwells and empty, foliage-filled openings lay naked to the elements. Harsh white lights dazzled from a jury-rigged wire. Massive insects crashed into the uncovered bulbs, eager to bash out their senseless lives. Other lamps blazed higgledy-piggledy from windows close to the helipad.

"No funny business, otherwise you'll have me to deal with, dig?" said the boy.

There was a warm vibe about him, despite the harshness of his words. Blue did a double-take. *He is the same height as me and I'm a stupid six-foot seven.*

At his side stood a wiry youth. He was by no means short—six foot, possibly six foot two, but both Blue and the blonde boy towered over him. A curious mixture of Hispanic and Asian, he possessed a skinny intensity of jerky movements and odd twitches. He preened at a poor excuse for moustache—more fluff than anything else—and shook his head in disdain.

"They spent all those years searching for these guys and this is what they end up with?" he said shrugging. "No wonder the future gave up on them."

Both boys were dressed in immaculate white uniforms—all-in-one romper suits made of a polyester-like material.

"Is this a rescue?" said Blue.

"Hey, we haven't even introduced ourselves." The blonde boy let loose his grip and saluted. "I'm Private Ammers."

The other youth, his thick black hair shining blue under the severe lights, pointed at a single bar on his collar. "See this? I'm *Second-Lieutenant* Singh."

Ammers winked at Blue. "And don't we know it."

Singh ignored him. "This shows I'm an officer of Our Very Earth, known to us simple soldiers as Earth Corps, okay?"

'Our Very Earth.' *The same words written on the jet-helicopter thing.*

Ammers grabbed him again. "Earth Corps is watching over you now. Listen up, Bucko. You're what we call a *Gote* and even though that's a whole box of rocks, you've lucked out big time. You get me?"

An officer? He's no older than Ammers. Just a kid. "What are you talking about? Where am I? Where are you taking me and what is a Gote?"

Compassion crossed Ammer's face. "Don't worry yourself, Son. This is B-Pal, the temporary HQ."

Singh patted Blue on the back. "Congrats, Buddy, you've made the program." They smiled knowingly.

"Are there any more survivors?"

They glanced at each other and grimaced. "Best save those kind of questions for the commander."

All this gung-ho militaristic macho crap was doing Blue's head in. *Their accents didn't come from anywhere he recognized and their uniforms? So white as to be dazzling. Like they are a part of some ill-conceived and poorly acted advert for militaristic washing powder. Why wouldn't they answer my question?*

Singh, urged him forward. "C'mon, Buddy-boy."

"I'm Blue."

Ammers chuckled. "No need to get depressed."

They're taking the piss out of me? What's wrong with them?

Ammers pushed Blue through an unimportant looking entrance into a neglected and fusty smelling corridor and stopped at a plain door. The thickset blonde boy ushered him inside. "In you go. S'okay. Take a gander."

Bare except for a table and two chairs. Cracked plaster hastily painted. Another doorway nailed shut with planks that had half-fallen off. A single brilliant bulb hung from a wire, bleaching the room into unforgiving alabaster. More stupid insects buzzed and hummed.

"The sooner we can get you into some whites, the better. You sure are a mess, Buddy."

Whites. Military uniform worn for dress occasions.

Blue's shredded jeans and trainers were caked in mud and Jonesy did nothing for his machismo.

They want to dress me up?

An older man arrived. Ammers and Singh jumped to attention. "Commander Dauntless, sir!"

Dauntless did not as much enter the room as take control of it. In his forties and well-muscled, this new visitor brought with him an air of controlled threat. Brown-skinned with a face that held a confusing mixture of racial traits, his shaved head shone in the harsh light of the cramped, neglected room. A deep burn cut across his nose, upon which sat tinted sunglasses. "Who have we here?"

"His name is Blue, sir."

The commander nodded. Ammers and Singh saluted and left. The man closed the door, his scarred face pulling into a menacing smile.

Blue liked things a lot more with the door open.

Dauntless sat opposite Blue and raised an eyebrow in apparent amusement. "You're scared. Don't be."

"You gonna tell me where, what and how? Cos I've had enough of this. You get me?"

"I get you, alright. I'm Commander Dauntless, the year is twenty-four fifty-four and if you want an easy life, you'll learn to call me *sir.*"

the past...
BOO-BOO

STILL woozy from his experience at the playground and wincing at the many sirens and rushing police cars, Blue made his way home. The image of the mashed car refused to go away. He'd read about blackouts, but nothing involving ripping vehicles apart.

Unless I'd had some 'Incredible Hulk' moment. What did that guy say? 'A door flung half a mile away'? Did I do that?

Blackouts. A period of unconsciousness or memory loss. They can occur as a result of brain damage or disorders affecting brain function, such as epilepsy. Can be caused by a recent traumatic event.

Bloody hell.

He turned into his dead-end street and opened the gate to the tip his parents called home. Blue loved his isolated excuse for a house, the warped walls and the broken back of its lop-sided, thatched roof. Round portal-like windows stared from under the rotting eaves like the watchful stare of some mangy owl.

Annie burst through the front door, a whirling dervish of tiny arms and legs. All blonde curls and excited green eyes. Not as dark as him, her almost white skin contained a hint of amber. She piled into Blue. "Boo-Boo home! Boo-Boo home!" she shrieked in excitement. "Jonesy missed you, Boo-Boo," she said, holding up her much-loved rag dolly.

"I've missed Jonesy too—and my blonde annoyance." Blue carried the two-year-old into the house, kicking a loose potato lying on the floor and grimacing at the ever-present stench of vegetables in various states of decomposition. Annie chatted loudly in his ear.

Eddi, his father, poked his head into the gloomy hallway of paint-peeling walls and spidery shadows. Tall, but crooked from a life spent digging and lifting, with straggly brown hair tied into a ponytail, he held a cup of herbal tea that he jutted at Blue in accusation. "What on earth are you doing home?" he said in his relaxed deep tones. "You should be at school. And you're covered in muck and dust." Intense emerald eyes frowned from a wrinkled brown face that like Blue's, held a mixture of racial traits.

Blue groaned inside, putting Annie down. The toddler hugged Blue's leg. *Dad has no idea about my life, of hating every nanosecond at school and being freak boy Number-One.*

"We allow you plenty of freedoms, but you can't keep drawing attention to yourself. You'll get a bad name."

'Getting a bad name at school' was a relentless theme of his father's.

Eddi took another sip of his disgusting brew and wagged a mud-stained finger in Blue's direction. "We didn't want to send you there, but home-tutoring involved all kinds of bureaucracy."

"Don't you get it? School is a daily hell. I don't fit in there. No one likes me." Despite being a melting pot of races, white, African, Hispanic, European, Asian, Mediterranean, South American, Arabic—whatever—Blue, although brown-skinned like his father and foreign in origin, did not resemble any of them. His features were odd. Rounded and pointy in all the wrong places.

Eddi stroked his curly black goatee beard. "Popularity is not everything, Blue. But you must keep a low profile, okay? Very soon, before you even realise, you'll be sixteen, and you can come and work with us on the Allotment full-time. But for now, you've gotta buckle under."

Stuck at home, covered in mud with the Mental-Lentils in a house held-together by cobwebs, was the last place Blue wanted to be. Eddi and Newt shunned electricity, didn't own a telephone, never answered the door and rarely went out. Neither of them worked a normal job. Instead, they spent all their time in *The Allotment*—what everyone else called a *back garden*. Here, they kept a few pigs, a hen run and a goat, growing vegetables most of the year round, the majority of which they stored in different places around their insect-infested homestead. Other than a sense of privacy and self-importance and a passion for science, the world outside their house held no interest.

Except… for the newspapers.

It's not the future I want for myself. No way.

As to what else he might do, Blue had no idea.

Newt appeared at Eddi's side, an eternal hippy in an oversized pink woollen bonnet from which long hair spilled in a riot of grey and blonde, her pale white skin, sun-reddened and peeling. She was taller than her husband, and older. Her coat was a home-knitted green thing hanging as low as her down-turned wellies. She stood knock-kneed, with an expression pinched into a frown, wearing an ancient pair of once-yellow marigold gloves. "What are *you* doing here?" She fingered an ever-present purple-black crystal on a silver chain around her neck.

Eddi pointed his mug at Blue. "Playing truant again."

Newt shook her head in disappointment. "Now what have we told y—"

"Boo-Boo home! Boo-Boo home!" shouted Annie, stomping her red boots on the crumbling floor.

Newt's thin lips turned downwards. "Don't call him that, Annie. We've discussed this before. His name in this house is *John*, okay?"

"John Smiiiith!"

"Good girl."

For someone with such a hodgepodge of ethnic traits—even Blue couldn't pinpoint his unusual blend of ancestry—Blue's real name John Smith was as ding-a-ling out there as it was normal.

Weren't they hippies? They should've named me *River* or *Storm* or even—*Blue*.

The toddler grabbed at the Cat with sticky fingers. "Annie take the caddapull, Boo-Boo? Put in the Cubby?"

Blue pulled the catapult from her reach. "No-one calls me John. Not even the teachers. I'm Blue to everybody. Can you guess why?"

"You're eyes are beautiful."

"Don't be daft. My googly eyes freak everyone out."

Newt pulled a practiced smile. "Be proud of them."

"You don't think I'm some kind of mutant then?"

His father appeared taken aback. "A mutant? Of course not."

Newt's smile disappeared. "You're like any other fifteen year old, confused and worried about everything. Me and Eddi think you're beautiful."

Blue gave Newt a withering look. "Yeah, right."

Eddi took a sip of his smelly brew. "We have more important matters at hand, as you know full well. You, young man, should be at school."

I'm not going back, no way. After bunking off, they'd only give me extra detention. "I've free periods all day, so I might as well stay here," he lied.

Eddi glanced at Newt. "Okay, just this once. But you have to promise me to attend every sesh?"

"They're called lessons." Blue headed upstairs.

"You're not off the hook. Go get changed and come help on the Allotment."

DAUNTLESS

The commander was one of the most immaculate people Blue had ever met. More than well dressed, his entire appearance radiated discipline, efficiency and a close-cropped intensity verging on style fanaticism. He wore the familiar all white uniform except for three gold bands and a star on each cuff. The same replicated in badges on his collar.

Dauntless lit a cigarette-sized cigar with a flip-topped golden lighter smelling of petrol and took a deep drag. He appeared in no hurry to talk, yet there was something urgent about his unhurriedness that convinced Blue it was time to get a move on.

"Where am I and what's happened to my parents, my sister? What caused the flood and the crocodile?"

Commander Dauntless leaned forward, his enormous shoulder muscles stretching the fabric of his well-fitting vest, the floorboards creaking. "You always address me as *sir*. You get me?"

"Huh?" Blue answered.

Dauntless clipped Blue on his temple. "Like I said, you call me, *sir*."

"You hit me?"

Another clip.

"Hey! That's against the law."

"The law? Don't make me laugh. You'll soon come to realise

I am the only law here. I can slap you around the face all night long until you start to show me some respect. Do we understand each other?"

"You want me to call you *sir;* otherwise you are gonna beat up on me, yeah?"

Dauntless took a long drag on his cigar. "I said: *do we understand each other?"*

"Yes, sir." Blue dodged a clip to the temple that did not come.

"Good. We are going to get along fine."

"This is all a bit mental."

Dauntless raised an eyebrow.

"Huh?"

Another painful clip to the side of his head. The commander smiled, he was enjoying himself.

Blue wasn't enjoying himself and pushed back welling tears. "Just tell me about the flood, sir. What's happened?"

"A flood? Yes, but that's not the full story. There's no easy way to break this to you and it won't help to soften the blow." Dauntless wiped a thin sheen of sweat from his shaved head. "You have heard of time-travel?"

Iciness crept over Blue. "Of course, sir." He'd seen how Dooleys Wood had changed, the water everywhere, the strange helicopter and, of course, the crocodile. Time-travel? Impossible, stupid. Yet? "You're not bloody telling me I'm in the future...are you, sir?"

"Don't you swear at me, Boy, or you'll feel the back of my hand."

"Sorry, sir. But time-travel? No way." As the words left his mouth, Blue remembered the predictions of Global Warming. *Everything makes dreadful sense.*

"You know I'm right."

"Do I, sir?" Blue's mind cast back to the odd collection of stars he'd seen in the night sky, earlier.

"Go on."

"All those new stars above the North Pole, sir?"

Dauntless blew thick cigar smoke from the ruin of his nose.

"*The Charles Darwin* and satellites, Earth's main spacestation and staging post. If you are lucky, you might spend some time on board."

Blue dreaded the next question most of all. "Where are my parents?"

The commander lifted an eyebrow again and Blue took the hint.

"—sir."

"Truth is they're not your parents, Blue. Never were."

"Of course they're my parents. Of course, sir."

"Despite your emotional attachment to them, you are wrong. No, no. They are what some in this time call *dangerous terrorists.*"

Terrorist. A person or persons employing terror or terrorism as a political weapon.

The word *terrorists* bounced inside Blue's head, screaming dementedly. *Terrorists!* it yelled. *Terrorists!* it warbled. **TERRORISTS!** it shouted in bold capitals with a significant underline.

Blue ground his teeth. "You were trying to capture my parents, sir?"

"Me? No. SEARCH brought you here."

Blue's brain had no room for any more words, especially for one that Dauntless emphasised with an ugly threat. "SEARCH? Who are they and who the hell are you?" he barked, ready for the clip that he managed to dodge.

Commander Dauntless twisted Blue's index finger. "I think you'll find the pain-learning response is a strong one."

Blue grunted in agony.

The commander let go and once again clipped him across the temple. "In your time, the use of corporal punishment was dismissed with disastrous results. We live in a more enlightened age. I fear our regime will come as a shock to you. Here, you respect your peers and your elders. Here, if you don't do what we tell you, when we tell you, you suffer the consequences. A simple and effective system you will learn to value." He flicked his lighter again and shrugged. "I'm sorry you've been lied to.

Your parents are criminals and you an innocent victim of their crimes."

Newt and Eddi not my mum and dad, but terrorists? That's Bonkers with a capital *B*.

"And Annie, she's gone as well, sir?"

"Annie?"

"My sister, sir, I lost her in Dooleys Wood."

"Was she your age?"

"A toddler, sir. I need to know she's okay."

Dauntless rubbed his chin and pondered for a few seconds. "Blue—she died hundreds of years ago."

They can't all be gone, be dead? Yet what the commander was telling him rang with dreadful truth. His mind rocked backwards and forwards. Blue's emotional denial hit the hard rock of stark rationality.

Dauntless sat back, enjoying another satisfying puff on his cigar. "You've plenty to deal with, granted."

Dazed and somewhat confused, Blue lurched back into the now. He took some deep breaths and regained his cool, lifting his head to stare once again into the impassive face of the commander.

"Good. You are physically and mentally stronger than you realised. Feeling better?"

Blue nodded. He didn't want to accept the harsh reality of Commander Dauntless and this flooded future, but he could not ignore his own terrible logic. "I can return home and save her, sir? Can't I?"

"I'm glad you've accepted where you are. A mature response. In answer to your question—I would be lying if I said going back was impossible."

"You mean you could send me home, if you wanted?"

Dauntless forgot to clip him. "Technically, we can open the rip and send you back to your time, but in reality, no, that will never happen."

A bright warm light switched on inside of Blue, illuminating the deeper recesses of his mind, driving away his confusion, doubt and worry. For the first time in his life, he experienced a real sense of purpose. *There is a way back. And I will move all the stars and planets to get home.* An awkward pause. "Now I'm here, in the future—what do you want of me?" Blue asked nervously.

"You ever noticed you were—how shall I say—different?"

Blue didn't even need to think about the answer. "Everything was way off with me and my family, sir. Way off."

"You were more intelligent? Stronger, fitter, taller?"

"I suppose so, sir."

"And you call yourself 'Blue', am I right?"

"Yes, sir."

"Named after those eyes?"

Blue reddened. "I'm the freak boy, sir. That's what everyone thinks, anyways."

Dauntless leaned forward, examining first one eye and then the other. "That particular enhancement is rare. You noticed how you have advanced night and heat vision?"

How does he know about that? "Er…yes…sir." *I'll never forget the twin sets of glowing footprints in Dooleys Wood.*

Dauntless shrugged. "I've only a few minutes before I jag out of here. Let me summarise. The year is 2454. You must face the fact that your so-called family and friends died over four hundred years ago. You left them all behind when you travelled forward in time. You need to make a new start, here in the future."

Blue shook his head.

"You've had a difficult experience. I apologise for the irony, but only *time* will help. Give yourself time, Blue and I will make it my personal duty to keep you busy while you get yourself back together. Your life won't be easy." He paused. "Congratulations, Cadet Blue, you are now a cadet of the Earth Corps Academy."

the past...

NEWSPAPER HOUR

THE afternoon spent on the Allotment passed without incident. The physical work took Blue's mind off the car accident and his blackout. When the reddening sun faded towards the horizon, he, Annie and his parents made their way back indoors. They sat in the depressing potato-filled kitchen. Eddi put on another pot of his herbal tea whilst Newt, who never rested, lit the candles on an ancient wax-covered candelabra and began to knit.

"Annie give Boo-Boo a lubby-hug?"

"Not now." Blue had given Annie enough lubby-hugs today to last her a lifetime. Did she sense something?

Her face dropped.

"Come here then, you annoying little turd."

Annie beamed. Blue lifted her into his arms. "Liddle turd. Liddle turd turd, turd."

Newt frowned at him.

"I lub you Boo-Boo."

"Thanks Annie, now bugger off." He put her down. "You need to get ready for din-dins—I mean dinner."

A knock at the front door. Eddi frowned at Newt. "Again? Why do they keep knocking?"

"Well how about this for an idea; why don't you go ask

them?" said Blue.

"We never answer the door to strangers, young man. A house rule."

Blue sighed, lit a candle and went upstairs to change.

A short while later, Blue emerged back into the kitchen and sat at the table. Dinner was another family ritual. They wouldn't be eating for ages.

No way.

First came Newspaper Hour. For a couple who had no interest in the outside world, Eddi and Newt had a never-ending appetite for news. Before every meal of the day, they would start on the newspapers (the national and local papers were delivered daily) reading them all before they went to bed.

Eddi and Newt's newspaper habit must make one humungous hole in the Amazon jungle.

He mentioned this to them once at breakfast. They said nothing, but were close-mouthed all day.

Hadn't they heard of the Internet? Weirdoes.

"Boo-Boo, Mommy. Lookie at Boo-Boo." Annie held up a copy of the local evening paper.

Blue stared agog at a photo of himself on the front-page. What the? Eddi and Newt hated photographs and never allowed school to take any pictures. That didn't stop the other kids snapping *the freak boy* with their smart phones, sending them to one another and sniggering. This was a more serious matter—his picture in the local rag. The Mental-Lentils will go—mental-lentil. Ack! Blue frantically motioned to Annie, but the irritating grass was too excited.

"Look Eddi! Lookie!" she shouted at ear-splitting volume, dropping the paper on to the table.

MYSTERY TEENAGER SAVES MOTHER AND BOY

—said the headline and an unmistakable picture of Blue.

The Aussie bloke must have taken a sneaky photo of me with

his phone. Blue was impressed. This isn't the guy I see in the mirror. Even my stupid eyes fit my face. Hey, I'm not the freak boy after all. He scanned the story below:

> A mother and her three-year-old son escaped with just minor injuries after a devastating car crash this morning at the famous accident black spot on Dooleys Road.
>
> The unnamed mother, knocked unconscious in the collision, is believed to be suffering from nothing more than a few cuts and bruises. Her son, Rooney escaped without a scratch.
>
> Police are baffled at the circumstances surrounding the accident. Debris was scattered over a wide area. They would like to talk to the mystery teenager pictured, who, they believe, helped rescue the two victims from the burning wreckage and who might hold vital clues to how this accident happened.
>
> This is not the first collision on this road. Local residents have complained to the council about-

Oh shit!

THE DEMOTION

An authoritative knock at the door and in walked a gargoyle-faced woman in her late thirties. She saluted lazily, an unmistakable edge of disrespect in her voice. "Captain Shelley reporting for Academy duty, sir."

Looks like she doesn't want to give knee to Dauntless either. I don't blame her; the man is a total dickweed.

Dauntless saluted back. "Well met, captain." He dropped the butt of his cigar to the floor and crushed it underfoot. "This is some demotion for you."

Overweight, with a double chin and an unflattering wide tyre around her waist, Shelley gave the commander a tired smile. "My demotion is of no concern to you, Commander. I can assure you that I am thrilled to be joining the Academy. How is Captain Lorenzo?"

"He'll live."

"Please pass on my good wishes and tell him I will do my best with his squad."

"Speaking of Saturn Squad, we have a new recruit. He arrived a few hours ago. One of your Gotes."

Captain Shelley glanced at Blue and gave him a good-natured wink. "Not one of *my* Gotes, Commander. I was thrown out of SEARCH when they demoted me, as you well know."

Blue's ears cocked. If SEARCH plucked me from the past, what am I doing here with Commander Cockwad in the Cadet Academy?

Dauntless didn't bat an eyelid. "This is Cadet Blue. Take him to the dorms. He has a long day ahead of him tomorrow and he will require rest." The commander stood and marched out.

Shelley motioned at Blue with a flabby arm. "A Gote, huh? That's all I need. Still, you'll find me better company than our good commander. C'mon it's late and I'm bushed."

"Why does everyone call me *Gote?*"

She led him to a grandiose double stairway, curving upwards to an imposing but rundown landing. Off-white, scuffed by the passing of many bodies and stained with mould. A corridor, doors on either side, some with patterned and rather posh veneers, others nothing more than rectangular holes rough-cut in the walls.

"This is B-Pal?"

The overweight captain ignored him again, opening a pair of doors to enter a dusky room from which came the sounds of sleeping. She switched on a torch and pushed him forward.

the past...
PHOTOS

NEWT dropped her cup on to the floor with a crash. "Oh no."

Eddi, grabbed the paper and scanned the article. "What have you done, Blue? At least they don't know your name."

"The door—they've been knocking all afternoon," said Newt, a flash of fear crossing her normally stress-free features.

"That's why I came home," Blue explained.

Eddi threw the paper down onto the table. Candles flickered crazily, mad shadows dancing across his face. "Why on Earth didn't you tell us?" His voice boomed accusingly.

"I dunno. I was freaked out."

Newt fingered the grape-sized purple stone hanging on the end of her necklace and frowned. "We told you to never let your photo be taken."

"Is that all you care about? A stupid photograph?" Blue studied the Blue in the paper. Bonkers blue eyes, yes, but warm and intense. Even the funny angles in my useless face seem to work. I'm a looker. Cool.

"You should've left well alone," said Eddi.

"What? And let those people burn alive?"

His mother sighed, shaking her head. "No, no, I suppose not. You did the right thing, but why allow your photo be taken?

After all we've said."

"Who cares anyway? Kids at school have been taking piccies of me for months with their phones. The world hasn't ended yet."

Eddi slammed his cup onto the table in an explosion of green tea. "You what?"

A short intense silence. His parents stared at one another with—

Was it panic?

"Listen, Son. Stay here and watch over Annie, okay?"

"Why?"

"We need a private chat. Then we'll talk to you. Don't go anywhere." They exited the dining room.

I'm not waiting around for an ear bashing I don't deserve. No way. Blue put his coat on. "I'm outa here."

"Annie wanna come. Put my coat on myself."

Blue said the first thing that came into his mind. "You can't. I'm going to Dooleys Wood."

"Dooleys Wood?" Annie's eyes widened with fear. "It dark, Boo-Boo and scary."

"That's why you can't come."

"Me not scared with you to look after me, Boo-Boo."

"Another time. I promise." He ran to his room, grabbed his secret stash of cash and put the Cat in his back pocket. Raised voices from Eddi and Newt's bedroom, but he was in no mind to eavesdrop.

He slid into the cool summer night. Above him, blotting out the inky sky, sat the outline of Dooleys Wood; the hill dominated the local landscape. Blue had no intention of entering the forested crag, but he had to tell Annie something.

No, I'm gonna get mashed on cheap booze, come home and chuck everywhere. Sure.

Blue headed off towards the Off-Licence, but found himself on a slow and roundabout journey to the abandoned playground. Long before he arrived, Blue spied police tickertape in the middle of a hayfield over a hundred metres from the scene of the accident. He climbed over a gate and went to investigate. The tape surrounded a car door half buried in dirt. A closer examination revealed the hinges ripped clean off.

The doors were attached to the vehicle before my blackout. What the hell did I do?

He shuddered.

Coming here was a mistake. I need to get back to Eddi and Newt, to Annie.

A short time later, Blue arrived home to a blacked out house.

No candles?

He stepped inside. Someone knocked him to the floor and held him down.

SLAP

Shelley pushed Blue to an unoccupied bed. "Here is your bunk. Make sure you get under the netting otherwise the mozzies will eat you alive."

"Mosquitoes?"

"I can't let you sleep in those filthy rags, not in my dorm. Even if we are evacuating." Her tone was adamant. "It's late and we're fusing tomorrow. First, the regulation shower." She ushered Blue through a rough opening and pulled a cord.

A bulb grew into slow life revealing a grim washroom. Rusted showerheads hung at regular intervals. A rack for towels. A large plastic tub screwed on the far wall. Cockroaches scuttled into crevices and cracks. The floor made of rough stone sloping to a central drain. No cubicles. Light reflected back into the dorm. Fifteen or so beds cramped together and covered in netting. Bodies sleeping beneath.

"Get undressed."

"Get what?"

"Put your clothes in a pile here."

Blue stood motionless, his brain in neutral.

"You take them off or I do. Your decision." She crossed her flabby arms.

This was no idle threat. Blue stripped to his boxers.

"And the rest," she ordered, nodding downwards.

"Not my unders."

She grabbed Blue's leg; overturning him to the floor; and his underpants were gone. Blue covered himself with his hands.

"Nothing I've not seen before, Cadet. Now get yourself clean." She spun a wheel on the wall and showers burst into furious life.

Intimate parts of Blue's anatomy threatened to spill everywhere, but he found his feet.

"Your clothes will have to go I'm afraid. We'll get you into some whites, pronto. Anything you want to keep, or can I burn the lot?"

"You're gonna burn my stuff?"

"Half of these things are torn to shreds anyway."

She's right, even my trainers are muddied and ripped. "I want the money and Jonesy." He pointed to Annie's rag doll, forgetting the vital function his hands were performing.

"Aren't you too old for a dolly?"

Blue tried to half tidy, half cover his bits again. "It's a keepsake, okay? Not for burning."

"Cool yourself Cadet. I'm giving you special compensation on your first night, but I'm *ma'am* to you unless I say otherwise. You get me?"

Ma'am. A shortening of the word madam. A female superior in the US military.

The same iron tone as Dauntless. "I get you, ma'am."

"You can keep your dolly, but you'll have no use for your credit sheets here."

"You're not taking my money. No way."

"'No way, ma'am. But okay." She nodded at Blue's cupped hands and sniggered. "Don't worry; I won't force you to salute."

"Thanks, ma'am."

"I will make a Level-One Heads and Beds Inspection tomorrow before we fuse. The less clutter, the more focused the cadet, is what I say. And don't worry, Mister Blue, you are an exception. Consider yourself inspected. Now get scrubbing, clean towels are on the rack." She yawned. "Can I trust you on your own?"

Blue nodded.

"You'll find a tub of Slap. Don't leave here tomorrow without a generous covering."

"Slap?"

"No more questions Cadet. Do as ordered." She waddled away.

The fact he'd been left on his own spoke volumes; Shelley didn't expect him to run off.

I need to escape, but not from this building with its mixture of decayed grandeur, whitewashed functionality and cockroaches—but from this time period. Eddi, Newt and Annie are waiting for me in the past. Regardless of how long it takes, I will return to them. I promise.

Blue showered, dried himself off and located the Slap—a tub of thick translucent disgusting gunk.

Yuck. No-way.

He padded into the poorly lit dorm to find his own, unoccupied bunk, pulled back the netting, slipped into the sheets and, determined to stay awake, fell at once into a deep sleep.

the past...

LOST

"WHO are you?"

A familiar voice close to Blue's ear. Eddi? The mental-lentil jumped me.

A match fizzled in the black and Eddi let him go. "It's John. Thank space."

Newt's face was a mask of worry in the light of another homemade candle. "Tell me you took her with you."

"You mean Annie?" Blue searched the flickering shadows for his sister. *Where is the blonde annoyance?*

Newt whimpered, her hand covering her mouth. "No."

Blue's father was as serious as Blue had ever seen him. "Did you take Annie with you?"

"I left her here. Why? Where is she?"

"We thought—*we hoped* you'd taken her with you."

"I told her I was going to Dooleys Wood," Blue spluttered. "Annie wanted to go with me."

"You mean she's gone there at night on her own?"

"She must've done."

"Didn't you see her?" said Newt on the edge of hysteria.

"No. I didn't go to Dooleys Wood. I said that to stop her coming after me. She's terrified of the place." Blue noticed packed suitcases at the bottom of the stairs. "Are you going somewhere?

And why did Eddi jump me?"

"No time to explain, Son. We must find Annie."

"Yeah, you're right. We should call the police straight away."

Newt stared deep into Eddi's eyes, a raw expression of pleading etched across her face.

Eddi shook his head. "We can't."

"Why not?" Blue asked.

"We can't, okay? You're in enough trouble already. If she went to Dooleys Wood, she won't be far away."

"How can you know that?"

"Enough discussion. We will all go and find Annie and be back here as quick as possible."

Newt clutched at her throat. "What if she didn't follow him, what if—?"

Eddi grabbed his coat and pushed Blue through the door. "Don't even think that. We'll find her, okay?"

Newt extinguished the light from the candle and the house was once again plunged into darkness.

The trees of Dooleys Wood grew in tight clumps, in other places the hill was bare; rough rock visible from beneath thin branches. Brambles, nettles and fern struggled against each other in the lean soil. Blue led Eddi and Newt along an invisible path. Eddi put his hand on Blue's shoulder. "Are you sure she came this way, Son?"

"I dunno, but I think this is the right place to be."

"You're a good boy, Blue."

As Eddi and Newt were blind in the inky night, Blue left them in the lower reaches of the wood.

"You be careful, Blue."

"I will be."

the past...
DOOLEYS WOOD

BLUE criss-crossed the rising ground, creating a perfect search pattern in the near total blackness. Dim light from a thin crescent moon was nothing more than flecks of ghostly white poking through the packed canopy. Gloomy, mysterious and dangerous, the crag upon which sat Dooleys Wood dominated the local landscape like the giant head of an old grizzled ape.

Blue rushed closer to the steep ridge, studying every bush, every tree and every broken twig for any sign of Annie, his missing young sister. Far below, muffled by the trees, Eddi and Newt, his hippy parents, distraught and panicked, shouted for the lost toddler.

A tiny footprint on the ground, glowing through thin foliage. He crouched, knees cracking. The print shimmered, fading before his eyes.

Annie?

At its side—an adult footprint. Both led along the trail to the cliff edge. Blue followed the fading tracks, running beside the steep, rocky path. He stopped at a sharp precipice, a frown creasing his smooth, brown, oddly shaped face. A tiny figure lay on the path, legs and arms twisted as if broken.

Jonesy. Annie's raggedy doll. She would never leave the miserable, moth-eaten plaything behind, unless—

"Boo-Boo, I'm scared!" His sister's voice coming from the bushes.

"Annie," he croaked from a hoarse throat. He turned towards that wonderful sound, but his world exploded into white and all became blackness.

Blue Into The Rip

SATURN

NOOBIES

Someone was shaking him roughly. Too roughly. Blue liked his sleep.

"Come on, lazybones, time to wake on up."

Blue opened his eyes aware something was not quite right. Where am I?

Two green eyes blinked back at him from the face of a plain Jane—a girl aged about fourteen—her features framed by sandy-coloured straight hair in an efficient bob lending her a comically boyish look. The girl straightened and saluted. "We are fusing at zero six hundred." Her voice was loud. Too loud for this early hour. Too loud for any hour.

Who is she?

And, like a montage from a cheap sci-fi movie, last night's events played themselves across Blue's mind. "The future? No."

A new voice, "I think the Gote remembered where he is." A boy about the same age as himself—all raven-black hair, hauntingly pale blue eyes like twin marbles, with a smirk for a smile and an air of 'I don't give a shit'—sat heavily on his bed and prodded Blue in the chest. "I'm Corvus," he said as an important announcement. "You can call me *Cadet* Corvus."

"Huh?"

Corvus, white-skinned and European with a pleasing hint of

Asian, sneered. "They're some eyes you have there, kid."

"I'm no kid."

"Of course not, you're a regular grown-up. Like the rest of us deadbeats."

The plain Jane pushed Corvus away, frowning. "What is your name?"

"I'm Blue."

"Pleased to meet you, Cadet Blue." Her voice reverberated off the bare walls and stone-floored dorm.

Blue winced.

"I'm Cadet Morgana. Let me be the first to welcome you to the Earth Corps Academy and Saturn Squad." Morgana drew herself to her full height and saluted. A well-balanced physique spoke of training and exercise. Morgana wore the same all-in-one white uniform as Ammers and Singh.

"Er…Hi."

Corvus yawned. "If there ever was a collection of deadbeats and misfits, it's Saturn. You should fit in nicely."

"Ignore him. Saturn has a long tradition of producing the Academy's best. You are in good company, Mister," said Morgana.

"Yeah. If you want to shine, Saturn is the squad. Although it's just as easy to crash and burn." Corvus grimaced at Morgana and Blue. "For some, that's gonna be easier than others."

"The Academy is Earth Corps' training school," said Morgana, her comical sandy-coloured bob bouncing in time to her eager and precise words.

A short boy poked his head between Corvus and Morgana. All serious-faced with a flock of rampant blonde hair, friendly eyes and the look of the lost about him. He clapped Corvus on the shoulder like an old friend and nodded towards Blue. "Who's the dink?" he asked with a nerdy, snaggle-toothed twang. His two front teeth crossed over each other giving him the appearance of a confused rabbit. But not ugly. His top lip stuck out.

Corvus brushed away imaginary dirt from where the boy had touched him. "Hi Parris," Corvus said with disdain. "The great commander sent us a Gote in the night. Meet Cadet Blue."

Parris' eyes widened. "A Gote? Interesting. You guys still landing in the future, huh?"

"Apparently."

"And you've joined Saturn Squad. Your choice?" The red skin of Parris' head was visible through his mad blonde hair, his blue-green eyes full of interest. "You jagged over here in the night, yeah? Have you met Dauntless?"

Corvus shrugged hopelessly behind Parris' back. "Give the noobie a break. The last thing he wants is a question and answer with the squad dork."

Noobie? *They have swallowed the news I'm some kind of time-travelling freak boy without any shock or comment. They were either seriously cool, or seriously not bothered.*

A flush of red spilled across Parris' face. "Sorry, Blue. I didn't mean to bother you. Laters?"

"Yep. Um…laters." *At least Parris seems interested, even if he does come across as a bit of a nut.*

"Brilliant." He spun around and marched away.

Corvus followed his retreating back. "What a spacehead. The guy has said zip for the last two weeks and now he's acting the excited puppy-dog. Typical of Saturn Squad, except for me, I'm the leader type. I bet you already noticed, huh?"

The thud of heavy feet and a thug of a boy—Blue guessed it was a boy—lurched into view. If an enormous slab of meat had been connected to Professor Frankenstein's machine, given life and a good kicking, the result would be something like what stood at the end of Blue's bed. Squat and squashed, as if an immense weight had flattened him, humungous muscles wrestled with one another under the tight fabric of his immaculate whites.

"Who dis?" the slab of meat grunted to Corvus in a peculiar guttural accent, pointing with a disapproving arm the size of a tree trunk. Two, pig-like eyes glowered at Blue from either side of his pug stub of a nose.

Morgana gave yet another salute. "This is Cadet Blue, a Gote from old Earth."

"Don't like Gotes."

"I'm starting to quite dislike them as well," said Blue. "And you are?"

"Keep out da way, unnerstand?" He stomped off.

Corvus whistled. "That, my friend, was Wurtz. You don't want to mess with him."

"He is also a noobie," said Morgana. "Do not take his bad attitude too personally; he has been like that with everyone."

"Well, not everyone, Morg'." Corvus grinned. "You must know he has the hots for you. I suppose where he comes from you're the looker."

"He's all—" Blue tried to gesture what he was saying by waving his hands around in front of him. "He's—"

Morgana saved him. "An off-worlder, a Berg, from one of the mining colonies in the Asteroid Belt between Mars and Jupiter. They are not famous for their social skills. The Bergs are miners specialising in H_3 amongst other rare elements and raw materials."

"H_3? You mean Helium-3?" Facts tripped into Blue's head in a steady stream.

A light non-radioactive isotope of helium with two protons and one neutron. Scarce on Earth and sought for use in nuclear fusion research. A leftover from the solar wind and the original solar nebula. Can be found upon the surface of asteroids.

Morgana continued loudly. "The Berg Empire supplies the H_3 used for Earth Corps fuse engines; including the rip. The power makes them a tad arrogant. King Wilhelm, a fair man, has put an embargo on all H_3 deliveries; until he gets his own rip machine."

Blue was lost. "I'm sure he did. Good on him."

Morgana saluted again. "You had better get ready. We don't want to be late."

"Late for what? Saluting practice perhaps?"

"No, silly. We're fusing. Breakfast is in the Hab."

Blue had no idea about *fusing* or *the Hab* but at least breakfast sounded promising. Under Morgana's excitable urging, Blue stumbled out of bed, wrapping his sheets around his waist. She stood there watching him.

"I may be a Gote, but I can dress myself, okay?"

"Oh." Morgana blushed. "I need to finish packing." Saluting her goodbye, she went back to her bunk at the far end of the dorm.

Brilliant morning sunlight shone through three towering vertical windows revealing the dormitory as squarish with a tall ceiling, which at some time had been rather posh and blingy. Whitewashed, curved eaves hinted at rich burgundy underneath. Cracked but quite splendid plasterwork, also whitewashed, surrounded the door to the showers.

This place has character—or did have.

A nudge and a girl with a flock of fiery, golden, curly hair and skin the colour of amber, flounced past Blue wearing only a towel. The most cra-mazing girl Blue had ever seen. All flashing brown eyes, flirty glances and a figure to die for. And she knew it.

"Hi there, Noobie," she said with a wink, letting the towel drop to the floor before disappearing into the showers.

Well that gets my attention. Wow!

Blue glanced around. Girls and boys in varied states of unconcerned, casual undress. Bits and pieces everywhere.

"Naked as a jaybird is the norm?"

"That's Sugar," explained a tall ginger-haired boy with rat-like auburn eyes. "And aint she just the cream of the crop? I'm Coop, her best friend. This is Ji." He put an arm around the shoulders of an Asian girl with thick black, blonde-tipped hair.

Ji pushed him away playfully. "I'm Sugar's best friend too."

"Yeah. Sugar, Coop and Ji, the Dream Team."

"Don't you mean, Sugar, Ji *and* Coop?" said Ji.

Coop shrugged. "Either way, I'd keep an eye on us three; cos we're gonna go all the way to the top."

Blue stared through the opening into the showers. "I'm… er…Cadet Blue."

"Cool name," said Coop. "It's certainly got something, hasn't it, Ji? I like it."

Ji yawned. "When's breakfast, I'm hungry."

Corvus appeared over Ji's shoulder. "Jag off will you and let the Gote get ready?"

"Sure Corv'," said Coop with a wink. "We'll leave him all to you." They slouched away, giggling.

"What a pair of droobs. Now, you better get showered and put on some Slap."

"I showered last night. Regulations apparently," said Blue.

"Fair enough, but if you start to stink, I'll go straight to Captain Lorenzo."

"Lorenzo? He's been replaced. I had a meet-and-greet with the new squad leader last night, Captain Shelley, from SEARCH."

"New captain? What happened to Lorenzo?"

"An accident. Shelley is a bit of a 'Crazy Amy'." Blue winced at the memory of the previous night's boxers moment. "She insisted on going through all my stuff."

"You were searched?"

"Yeah. She's gonna perform some kind of inspection on the rest of you this morning. I'm exempt. Lucky me. Not that I've much left to inspect. She's seen just about everything."

"A heads and beds? Space!" Corvus walked away.

Shrugging, Blue opened his locker to find three identical white uniforms, two pairs of canvas shoes and a kitbag with *CADET BLUE: SATURN* printed in rough black capitals.

They're efficient if not imaginative.

The suit was the same one-piece the other cadets wore—hooking over his feet and fastening with a row of buttons on one side. No pockets, just an extra padded area over the groin with two penny-sized badges on the collar. A single word, *SATURN* and a Saturn-shaped black pin.

Saturn was the coolest planet, sure.

The sixth planet from the Sun and the second largest planet in the Solar System. A gas giant with an average radius about nine times that of Earth. Named after the Roman god of agriculture, Saturn has a prominent ring system made of thousands of individual loops composed mostly of ice particles with a smaller amount of rocky debris and dust.

Smiling at his super cool, top end memory, Blue grabbed Jonesy and his money, ready to stow them in his kitbag and turned to find Wurtz standing next to him.

"What's dat?" grunted Wurtz, grabbing at Jonesy, his piggy eyes narrow and eager in his squashed, brute of a face.

"Hey you twacker, that's mine."

"Let me look." The Berg knocked Blue on to his bunk, pinning him with a heavy knee.

"Get off."

"Wurtz want," he growled, wrestling Jonesy from Blue's hand. "Thanks. Will help Wurtz sleep at night." Grunting with satisfaction, the Berg removed his knee and lumbered away.

The stocky frame and blonde head of Parris appeared behind Wurtz's back. "Oi! We don't steal in the Academy."

Blue rolled to his feet, clutching at his chest. "You git! Give him back, otherwise," he shouted to a few nervous laughs and giggles from the other cadets, "I'm going to make you."

The Berg ignored him.

"I said give him ba—"

Wurtz raised an enormous ham-sized fist and knocked Blue sideways. He fell on to a wooden chair, which collapsed under him. Some of the cadets were laughing, including the attractive black girl he had seen earlier.

"You total thieving scumbag!" The sudden venom in Blue's voice made everyone jump.

Morgana jogged over. "Fighting is against the Cadet Code. Wurtz? What are you doing?"

"Let the captain deal with him," said Parris.

"No way!" shouted Blue. He grabbed a leg from the broken chair and raised it above his head. Before he could smash it into Wurtz, Morgana jumped onto his back, wrapping her arm around his neck.

"What the—?" Blue gasped for breath and tried to struggle, but Morgana squeezed harder. The chair leg dropped to the floor with a clatter.

Wurtz turned and laughed. "Beaten by girl, hah."
Unable to breathe, Blue passed out.

B-PAL

A hot salty breeze blew across Blue's face. The sound of water lapping in the distance, gurgling through hollows, shingle splashing against rocks. Seagulls chattered and screeched.

"I am sorry, Cadet Blue."

Blue pushed his eyes open and found Morgana and Corvus staring at him. He was leaning on the stone posts of an eroded and unsafe balcony outside the dorm. Two impressive, fattened columns stretched up to a creaky looking lintel.

Morgana smiled apologetically. "You're back."

Blue rubbed at his throat. "Why did you stop me?"

"Wurtz might appear like a lumbering oaf, but as he is from a Two-Gee environment, his reflexes are catlike."

"I was gonna bust him up."

"You sure?" Morgana stood back, her hands on her hips, examining him. "Wurtz is one hunk of muscle and you? You're a bit on the slight side."

"Thanks."

"You need some serious body-building before even thinking about combat. You showed no technique whatsoever."

"Okay, I'm a wuss." Blue raised his hands in defeat.

"I am offering you basic advice. A good cadet always listens. Secondly—"

"Just leave me alone."

"But—"

"You heard the noobie. Scat," said Corvus.

Morgana shook her head, saluted and marched back inside.

Corvus smirked. "I think she likes you. No fighting between cadets is an Academy rule and Morgana loves the rulebook. At least she stopped Wurtz turning you into a bloody pulp."

"This is not over. Jonesy belonged—*belongs* to my sister. I have to get him back, even if the Berg git kicks my head in."

"The rag doll is important to you, yeah?"

Blue nodded.

"I'll have a word with Wurtz, okay? Maybe I can make him see sense."

"Oh… That's unexpected."

"What d'ya mean?"

"I dunno. You just don't seem the type who'd bother helping anyone out."

"Sometimes I surprise even myself."

"Thanks Corvus. To be honest, I don't really want to fight him again."

The sneer reappeared on Corvus' face. "You call that a ruck? Here—" Corvus pulled Blue to his feet.

What met Blue's eyes made him stagger backwards in shock. Intense sunlight rained down on a half-submerged city. Waves crashed between buildings that stood like waterlogged tombstones. Skyscrapers of smashed glass and twisted rusting metal jutted from the churning swell as islands of broken dreams. A familiar tower with a familiar clock face—*Big Ben*. London stared back at Blue. What was left of it. A sea-drowned cemetery for a time and a place long dead.

"You alright, Gote?"

"No, I'm not bleedin' alright. How can I be? This was London and now look at it."

"Yep, been like this for hundreds of years. Rising waters and all that. You're not gonna blub are you?"

Behind Big Ben, stood the mostly submerged London

Eye, the top-most part of the now bent and distorted wheel blackened, the once gleaming capsules broken and stained by thick bird droppings.

Corvus grimaced. "Sure is a dump."

Blue let his gaze wander over to the north bank to Piccadilly. The waterline was a collapsed muddied wasteland of concrete blocks and twisted wire. Where the waters did not reach, Blue glimpsed ruined buildings poking through dense verdant undergrowth. Avenues of jungle crisscrossed each other, following the lines of the ancient once famous streets.

"We are here for squad orientation. A couple of weeks in this damp hole to 'get to know one another'. Still, living in the Hab means we don't go Topside often. You listening to me?"

Blue stared at the balcony and at the building behind him and back at what once used to be The Mall. "Of course."

"You okay, Cadet?"

"Have you any idea of where we're standing? It's B-Pal. Don't you get it?"

"Go on," said Corvus, "spill those beans."

HEADS & BEDS

"It's only bloody Buckingham bloody Palace! I can't bel—" shouted Blue, his words drowned by a deafening roar. "What on Earth?"

Corvus grabbed Blue by the shoulders and pushed him back inside the dorm. "Hey, Veeva." He called to a beanpole of a girl with bright ginger hair in long, thick, red dreads.

She glanced up. A serious cadet with pinched eyebrows, emerald eyes like saucers and a pointed hedgehog-like demeanour.

"I've gotta find me a Berg," said Corvus dismissively. "Tell the Gote what the din is."

Blue shouted in Veeva's ear. "What's the noise?"

"Old Dinger."

"Old *what?*"

"To take us back home to the Hab. I can't wait. This place is damn clammy and the flies get everywhere. Plus Slap gives me spots." Veeva was pale, apart from where her skin had broken into red blotches. The deafening noise stooped. "So, you're a Ringer now?" Veeva shouted in the sudden quiet.

Blue nodded, aware of the groans coming from other cadets.

"Welcome to Saturn." Veeva smiled. One of those smiles you never forget. All warmth, big eyes and white teeth. Her dour features replaced with unexpected beauty.

Blue, who did not normally speak to girls, blushed.

"Here." Corvus pushed Jonesy into Blue's hands. "I had a word with Wurtz. You might be the runt of the pack, but I'm aware how you Gotes get attached to your belongings."

Veeva's serious expression returned and she stalked away. "See you, Blue."

"Bye, Veeva."

"Hey, don't I get a thank you?" said Corvus.

"Thanks Corvus. That's brilliant. The thought of having to fight that bully—"

"Wurtz didn't mean to be an ass. I think he was trying to make a point,"

"About what?"

Before Corvus answered, Captain Shelley waddled into the dorm.

"Officer on deck!"

Blue stumbled back to his bunk and tried to stand to attention like the others and was surprised by a boy at least a foot taller than the tallest cadet.

Not just tall, but elongated. An alien?

"At ease cadets. You were expecting Captain Lorenzo, but he's had a minor accident. Until he recovers I, Captain Shelley, am his replacement. And do not judge by appearances, you will find me more than capable, you get me?"

"We get you, ma'am!" they all shouted, Morgana the loudest.

"Let me introduce our newest recruit, Cadet Blue. I want you to welcome him into your ranks and help him readjust. You Ringers give the kid a bit of leeway, okay?"

"Yes, ma'am!"

"Cadet Wurtz, a Berg, joined Saturn Squad a few days ago here in B-Pal. I take it you are aware of the unfolding political situation involving the H_3 embargo? Understand that I will take any discrimination against him very seriously indeed. Good. Now before we fuse this morning, I am making a Level-One Heads and Beds inspection. See it as my way of getting to know you. Cadet Blue, you are of course excused."

Shelley took a long time chatting to her new cadets, particularly Wurtz, going-over every inch of his gear. When she had finished, Blue's stomach was rumbling.

"Leave your things here. I will get your kit bags repacked and sent to the Crater, asap," said Shelley with—

Was it irritation?

"Cadet Corvus, you are in temporary command."

Shelley saluted and left.

"I'm not leaving my kitbag," announced Blue, shouldering the bag. "No way." *They still might try to burn my money, or even worse—Jonesy.*

Corvus beamed. "Of course not. You're a Gote, which means special dispensation, just as the captain ordered."

"What are you so pleased about?"

"I'm in charge, Buddy. The cream always rises to the top."

Corvus was hiding something, Blue was sure.

"Right then, Cadets," Corvus hollered, his pale blue eyes intense and commanding. "With me!"

THE SERPENTINE ROAD

Ten minutes later, Blue found himself with the rest of the twenty or so Saturn Squad cadets tramping into the dense jungle that used to be Hyde Park, heading north towards Mayfair, his new kitbag slung over his shoulder. Part of the general exodus of Buckingham Palace.

Oppressive and blazing, the early twenty-fifth century sun tickled his scalp even through his mammoth afro. They came to a wooden pathway raised above swampy waters, following the old Serpentine Road. A simple construction of crude planks and uprights snaking amongst a rich, verdant explosion of trees and foliage. Bugs buzzed on the waterline, while creatures snaked and scurried underneath.

Blue knew London's streets, public buildings and parks backwards, but the capital was unrecognizable—an unkempt nightmare of colour and noise. Insects and mysterious animals filled the Piccadilly and Knightsbridge jungles with a riot of squeals, strange calls and chirrups.

Multi-coloured parrots squawked, bouncing on the topmost branches of vivid green trees, whilst what appeared to be huge-winged birds of prey circled above. He glimpsed primates of some kind swinging amongst the heavy canopy as well as other exotic plants and animals.

Blue wanted to explore, to stand in Piccadilly, to experience what now must be an overgrown relic of an indulgent, self-destructive cracked-out past. All those cars, buses, people—the rushing, the noise and the lights; replaced by jungle, the cacophony of birds and insects and the lapping of water.

How much remained intact? The museums and the galleries, the theatres and cinemas? Or had over four hundred years' decay eroded the once proud buildings into abandoned temples like those of ancient Greece and Egypt? One day, there would be nothing to show a city stood here at all.

Parris clapped him around the shoulders. "Hi, Blue."

"Ah, my excitable friend from the Dorm. Hello."

Parris turned to face him, walking backwards along the precarious plank way. "A bit of a change from what you remember? Yeah?" He smiled, revealing his twisted front teeth whilst gesticulating at the jungle with mad hands.

Blue was pleased to talk with the cadet. Corvus was too busy to bother with him and Veeva lost in her own thoughts. Coop, Ji and Sugar chatted to one another; as if all they needed was each other's company. Morgana had tried to teach him some combat basics, but Blue's lack of enthusiasm convinced her otherwise. "I'd think twice about taking the Tube, that's for sure."

Parris pulled a confused face.

"I've never been to London before, although I've seen maps and pictures in books and papers. It was, I dunno, busy."

"The place is still thriving."

"I suppose there has been some unforeseen immigration. Scientists in my time predicted the return of a destructive ice-age, with the world's warming currents switching off and Europe becoming a snow-covered wasteland. Yet the climate here is hotter, not cooler. What's all that about?"

"Your Gulf Stream stopped in the late twenty-first century before any of the predictions thought possible. But carbon in the atmosphere combined with serious ozone depletion meant the Earth stayed warm. Became warmer. Like this place. Earth is still warming. But there'll be a full-blown ice-age. Within a few hundred years. At least."

Parris seemed like someone who knew things, even if he did speak in short sentences spat one after another with a nerdy twang and half the words missing.

"This heat is bloody diabolical." Blue pulled at his collar, rubbing at the back of his neck. The sun scorched him.

"Met Dauntless yet?" asked Parris, still walking backwards.

"The commander? Oh yes. Me and him are tremendous buddies. Although, he did mention my parents were terrorists and dead and then beat up on me. Not a marvellous start. But other than that, he's lovely."

Parris' confused expression returned.

A wave of irritation swept over Blue. "The man is a heartless git!"

Heads turned around to stare. Sugar smiled and gave him another wink, whilst her two friends, Coop and Ji, tittered.

Parris frowned. "You okay?"

"Soz, Parris. I'm going a bit mental-lentil. Not your fault. Maybe you can tell me what the hell I'm doing in the future?"

"Long story. To do with how the time rip works. You Gotes have been arriving here and there for the last hundred years."

"—Go on."

"To snatch someone from the past using the rip is a precise calculation." Parris' eyebrows furrowed as if he was attempting the math. "They can pinpoint time and place with uncanny accuracy. Open a rip and wait for someone to be pulled in. Brilliant. Yet with all their complex physics and advanced computation, they cannot predict when the return rip will burst into the future. No idea. Could be a day or a week, a month, a year, or a century later. Rubbish. Utterly unpredictable, as your arrival confirms. In the end, the whole project was abandoned. SEARCH lost interest in you Gotes over seventy years ago. You keep on turning up though. More of an inconvenience these days than anything else."

"You're saying…SEARCH moved hell and heaven to get me here in the future and now I've arrived, they don't want me?" Is that possible? Can Earth Corps be that heartless, that scummy?

"You've not been given a full debrief?"

"Unless you mean Captain Shelley's advanced underpants removal skills, then no. Dauntless didn't say anything, other than to call him *sir*. He was quite keen on that."

"We have to call them *ma'am* and *sir* at all times. The commander is one cool customer. He runs the Academy with a rod of iron."

Cool is not the word I would use. Git is my choice. Or shithead. Is that one word or two?

The blonde boy didn't have time to answer. Wurtz, who had stopped a few feet ahead, tripped Parris over with a stubby leg. His friend landed on his back and nearly rolled into the boggy waters.

"Dats for tryin' ta help da Gote," he spat.

"Oh hi, Wurtz," said Blue wincing. "Nice to see you again or do I mean, 'Get lost you aggressive thug.'"

Wurtz squared up to him.

He wants something? A fight? What is wrong with the Berg bastud?

Veeva, her thick red dreads bouncing, ran over, followed by Corvus and the other cadets. Corvus pushed Wurtz away with the flat of his hand. "What are you doing, Wurtz?"

The Berg shrugged.

"Leave the Gote alone and get to the front of the squad. Now!"

Wurtz did not like following orders. That much was obvious, but instead of turning his ire on Corvus, he lumbered away, knocking into the lanky alienesque boy Blue had spotted earlier in the dorm. Morgana went after him. Blue guessed she was giving the Berg a much-needed ear beating.

"Who or what is the weird looking kid?" Blue asked Parris a short while later, pointing at the elongated cadet Wurtz had winded. He stalked along as if on stilts, struggling to keep in step with the squad. He appeared the exact opposite of the flattened Wurtz. "Is he—an alien?"

"The Minnie? Nah. That's just Hermans. Hey, we're here."

With the commotion caused by Wurtz, Blue had not realised they were at the end of the walkway. He descended a wooden ramp onto a muddy shoreline. Ahead was a circular concreted area the size of two football fields upon which sat a gigantic silver rocket.

"Yep, there she is," announced Parris. *"Old Dinger."*

THROWING THE BOLTS

Blue gasped. "It's like every toy rocket I've ever seen."

Three long fins swept down the spaceship's length, doubling as landing feet. A single retractable ladder stretched from an open hatchway midway along the dented and burnt silver fuselage. The engine was a smoking blackened stub at its base.

Nothing more than a manky tin tube with extra shiny bits added for show.

Two words on the rocket in bright red lettering. *Old Dinger*. Underneath and somewhat faded, was the rocket's true name: *The Erwin Schrödinger*.

Erwin Rudolf Josef Alexander Schrödinger. Nobel Prize winning physicist. Born in Vienna 1887. Famous for his interpretation of quantum mechanics using the paradox of 'Schrödinger's cat'. Opposed Nazism. Lived with two women.

Go Schrödinger!

"The idea was a fantasy in your day, but rockets are pretty much commonplace to us," said Parris.

"No, no. We had rockets too. They were, I dunno, more complicated with thousands of men and women working on all their different systems and stuff." Blue grimaced at the scorched bent metal. "Took them months to organise a take-off," he added hopefully.

"Thousands of people? The only person who looks after *Old Dinger* is the pilot. The fuse engine will last for hundreds of years. You switch on and hope."

"Perhaps I'm sounding over-cautious, but it doesn't appear that safe."

"Nothing is safe when you're in the Academy, Cadet. *The Bessler* went down a few months back. All hands lost. Pilot error they said. Or weather attack. But wondering if the old bucket of bolts is gonna stay in one piece is part of the fun."

"Sounds like a barrel of laughs. What is a weather attack?"

"Any kind of unpredictable, killing atmospheric conditions. Wasn't the climate like that back in the past? Or were you from the generation of lunatics who used to sunbathe? They wouldn't last ten minutes without Slap." Parris drew himself to sudden attention.

"Hey, if it isn't the Gote," said a familiar voice. Second-Lieutenant Singh, the young twitchy pilot from the night before, strutted over to Blue and saluted. "I said the sooner we put you into some whites the better—seems like I was right."

Blue clumsily saluted back.

"So, I'll be flying you again. You sure are one lucky cadet."

"You're flying this?" It was bad enough this teeny flew the copter last night, but for him to pilot this excuse for a rocket? Bananas.

Parris tensed at his side, "Sir. You call him, *sir.*"

Blue sighed. "You're piloting *Old Dinger*, sir?"

"That's better, Cadet. These stripes mean I'm *sir* to you at all times. Don't you forget."

"I won't, sir. Instead, I will make a concerted effort to remember that information as long as possible."

Singh ran jittery fingers over the pinned badges on Blue's collar. "They put you in Saturn, yeah? That's some squad to live up to." He lowered his voice. "Don't let the Ringers down okay? Or you'll have me on your back. Now, who's in charge here?"

"Me, sir." Corvus swaggered over, his pale-blue eyes flashing with pride.

"Excellent. Well how about joining me in the co-pilot's seat?"

"That would be cool times-two, sir."

"Good. Give me a visit when you've installed your squad." Singh ascended the ladder to disappear into the belly of the rocket.

"Always bloody Corvus," muttered Parris.

Corvus shushed him. "You heard the boss; time to get installed."

The cadets followed Singh, but Blue's feet were rooted to the ground.

Parris caught Blue's expression. "You can't stop here."

"Why not? Here is not at all bad. I've always wanted to live in London. Sure."

"We're shipping out today. Everyone in B-Pal. All ranks. They won't leave you behind. No way. They'll force you into *Old Dinger*. Kicking and screaming if they have to."

"I could find a place in Islington. A nice bedsit."

"Get on the ladder. One rung at a time. Yeah?"

"I'm not sure if—"

Parris pushed Blue forward. "The Gote's going next," he announced.

The hatch was at least one hundred and fifty feet above the ground with no safety ropes, no cage—just a thin ladder.

Don't they know about Health & Safety in this century?

Blue had no time to think, for as soon as he followed Parris, who raced away, the rest of the eager cadets climbed onto the ladder behind him. Urging him on.

"Hurry yourself Blue, or I'll make it my personal duty to ensure you miss breakfast," shouted Corvus. Same for you, Hermans." The incredibly tall boy was also having trouble with the ladder. At least Blue wasn't on his own.

Blue pushed on. After a daunting and exhausting climb, he stumbled into the claustrophobic interior.

Rundown, worn, the floors and walls scuffed by the passage of countless hundreds of bodies, the spacecraft's squalid, cramped insides did nothing to quell Blue's growing anxiety. A sharp odour of sweat and vomit slapped him in the face. "Yuck."

Parris breathed in deeply, relishing the smell. "You kinda get used to it."

Where are the flashing lights? The cool spacey stuff? "Is this some kind of test? Are you trying to see how much you can scare me? Cos I'm putting my hands up. I am bloody scared. Okay? Wussed out," said Blue. "To the max."

"Sure, you're a bit nervy. You didn't have the chance to jag into space. Not in your time. But they do this day-in and day-out. Routine."

"I'm not one hundred per cent convinced."

"It'll be fun. Hardly spaceflight at all. No. We're skimming the atmosphere. Letting the Earth do the hard work. Spinning below us. Then jagging back down when we're over the Hab."

"The Hab?" asked Blue wishing Parris would shut up about jagging.

"Your new home."

A deep clang and the sound of heavy bolts falling into place. The hatch closed behind him.

"There's no going back, Blue," said Parris with his rabbit smile.

"I can't, I've never, I—"

"Do you want make a fool of yourself? In front of the others? In front of Corvus, Veeva and Morgana? In front of Wurtz?"

"Don't you mean, *make more of a fool of myself?*"

"Like I said. These things fly every day. Safe as underground."

"In my experience underground is mostly dead and certainly not safe."

"It's like waking up. Or using the can. It's nothing. C'mon. I'll show you to your bunk." Parris grabbed a hesitant Blue and pushed him forwards through featureless rooms the colour of gun metal and no different from submarines in movies.

"Flying into space is definitively not nothing."

They ascended stairs spiralling around the inside of the fuselage. Occasional landings lurched into the rocket's interior, protected by massive hatchways. Parris guided Blue through one of these doorways into a huge ovoid compartment roughly the same width as the ship. The floor sloped to the centre before rising again at the edges. Naked bulbs illuminated grey-panelled walls held together by massive rivets. A bank of well-used lockers, paint worn and scuffed, stood adjacent to the hatchway. Rows of oddly shaped bunks—metal tubing covered in thick netting and bolted to the floor—stretched to the far side of the compartment. Saturn Squad and about fifty other military-looking personnel busied themselves, slipping between the mesh of the bunks and securely strapping in. Cocooned. Chatting to each other as if this was every day.

Wurtz hung in one of the wider bunks with thicker latticework, no doubt designed for cadets of his build.

Hermans lay next to him in another special bunk. An elongated human torpedo in tight netting. Penetrating eyes stared from under a high forehead, sitting atop a lengthy nose. Think of an extended hairless head with drawn-out features. His mouth was a slit above a prominent chin, his ears long thin flaps. Fingers twice the length of Blue's, wriggled like snakes within the mesh.

Not alien. No. A stretched human. What happened to him?

A siren sounded, making Blue jolt. The cabin lights flicked to amber, bathing everything in shades of yellow.

"Nothin' to worry about," said Parris.

"More *nothing*. There certainly is plenty of *not very much* for me to be frightened of, especially when I was thinking—this is scary as hell."

"Just the Five Minute Warning."

Blue swallowed. "We're taking off in five bloody minutes?"

"Yeah. Give me your kitbag."

"You're not touching my stuff."

"You want your pack flying around? Loose? During take-off?"

"Oh."

Parris opened one of the lockers and Blue stowed his kitbag away. "Easy."

Blue said nothing, his mouth dry.

"That," Parris pointed to one of the mesh-covered weak tubular frames, "is what we call a Gee-Bunk. Your pit. For take-off and landing." He lifted one side of the mesh and motioned for Blue to lie down.

"A Gee what?"

"I know Singh. When we fuse, we're gonna be hit with five, maybe six Gee. If you're caught away from your pit, well, let's say you'll be injured bad. Very bad. Time is running out."

"You're right. I think I need a lie down." Blue took a deep breath and entered the bunk. "I'm going to be okay, sure."

Parris fastened the netting, before getting in the pit next to him.

Another siren and the lights turned red. "Here we go. He's gonna light the fuse. Any sec—"

The growl of the engine below filled all sound. Blue tried to scream, but an elephant sat on his chest. The mesh held him, pressing into his back. He struggled to open his eyes, trying to breathe. Stars exploded across his vision. With a grunt, Blue slipped into unconsciousness.

HUGHIE & RALPH

I'm falling!

Blue woke with a start, grabbing at the tubular frame of his bunk.

"Hey. You're back." Parris unclasped his protective netting and floated over, his blonde hair sticking out like a manic dandelion. "Zero-Gee is a bit of a shock at first. But nothing to write home about."

Nauseous and disoriented, his head stuffy, any thoughts Blue had had about breakfast vanished.

The red cabin light turned to amber and to white.

"You're not looking good, cadet."

Ignoring Parris, Blue made a strenuous effort—to not move a single muscle. Up and down had disappeared. If he let go of his bunk, he would fall. But in what direction?

The other cadets released themselves and milled about, apart from Hermans who had passed out. *At least I'm not the only wuss.* Sugar, the cra-mazing girl with the amber skin, spun elegantly, her long, golden hair rampant in Zero-Gee.

"C'mon." Parris unhooked Blue from his netting and grabbed his wrist.

"I'm very happy where I am thank you very much."

"You can't miss this." Parris braced himself against the floor and launched Blue upwards.

The roof of the vast compartment flew towards Blue at tremendous speed. "No, no, no, no, no," he gasped, his arms flapping like an agitated penguin.

At the last moment, Parris somersaulted, landing on bent legs, stopping Blue crashing into the ceiling.

Blue hung onto Parris for dear life, the back of his throat burning with acid from his stomach. "I don't feel so good."

Parris smiled. "If you're gonna chuck—and believe me, being a cadet means you chuck all the time—you won't make many friends if you don't use the appropriate equipment. Here." Parris offered Blue a brown paper bag. "I thought you might need one of these."

Blue grabbed at the bag and vomited. Cheers and hoots rang out from below.

"That's why we didn't get breakfast before fusing. Saves on cleaning. You broke your duck. That's some achievement. No matter where you're from."

Blue put his face in the bag again and had a rather intense conversation with his new friends, Hughie and Ralph.

"You're not one-hundred per cent weightless—you are in a state of free-fall. Your vestibs are causing the problem. Won't take long for them to adapt. You are a son of Our Very Earth after all."

Blue grunted in between retches, his new whites soaked in sweat. "Vestib-*what?*"

"Your vestibulars. The part of your ear telling you which way is up."

The vestibular system. Based in the inner ear. Contributes to movement, sense of balance and spatial orientation. Healthy function can lead to motion sickness.

"As your up-and-down is all over the place, your vestibs are confused. Once your brain decides to ignore them, you'll be as right as re-entry."

"Thanks. Nice voiceover. Some interesting facts." Blue retched again, but his dizziness was disappearing.

"We have a few minutes. Before descent. I've something to show you."

"Can't you just leave me be. I'm happy here on the ceiling. Puking. Sure."

"You'll love it. Honest."

Parris guided a reluctant Blue through a door in the far side of the room and entered a small chamber. The blonde boy punched a button on the wall. Muted hydraulics and a circular panel on the outside of the ship slid open, revealing the blackness of space beyond and the beautiful curve of planet Earth. Parris beamed. "There she is. Terra."

Terra. The Latin name for Earth, the third planet from the sun. Home to humankind and all known life.

Earth filled the window, an awe-inspiring oasis of never-ending azure, fluffy white clouds and vast continents. Blue identified Africa and Northern Europe, their coastlines very different from what he remembered. He forgot all about vomiting and his annoyance with Parris.

"That's why I brought you here. Too brilliant to miss. I did good?"

Blue nodded. "It's aw-wonder-sum."

"She's a real beaut'. You're not too peed off with me?"

"No, I suppose not. I wouldn't have missed this for the—well, for the world."

A warning siren and the porthole closed.

"We'd better get you back in your pit."

After more help from Parris, Blue was once again installed in his Gee-Bunk. The lights turned from amber to red and a few seconds later, gravity pulled at his back. A terrific roar of engines lasting for many minutes, a heavy thump and all went quiet.

If possible, Blue was even sweatier. "We're down?"

THE SCORCHED EARTH

After retrieving his kitbag, Blue shakily headed towards the hatch. Saturn Squad, instead of making fun of him, showed him some respect at last. Parris whispered into his ear, "You did alright, Blue."

Blue's mouth tasted of vomit. "Huh?"

"Don't you realise? They were all waiting for you to freak out. Damn impressive. For a Gote. That's why I took you to an observation room. To keep your mind occupied."

"I was puking and everything."

"Who doesn't chuck? The first time?"

Blue was sure he'd made a complete knob of himself. I sounded like some drowning moose.

Morgana pulled her familiar salute. "Well done, Cadet Blue, you handled yourself admirably."

A heavy hand knocked Blue off-balance. "Good, Gote. You did good," bellowed Wurtz, pushing past. "You still a wuss tho."

Parris grimaced at Wurtz's bear-like back. "See."

"But I nose-dived? Literally. Into a sick bag. Nasty."

Parris steered Blue towards the hatchway. "No you didn't. Zero-Gee aint like riding a bike. Or flying a hellijet. Either you have it or you don't. Some recruits, even with weeks of training, can't handle themselves as well as you did." Parris offered Blue his hand.

Blue wasn't frightened of physical contact, rude or worried about catching the next superbug (he'd not had a day's sickness in his life), but the shaking hands thing never happened to him. He did nothing.

"My hand not good enough for you?"

Before Blue could apologise, Parris launched himself through the door and disappeared, sliding down the one-hundred and fifty feet of the ladder with practised ease.

Someone tapped his shoulder. "That was kinda rude of you, Blue. After what he did, you should be trying to make friends, not losing them. Get me?"

"As far as I'm concerned, the friendship thing is way too difficult for my liking," said Blue before he realised he was chatting to Sugar, the most attractive cadet in Saturn Squad and—for that matter—the hottest girl he had ever met. Her wide eyes had a smile all of their own. Blue tried to think of something to say, but was flummoxed. *Space travel I can just about manage. Girls are far scarier.*

"Now you make quick amends, Parris isn't as confident as you may assume. Till you arrived, he'd not said a word." Sugar climbed through the hatch on to the ladder and gave him a playful kiss on the cheek before sliding down to the tarmac.

Coop pushed past, holding his nose, followed by a giggling Ji. "Man, you need some mouthwash."

Blue took a deep breath, steadied himself—mostly from the kiss—and stuck his head through the door. A concentrated blast of heat and bright sunlight hit him in the face. A vast, barren, desert-like landscape, baked by the sun, dominated by an enormous artificial hill of some kind. Dry air snatched his breath and took the moisture from his sweat-sodden whites. He spotted other similar rockets and hellijets parked on a raised concrete plateau above which sand swirled and twisted in a slight breeze.

Whatever pride Blue experienced moments ago disappeared. The cadets hand-clapped him down the ladder, one rung at a time. Once on the tarmac, Blue found Parris standing on his own. "Soz about earlier."

Parris said nothing.

"No one shakes hands at school. The only physical contact they seem to enjoy is punching and kicking each other. I try and stay well clear of that, although it's fun to watch. *Dancing Twats* I call them."

"I thought the Gote would be different," said Parris. "You're just like the rest."

"'Different'? Of course I'm different. I'm four-hundred and fifty years different. Give me a break."

"I'm just tired of being treated as the squad dork."

"All this shaking hands and saluting stuff is kinda new for me, yeah? I'm sorry." He offered his hand. "Thanks Parris. I really appreciate what you did."

"You do?"

"Of course I do. I'm not used to people being friendly. I was also the freak boy at school. No one talked to me, and if they did, I usually wished they hadn't. Shake?"

Parris grabbed Blue's hand and shook. "Taking my hand is important."

"I can see that. High five?" Blue raised his palm.

Parris pulled a perplexed expression.

What was I thinking? Blue had never high-fived anyone either. He dropped his hand. "Er—where the hell are we?"

The blonde boy smiled at the sun-baked sand. "This is home."

"You mean the desert? Are we in the Sahara?"

"No." Parris furrowed his eyebrows. "The Amazon. A famous place. From years back."

The Amazon Jungle. The Lungs of Planet Earth. Produces more than twenty per cent of Earth's oxygen. Represents fifty-four per cent of the total rainforests left on Earth. Covers an area of 2.5 million square miles and nine countries.

"The Amazon?"

"Yep, 'fraid so. Things have changed since your time. The jungle lasted for thousands and thousands of years. Persisted even during the many ice-ages. Took your lot only eight decades to demolish the lot."

"You mean the bloomin' fools went and cut it down?" Blue had read about the predicted demise of this most famous of all jungles, but never believed humankind would let such a terrible thing happen.

Idiots!

"Your people were not forward thinkers. They all paid in the end. The climate is way too complicated. Even for the eggheads to understand. One thing is for sure though—if you mess with the environment, bad things start to happen. The Amazon was far more important than anyone ever imagined. The jungle is not quite dead. The occasional oasis, teeming with life, pops up when underground water makes it to the surface. The eggheads go bananas for them. They think they might be the key. To bring back the jungle. Dunno how."

Blue shook his head, not believing this barren wasteland was all that was left. "Eggheads?"

"Scientists types. The mega-brains. *Eggheads*. They live Topside. Best place for their observations." He pointed to an immense single-story structure dominating the landing field. Grey, with a roof like a white cap stretching off into the distance. "That's the Run-To. A building we have to literally *run to* when the weather gets bad. And when it gets bad? You don't want to be stuck with no cover. The Run-To doubles as a machine shed. Outpost. Labs. And temporary accommodation."

They arrived at a tank-like structure, three to four times taller than Blue. All bulbous, riveted metal painted in the same military grey as the inside of *Old Dinger*. It sat under a sun-bleached awning giving welcome shadow.

"Grey is certainly a popular colour in this century. I'm really starting to love it," said Blue to a confused Parris whose ability with sarcasm was somewhat underdeveloped.

A creak of metal and Parris opened one of many cabinets. It was full of glass flasks. Water dripped from a rusty tap. He filled one of the bottles and passed it to Blue. "A Hab rule. Topside, we all carry H_2O."

Blue sat in the welcome shade and gulped at the warm, slightly discoloured, brownish liquid. They call this water? Yack.

In the distance, more military personnel disembarked from *Old Dinger,* making their way to the Run-To. The unstable-looking rocket stood in the middle of a large burnt circle. Other similar beat-up rockets on either side. Dotted here and there, like a yard full of a child's abandoned toys, were hundreds of outlandishly designed vehicles. Some were colossal in size, others tiny in comparison. It was difficult to tell through the heat haze. Apart from a row of golden, gleaming hellijets, the future did not seem particularly blingy. Far from it. Blue sighed.

Saturn Squad milled around, pleased to be home.

"You did a good job in orbit, Cadet," said Veeva, her thick ginger dreads tied up to reveal a thin, if not attractive face.

"Yep. I blew chunks like a veteran. Apparently, this means I'm a puking success."

"You are. I took ages to get my flying legs. Sure, you hurled, but you adapted in no time. I'm still nauseous and not getting better."

Blue quickly changed the subject. "What is Earth Corps doing in this god-forsaken place? Hardly *Our Very Earth,* more like a wasteland." He stared at what used to be one of the most alive places on Earth and grimaced.

The Amazon contains a wider variety of plant and animal life than any other place on Earth. Home for one-third of all species. 2,700 million acres of the Amazon are destroyed each year. Such large-scale deforestation will have a serious impact on the world's climate.

Veeva twirled a finger in her favourite ginger dread. "As the climate went awry, a few forward thinkers were already searching for survival spaces. What they found in the Amazon Basin was ideal. Most of the survivors moved here over the next fifty years. Earth Corps formed decades later."

"Ideal? Where's the water, the fields, the crops?"

Parris snorted. "You don't think we could survive here? On

the surface? Do you? We'd burn to a crisp."

"You live underground?" Blue stumbled to his feet and took another gulp of the nasty, brackish water.

Why am I so thirsty?

"Hey, Gote, stand still," warned Wurtz.

Blue turned to face the Berg. "You got the hots for me or something? Cos I'm start—"

The Berg cut him off. "Wurtz said stand still!"

"Cadet Blue, listen to him," warned Morgana in alarm.

The other cadets stopped speaking and turned to stare at Blue with anxious faces.

"You're in trouble, Honey," trilled Sugar. "Do as he says."

Blue sighed.

"Don't move a muscle, Recruit," Corvus barked. "That's an order." Morgana stood at Corvus' side, her hand clutching her mouth.

Something heavy crawled up the back of Blue's leg—the type of crawling Blue could quite do without. He'd been knocked unconscious, transported against his will through time, roughly undressed, shocked, robbed, strangled, sent into space, sort of kissed and now a possibly nasty and dangerous creature had decided to add itself to the general sense of 'what the hell is going on'.

The *something* chattered and hissed close to his nether regions. "I've just about had enough of this."

"Quiet," Wurtz grunted.

A blow to the back of his knee and Blue crumpled face-first into the sand.

TOPSIDE

Blue opened his eyes to the sound of cheers and applause. Wurtz held a writhing sand-coloured centipede as long as his arm and half as wide. Multitudinous shiny legs rippled as it screeched and hissed.

Gi-normous.

A thick liquid bubbled from a nasty pair of chitinous fangs. In one swift motion, the Berg ripped the creature apart and flung the remains aside. Coop and a few other cadets jumped on the still twitching insect.

Blue shuddered. "I didn't think I'd ever say this, but thanks, Wurtz."

The humungous boy shrugged.

Blue struggled to shaky feet, brushing sand off him. "What was that?"

Corvus laughed. "That was a Crawler. One bite, and without some serious medical help, you'd be a dead cadet. They like the moisture and shade, and you're about the wettest cadet I've ever met." Saturn Squad erupted into laughter.

Wurtz stuck up a stubby finger. "Now you owe me one, Gote."

The experience with the centipede had wounded Blue's cool. "I'm pretty sure that I don't owe anybody anything, okay? I'm the one who should be owed stuff. It wasn't my choice to come to this wasteland. I want to go back home."

Corvus sneered. "Well, you can't."

"I hate the future. Okay? Bloody hate it."

Sugar came over and brushed sand off Blue's face with a perfectly formed brown thumb. "We understand, hon', but you gotta know there's no going back. One way ticket, yeah?"

Blue could not hold on to his anger with Sugar standing close to him. *And why does she have to be so nice. I've no hope.*

Sugar smiled. "Time to stop worrying about the past and start thinking about where you are now, dig?"

"And chill out," Ji added with annoyance. Coop nodded in agreement, giving Blue an encouraging smile.

Chill out? Don't these mega-twats realise I've lost everything and everybody?

"You filled your bottles yet?" asked Corvus, ignoring the answers. "Cos we need to get on. Saturn with me!" He stomped off along a pathway leading upwards to the steep hill Blue had spotted earlier. Bare, except for a few clumps of sad vegetation, the obviously man-made mound towered above them, eight, maybe nine hundred feet in height. A tarmac road seesawed up its side to a cave-like entrance halfway up.

Feeling the need for space, Blue jogged past Corvus and the rest of Saturn.

"Hey Blue, stick with your squad," bellowed Corvus.

Blue kept going, the unbearable sun scorching him. *The sooner I find shade the better. I need time to myself. All this is too much to take in, to deal with.*

"You think the Crawlers are all you need to worry about here in the open?" Corvus shouted. "We stick together Topside for one thing only. For safety. Unless you know better of course."

The incident with the poisonous centipede still close to his mind, Blue slowed his footsteps.

Corvus appeared at Blue's shoulder, Veeva following behind. "And besides, we've a Minnie with us." He nodded towards Hermans.

"A what?" Blue's need for space was forgotten. He gawked at the tall thin boy struggling to walk under his own weight. His long, stilt-like legs reminded Blue of an enormous stick insect.

Veeva grimaced. *"Minnie* is not a nice word. Insulting. Hermans is from Ganymede."

Ganymede. Jupiter's largest moon and the largest moon in the Solar System. The terrain consists of enormous criss-crossing grooves of over seven-hundred metres in height running for thousands of miles across its surface. Thin oxygen atmosphere. Named after a handsome mortal prince from Greek mythology abducted by Zeus to become cupbearer to the gods.

"'Ganymede'? You mean the seventh moon of Jupiter? He's from there? Wow."

"There's no 'wow' about it," Corvus sneered, "he's slowing our progress and we need to get on."

Ji yawned. "He's used to One-Third Gravity. Walking here on Earth must be like swimming in treacle. He'd better get a move on, I'm starving."

"I think it shows strength of character," said Veeva smiling at Hermans.

Corvus laughed. "I heard the sucker passed out under acceleration. Still, the Academy will soon beef him up or send him back home—which would have my vote."

"You shouldn't talk like that, Corvus," said Morgana.

"Who is in charge of this outfit?"

Morgana saluted. "You are in temporary command, sir."

"That's right, consider yourself dismissed."

"But, sir."

"Do I need to repeat my order?"

Morgana shook her head in annoyed defeat. "No, sir."

"Good."

She saluted again and marched away.

"Mmm. Power is excellent. I can't wait until I'm an officer. I'm going to have one helluva time ordering everyone about. Especially dunderheads like Morgana."

After a tiring climb, they reached a wide, steep ramp leading directly to a cave-like entrance above. Morgana, a few steps ahead of Blue, glanced around with a worried expression. "I don't like this wind."

Blue disagreed. *The breeze has a refreshing edge. I'm starting to understand why people in this century think sunbathing is mental-lentil. The sun here is an oppressive force. Unrelenting. Blistering. Beating everything into submission.*

Corvus appeared nervous. "Yeah, we'd better get moving. You okay with that, Hermans, cos we're not going to wait for you."

The tall boy nodded, taking enormous steps.

The well-worn road became steeper as they ascended, before it finally flattened out to reveal a wide section cut out of the side of the hill. More vehicles were parked here and a few golden hellijets tied down under thick plastic blankets. Tracks led towards an artificial semi-circular entrance roughly fifty-feet away constructed from thick metal painted eggshell blue and big enough to drive a double-decker bus into.

Blue took a step forward and found himself shivering.

Sugar squealed. "Oh no!"

Corvus galloped towards the tunnel entrance. "Run!"

"What?" As the word left Blue's mouth, cold swirling sand engulfed him. Visibility dropped to less than a metre. He forced himself forward, blinded by unremitting dust and grit.

Sandstorm. A climatological phenomenon common in desert and other arid regions. Strong winds containing loose sand and small stones. Can cause widespread damage and death to wildlife and humans.

A highly pitched, precise voice. "Felicitous greetings to you and your family unit, Cadet Blue."

"Hermans?" guessed Blue, struggling in the hail of sand.

"Yes, This One has allowed his name to be known to those within the Academy and the organisation identified as Our Very Earth."

"Oh."

"This One believes that, in our present and dangerous

circumstance, the best course of action is to suspend our introductions forthwith. Indeed, This One urges that it is more than propitious to discover a safe haven."

"Er—you mean we need to find shelter? C'mon then." Blue grabbed at Hermans' thin out-stretched arm, dragging him along.

Sand grated against him. *If I stay out here any longer, my skin will be flayed off.* A cold lump of sandy ice cracked into the side of Blue's head.

Hailstones? What the—? This is like no sandstorm memorised by my stupid brain. It must be some future phenomenon I've never heard of.

Covering his face with his free arm, Blue pushed himself forward. Behind the rattle and hiss of sand came the faint sound of shouting. He followed the voices, struggling against the clogging storm, pulling Hermans with him.

A stubby hand grabbed at him. "Dis way, Gote."

GOING UNDERGROUND

Blue stumbled, sand burning his skin, holding tightly onto Hermans. Wurtz roughly pulling at him. A screaming, banshee-like freezing squall. The sandstorm rattled and rasped, but became more distant with every footstep. Their feet now clanging against metal…until the tempest was behind them.

"You now owe me two, Gote," grunted Wurtz.

Too relieved to reply, Blue splashed water into his eyes and said nothing. He was drowning in freezing sand until the Berg grabbed him. Despite his aggressive features, his gruff accent and his odd if not violent sense of humour, Wurtz was somehow all right. He might trip people or try to steal their belongings, but Blue had the distinct impression he possessed an honourable streak.

What a total git.

Blue dried his eyes with his sleeve cuff and took a violent step backwards, bumping into Hermans. The entire hill was hollow, plunging downwards thousands of feet, plummeting past the roots of the artificial mound and far into the earth. Nothing in Blue's short life prepared him for the sheer immensity of this space. Massive bolts, like outsized cars, held together humungous-sized metal plates in a vast, complex honeycomb.

The other cadets stood or lay sprawled by the opening,

brushing wet sand from their eyes, ears and hair.

The cave entrance was of unremarkable proportions, a simple access way. It led to a wide lip from which a steep road, as broad as two football pitches laid side by side, leapt downwards through the artificial hill and into the earth.

Corvus frowned. "That was a close one. Oh, and Hermans made it." He seemed disappointed. "Thought we'd lost you for a minute or two. I'd hate to get some *deceaseds* on my first command."

"This One offers the Cadet known as Wurtz his most heartfelt thanks." Hermans bowed to the stoic Berg, who waved the tall boy away with a stubby hand.

"The storm came on us so fast," said Blue.

Morgana bounded over to where Blue and Hermans lay and saluted Wurtz. He gave her a curt, if not pleased nod in return. "You were lucky Wurtz managed to find you," she said, saluting the Berg again.

"I was all but stiffed."

Corvus shrugged. "Another twenty feet and we'd all be stiffed."

"I don't understand, one moment I'm suffering the hottest day ever and the next I'm shivering my bits off in a lethal, ice-cold sandstorm thing."

"Be thankful you escaped," said Corvus. "Otherwise you'd now be a pile of white sand-polished snow-covered bones."

"Thanks Wurtz," said Blue. "I didn't expect you to come after me."

Wurtz shrugged and lumbered off.

"Don't worry about him," said Morgana. "Bergs are well known for being enigmatic."

"The guy is a puzzle, that's for sure. And just when I was starting to dislike the turd. Typical." Blue shook sand from his hair. "What happened to *Old Dinger* and the hellijets? Those people I saw on the landing field?"

"They will be safe inside the Run-To, Blue," explained Morgana. "As for *Old Dinger,* a quick fuse burn will clean her tubes. The hellijets are kept undercover. They have special tarps to resist the sand and even if they were exposed, a thorough strip down is all they need for flight. You two okay?"

"Experience of hardship is sometimes its own reward," replied Hermans, his trilling optimistic voice amplified by the cavernous structure.

"And what about you, Blue?"

"Me? Well let's see. After everything that has happened since I've been here—I won't go into the full list, but it now includes insect attack and almost kicking the bucket in a sandstorm—I'm veering towards a *no*. I'm not quite brilliant. In fact, I'm all upside down and psyched out. Does that answer your question?"

"I am sorry you are having a bad time, Blue," Morgana continued brightly, "but you will settle in soon. I suggest you stick next to me in the future; I can make sure you stay clear of trouble. Same for you, Hermans."

Blue grimaced. "I'm doing well on my own thank you very much."

"Really?"

"I'm certainly less likely to be strangled when you're not around. So I'll take my chances."

"I'm sorry that that is your opinion of me, I was only trying to help." Morgana saluted and went to talk to Corvus.

Hermans turned towards Blue "This One is indebted to Cadet Blue. His family unit thanks you most profoundly for your help." He bowed at Blue, waiting for a response.

"Um…thanks."

The Ganymedian lifted his head and fixed Blue with steely eyes. "This One must also admit he is distressed and confused by the discourteous refusal of assistance freely given in good faith and friendship by Cadet Morgana." In Herman's high-pitched whiney accent, it was like being told off by a rather posh nanny.

"Oh."

Hermans bowed one more time and stalked away.

Parris came over with Sugar, followed by her ever-present companions, Coop and Ji. "Wurtz rescued you again, huh?"

Blue groaned. "Yeah."

Ji rubbed at her sand-encrusted red-rimmed eyes. "Pretty cool to have a guardian angel—or do I mean guardian thug?"

Parris ignored her. "Never been in a sludge-storm before. Heard about them. Seen pictures of them. But space, I don't want to experience one that close again."

Coop agreed. "You're not wrong. My whites are ruined."

Blue glanced back to where the storm raged outside. "Are sludge-storms common then?" Sand swirled for a good few metres into the entrance, ice-stones and slush staining the floor. He shuddered.

"The local climate is buggered," answered Parris. "That's why the landing field is on a high plateau. And why the entrance to the Hab is not at ground level. Otherwise, everything would wash away. We've even had full-blown blizzards. I sometimes think the hill attracts bad weather."

"Quit your jawing and get your legs sawing!" ordered Corvus over their conversation.

After a long downhill walk (the golf cart-like personnel transports were out-of-bounds to cadets), the road gradually flattened out.

Corvus talked about himself all the time, about what good a pilot he would make and how his father, a rich off-world trader, had sent him here to become an officer. He complained about Saturn Squad, about what a poor intake they had; oblivious to the fact half the cadets heard him.

Sugar was lost in deep conversation with Ji and Coop. Wurtz walked next to Morgana, making Blue wonder if the Berg really did have the hots for her as Corvus suggested.

How can anyone read the body language of such an outlandish physique anyway?

Hermans admitted to Veeva in his rather ornate and convoluted speech that he hadn't piloted anything in his life, apart from his boat back on Ganymede.

Boats? On Ganymede? Jupiter's moon was a ball of frozen muddied ice. The Ganymedian made no sense.

Veeva gave uninterested noises in reply. Parris also tried to talk to her and received the same treatment. Blue guessed his new friend had somewhat of a soft spot for Veeva.

He hadn't gotten anywhere with her either…Cool.

Blue caught his own thoughts.

I shouldn't be concentrating on girls when my plan is to split this era as soon as possible. Getting jealous about Veeva or even Sugar is a waste of time. I owe these people nothing. They might give the appearance of friendliness, but they care more for the Academy, Our Very Earth, their orders and Commander Dauntless than trying to help me get back home. Don't they? Eddi, Newt and Annie are alive in the past. I should be thinking about them.

Veeva smiled at him.

Damn. All this ignoring girls is not going to be easy.

A side tunnel led away from the road to a half-lit cavern of shacks and derelict low houses widening into a jumble of faraway dwellings.

Parris followed his gaze. "That's the Nest. Where everyone lived while they built the Hab."

"Well creepy."

"An absolute maze of tunnels and cramped quarters. Been deserted for hundreds of years. No one goes there. Off-Limits."

Blue noticed footprints in the dust leading into the Nest but said nothing.

They came to twin gargantuan metal doors standing flat against the road's walls, buckled by their own immense weight (Blue guessed they had been open for centuries) and entered yet another vast circular chamber carved from solid rock stretching far away into the distance. An underground cathedral. A ceiling curved upwards to form a perfect dome. Peculiar globes of warm light (unlike the bare bulbs of B-Pal) dotted along the walls at regular intervals, outlining the cadets in soft, creamy whites.

At various places throughout this space, some far off in the distance, others closer, stood identical mechanisms. Like everything Blue had seen on this journey so far, they were of epic proportions. Altars to an advanced, enlarged technology.

Corvus led the cadets towards one these contraptions. Eight metal pillars, each as wide as a roundabout and as high as the chamber's ceiling, encircled a raised circular platform large enough to park a jumbo jet. Thick black cables, the width of Wurtz, snaked throughout.

"What is it?" asked Blue.

"You'll see," Parris replied with a wink.

They walked between two of the gargantuan pillars and up on to the vast platform. Like ants crawling onto a dinner plate. The rest of the cadets chatted without concern.

Corvus busied himself with an elevated metallic pod of buttons and bulky switches. Amber lights followed by red, a thump, a few bangs, a loud klaxon and the entire platform started to descend.

Blue gave a sigh of relief. "An elevator. I thought—I dunno, maybe we were gonna beam down or something."

Parris pulled a confused face. "You sure say some stupid stuff, Blue."

Silence fell on the group. The cavern quickly disappeared, replaced by featureless grey rock lit from within by the elevator's own ambient lighting. They descended. The slow whine of hidden motors increasing in volume and intensity.

Blue's stomach groaned. He crouched, holding his head, taking his darting eyes away from the rushing walls, ignoring the laughs and jibes from Coop and Ji and the other cadets.

He lost all sense of time, of how far they descended. It didn't matter one bit where the elevator led to; this whole planet was one awful penal complex.

Thousands of miles and over four-hundred years from where I need to be.

With the grinding of heavy gears, he emerged through the roof of the world.

EARTH-HAB

The dawn of a new day.

No way!

An artificial elongated sun crept into slow life. An immense, man-made, red neon tube stretching for kilometres, hanging below the rock roof through which Blue and the elevator had just appeared. Crimson turning to orange. To white. Warming. Revealing a bizarre underground cavern.

The Hab. Of course—

Artificial Habitat. A regulated replica of Earth's climate.

—Beyond imagination, beyond all and any experience—even flying in space.

The colossal elevator sped through clouds. Emerging from the floating cumuli to reveal an exotic landscape. Blue's skin glistened with moisture, his face a mask of shock and wonder. Cities and towns, roads and rivers, forests and lakes and the patchwork of fields. *Satellite view* from an online map. But the vista paled in comparison to the blood-red tinged stalactites stretching from cavern ceiling to floor like mammoth termite hills. In these columns, thousands of windows shone with the bright light of habitation.

Five, six, no—seven of the massive stalactites, Blue counted.

Stalactites. Formed by calcium carbonate and other minerals deposited by mineralized water dripping from the roof of underground caverns forming rocky icicles. Not to be confused with 'stalagmites' rocky protrusions made on cavern floors by the same dripping, mineral laden waters. Stalactites and stalagmites grow in pairs over hundreds of thousands of years. Often stalactites and stalagmites will connect becoming one single column

This was no manufactured cavern but naturally formed. The reason for all the tunnelling above. To reach this cra-mazing subterranean survival space.

Morgana caught Blue's stunned expression. "Before the desert, this cavern was a giant underground lake," she said matter-of-factly. Wind blowing her sandy bob to reveal petite well-formed ears. "The Hab waited beneath the Amazon for eons. The dripping waters from the jungle above created these vast conjoined stalactites over hundreds of thousands of years. Ironic that after the lake drained away it became the home for all mankind."

The growing light from the neon-tube like sun revealed a green undulating landscape stretching away from him in all directions covered by a gentle mist. An explosion of cultivated fields similar to the English countryside, or at least any countryside in a temperate zone.

The dawn chorus started.

"You have birds?"

A delighted smile leapt across Morgana's face. "Yes. The whole self-contained scenario. Plants, animals, soil and atmosphere. The same Hab technology they use on Ganymede or in the many hollow asteroids of the Bergs and even the Martians."

"I don't know why I'm surprised, this is about the twentieth time I've been amazed today and I haven't yet managed breakfast."

Corvus tapped Blue on the shoulder and pointed to a peculiarly shaped red stalactite dominating the local scenery. "You see that?"

A skyscraper sized alien skull. Elongated. The dripping waters had guttered down the stalactite's side, creating a thick, artery-like latticework of solid rock.

"It looks like a melting face. Very nice. Not creepy at all."

"That's the Academy Column. Your new home and our base for the foreseeable future. If you don't die or get kicked that is."

Blue Into The Rip

ACADEMY

Blue Into The Rip

PHASE ONE

Blue stepped onto clipped green grass. Plumes of water from mechanical watering systems gave the underground air a dewy summer morning feel. Automatic machinery tended to plants and trees. A mower purred past, trimming the iris of lawn surrounding the elevator's vast disc.

"This One will never cease to be astonished by the extraordinary feats of human ingenuity," said Hermans suddenly at Blue's side.

"This is the most aw-wonder-sum place I've laid my big blue eyes on," Blue replied. "The elongated sun, the clouds, the immense stalactites—and we're underground. I'm gobsmacked."

A shadow of confusion passed over Herman's face. "This One begs your pardon, Cadet Blue, but he does not entirely understand your ancient vocabulary."

"Humans are amazing," explained Blue. "Slick. They created a place like this, yet did bugger all to stop Global Warming."

"And that is *gobsmacked?*"

"Language is a beautiful and wondrous thing, Hermans; don't let yourself get all disconfuckulated."

Corvus guided them towards the alien skull sitting atop the valley side, a vast, red-tinged stalactite. Early morning mist rose to meet swirling clouds. Empty alien eye-sockets stared mournfully through the haze. Watching. The millennium-long dripping waters had converged here, creating this peculiar natural formation. The illusion did not falter as they ascended.

"We live in that?" asked Blue.

"Pretty cool, huh?" said Corvus, meaning it. "And you aint seen the best yet. C'mon."

A well-worn road coiled up from the elevator towards the Academy Column, but the cadets took a direct route, trudging straight up the valley side, finally arriving at the foot of the immense stalactite. The road disappeared into the base of the Academy Column, but Corvus guided them to a more formal entrance. A set of fanned steps led to an impressive marble archway.

A statue of an imposing spacewoman—at least twenty feet tall—hand raised, pointed to the stars, a helmet held under her arm, her chiselled features speaking of dedication and service. Opposite stood a towering stone rocket, the Earth Corps insignia carved on its belly. Above the entrance, between them both and deeply engraved like a threat into the unyielding rock, was one word: *ACADEMY.*

Blue swallowed. "This is the big one."

Morgana stopped and saluted the statues. Coop bumped into her, nearly knocking her over, much to Blue's amusement. Veeva hung back, her expression one of worry. Sugar fiddled with her flock of beautiful golden hair, brushing sand from the twisted strands, straightening her uniform. Blue guessed there was some lucky dog in the Academy she wanted to impress. Hermans stalked up the steps, his breathing heavy and rasping with effort. Wurtz, as ever, remained dour and silent apart from the hefty thud of his immense feet.

They entered a modest circular entrance hall hollowed from the reddish rock of the column. Footsteps echoing from bare walls and the high, vaulted ceiling. Hundreds of yellowed photographs of previous students and weird aircraft poked out from twisted frames. An enormous display of memorabilia from NASA, the Russian and Chinese Space Agencies and *Virgin Galactic* and others filled part of the wall. There were mission patches, models of a Saturn V, a Sputnik, a Vostok-6 and SpaceShipTwo as well as some *future artefacts.*

Blue was geeked to learn about Moonbase Two, Earth's first station on the Moon. Moonbase One was the honorary name given to the landing site of Neil Armstrong and Buzz Aldrin way back in 1969. Spellbound, he let his eyes rove around until, with a loud "No way!" he glimpsed a lump of moon rock brought back from that historic Moon landing and picked it up. Nothing more than a drab piece of pumice encased in a scuffed plastic block. And so light.

The Apollo missions collected 2,196 rock samples weighing 382 kilograms. Half of which have gone missing. Moon Rocks presently cost around fifty-thousand dollars per gram. One-hundred thousand times more expensive than silver.

Actual moon rock in my hands. Back home this is worth millions.

Without a second thought, he stuffed the priceless artefact into his kitbag.

Veeva appeared at his side, a riot of red dreads brushing against him. "If you like this stuff, you might want to visit the Museum of Indulgence. It's crammed with paraphernalia from the old days," she said brightly.

Blue fastened his pack. "I'm not going anywhere except home, okay?" He turned to see Veeva's beguiling smile fall from her face and immediately regretted his harsh tone.

They marched along a well-lit tunnel with circular doors and tunnels branching off. Blue walked at Veeva's side, trying to think of something to say in apology, but before he had the chance, Parris started to narrate.

"Let me tell you about the Academy Column," Parris began. "These tunnels to the left and right? They lead to training seshrooms. Where we will be spending most of our time."

They arrived at a high-ceilinged curved tunnel. Wide enough for twelve people to walk abreast. Various military personnel marched past in both directions, ignoring the lowly cadets.

"This," Parris continued, "is what we call the *Wheel.* From which you can find the Crater. R&R. The Sanatorium. Everything. The Wheel surrounds the Academy Mess."

Mess. Called a messdeck aboard ships. The place where military personnel eat, socialise and sometimes live.

"Mess? Where they throw away all the rubbish?" Blue nodded at Veeva, hoping for a return of her smile.

"The Mess is the canteen. Jeez, they should call you Green, not Blue," Coop said to laughter from the other cadets.

Twenty or so boys and girls jogging in shorts, T-shirts wet with sweat, led by a young man barking in military cadence appeared from around the curve.

"That's Venus Squad," said Parris, pulling Blue out of the way. *"Running the Wheel* is just one of the many Academy punishments.

Blue grimaced. "How long is the Wheel?"

Parris scratched his head, his lips pursing to reveal his rabbit teeth. "Dunno. And I don't want to find out."

"What rule did they break?"

The pursed lips returned. "Could be anything. Take my advice, Blue. Keep your head down, don't speak back and call everyone sir."

Blue rubbed the temple where Dauntless had repeatedly clipped him last night. "I'll keep that in mind."

Corvus ushered the squad to an official notice board hung by an entrance through which the rank stench of over-boiled vegetables leaked out. The cadets gathered around.

BERG KING IN TALKS
WITH EARTH CORPS

```
King   Wilhelm's   Royal   Barge   has
successfully  docked  at  Charles  Darwin
```

```
spacestation in advance of talks to
resolve the Helium-3 Embargo. Squads
are reminded to treat all cadets with
respect whilst this difficult situation
is being resolved.
```

Blue's stomach rumbled—was he hungry or still nauseous? "This political stuff is important then, huh?"

"Yeah," replied Corvus, pretending to yawn. "A warning to us cadets not to give Wurtz and others like him a hard time. Blah, blah, blah."

"King Wilhelm is worried that the Berg Empire will stagnate," butted in Morgana, raising her crescent eyebrows at Corvus. "He has stopped the flow of H_3 to Earth in an audacious move to get his own rip machine."

Blue's ears pricked. "Rip machine?"

Morgana nodded with enthusiasm. "Yes. H_3 is the stuff keeping Earth-hab running; the fuse fuel for the rip, the hellijets, *Old Dinger* and even Earth-hab's sun."

"You mean they might all go kaput?"

Morgana shook her head as if the matter was beyond doubt or discussion. "Wilhelm won't let such a thing happen. He has kept the warring Berg families at bay for a generation. Besides, Earth Corps have a significant stockpile of H_3. Enough to keep us going for months. Nothing to worry about. But Fleet-Admiral Apache and the rest of the Council have their work cut out for them. Wilhelm is a tough negotiator. Right, Wurtz?"

Wurtz replied with a dismissive shake of his squashed head.

"Suit yourself."

An excited Coop pointed at a sheet of rough paper pinned under the title: *SATURN SQUAD*. "Hey boys, they've posted the Itinerary."

Everybody crowded around. Blue stared at the list, his mouth hanging open.

Blue Into The Rip

```
       SATURN SQUAD
      TRAINING PHASE I
```

Note: a pass in all subjects marked with an asterisk (*) is required to qualify for PHASE II

```
UNIT ONE
London Swamps (B-Pal)
SQUAD ACCLIMATISATION
Duration: 2 Weeks


UNIT TWO
Earthhab Academy & Topside
BASIC TRAINING & PREP
Duration: 8 Weeks
Hellijets: Piloting & maintenance*
Gym & Self Defence
Endurance & Survival
Ripwalking*
```

"Piloting?" Blue whispered.

Parris blew on his fingernails. "I've always fancied myself. On the stick."

"Aint that right," said Coop to giggles from Sugar and Ji.

```
UNIT THREE
Earth Orbit; The Charles Darwin
ASTROPHYSICS & SPACE
Duration: 4 Weeks
Astrophysics & Astronavigation*
Spacesuit & Vacuum Training*
```

"We—we're going into bloody orbit!" The words burst out of Blue's dry throat like an explosion.

"Astronomy is what I'm interested in. I want to specialise in Astronav'," said Veeva nervously. "I'm hoping that's the one thing I'm gonna be good at."

Morgana's eyebrows screwed into the bridge of her perky stub of a nose. "That is not quite the Academy Spirit, Cadet. Put the effort in and you'll be fine. You are here and that is one big tick in my book. Besides, we take care of each other in Saturn."

The barest shake of Veeva's head said everything.

Blue found his regular voice again. "The schedule is bonkers. There's no way we can cover all this in a couple of months. Astronauts train for years. Nutsoid."

Corvus crossed his arms and leant on the curved wall of the Wheel. "Get with the program, Blue. We are not those monkeys you grew up with. This is the Hab, not Kindergarten."

Blue ignored him and kept reading.

```
UNIT FOUR
Earthhab Academy
R & R
Duration: 2 Weeks
Gravity Reorientation
End of Phase Fest

END OF PHASE I TRAINING
```

I might have been the Boy Wonder back at numb-nut school, but here I've no chance. Blue read the list again. Something he'd missed earlier jumped out at him.

Ripwalking.

He grabbed Parris' arm. "We're time-travelling?"

"Time-travel? No. That's basic void walking. Stepping between planets. And back again."

"You travel to planets?"

"You don't know? About the void?"

"Mess!" shouted Corvus and the cadets hurried through the high and intimidating wall of the Wheel and into the central room beyond.

FOOD ON THE MOVE

The Mess. A cavernous circular utilitarian room, but not too vast to be unwelcoming. Harsh bright lights cast stark shadows on whitewashed walls. A vaulted ceiling curved into a low smooth hemisphere. Painted at head height, the 'Academy Ethos' in huge black letters:

YOUR SQUAD LEADER IS YOUR CAPTAIN AND YOUR FRIEND

A CADET SHALL NEVER DISOBEY HIS OR HER COMMANDING OFFICER

REMEMBER: WHEN IN COMMAND THE BUCK STOPS WITH YOU

WHEN TOPSIDE PLEASE REMEMBER TO TAKE CARE

ALWAYS REMEMBER: FORK IN YOUR LEFT, KNIFE IN YOUR RIGHT

K.J. Heritage

WHERE YOU STAND: THE CORPS » THE ACADEMY » YOUR SQUAD » YOU

COMMANDER DAUNTLESS IS ALWAYS RIGHT

"This place is seriously messed up."

Hermans tilted his elongated head in Blue's direction. "The Academy does seem to favour idiosyncrasy, obligation and duty. This One sometimes wonders why his family unit chose to send him to the Cadet School. The island paradise of This One's birthing is sorely missed."

"So you're here against your will as well, right?"

"Cadet Blue has made a most astute observation. Nevertheless, he believes Cadet Blue and This One must endeavour to find enthusiasm for this new and singular experience."

A circular wooden table, surrounded by six long benches radiating outwards like spokes in a wheel, dominated the centre of the Mess. Each could seat about twenty to thirty cadets. Another table, a showy, grand affair, stood on a raised area behind a thick dotted line painted on the floor and labelled *OFF-LIMITS* in red imposing letters. For Dauntless and his cronies, no doubt. Behind the table an exit—stairs leading upwards.

"That's to the Officer's Mess," said Parris, dragging him over to a long, straight, white line also painted on the floor. "And this is the Saturn line. We have to Stand-the-Line. Before we can eat."

"Of course we do. I think everyone should have a line to stand on before breakfast. Makes total sense."

Parris' eyebrows furrowed.

"It's called sarcasm," said Blue. "Give it a go sometime. Works wonders."

"Squad attention!" Corvus marched over to a hatch and rapped on the metal shutter. "Saturn reporting for breakfast, sir."

The hatch opened and a man's face, not unlike a pig, stared out. Swarthy in complexion and wearing a pair of golden earrings, he glowered down the line. "Past oh-six-hundred and you're late," he accused, shaking a white turban-wrapped head. Low guttural tones reverberated off smooth walls. "Do you think I want to waste my time waiting on you lot? I've a life outside this kitchen. Not that you brats give a wet one."

"That's Cookie," explained Parris. "He's famous for that bad attitude."

Corvus saluted. "We've just fused in, sir. Delayed by a sludge-storm."

"You all make it?"

"Yes, sir."

"Good, the last thing we want is to lose a squad before training has started."

Blue baulked. "Losing a squad actually happens?" *The sooner I escape from here the better.*

Cookie gave Blue a hard stare. "I've got some good news and some bad news. The bad news is that you're all gonna miss your rationed breakfast. The good news? You are ordered down the Cubby Hole, pronto."

The shock of this statement reverberated through Saturn Squad.

"Still, we can't send you away empty-handed." Similar white-turbaned kitchen staff opened the many hatches. "I've prepared food-on-the-move—Squad to the hatch!"

THE CUBBY HOLE

Food-on-the-move turned out to be flavourless corn on the cob and a slice of bread. *If this is a treat, I'm not holding out much hope for the regular rations.* His hunger somewhat satisfied, Blue felt better, although his occasional bouts of dizziness did not go away.

They made their way from the Mess, around the Wheel and through an entrance marked *EXAMINATIONS* arriving at a bright reception-size waiting area with a few doors and corridors leading off and the same *OFF-LIMITS* line he had seen before. Corvus brought the squad to a halt.

Ji played pulled at her long black blonde-tipped hair with unease. "Well this is a box of rocks."

"A box of what?"

"You don't know?"

"Of course I don't. I'm the useless Gote, remember?"

Sugar put her arms around Ji's shoulder. They made a striking pair. "The Cubby Hole. Don't you understand?"

Coop stood behind them, his whitish skin paler than usual, freckles hidden by the bright illumination of the corridor. "Too soon. Too soon by far. I thought maybe Phase Two or Three, not the first jazzing weeks."

"Wurtz don't like," the Berg said to an agitated Corvus.

Blue tried to speak but was ignored by a long discussion about all and everything 'Cubby Hole'—and he was still none the wiser on the subject. What seemed like an age later, Blue spotted Commander Dauntless standing in a doorway.

The commander took a deep breath. "Welcome to the Cubby Hole," he began in the same unhurried and yet rather urgent fashion Blue associated with the self-important git. "This will be your first taste of the room countless cadets have come to dread over their time at the Academy. In the Cubby Hole, you will either succeed or fail. There is no middle ground, no second chance. However, a flop in the Cubby Hole is as good and, some say, a better teacher than an A-one Top-Ten finish. Listen to me carefully—all the trials you will face in the next room will have a bearing on your future. Some are more obvious than others, some are more dangerous and a few are life threatening. What you need to remember is—they are all sig-nif-ee-cant."

There were murmurs and gasps, most of them from Blue. *This test can kill me?*

"Don't worry, this, your first assessment, although important, is not life-threatening. You will be uninjured—this time. You get me?"

"We get you, sir," the squad answered in unison, all except Blue.

"I hope that includes you, Cadet?"

"Yes…yes, sir."

"Good, you're first in."

SWITCHED

Blue entered a dim room. Bare, apart from a circular open door on the far wall leading to a chamber. Inside, bright lights glinted off a substantial metal cylinder mounted on powerful hydraulic springs, the end blackened as if burnt by heat. Rough white letters spelled out the words, *PULSE CANNON* along the barrel. The whir of hidden motors and the rounded door closed with a heavy bang. A single bulb blinked on to reveal a console in the shadows. Three switches. Each with an OFF and an ON label. A simple note was taped above:

> ```
> Cadet, you observed the laser pulse
> cannon mounted in the now sealed and
> soundproofed chamber. There are three
> switches to the right of the closed
> door. Only one will activate the
> laser. All switches are set in the OFF
> position. You can change the switches
> to any position you desire, however,
> you can open the door to observe the
> laser only once.
>
> Now, Cadet, using clear and logical
> thinking,    determine    which    switch
> ```

```
operates  the  cannon.  You  have  ten
minutes. Please explain your reasoning
before attempting a solution.
```

Blue was stumped. Three switches and only one operated the beam? If I turn Switch One to *ON* and open the door, I have a one-in-three probability of observing the laser getting it on 'beamwise' and that would use chance, not logic. If I switched them all to *ON,* I'd be sure of observing a working laser beam, yet I'd still be no wiser as to which switch was active. Three switches and one chance to make an observation impossible. The test is flawed, unsolvable. Isn't it?

Blue thought back to when he'd first arrived, to the chamber with the blackened laser.

Why show me that at all? A clue maybe?

Then, like the hot beam of the laser burning in his mind, the solution came to him. The answer was literally at his fingertips— simplicity itself. Blue gave his explanation and flipped his chosen switch.

A few minutes later, Blue was ushered into a cramped whitewashed geometric square room. Bare walls. An ancient wooden bench of burnished oak, worn and cracked and chiselled with the names and dates of countless cadets, sat opposite the door.

How many have passed through here?

Blue sat down, running his long brown fingers along the carved grooves, into the names that had been there for hundreds of years, into the ancient dates engraved more than a century after Blue's time. After he was cruelly snatched from Dooleys Wood.

I'm four-hundred and fifty years in the future. Here, now, in this place Eddi, Newt and little Annie are long gone.

He tried to take his thoughts away from this fact, to think about London submerged, or flying in space, the sludge storm and even this fantastic underground habitat. No good. His mind kept coming back to the awful knowledge that somewhere in what was left of Britain, lay their long-dead bones. His family were still alive in the past, but he couldn't ignore the terrible certainty of now.

And if I achieve my goal of returning home? What then? …My bones are somewhere out there too.

Just when Blue thought that waiting in this room was another part of the Cubby Hole test, the door opened and in walked Hermans, stooping to avoid bashing his head on the low ceiling.

Briefly, the Ganymedian's eyebrows knitted together in a marriage of disbelief. "Greetings Cadet Blue. This One is… um…delighted, if not surprised to discover you in this auspicious chamber."

"Don't sound too astonished. I'm not a total dimwit numb nut."

"This One must apologise most profusely if his excitement at finding his esteemed comrade was in anyway discourt—"

Blue waved his apology away. "You sussed the switches as well, huh? Coolio."

Hermans' lips curled around his elongated jaw to point upwards at his ears. Then Blue realised—the Ganymedian was smiling.

"This One will admit that at first he was perplexed, but calm consideration won out in the end. Nevertheless, This One had hoped more cadets would be on hand to congratulate him on his remarkable success." The stretched boy sat down, grimacing in pain.

"Nope, just me. Er…congrats fella."

Hermans bowed solemnly. "This One and his entire family unit thank you for your heartfelt wishes."

"Do they? That's very nice of them—so what the hell are we doing here? Is this like the Winner's Enclosure?"

The Ganymedian's squeaky voice took on some extra bass. "This is the Waiting Room," he said as grandly as his vocal chords would allow.

"Sounds a bit mundane. Where are the women's magazines and screaming kids?"

"Cadet Blue," Hermans began earnestly, fixing Blue with what he guessed was his best attempt at a steely stare, "visiting the Waiting Room this early in the Academy training schedule is a superlative and unexpected honour."

"Maybe, but it's a little small."

"Yes. The lack of space is somewhat disconcerting for one used to outdoor living. This One had expected a more ostentatious chamber."

"You're claustrophobic?"

Claustrophobia. An anxiety disorder. The fear of cramped spaces or rooms.

Hermans' eyebrows knitted together again, his head tilting to one side. "It would be pertinent to mention that This One suffers from a certain condition relating to restricted spaces. Nothing Cadet Blue need concern himself with."

"Fair enough. So just us two have passed, yeah?"

"Cadets Sugar and Corvus have yet to brave the test. This One fervently wishes them success."

"Can I ask you a personal question?"

"This One would be most honoured to engage in a conversation of a more intimate nature if that would be pleasing to his new colleague."

"Do you always have to talk like that?"

"Is This One correct in thinking Cadet Blue finds the Ganymedian speech patterns intriguing? This One is aware his off-world vernacular must sound perplexing to twenty-first century ears."

"*This One* this, *This One* that and all those long words. You're kinda odd."

"The way This One addresses his peers is a sign of deference deserved of a respected associate and is not out of the ordinary."

"You're saying this is not how you normally speak?"

"Cadet Blue's assertion is accurate in this instance. Informality of speech is reserved for those within the family unit and for those who by action or deed have gained the accolade of *friend of the family*."

"A bit like having to wear a suit and tie on formal occasions, when you'd prefer to be in jeans and T-shirt, yeah?"

Hermans shrugged. "This One has not heard of the things you mention, but there is nothing onerous in giving his colleagues the honour they deserve."

"Well, you're free to talk however you please with me, I won't be offended."

"This One finds the informal way cadets interact with each other enlightening. He is constantly impressed at their effortless verbosity. Nevertheless, it would be inappropriate for This One to even contemplate the relaxation of what Cadet Blue might call *etiquette*."

Sugar breezed through the door; her thick golden curls an absolute riot. "Space, you were lucky Blue, getting to go in first like that!" she shrieked, pushing back her luscious locks with one petite hand, the other resting on her hip. "I never get nervous, but that was a ride I don't ever want to repeat. Hey, and you made it too Hermie. Well done, I kinda guessed you'd be top at logic."

The peculiar smile returned to Hermans' elongated face.

"I'm in the Waiting Room guys," Sugar continued. "That means we are the elite. And well done to you Blue. You sure are the dark-horse." She strode over on long legs, draping her arms around him, squealing and stamping her feet. Sugar seemed more approachable without her two constant companions Ji and Coop. "I was all panicked, but I forgot about those stupid switches and saw beyond them."

Blue was going to agree when in walked Corvus. Sugar disentangled herself, ran across the room and, with a yell of pure joy, jumped on him, wrapping her legs behind his back.

Corvus winked at Blue over Sugar's shoulder. "Yep, seems like the cream has risen to the top," he said proudly, as if there was never any doubt about the fact.

The Waiting Room might be important to everyone else, but Blue wanted to leave here as soon as possible. His dizzy spells were getting longer.

The door flung open. Commander Dauntless stood to attention in the entrance and saluted.

Begrudgingly, Blue saluted back with the others.

"At ease and well done cadets," said Dauntless. "A merit will be placed in your records." He turned to Blue. "And special congrats to you, Cadet Blue. You solved the Cubby Hole in top time, beating my own long-standing record."

Hermans, Sugar and Corvus stared at Blue with a mixture of admiration and surprise.

"Er…thanks, sir."

Dauntless led them back to Saturn Squad, a dejected bunch standing next to the OFF-LIMITS line.

"Cadet Blue," said Dauntless, his shaved head gleaming in the light of the corridor, "in recognition of your fine record-breaking Cubby Hole performance, you are now in charge. Take Saturn Squad to the Mess. Enjoy some lunch and a special period of R&R."

R&R. Military slang for 'rest and relaxation'.

Blue stood transfixed.

"Did you hear me, Cadet?"

"Yes, sir."

"Carry on." Dauntless marched away, laughing to himself.

Blue motioned for Parris to come to his side. "Saturn…er… with me."

SQUADS

"Go on," Veeva asked Blue as they returned to the Mess. "How did you solve the problem of the switches?"

"Huh?"

"The Cubby Hole Test, silly, I was stumped."

"Are you sure you want to know?" Blue teased, feigning disinterest.

"Of course I do," Veeva answered.

Blue jokingly puffed out his chest. "It was easy. One of the three switches operated the laser cannon in the other room, remember? I turned a switch to ON, waited a few minutes and switched it OFF again."

"But which switch?"

"That's not important. I could have selected any of them."

The ginger girl's face radiated confusion. "—Oh."

"Then I switched one of the remaining two switches to ON. Yeah? I opened the door and the cannon was off. So I went into the room and, this is the clever bit, *I touched the barrel.*"

Understanding bloomed within Veeva. "You're brilliant, Blue," she exclaimed.

"And guess what?" Blue continued. "The metal was warm. So, logically—"

"—The first switch must have turned it on," she finished for him.

"Right. If I had opened the door and the cannon was operating, I would know it was the second switch. If the cannon was off and the barrel cold, it had to be the last, unused switch."

"That's so easy now you've told me." The familiar frown returned. "I should've got that."

"Explain again?" said Parris.

Blue pulled himself up to his full height and ran his fingers through his rampant afro. "Observation can be about touch as well as sight, Parris," he said like an old master to his youngest student.

Parris didn't appear any wiser.

In the Mess, Blue discovered five other groups of cadets standing to attention. He guided Saturn to their line and waited.

An enormous black man dressed in casual fatigues emerged from the stairwell leading down from the Officer's Mess. Bear-like, well muscled and around fifty years of age with military written all over him, he was built like the proverbial *brick shithouse*. Cropped greying hair, trimmed into a tight sponge, sat atop his sprawling face. Tinted sunglasses, similar to those worn by Commander Dauntless, were jammed into his glossy black skin. He marched over to the circular table at the centre of the Mess with controlled efficiency and some considerable formality.

"Who's the stiff?"

Coop turned his smiling rodent-like eyes in Blue's direction. "That's Captain Khan of Jupiter Squad."

"There's something about him. I dunno…a confidence. But more."

"You noticed, huh? Well, he inherited the long-life gene. He's over one-hundred and fifty years old."

"Wow."

"And that old man is courting Captain Sekhmet. She's about the best looking babe on campus."

"Oi!" complained Sugar.

The oldest man I've ever laid eyes on and he appears only a third of his real age. Isn't he too old to be courting?

Courting. Part of the courtship and mating rituals of human adults. To gain the affections of; to woo; to seek marriage with.

"I'd like to meet this Sekhmet," said Blue. "She sounds… um…interesting."

Parris tapped Blue on the shoulder. "You need to choose two cadets. For hatch duty."

"I have to do what?"

Corvus pushed Parris aside irritably. "Pick two *someones* asap. I'm hungry and someone has to go to the hatch and bring our food over, yeah? The commander put the Gote in charge. As far as I remember, that's you, Blue."

"Why don't you go get lost, Corvus," Parris spat.

Sometimes when Parris spoke, a surprising fury overcame his body, as if every one of his atoms experienced that emotion directly and at once. Blue was reminded of the time on *Old Dinger* when he had refused his handshake.

Corvus tilted his head and sneered. "What is your problem, Parris? Time of the month again?" he said to outbreaks of laughter.

The excitable blonde boy squared up to Corvus and everyone was suddenly quiet.

Blue pulled Corvus aside. "I'm in charge, and I'm choosing you, Corvus. Okay?"

Corvus replied sardonically. "Yes, sir. Whatever you say, sir."

"You and cadet Morgana."

Hearing her name, Morgana jumped to attention and saluted. Both she and Corvus ran over to the hatch.

"I thought they might try and pretend to be more annoyed," said Blue. "You alright, Parris?"

"It's Corvus. I can't stand him."

"I can see that. You need to take a chill pill and calm down a little bit."

"Huh?"

"He's a loudmouth, but that's all. Don't let him get to you. He's not that bad. I kinda like him."

"What?"

"Squads fall out!" Khan ordered. The cadets found their tables and sat down, Blue and Saturn Squad amongst them.

Parris lowered his voice. "Why didn't you choose Wurtz? After all he's done today." His face was pale, his eyes sparkling with remembered rage as they followed Corvus across the Mess room.

"You're right, but I don't give a jot what happens here. I can't let anything get to me, okay? I'm off home at the first opportunity. Sure."

"Home?" The sparkling eyes blinked back to Blue. "You mean the past?"

"Like I said, I'm gone as soon as I can find a way."

Parris' blonde head twitched in the negative. "No chance."

The food, when it came (efficiently delivered to their tables by Morgana and an over-courteous, smarmy Corvus) was basic. Potatoes, carrots, peas and some other vegetables Blue couldn't identify accompanied by a strange paste. He poked a long brown finger into the mush and grimaced. "We all supposed to be veggies then?"

Ji shovelled food into her mouth as if her life depended on it. "What on Our Very Earth is a *veggie?*"

"I'm asking if we get any meat. Cooked dead things. In gravy."

Ji rolled her eyes at Coop. "Meat is for the Top Table and Hermans. Special rations cos he's from Ganymede. The boy needs beefing up. For us it's regulation protein paste."

Blue was surprised to see a bloody steak on Hermans' plate and twice as many vegetables as everyone else. He compared his own reedy frame to the other cadets. They were all well-muscled and proportioned individuals. I also need beefing up.

Commander Dauntless and a few other Captains, including Shelley, entered the Mess. The squads jumped to attention, Parris hoisting Blue to his feet.

Dauntless took in the amassed cadets for a second. "Be cool."

The squads sat down. Morgana and Corvus stayed on their feet, as did cadets serving the other squad tables.

"Saturn," chose Dauntless. Corvus and Morgana hurried off to tend to the Top Table.

Blue's nausea wasn't getting any better and the taste of this so-called food was threatening to make him chuck. He passed his plate on to a grateful Parris who had to fight everyone off. "Who and what are the other squads?" Blue asked to take his mind off his own discomfort.

"Well, we've the *Spotties*—Jupiter—the squad who are," Parris put on an arrogant voice, "most likely to succeed. Where all the officer material ends up. All said and done. Jupiter is the Academy's elite squad."

Blue caught a flicker of envy in Parris' tone but said nothing.

"Then we have Mars Squad. Or the *Grunts*," Parris continued. "Led by the lovely Captain Sekhmet. They're not the brightest bunch. Foot soldiers. Doers. They're the squad the high-fliers in Jupiter will be ordering around somewhere along the line. So plenty of competition."

"I don't understand. Cadets are equal, yeah? But you're telling me Mars Squad is unlikely to pass?"

Sugar flashed wide eyes at Blue and smiled. Her teeth were dazzling. "Success at the Academy means getting through all nine phases of training and making it as a Private, the lowest Earth Corps rank. Get me? The squads are traditional and cater for different career paths in the Corps, should they manage to reach Phase-Ten."

"Phase-Ten?"

Ji speared a potato on Parris' plate with an urgent fork and thrust it whole into her mouth. "Getting to Phase Ten," she said between chews, "means you've made it all the way without being kicked or killed."

"Oh," said Blue.

Sugar caught the eye of a handsome Jovian cadet who smiled back at her. "The usual Jupiter Squad career path is in command. And I do like the leader type." Coop and Ji giggled knowingly.

Parris pointed to a table of nerdy boys and girls. "Don't forget the *Moonies*."

Blue pulled a confused face.

A frown crinkled Veeva's freckled nose. "He means Titan Squad, named after Saturn's largest moon, where the important science labs are built. They are intelligent types, eggheads, aiming for a career in Science and Research or if they're ambitious, they'll try for SEARCH. The Moonies get an easy ride for the more physical aspects of training." Her teeth gritted together momentarily, a flash of resentment in her beguiling emerald eyes. "Some say *far too easy.*"

"They look like a right bunch of geeks," Blue snorted; aware he was called that at school. When anyone bothered to speak to me that is.

Ji waggled her index finger in Blue's direction. *"Geeks?* I hope that's not insulting. Titan Squad is for those who want a career with real power."

Sugar spooned a large glob of paste into her mouth. "They're not going to let any egghead fail. They're too valuable to the Corps." The amber-skinned beauty turned towards Hermans. "I never understood why you are in Saturn, Hermie, I thought you being a Minnie was a sure bet for the Moonies."

Veeva narrowed her eyes, her normal dour expression, if possible, even sterner. "Hey Sugar, don't you know *Minnie* is an insulting name to anyone from Ganymede?"

"Oh can it, Veev'. I think Minnies are real cute." Sugar pursed luscious lips in a mock kiss, giving Hermans a good-natured wink. The Ganymedian turned red.

"Which leaves the *Lovelies* and the *Body Snatchers,*" announced Ji.

"Venus and Pluto Squads to give them their proper names," added Coop.

"Venus, the Lovelies, are allied to Titan," explained Ji before Coop could continue. "They're technicians, engineers," she added.

Blue got the impression that even though Ji and Coop were good friends, they were rather competitive. "The Body Snatchers are Pluto Squad, right?" Blue asked with a bemused smile, wondering who would answer first.

Both drew breath to speak, but it was Veeva who answered. "They're the Medic Corps."

Coop raised his fist. "That leaves Saturn. The dregs and misfits. The Ringers!" he bellowed. A slight pause and everyone on Saturn table cheered these words with military enthusiasm. Not to be outdone, the other tables roared their own squad names.

"How quaint." Blue grimaced. "Rivalry between the squads is rife then, yeah?"

"Not at all," answered Sugar. "Competition is disallowed in the Academy. But having said that, everyone knows that Mars and Jupiter are always seeking to outdo each other. And nobody wants to take the Drop."

Morgana and Corvus returned from serving at the Top Table. Morgana beaming, Corvus smug and pleased with himself.

I've made the twin twats *as happy as Larry*. Great.

On the raised area where the captains sat, Dauntless pushed back his chair and stood up, his gaze expectant, commanding.

Everyone in the Mess lurched to their feet, Blue with them, although he was still dizzy and his ears throbbed.

"Listen up," the commander began. "I have a few announcements. This afternoon, Saturn was the first squad to attempt the Cubby Hole."

The other squads turned to stare at Saturn with a mixture of worry and respect.

"Four students passed."

Corvus puffed out his chest, whilst Sugar beamed.

"An impressive performance. You would do well to emulate them."

Blue tried to stand taller. Coop chuckled next to him, poking Blue in the ribs. "Gerroff," Blue whispered, pushing him away.

Dauntless carried on. "It is my duty to announce that at the end of Phase One, the Drop will be a six week stint patrolling the Asteroid Belt and then on to Saturn."

"The Drop?" Blue blurted a little too loudly.

Dauntless glanced over at Saturn's table. "For those unfamiliar with the phrase, the Drop is what I like to call an 'intense character-building period'. The squad that performs, in my sole opinion, the least adequately, will miss their inter-phase six-week break and instead be ripped to the Berg capital between Mars and Jupiter, where the patrol begins. The tour ends with Saturn and its many moons."

"That's a punishment?" Blue whispered. "Sounds like the most wonderful journey imaginable."

Coop tilted his freckled head to one side and raised a finger. "Hey, nothing's decided yet. Saturn has what it takes to be a top-notch squad."

Corvus smirked. "Yeah and what's that?"

Coop hugged a smiling Sugar and Ji. "The Dream Team."

Corvus' smirk mutated into an expression of utter disdain. "Looks like we're going all the way down."

Dauntless continued, "I am also very proud to introduce a new member of the Academy. Please give an all-squad welcome to Captain Shelley."

"Well met, ma'am!" the cadets shouted as one, before applauding, the loudest clapping coming from the Titan table.

"We are lucky to have Captain Shelley, recently transferred from SEARCH, to take leadership of Saturn Squad. I'm sure she will be a fantastic asset to our already outstanding team of captains. Be cool." Dauntless sat down, followed by everyone in the Mess.

A few moments later, the new captain of Saturn waddled over. The table of cadets leapt to attention.

All this jumping up and down was seriously affecting Blue's cool. Occasional bouts of nausea threatened a repeat of his earlier vomiting antics. *The last thing I want to do is chuck up on the new captain*, he thought, swallowing.

"Good afternoon, cadets," Shelley said, her flabby jowls twitching. She eyed the upturned faces and nodded as if in appreciation. "Our good commander has ordered a period of R&R where I am to meet you all for a one-to-one sesh, heh."

The captain turned her attention to Blue. "Has Mister Blue been quartered yet?"

"No, ma'am," Morgana answered.

"Then quarter him with Mister Hermans." Shelley glanced at the Ganymedian. "You did well today in the Cubby Hole, Mister. Your parents will be proud."

Hermans saluted with a hand like a paddle. "Yes, ma'am."

"And you, Mister Wurtz, I suppose you'll need a partner?"

Corvus stood to attention. "Dauntless ordered Wurtz to bunk with me, ma'am."

"He did? You wouldn't have been my choice, Mister. But who am I to interfere with our great leader? Well met, squad, well met. Miss Morgana, you are in charge."

"Yeeees, ma'am!" Morgana shrieked, jumping to her feet and saluting.

Next to her, Corvus pulled a sarcastic face not missed by their new captain.

Shelley turned towards him. "Unhappy, Mister?" Her tone contained an unmistakeable edge.

Corvus did not blink. "No, ma'am."

"Excellent. I have many unpleasant duties for unhappy cadets. Do I make myself clear, Mister Corvus?"

"Very clear, ma'am."

"Good, heh."

Blue noticed how Shelley had the habit of ending her sentences with a half-laugh. It was quite endearing.

"Now, Miss Morgana, take Saturn to the Crater. I will be interviewing you all later this afternoon." With that, Captain Shelley waddled back to the Top Table.

"Saturn with me," barked Morgana to a chorus of groans.

THE CRATER

Saturn squad exited the Mess strolling behind Morgana and entered the broad expanse of the outer Wheel. After a short walk around the circular well-used corridor, they arrived at a rock-hewn stairway spiralling downwards into a murky dimness. They descended, chatting about the Cubby Hole and Captain Shelley. Blue became aware of a growing rumbling sound. He tapped Hermans on the shoulder. "What's that?"

"This One prefers not to divulge the requested information," he warbled between puffs. "He is sure this withholding of knowledge will reap significant dividends in the near future and hopes Cadet Blue can forgive him this slight indulgence."

"You're not telling? Fair enough."

Hermans waited expectantly.

"Yes, yes, I forgive you."

The rumbling increased in volume. The stairs ended and, pushing through a series of translucent, thick, scuffed plastic barriers, Blue stepped into an overwhelming greenness. A ginormous cavern containing an overgrown rainforest. He did a double take, stopping in his tracks so that the cadets behind bumped into him. An underground Jungle!

Trees and plants of all types, sizes, shapes and colours vied with one another, stretching to touch the arched ceiling high above from which in the distance shone, he guessed, another smaller artificial fusion sun. Everything around him breathed, growing and reproducing. Vines and creepers hung from the canopy, whilst a rich variety of exotic plants exploded in massive abundance at his feet. A continuous spray of water fell from diffusers somewhere high in the mist. "Wow."

All the cadets, apart from Hermans and Morgana, ran past Blue along a well-trodden jungle path. Morgana shouted for order, but giggling and shouting, the cadets ignored her. Stunned, Blue followed Morgana and Hermans, still unable to take in the living rainforest.

They approached the cavern's centre, the sound of rushing water now over-powering. The vegetation parted to reveal a cavernous crater-like hole plunging a good fifty feet. Reddish grey rocky walls, from which poked rounded openings spaced at regular intervals, looked down onto a central circular pool the size of a small lake. Cadets swam and larked about in the deep pool, including the outsized bulk of Wurtz. A noisy waterfall cascaded over the lip, crashing into the waters below. A fast, powerful invigorating torrent.

Blue staggered, overcome by an all-engulfing dizziness, as if everything he had seen and done since waking in Buckingham Palace had caught up with him. Like he was not here at all, but watching from some faraway land. "I really could do with a lie down of some kind," he said like a dream. "And maybe some tea. I could definitely do with a cup of tea. Tell me they have tea in this bonkers mad, crazy future?"

Morgana appeared at his side. "This is the Crater, Blue. And all ours till we finish training. The Top Brass can visit, but here we are free to do as we please."

"Just tell me where I need to go, cos I'm starting to lose it big time."

"You are wondering where our quarters are, yeah?" Morgana asked with a mischievous expression. "This way!" She ran to the Crater's lowest point, still a good thirty feet high, and plunged into the pool, twisting in the air to hit the water as a long thin dart.

"This future of yours is really starting to do my head in," said Blue, following Hermans down a steep stone staircase. "Is it far?"

"Do not concern yourself," wheezed Hermans. "Cadet Blue will be relieved to hear our shared quarters are on the upper landing. However, This One must regretfully inform him the showers and the heads are both located at pool level."

"Heads?"

"In the vernacular of your day, I believe Cadet Blue would call them *toilets.*"

"Oh. The bogs. Right." A sudden thought struck him. "You're from Ganymede, yeah? A moon of Jupiter with one third of the gravity of Earth. All this climbing up and down for a Jimmy Whiz will do you in, mate."

"Cadet Blue makes an astute and frank observation."

"So why don't they bunk you somewhere more suited to your needs?"

Hermans blew air over his thin lips, making a high-pitched sound, shrugging. Blue guessed that was Ganymedian for a sigh.

"This One was adamant to be quartered here."

"Sounds like you're a sucker for punishment."

"This One is flattered by your constant forthrightness, Cadet Blue. In answer, This One could not possibly ask for special treatment. He is a member of Saturn Squad and that is an honour he must respect."

Despite his formal words, Blue wasn't convinced. "Really?"

"This One does not always weigh the consequences of his somewhat impulsive decisions."

"So it's not just me who makes dumb choices. That's a relief. But it's gotta be tough on you though, yeah?"

"This One sometimes unjustly wishes his family unit had not been so eager to send him to Earth. He fervently misses home."

"You and me both."

They arrived at a landing, a narrow pathway with rock on one side and a fifty-foot drop on the other. A short walk, where Blue attempted to explain the notion of Health & Safety to a perplexed Hermans, and they stood in front of one of the circular openings. A doorless Hobbit-hole lit with a lambent light from within and high enough for Hermans to enter without stooping. The entranceway bent right, left and right again. The waterfall's thunder became a soothing rumble. They arrived in a plush and accommodating multi-bubble-shaped space, nothing like the ramshackle dorm back in B-Pal. More organic, more swick; as if the tunnellers had stumbled into natural rock hollows. Gentle lighting revealed different coloured layers of striated stone.

The most amazing aquarium followed the curve of the wall, a tube of thick rounded glass feeding into tanks huge enough to swim in, containing corals, fish and creatures of many types and sizes. Substantial crystal-clear pipes disappeared into the rock, appearing a few feet later, snaking throughout their quarters—snaking throughout the Crater. Shoals of iridescent darting fish flitted from one tank to another.

Even though Blue was possibly miles underground, the room, like the others he had encountered so far, was curiously warm. He ran long brown fingers along the rounded wall. The heat came from the rock itself. Warmed by some unknown mechanism.

Two bunks complete with bedside tables and lockers sat opposite one another. At either side were twin well-lit alcoves fitted with desks and wooden chairs. Pinned to a single noticeboard was a picture of what Blue guessed represented home for Hermans—Ganymede. An enormous complex of interconnecting insect eyes sitting on a frosty horizon above which hung Jupiter in the deep blackness of space. How Hermans lived an outdoor life was beyond him.

"This One must apologise for such a breach of manners, but he is quite unable to stay upright any longer." Hermans collapsed onto his bunk, an angular mess of sharp, pointy limbs, his long legs sticking out a good two feet over the end of the bed.

Blue stared open-mouthed. "The fish?"

Hermans closed his eyes. "A rather magnificent self-contained system, yes. An early experiment in self-sufficiency from way back. The Crater is a strictly controlled mini-habitat, an abandoned but superlative hydroponics and ecosphere trial taken over by the Academy when they occupied the column."

Hydroponics. Plants and trees grown in an inert medium without soil. Perfect balance of pH. Nutrient solutions and highly oxygenated water delivered to root systems.

Ecosphere. Self-contained and self-sustaining water ecosystem containing micro and macro organisms.

"I was expecting more of the same whitewashed walls and hard bunks. The normal kind of harsh Academy rubbish."

"This One is quite used to artificial constructs. On Ganymede, This One often swam with dolphins and was sung to sleep by whale song."

Blue examined Hermans' picture of Ganymede again. It didn't seem like such a bad place to live after all. "I can guess why you don't want to bunk anywhere else. The Crater reminds you of home, yeah?" No reply. "You nodding off?"

A shadow appeared in the doorway. "I am here to give you a formal apology, Cadet Blue," Morgana said, saluting. Even with the rumble of the waterfall outside, her voice reverberated loudly around the curved walls.

"You can't come barging in here," protested Blue somewhat taken aback. "Can you?"

"You are still very angry with me. I can tell."

"Well you did strangle and humiliate me in front of everyone. And on my first day. That's quite some going."

"I'm here to say I am sorry." She saluted again. "You forgave Wurtz."

Blue grimaced. "He did save me from the crawler thing and dragged me from the storm. Besides, he's a noobie as well."

"Can we start again? I think we should be friends, okay? I do not like conflict."

The girl was an irritant, that much was for sure, but he didn't have the heart to tell her to get lost. "Alright, apology accepted. And stop saluting, you're embarrassing me."

Morgana's hand dropped to her side "Thank you, Cadet Blue.

I sometimes do not know my own strength; I did not mean to make you pass out."

"Don't bloody remind me."

"You really need to watch that mouth. It will get you into a lot of trouble."

Blue took a deep breath and counted to ten. "I'm kinda tired." He nodded towards the doorway.

As she raised her hand for what appeared to be yet another salute, Corvus strolled into the room. "My, my, Morgana. You are keen."

She reddened. "I'm only here to apologise and besides—"

"So, Blue, I see you've met the fish?" Corvus asked, cutting her off in mid-sentence.

Blue sat on his bunk, a little overwhelmed. "Doesn't anybody knock in this century?"

"Sorry, Bud, but since you passed the Cubby Hole test, I thought we ought to get to know each other better." He glanced over to Hermans who was snoring.

Blue rubbed his head, his dizziness returning. "He went out like a light."

Corvus turned his attention to Morgana. "You still here?"

Morgana saluted. "I will be going then. Bye, Cadet Blue."

"Yeah, bye."

"You two friends again?"

"I guess so."

Corvus' face curled into a frown. "You look kinda rough. You okay?"

Blue sighed. "I have no idea if I'm bloody okay or not." A shark emerged into one of the tanks, startling a shoal of smaller orange and purple fish. "I've travelled so far forward in time that everyone is…well, they're dead, all dead. The Academy? Full of nutsoids, mad-whackers and cracked-out crazies. I'm not okay, not even slightly."

"I suppose the way you've been acting sort of makes sense. You are the new boy. That's gotta be rough."

The new boy? These guys have no idea about anything I've

gone through. Blue drew breath to tell Corvus exactly what he thought. "Don't you realise—"

"Shush. Shelley's started the Meet-and-Greet. You're first in line again. What's it like being popular?"

"Huh?"

"Huh?" Corvus repeated with sarcasm. "Didn't you hear our captain earlier? Shelley is meeting us all for another get-to-know-you sesh. Go back to the Mess, pronto and wait by the Off-Limits' line."

Blue stared mournfully at his pillow. "But I was gonna have a lie down."

"Get your act together and your ass in gear. Orders."

Blue resentfully grabbed his kitbag and went to leave.

"You gonna take your bag with you everywhere?"

Blue thought about the moon rock, the money and Jonesy and nodded. "I'm taking no chances. Since Wurtz stole from me, I'm keeping everything close."

THE GENETICS OF IT

"How are things, Mister Blue?" Captain Shelley lounged opposite Blue on a comfortable if not worn divan.

The officers' quarters were a squalid affair, her room a rough square with enough space for a desk and a single bunk. The divan was Shelly's addition and only just fitted in the cramped chamber. The Crater, Blue realised, was quite a perk.

"This needs to be quick; I have plenty of cadets to get through." Shelley fiddled around in her desk drawer and produced a humungous homemade biscuit in one flabby hand. "Chomp on one of these. I asked Cookie to do me a batch. They are somewhat special, heh."

"No thanks, ma'am." Blue sat perched on a stool, clutching his backpack like a security blanket.

"History is a passion of mine." Shelley took a bite from her biscuit, crumbs flying everywhere. "You can tell by my interest in your century's pop art." She waved the cookie towards a framed faded poster of a female tennis player with no knickers scratching her bottom.

"Yes, very…er…*nice.*"

Shelley nodded with approval. "I knew you would appreciate my taste in historical art." She took another bite. More crumbs made a desperate attempt for freedom. "How are you settling in?"

Despite the warm vibes he received from Shelley, she appeared as unsympathetic as Dauntless and the rest.

"You're finding the adjustment an easy one?"

Blue thought back to Dooleys Wood and the dreadful moment he fell into nothingness, of the twisted, empty, drowned future he had woken to. "Why?" he said, his voice full of loss. "Why did they do this to me? I've lost everything, everybody."

The captain continued chomping on her biscuit. "How awful. I can imagine."

"Can you? I was searching for Annie, my little sister, when they stole me away. I have no idea what happened to her."

"You lost her as well as your parents? How horrible." Shelley spoke in platitudes, her voice devoid of emotion or empathy.

She doesn't give a shit.

"It's hundreds of years in the past, but still yesterday to me. I can't stop worrying about her." He rubbed his eyes, hoping not to get a full on blub in front of his new captain. "The worst thing? No-one will tell me why I'm here or what any of this is about. And why leave my family, the so-called terrorists, behind?"

"I'm afraid I don't have time to give you a complete explanation, Mister. You might think you've had a busy day, but I've been demoted, ripped to Earth-Hab from Titan and then flown to B-Pal and back again. All with no sleep. I was kinda hoping for a quick meet-and-greet and forty winks, heh."

Blue narrowed his eyes.

"Something to say, Cadet?"

"I dunno. I thought you were different from Dauntless. Better somehow. I thought you might explain to me what the hell I'm doing here."

Shelley stopped in mid-chomp. Stabbing eyes, wet like a baby, regarded him sternly for a moment. "This may be your first day at the Academy, but you will learn to show more respect to your captain, otherwise things will not go well for you, get me?"

Blue had seen her turn on Corvus like this before. It was terrifying to be on the wrong end of her anger. "I get you, ma'am."

She fixed him with a cold stare for a few seconds and, as suddenly as it had disappeared, her smile returned. "Good. Still, I can't have any of my cadets thinking I'm anything like the great commander. I suppose I can indulge the time-traveller. But remember, you are a cadet in my squad. This is the last time I'm giving you leeway. You get me?"

Blue nodded.

"What do you want to know?"

"Why am I here? How come my parents are considered terrorists and," Blue sighed, the breath leaving his body in fits and bursts, "I need to know who or what I am."

"I see. There's no quick answer, but I'll try…You've seen the Hab? Its columns, cities and agriculture were created as an underground refuge against the devastating shift in climate. Over time, the Earth's surviving populations (what was left of them) found their way here, slowly coming together to live as one community known as Our Very Earth. In preparation for the oncoming ice age, and to ensure our survival, we started to alter our genetics to make the remaining human stock stronger, fitter and healthier. A form of positive eugenics enabling us to survive on a harsh, cold Earth and some of the more extreme planetary bodies of the Solar System. You get me?"

Eugenics. Improving the qualities of the human species or a human population by discouraging reproduction of genetic defects or undesirable traits (negative eugenics) and encouraging reproduction of desirable traits (positive eugenics).

Blue had heard of Eugenics. It had a nasty history associated with ideology, racial cleansing and the Nazi Party. The skin on his back began to crawl. "Genetic manipulation?"

"We put all our efforts into this endeavour and we can observe the results of their work today. Humans have never been so fit and healthy." To emphasise the point, Shelley stuffed the remaining biscuit into her mouth. "That's what makes us superior, you see?" More crumbs fell on her uniform, her divan and the floor. "With the discovery of the rip, everything changed.

Humans left in their droves to go populate the New Worlds. An exodus of sorts."

"But I'm guessing the genetic experimentation didn't stop?"

"No it didn't." Shelley reached for another biscuit. "Are you sure you don't want one, they are very more-ish."

Blue shook his head.

"Suit yourself. The Eggheads wanted and did continue with their experiments. They became obsessed with the notion of the Super Human. Nothing would stand in the way of their noble goal."

The Super Human. A genetically superior human being. The objective of Nazi leader Adolph Hitler to turn Earth into a utopia of god-like beings with perfect physical bodies of one racial type.

"That sounds worrying."

"Scientific endeavour can sometimes be extreme, but unlike your unfortunate time where racial concerns dominated everything, here, at least, their intentions were honourable. There is nothing wrong in making humans as strong, as fit and as intelligent as they can be. They eradicated genetic diseases from the genome, located the DNA sequences for photographic memory, high intelligence and enhanced constitution and were working on the long-life gene when a faction decided to intervene."

"My parents?"

"A group of militant activists, which must have included your parents, yes. They broke into the egghead labs, destroyed the priceless gene-sequencers (the last of their kind) and stole their genetic material. Over one-hundred eggs already present in their auto-maturation flasks." Her flabby lips quivered over her biscuit. "You know your biology? The name for fertilised ova capable of growing into life?"

Blue nodded.

Ovum. An initial cell formed when two gamete cells are joined by sexual reproduction. A fertilized egg. An embryo. A diploid cell. A zygote.

"I was one of those eggs? One of the zygotes? A Gote!" Blue's mind came to the obvious conclusion. "I came from a flask?"

The biscuit disappeared into Shelly's mouth, her jowls bulging as she chewed. "What the activists did next confounded everyone, including their so-called supporters. After taking all the flasks and setting fire to the labs, they turned their attention to the Hab's rip machine. It took thirty years to build, a priceless asset. The terrorists stormed the Rip-Room and removed its heart—a single, irreplaceable and yet unremarkable crystal in which rested the co-ordinates of the *New Worlds*. Without this Nub, as it was called, the rip imploded, scattering your parents, the zygotes and their co-conspirators into history like so many leaves in the wind. The New Worlds were left cut-off, possibly lost forever. SEARCH was created to scour the remaining records; the electronic archives, libraries and even the surviving newspapers and magazines; any and all information from the Great Meltdown in the hope of finding those hiding in the past."

No wonder Eddi and Newt went Crazy Amy at my picture in the local paper. My stupid blue eyes are such a giveaway.

"SEARCH wanted to bring these terrorists to justice and, more importantly, to retrieve the Nub. We can tell by your unplanned arrival that the process was, and still is, unpredictable and time-consuming. Months are needed to program a time rip and to be blunt, the results went skew-whiff from the start. Not one terrorist was recaptured, but you Gotes couldn't stop falling into the void, appearing willy-nilly all over the planet. In the end, SEARCH, now powerful within Earth Corps, turned their attention to rediscovering the *New Worlds,* or as we call them nowadays, the *Lost Worlds*. They have been more successful in this endeavour, but the search goes on."

Blue wiped at a sweaty forehead, a wave of dizziness sweeping over him. "So SEARCH opened the rip to seize my parents and they captured me instead." An unsettling thought jumped into his mind. "Why the rip in Dooleys Wood and not at the abandoned playground?"

"Playground?"

"I'm confused as to how SEARCH knew where to capture

me," Blue said quickly.

"Historical records of all kinds survived to our time here in your future. Everything that was saved, salvaged and restored found a way to the Hab; a wealth of information sifted through and examined by SEARCH hoping to find the out-of-ordinary, the strange and the peculiar. The giveaways of those hiding in the past, alerting SEARCH hundreds of years later."

If it wasn't the article about the car crash in the local paper, then what alerted SEARCH to my parents' presence? Maybe something dreadful happened to them and Annie in Dooleys Wood? "I just can't believe Eddi and Newt are terrorists. It makes no sense."

"Eddi and Newt?"

"Mum and Dad. They were a bit eccentric."

Bright stars swirled across Blue's vision. His head swam with thoughts of Annie, Eddi, Newt and the missing zygotes. He quite forgot how to sit on his stool and fell to the floor in a dead faint.

SANATORIUM

Blue lay on the verge of waking. A vague, unhurried chilled-out place he had no need to leave anytime soon. But heartbeat by slow heartbeat, he became aware of hushed voices, a hand holding his wrist and a strong overpowering smell of antiseptic.

"Yes, he was a real dink going Topside without any Slap." A clipped female voice to his left. "Still, he has the typical Hab constitution, even if he is a Gote. The burns are mild. He'll be itching. That's about all."

"Thanks Phelps, you've put my mind at rest, heh." Another female voice carrying a hint of laughter.

Captain Shelley.

Blue opened his eyes to a crack. Searing whiteness threatened to incinerate his brain. "Turn out the lights," he croaked through parched lips.

"Ah, Cadet," said the first efficient voice, "despite all your attempts at the contrary, you are still in the land of the living."

"The land of the living doesn't seem that clever to me."

"You silly boy," she admonished. "People in your century might have bathed in sunlight, but here and now, the sun is not our friend. You're suffering from sunstroke."

Sunstroke. Potentially fatal condition caused by over-exposure to direct sunlight. Symptoms include hot, dry skin, exhaustion, vomiting, delirium and coma. Urgent medical treatment is required, possibly in an intensive care unit. Recovery is usual within a day or two.

"Oh."

A tall woman in a white lab coat with red epaulets on her shoulders grabbed his wrist tightly. Pinched eyes stared at a small nurse's watch on a chain, long hair piled in a bun, thin wisps escaping to bounce around her elongated pointy face. "First case I've had in years. We've salved the affected areas and put you on a re-hydration drip. You should be fine and dandy in a few hours, apart from some sores and dizziness." Her skin was white, as if bleached, her hands calloused and rough.

Blue lay in an antiseptic bed in a cold hospital ward reminding him of his school refectory. The room, containing six beds, was not cosy. Artificial sunlight shone through elevated windows high above. Unlike most other rooms in the Academy Column, this space was all straight corners and imposing geometric arches. Colourful anatomical diagrams of the more disgusting diseases and afflictions adorned the walls. Old glass jars (including a foetus, a brain with the optic nerves and eyes still attached, a left hand and a decapitated staring head) packed the shaky shelving.

"Nice décor. I really like what you've done with your collections of brains. I have one question. Where the hell am I?"

"The Sanatorium, where else?" the tall woman answered.

Sanatorium. A medical facility for patients infected with tuberculosis (TB) before antibiotics. A hospital. A place for the treatment of mental illness.

"Sanatorium? I've not gone nutsoid, have I?" Blue asked hopefully. "Cos that would certainly explain what has been happening to me."

"The Sanatorium is the Academy hospital and I am Physician Phelps. You are a lucky young man. Sunstroke in this century is an easy killer."

"Lucky?" broke in Captain Shelley. "Stupid more like. He was ordered to apply Slap twice."

"How was I supposed to know what Slap was for? I'm not

telepathic."

"Listen, Mister." Shelley was furious. "In Earth Corps, in the Academy and most importantly of all, in my squad, you will be told to do things you may not understand. We do not always have the time to explain our reasoning. But understand this: if you disobey any other direct order, I will make it my personal duty to get you expelled. Do I make myself clear?"

"Yes."

"Yes what, Mister?"

"Yes, ma'am."

"That's better." She squeezed Blue's other hand with flabby fingers. "Don't do anything as stupid again.

"I'll try my best."

"No-one tries in my squad. *We do,* we do not try."

These gung-ho nutters are doing my head in, sure. "I will do my best, ma'am."

"Good."

The Physician let go of his wrist and nodded as if satisfied, fixing Blue with a quick stab of her eyes. "I'll leave you to it." She saluted and walked away.

"Phelps might be a tad eccentric," said Shelley with a wink, "but she is the very best. You gave me quite a fright collapsing like that."

"I'm sorry, ma'am. Have you seen my kitbag?"

"Relax, Cadet, as I said to you back at B-Pal, I know how you Gotes get attached to your possessions. It is in the bedside table."

"Thanks, ma'am." Blue sighed with relief. His personal stuff was not much, but it was all he had.

"You may think this *ma'am* business is tedious, but you must always call me *ma'am* in front of the other officers. Another rule of the Academy and Commander Dauntless does love his rules."

"The stuff written on the Mess walls is his idea then?"

Shelley grimaced comically, her eyes smiling in mock horror. "He takes that thing way to seriously, heh. Don't pass that on, okay? He mostly speaks guff, but he is right when he says 'Your squad leader is your captain and your friend'."

As if on cue, in strode Commander Dauntless. He marched over to the bed. "How is he doing, Captain?" he said, his eyes hidden behind his ever-present tinted sunglasses.

"He's on the mend, sir," Shelley said casually with a half-hearted salute.

"Is he?" Dauntless replied like someone robbed of good news. He then went on to berate Blue about refusing orders. But Blue guessed something else was on the commander's mind and he was getting the brunt of it.

Afterwards, Blue closed his eyes and said nothing, pretending to fall asleep.

Dauntless turned his attention to Shelley. "Captain, how are you finding life back on Earth? Quite some come down after the vaulted heights of SEARCH?" he asked, lowering his voice. Blue had to strain to hear.

"If you sought to gain influence from your association with me, I'm afraid you are mistaken, Commander. As far as SEARCH is concerned, I no longer exist. Which suits me down to the ground. May I be dismissed, sir?"

A slight pause. "On your way, Captain."

Shelley pushed back her chair and walked away.

"Physician Phelps!" Dauntless barked, making Blue jump. "In your office. Now."

Phelps poked her head from a side room. "Of course, Commander."

"Good…And Blue? I'm ordering you to get better, you get me?"

Although he was pretending to be asleep, Blue nodded.

SHADOWS & LIGHTS

Blue spent the evening dropping in and out of consciousness, his feverish mind back in Dooleys Wood and the swamps. Dreadful fumes assailed him, the fetid air tasted scummy and the constant buzz of insects drove him mad. A manky place full of bad dreams, demons and an over-riding *hellacioiusness*. An awful grief sometimes consumed him, but he would open his eyes and find himself back in the Sanatorium and be comforted.

By mid-evening, the damp mudlands of twenty-fifth century Britain seemed a long way away. A crash of doors. Phelps and a group of medics wheeled a sturdy bed into the ward. Two muscled squat men of similar stature to Wurtz followed behind.

Bergs.

They shared Wurtz's heavy eyebrows and low forehead and seemed, if possible, even angrier. Exposed areas of skin on their arms and faces featured what appeared to be geometric tattoos and ritualistic scarring of a similar design. They were showy, dressed in reds, oranges and greens, carrying ornate rifles with spikes and jaggedly serrated edges. Close-set eyes menaced from below golden, blingy helmets.

Phelps ushered the curious group into a side room. Blue waited for long minutes, hoping to ask the physician about the bed's mysterious occupant, but tired after his meal and still dizzy, he fell back into slumber.

Hours later, disturbed from a deep sleep, Blue opened his eyes and was at once wide-awake. His eyesight flickered—the Sanatorium revealed to him in black and whites. His ability to see in darkness still amazed him. What amazed him more was a strangely shaped scary shadowy-type-thing, creeping along the opposite wall towards the side room where the medics took the unknown Berg.

An intruder. Wearing some form of stealth-tech. That can't be good.

The shadow reached the doors and stole inside. A rasp of metal, a grunt and something heavy hit the floor.

Unable to lie back and do nothing, Blue jumped to shaky feet and lurched into the room. He found two Bergs. One motionless in a bloodied heap, the other clutching at a sliced throat, the shadow thing standing over him. The shade whirled. Blue ducked, the swish of a long blade passing over his head.

To his right a light switch. Blue rolled forwards, punching the button, the sudden illumination momentarily blinding him. "Help!" he bellowed, surprised by the volume of his voice. "Someone help me! Intruder!" His eyes adjusted to the brightness and found himself standing between the mysterious patient and what was now many shimmering orbs of light. Under the intense lighting, the shadow appeared as multi-disco balls of different sizes popping in and disappearing out of existence.

"Move aside, Blue." A voice, twisted and distorted by the stealth-tech and yet commanding and dangerous.

This person knows me?

Blue stood his ground. "No way!" he yelled, not one hundred per cent sure why he was protecting the bedridden stranger or how he would fare in a ruck against a ball of gleaming, sparkling light armed with a lethal blade. From outside came shouting and the thump, thump of running feet. "In here! Quick!" Blue hollered. With a scowl, the glistening balls turned as bright as to blind him and disappeared.

Seconds later, Physician Phelps burst in, followed by medics and four more Berg guards. Phelps pushed Blue aside and examined the huge bedridden man. "What happened, Boy?"

"I thought I was a gonner for sure. Didn't you see those balls of light leaving the room?"

Phelps shook her head and stared into his unusual eyes. "But you did, didn't you?"

Blue nodded.

"Did they carry a curved blade?"

"Yes. Nearly took my head clean off."

"As I guessed. A SEARCH assassin." She grabbed at a passing medic. "Ring the alarm and send word to Dauntless."

"Assassin?"

"Silent and invisible unless you can perceive the infra-red spectrum. They will be long gone. At least the intruder didn't get a chance to kill—" She stopped herself in mid-sentence.

"Who?"

"He is safe, which is all that matters."

Bells rang and sirens wailed. Blue turned his attention to the figure lying in the bed. The man was immense in stature. Long greying hair, held back by a golden band, framed an expansive but kindly face. Ritualistic scars, decorated his cheeks, chin and forehead in geometric patterns—inked with tattoos of red and black. Both imposing and stately. The squashed Berg features were noble even in sleep. Like some fallen god. "He's an important Berg, isn't he?"

Phelps' cold eyes glared at him. "That's not your concern, Cadet. Get back to your bed."

More people arrived and went into the room. Some of them official Bergs. After a lot of coming and going, Commander Dauntless burst into the ward. He chatted with Phelps whilst glancing at Blue, before striding over.

"Tell me everything."

Blue did so, although caution told him not to reveal the assassin knew his name.

"They let you go?" growled Dauntless when Blue had finished. "You should have been cut down without a second thought." He seemed almost disappointed.

"Phelps said the intruder came from SEARCH, sir. And who is that Berg?"

"That's nothing you need to know about."

"But, sir."

"Quiet. Physician Phelps informs me you're fit enough for active duty."

Fit for active duty? I don't feel fit for anything.

"Get dressed. I'm ordering you back to your quarters." With that, Dauntless left.

A short while later, a despondent Blue opened the hermetically sealed doors to the Crater. Even with his night-vision, the pathway was almost lost in the intense jungle gloom, but he had the sound of the waterfall to guide him. When he reached the Crater's rim, he was surprised to hear raised voices from one of the many openings: Corvus trying to calm an agitated Wurtz. Blue had no time for contemplation. He was bushed. Stashing his kitbag in his locker, he climbed onto his bunk, glanced at the sleeping Hermans, closed his eyes and drifted off to a welcome sleep.

ENDURANCE

"Cadet Blue. This One is in the unfortunate position of having to wake his stricken colleague from his much deserved slumber."

"What the—?" Blue muttered from a dry mouth tasting like a herd of sheep had slept in it, but had mostly used it as a toilet. *I only just closed my eyes.*

"This One offers his most heartfelt wishes to his esteemed bunkmate on his return from illness. However, he must regretfully inform Cadet Blue that the breakfasting hour is upon us and a serious breach of Academy protocol would occur if he does not attend. Indeed, This One fears this is a direct order from the commander himself."

Blue pulled the sheets over his head. "I'm having a lie-in."

"This One understands more than most how tiring the Academy regime can be. And such is the onerous task of climbing the stairs to the Wheel, This One must leave now or be late for Mess. Can he trust Cadet Blue to follow him forthwith?"

"Yeah," replied Blue from under his sheets. Hermans left the warm and comfortable bunkroom. A short time later, he was startled back into wakefulness by someone prodding him.

"Oi, Cadet. Get your arse in gear."

Corvus and he doesn't sound happy. Blue pulled down the sheets to discover the stern face of the raven-haired boy staring at him. "What do you want?"

"What I want, Recruit, is you up and dressed pronto, understand?"

"Well, what if I don't want to get dressed pronto?"

"Nothing personal, Gote, but if you, or any of us don't arrive at Mess on time to stand the line ready and dressed, we are all gonna take the jump. You understand? No way I'm gonna do Kitchen Duty on your account."

"I'm not well, okay?"

"Last thing I heard, you're fit for duty, Buddy." Corvus stood back and smiled. "There's two ways of doing this, one is for Wurtz to drag you to the showers, scrub you and dress you; and let me warn you, he's in an angry mood this morning. Or two, you can get your stupid Gote act together and sort yourself out."

"Okay, okay." Blue didn't want to face Wurtz again, and besides, the no-necked thug would beat him to a pulp.

"You may be suffering from a severe rectal cranial inversion, but you are no different from the rest of us. Saturn Squad takes care of one another. Otherwise, all our necks are on the chopping block. I don't want to be the one to make you pull your socks up, but the squad sorta expects me to knock heads, yeah? Lose the attitude."

"Attitude? I just fancied a lie-in. What's a rectal cranial inversion?"

"You'll suss it as soon as you get your stupid big head removed from out your fat ass. Now get showered, get into some whites and get yourself to the Mess asap." Corvus turned around and left.

After an embarrassing shower amongst naked cadets—nudity didn't count for anything in the Academy, bits and pieces everywhere—Blue dressed and struggled up the many steps to the Wheel, keen to check the Board for any mention of the previous night's assassination attempt. Nothing, except for one new posting: a single information sheet:

K.J. Heritage

FYI: THE BERGS

```
For those unfamiliar with the Berg
Empire, here is some background info
you might find useful:
```

There was a potted history of the first miners who made their home in the Asteroid Belt; their growing society and customs; a quick mention of the warring families and feuds; the foundation of their empire, their preference for a higher Gee environment and a section on succession, dealing with their most potent symbol of kingship—a golden signet ring set with a single sapphire. Passed from king to king, the heirloom had been the cause of many intrigues, deaths and assassinations.

The mysterious patient in the Sanatorium last night wore no such ring. If the important looking Berg isn't the king, just who is he? He read further. Technical stuff about H_3 and nothing at all about the attack. Dauntless must have hushed up the whole thing. Typical.

Back in the Mess, food was basic rations. Mutated porridge and a failed attempt at a hash brown seemingly made from sawdust. Ack.

The ostentatious cutlery, a mixture of silver and gold, was showy and expensive. The Hab must be stuffed with treasures like this. Blue licked his knife and fork clean and slipped them into his kitbag. *Easy. If I return home, they'll be worth a fortune. I'll grab as many as possible.*

Afterwards, a commanding and curvy olive-skinned woman in military fatigues—a less formal uniform of tight-fitting camouflage green—emerged from the steps leading down from the Officer's Mess and sauntered over to their table with controlled feline efficiency and some considerable grace. Well-muscled and lithe, a simple red band framed her thick black luxurious hair. She took in the Cadets of Saturn Squad with mysterious brown eyes and a face that reminded Blue of Tutankhamun, or at least, the female version on the pharaoh's beautiful golden death mask.

Heavy eyebrows, high cheekbones, and thick, dark red, pursed lips. A mixture of Middle-Eastern, Asian and Hispanic. Like the pharaoh, her calm expression held one of simple, but god-given command.

"Saturn with me!" she barked and Saturn Squad quickly fell in behind her.

"Who *is* that?" Blue whispered.

"Captain Sekhmet of Mars Squad of course," said Corvus.

"Of course."

Sekhmet. The Egyptian warrior goddess of war and healing. Commonly depicted as a lioness.

Blue tried not to stare, but could not help himself. "She certainly is…um…all woman."

Corvus sniggered. "She might be a total babe, but she'll come down on you like a shower of iron-rich meteorites if you're not careful."

"I shall be walking you to the Endurance space myself," Sekhmet explained in warm, relaxing yet authoritative tones, guiding them forwards. "Next time, I expect you to know the route and be waiting for me. You dig?"

"Yes, ma'am, we dig you," they replied in unison, apart from Hermans who said *sir*. There were laughs and giggles at the Ganymedian's wordy and protracted attempt at an apology.

"The time for humour is over," Sekhmet informed them and everyone went quiet.

"I want to ask you about something," Blue whispered to Corvus, a few minutes later. Blue relayed last nights' events in the Sanatorium including the mysterious assassin, deciding against revealing the intruder knew his name.

"We're humble cadets, Blue," said Corvus. "Lots of stuff goes on here we know nothing about. Stuff to do with SEARCH, the Bergs and even the Lost Worlds. Political stuff. We're never gonna know what's really going on until we get rank. And that's a long way off. I suggest you thank your lucky stars you lived through last night and let it rest. And don't pester me or anyone else with your constant questions. Okay?"

"Oh."

"Good, let's get on. We've a busy day with the Academy's best babe."

The Survival Space was an elongated cavern with a curved roof like an army barracks shed. Bare bulbs hung from thin wires running down the centre creating a mixture of shadows and highlights. Tables and chairs lined in front of an old-fashioned blackboard at the far end. A shelf ran around the other three walls full of quacky instruments, plants, bottles and weird stuff.

Sekhmet positioned herself behind a desk upon which sat a tall, rounded, mud-filled jar wide enough to take a clenched fist. She pursed her lips and waited for silence. She did not have to wait long. The captain generated instant respect and a little fear. "Your most important lesson is learning to stay alive in extreme environments," she began. "At different times throughout training, whether in space or off-world, I will be instructing you in the many and varied arts of survival. Listen up and listen up good. The information you learn from me will save your life sometime in your Academy training." She paused, letting the words sink in.

Blue paid attention carefully. *Surviving is one of my favourite interests.*

Captain Sekhmet picked up the glass jar and gave it a shake. Long shapes, writhed and wriggled within. "Can anyone guess what I have in here," she asked to blank faces. "Not to worry, you'll find out soon enough." She sauntered over to her blackboard and wrote *Swamplands* with the soft scrape of a chalk stub. "Swamps are commonplace Topside. This first sesh deals with basic survival in such environments. Think of me like a chef. I will be explaining where you can find a whole range of life-sustaining delicacies and how to prepare them for consumption." She then spent the next twenty or so minutes talking about food groups, diet and nutrition, and the ways and means one could extend life until rescue. The captain then raised her black eyebrows as if in amusement. "Before we have a break, I think a practical demonstration is in order." She removed the jar's stopper and tipped the contents onto a lab table.

Blue stared aghast at what writhed and crawled there. About twenty of the fattest orange-bellied slugs he had ever seen, all exuding thick slime.

Slug. A snail without a shell. Can reproduce by themselves, although a mate is preferred. Has green blood.

Slugs were common in his parents' allotment, but these were humungous. Some the size of small cucumbers. *Yeuey.*

Sekhmet held one of the glistening, muscular creatures, writhing in her grasp. "The species has a rather long and unpronounceable Latin name, what we here in Earth Corps call a *slimer*. For obvious reasons." Goo dribbled down Sekhmet's finger. "Their ancestors have been around for millions of years. Common in the swamplands and an easy source of low nutrition food if you are starving."

Predictable noises erupted from the cadets.

I agree with them. Disgusting.

"You find this creature unpalatable? Believe me, he could be the difference between life and a horrible, painful and slow death. That's why—" she paused with a wide smile, "—I want you all to eat one for me."

The cadets became silent.

"Not hungry?" With one fluid motion of her hand, Sekhmet popped the slug into her mouth. A few brief munches and it was gone.

The cadets reeled, gasping in horror.

"I've had worse. And you will too in your time at the Academy. Now come over here and choose a slimer. Cadet Corvus?"

"Yes, ma'am?"

"You can be first."

"Thank you, ma'am." Corvus went over to the table, chose a slimer, put it into his mouth, chewed for a few moments, retched, retched some more and swallowed.

"Well done, Cadet," said Sekhmet. "That was cool."

Veeva ate hers efficiently, determined to enjoy the experience. Blue guessed her failure in the Cubby Hole had dented her confidence and she wanted to make amends. Wurtz chomped his slimer with no show whatsoever, as if it was beneath him. Parris swallowed without chewing, although Sekhmet warned him the hardy creature would stay alive in his stomach for at least a few hours. Parris turned green. Hermans had no problems, the boy was permanently hungry. He thanked Sekhmet for what he called 'an intensely interesting and gastrically challenging experience'. Sugar made a show of hers, pulling some gruesome faces along the way. Not to be outdone, Ji and Coop did the same. Morgana was the only one to be sick. Everybody cheered when the chewed remains of the slimer made an unwelcome reappearance all over the seshroom floor.

Sekhmet turned her attention onto Blue. "Your turn, Cadet."

Blue went over to the table and stared at the writhing slimers. "I get how this is a bit of introductory fun, sure, but why do these creatures need to die to make your point. It's cruel."

"Cadet Blue," said Sekhmet, "In the Academy and in Earth Corps, we are sometimes forced to do things we don't want to. Do you somehow think you are better than the rest of your squad?"

"Of course not."

"I asked you to eat the slimer, now I might make it an order." Her soft voice contained the unmistakable Academy edge.

Wurtz made a threatening noise behind him.

Blue turned to the other cadets "She can't do that, can she?"

Sekhmet crossed her arms and nodded towards the slimers. "She can do anything she wants, Cadet," she said, giving every impression she would quietly force the thing down his throat if he didn't comply.

"Let me get this right. Not content with ripping me from my home and my family and making me take part in all this Cadet Academy nonsense, you now want to force-feed me creepy-crawlies? You are all quite, quite insane. And just what is the point of eating these miserable creatures when we're not even starving? Why bother? You might as well explain dehydration by giving us water to drink when we're not thirsty." Blue searched the seshroom for support. The series of frowns and shaking heads convinced him he was on his own. Only Parris and Morgana met his eyes and their faces spoke volumes.

"You make a compelling argument, Cadet Blue," said Sekhmet, still like a snake, her words stony and full of silent threat. "As a Gote, you are typically rebellious and questioning. Others in your squad can learn from such an admirable trait. Now for you all to appreciate the true meaning of starvation, as Cadet Blue so aptly pointed out, I am suspending Saturn Squad's food rations for a period of twenty-four hours. Cadet Hermans is of course excused this suspension."

A chorus of consternation and annoyed hisses erupted behind Blue.

"Thank you for your help, Blue," said Sekhmet, an expectant glint in her dark brown glass-like eyes. "Now we have a valid reason, I believe you need to do something for me." She picked up the most hellacious looking slug and passed it to Blue. "Enjoy. You won't be eating again for another twenty-four hours."

"But that's not fair," Blue blurted.

Sekhmet's head tilted the barest amount. "Commander Dauntless briefed me on your attitude problems, Cadet Blue. Now, shall I increase the starvation period to forty-eight or maybe seventy-two hours? All I have to do is make the order. Your decision, dig?"

The eyes of Saturn Squad burned into him.

"And I have a whole range of special punishments I can hand out, all of which I guarantee, are more disgusting than eating our sticky friend here. But that will not be necessary, will it, Cadet?"

Sighing in defeat, Blue sullenly grabbed the slug, bit off the head, sucked out the contents, chewed the remains and swallowed. The most disgusting mental-lentil thing Blue had done in his life. And yet the flavour was familiar. *That makes no sense.* He found himself perversely enjoying the salty taste. He reached over for another slimer, stopping at the last moment.

Captain Sekhmet raised a single eyebrow. "That's all for the morning sesh. Dismissed."

OFF-LIMITS

As soon as they left the seshroom, Corvus grabbed Blue around the throat and pushed him against the smooth rock of the corridor wall. "You dumb Gote!"

A fuming Saturn Squad surrounded them.

"What were you thinking, talking back?"

"I didn't mean t—"

Ji's face twisted into a scowl. "What is wrong with you?"

"You're not in your horrible stupid past now," spat Coop close to his ear.

"Hey!" shouted Parris. "You heard Shelley's orders. He's a noobie. Leave him alone."

Sugar pushed Parris aside and waved an angry finger at Blue. "You gotta learn never to speak back to an officer. Never. You hear me?"

"He'll need to do more than keep his mouth shut," threatened Corvus, his pale-blue eyes narrowed and full of ire. "I'm putting him Off-Limits."

"*You* are putting him Off-Limits?" said Morgana with indignation, pushing her hair behind her ears and glaring. "Who said you are in charge?"

"You have a problem with that, soldier girl?"

They glowered at each other for intense seconds, but it was

Morgana who dropped her eyes. "No," she conceded grumpily.

"What's Off-Limits?" Blue croaked, hoping Corvus would remove his hand from his throat sometime soon.

Parris' eyebrows knitted together in his familiar grimace, his face reddened. "He means no one is allowed to talk to you. Unless they absolutely have to."

"Enough, Parris." Corvus released his grip and stalked away.

Morgana touched Blue's shoulder for a second, smiled apologetically and chased after Corvus.

Blue glanced at Veeva and the others, but they had no eyes for him. "Well this is what I'm going to call 'one big bollocking mess.'"

Parris, shrugged and said nothing

"Right, you can't speak to me. I'm Off-Limits. Aint this the whiz-bang. My first proper day at the Academy and everybody thinks me the freak boy. Just like old times."

::

Back in the Mess for lunch, Cookie ordered the Squad to queue at the hatch. Blue wondered why, seeing as the demure but mental Captain Sekhmet was officially starving them. As ever, Corvus was first in line.

"Starvation Rations, Saturn Squad!" Cookie bellowed at the top of his voice. The other squad tables erupted into a tirade of catcalling and laughter. Corvus stood even taller, ignoring them. Cookie produced a tray of water bottles and passed one to Corvus. "Now listen. This is your one source of water, okay? You can fill your bottles here as and when you need. No food or fluids from anywhere else. Orders."

"Yes, sir." Corvus saluted.

As Saturn Squad passed, one-by-one, Cookie distributed the bottles until Blue's turn. "Good news, Cadet Blue." Cookie's voice reverberated around the Mess. "You are exempt from starvation rations."

"What?" exclaimed Sugar behind him. "He's the palm jockey

who put us into this damn situation."

"That might be the case, beautiful," leered Cookie, his voice, if possible, getting even lower, "but I have a direct request from Physician Phelps. This cadet is recovering from heatstroke, is undernourished and needs building up. Take a look at the skinny runt. Same for the Minnie."

"Well that's just—" Sugar was unable to finish her sentence in exasperation.

Blue joined the squad at the Saturn table and sat down; the other squads grinned at them, laughing. Blue had been hungry until he'd received his plate of food. Guilt stole his appetite away. Sitting next to him, Hermans possessed no such qualms. No one would begrudge the Ganymedian his full ration. The same wasn't true for Blue. Saturn Squad scowled at him. In the end, he pushed his tray away.

"Cadet Blue!" Cookie's pig-like face in the hatch. "You have a direct order to eat your food, you get me?"

"I get you, sir," replied Blue.

"I can't hear you."

"I get you, sir!"

"Good, I want a clean plate, you understand?"

"Yes, sir!"

::

The afternoon sesh was Endurance again and Blue had to endure every long second of it. Around him the sound of empty stomachs rumbled. This time, Blue kept his mouth shut and instead concentrated on the training. Captain Sekhmet went into more detail about the Swamplands and survival, and Blue soon realised the slimer was a treat compared to some of the gruesome things available in a 'starvation situation'. True to Corvus' order, no one uttered a single word in his direction, which had one positive outcome; with no one talking to him, there was every chance he wouldn't say something stupid again. Nevertheless, letting Saturn down dismayed him somewhere deep inside.

Later on, at the evening meal at which Saturn attended with

only their water bottles, Captain Sekhmet announced to the Mess, "…thanks to Cadet Blue, Starvation Training will be a compulsory part of all squads' Endurance Introduction. Details of the next squad to experience this training can be found on the Board."

Despite the rest of the cadets in the other squads giving Blue daggers, Saturn cheered.

"This doesn't mean the Gote is no longer Off-Limits," Corvus warned, but he seemed pleased.

Having the entire Academy against me is easy; having Saturn on my case was too much to bear. Like it or not, Captain Shelley and the squad are all I have. He tucked into his meal of over-boiled potatoes, roasted vegetables and a steak, aware that Cookie was keeping an eye on him. Physician Phelps had put him on the same diet as Hermans.

"Saturn Squad!" The commanding voice of Captain Shelley standing at the end of the table. They all jumped to attention. "It has come to my notice that our newest cadet here, has not, shall we say, been welcomed with open arms."

The squad shifted uncomfortably whilst Blue groaned inside.

"I ordered you all to give Mister Blue some leeway. None of you has the smallest idea of how he has been suffering, nor the terrible journey he has been through over his first days in a new world."

Corvus smirked and Shelley pounced on him.

"You think I don't know who put Mister Blue Off-Limits? You think your new Captain is perhaps easy to manipulate, to dodge?"

Blue closed his eyes and sighed.

"No, ma'am," Corvus replied without flinching.

"I admire your restraint, Mister. I am no fool, which you will all come to learn. I know people like you, with your dashing looks and family connections. You will have to do much more to impress me, you understand?"

Corvus swallowed, and Blue was surprised to see him shaking. "I understand you, ma'am."

"You and no one else in my squad will put anybody Off-Limits again. Do I make myself clear?"

"Yes, ma'am."

"Good. Mister Corvus, come to my Ready Room at twenty-hundred hours. Squad dismissed."

HELLIJETS

***"You dumb** Gote."*

"Stargazer."

"Stupid green ass!"

Now Captain Shelley had blocked the Off-Limits command, Blue became the butt of every insult going. He was jostled, bumped into, pinched and sworn at. Blue ignored the barracking with quiet dignity.

Today, Blue was excited; so excited he failed to hear the rumbling of stomachs around him as the twenty-four hour starvation training deadline approached. Saturn Squad were to spend the morning studying the hellijet's systems and maintenance in the aptly named Flight Room, a circular space dominated by pictures of spaceships and flying machines of various types and designs.

Swick.

Captain Khan, the long-lived leader of Jupiter Squad, waited for them in the room's centre, heavy black fingers pressed together expectantly, eyes hidden by tinted sunglasses. His square sponge of greying tightly clipped hair seemed almost white under the room's single naked bulb. He was, Blue reminded himself, over one-hundred and fifty years old and, according to Academy rumour, Captain Sekhmet's boyfriend. A model of the golden hellijet that had plucked Blue from Dooleys Wood—

Was it only days before?

—stood on Khan's desk.

The captain removed his sunglasses. Tired-looking milky green eyes, flickering with a constant tremor, swept over the cadets. His true age shone out from them, packed with wisdom, experience and a hint of sorrow. "Gather round, Cadets," he boomed cheerfully. Khan took the model apart, his sausage-like fingers nimble and practiced. "This is the Mark Two-Point-Three Hellijet. One of the most important atmospheric vehicles used by the Corps." He talked efficiently, taking them through every part of the hellijet's complicated systems. After this introduction, the cadets seated themselves and Khan pinned up the craft's schematics on a board, distributing extra-information on scuffed, well-used plastic sheets.

Parris smiled at the plans, as did Hermans and Wurtz. Ji and Corvus were in some sort of heated discussion, whilst Morgana, sitting with Sugar and Coop, appeared confused. The other cadets exhibited a mixture of gloom and excitement. Blue found the schematics mesmerising.

Complicated? Sure, but I can see beyond the blueprints. As if I already know all about aerodynamics, thrust vectors and cool jet turbine stuff.

The prop, unlike conventional helicopters did not give lift, but lent the craft better stability. The machine possessed a regular fuel system, used to kick-start the prop at take-off. Before Captain Khan moved on to explain the control systems, Blue had already worked out what they would be.

I'm learning in a way I never did at school. A new resolve came over him. If I can grasp complicated stuff like these hellish schematics as fast as this, all I have to do is learn everything about the rip and get myself home, sure.

The lesson continued. Maintenance and safety aspects, as well as the different classes of hellijets, some designed for manoeuvrability, others for speed including a list of manoeuvres from basic turns to barrel rolls and looping the loop.

Captain Khan sat back and narrowed his eyes. "Now who's understood all that?"

Parris, Corvus, Veeva, Wurtz and Ji raised their hands. Sugar and Coop appeared betrayed. Ji bounced in excitement. Blue also lifted his hand.

Morgana, Sugar, Hermans and the rest did nothing.

"Right, those with their arms raised can meet us Topside after lunch for your first flying lesson." Khan turned to an open mouthed Blue. "You okay, Cadet?"

Blue nodded, his eyes widening in shock.

Khan pushed himself up onto sturdy legs. "The rest of you take a short break. Meet me back here in fifteen."

Blue noticed the captain had left his sunglasses behind and, before he knew what he was doing, snuck them into his kitbag.

With the excitement of the flight, Corvus and the rest forgot their annoyance at Blue, although Parris had been babbling at him non-stop since the Off-Limits punishment had ended. They made their way back to the Crater and after ascending another carved stone staircase leading from the amazing jungle greenness below, they passed through more hermetically sealed doors to enter the stark R&R room.

Unlike the other rooms and chambers in the Academy Column, this space housed a vast window of the same thick glass used in his bunkroom's aquarium, giving wonderful views across the natural underground cavern. The rock walls replaced with vast metal plates, bolted together much in the fashion of *Old Dinger*. Well-spaced sturdy columns held up the roof, but the feeling was one of security. Sofas, tables, chairs and even an ancient Ping-Pong table dotted haphazardly.

Blue rushed to the window, joined by Veeva and Wurtz. They were low down on the side of the column, but high on a valley side. Wide rolling fields of green stretched off into the far distance where they met a gleaming city. Not exactly the size of skyscrapers, tall glass buildings made hazy by the distance caught glints from the artificial sun.

"Did I hear Khan right? We're flying hellijets this afternoon?"

Blue asked, his eyes skimming over to the other columns—magnificent and imposing stalagmites stretching from floor to ceiling.

Parris lounged in an ancient armchair. "Yes. Yes, we are."

"Okay, that's mental, but I'm on board with it. I'm sort of getting used to the shocks," said Blue pulling himself away from the window and its cra-mazing vista. "I may need more lie-downs though. And some form of tranquiliser. My main question? Why are we here, when the others are still studying?"

Corvus went over to the Ping-Pong table and sneered. "You don't know anything do you?"

"I know a great deal of things. The only problem? They mostly relate to a time half a millennia away...or had you forgotten I don't belong in this stupid century?"

Corvus snatched at a Ping-Pong bat and made experimental strokes. "Your real question should be: 'how did a pair of dumb asses like Parris and Ji find the lesson easy when the likes of Hermans and Sugar are struggling?'"

"Hey," protested Parris.

"That's not on, Corvus," blurted Ji, pushing long black, blonde-tipped hair away from her face to reveal an injured expression.

Corvus turned to Parris and smirked. "Can you see in the dark?"

Parris shook his head.

"Neither can I, nor Veeva nor Ji, nor most people," Corvus continued. "And what about you, Blue. You can see in the dark can't you?"

Blue remembered the assassin in the Sanatorium and shuddered. "You're saying even though we are all the same, some of us have different genetic talents?"

"That's right, Buddy. Here in the Hab, either you have a skill or you don't. A simple fact of life."

"I do have one skill...I remember stuff. Facts and information. Everything I've ever read. Pops into my mind all the damn time. If I want it to or not. Stuff I don't remember ever knowing. Does that make any sense?"

"Improved memory is standard kit for us advanced humans."

"Oh." Blue thought back to his freak blackout in the playground of over four-hundred and fifty years ago. "What other talents are there? Anything...er...way out there?"

"Some lucky spacers get the long-life gene. Like Dauntless and Captain Khan," said Parris. "Others have a form of limited telepathy. Although they tend to be a little peculiar."

Corvus pushed back his thick raven hair in mock exasperation. "We're much better off than those awful *unsats* from your time. They sounded like a right bunch of disease ridden jankers to me."

"They were not jankers," Blue protested, unsure what the word meant, but guessing it wasn't a compliment.

"No?" questioned Ji with a spark in her eyes. "From what I've learned, infection and sickness was widespread."

Veeva fingered her favourite ginger dread. "She's right. Humans in your time suffered from many genetic conditions: mental disorders, bone diseases, arthritis and cancer and many more. Most of which are eliminated and protected against in Earth-Hab. But we still get colds and flu."

"And no one from your century could read those schematics. Grasped the info. Like we did in the Flight Room," added Parris in his stunted fashion.

"Still, I can't believe we'll soon be flying."

"Wurtz fly before," the Berg butted in with his familiar gruff pigeon English. "Not in such flimsy craft. It break under my feet."

"That I don't doubt," said Parris and they all laughed.

::

Lunch was a meagre affair prepared by Cookie himself. Even though the Squad complained about the inadequate portions, none of them finished their plates, apart from Blue and Hermans. Sated and ready for their lesson, they made their way through the maze of tunnelling to emerge outside the Academy Column.

"We'll have to rush to miss the downpour," said Corvus pointing at a series of dark clouds slowly creeping up the valley."

"It rains down here?" Blue blurted.

"You better believe it, Kiddo," Corvus answered. "Although I doubt you can get any wetter."

They ran down the valley side, joining various other military personnel waiting on the immense disc of the elevator and were soon ascending towards the habitat's roof. A short time later, they exited the Mound and arrived at the landing field.

Topside in Desert Amazon at midday, the sweltering heat was like a weight upon his back. Grinding him into the sand. Blue was more than thankful for his generous covering of Slap. *Last time the sun nearly killed me and that was just in the morning. I was damn lucky. I won't make the same mistake twice.*

He was met by two familiar faces.

THE CLIPPED BOARDS

Second Lieutenant Singh glared at Blue with familiar twitchy intensity, a flicker of a smile hovering upon thin lips, above which sat his poor excuse for a moustache. "I heard you did well in the Cubby Hole. Great news for Saturn. Although I'm reliably informed that you also excel at starving your own squad. Not so great."

Blood shot to Blue's face.

At his side, Ammers guffawed, the thickset youth's greenish-blue eyes sparkling in his enormous curly-blonde head. The familiar lop-sided grin flicked in Blue's direction. "Good one, Singh."

With a mocking rise of his eyebrows, Singh spun around to address the rest of the squad. "This is where the fun begins. You get me?"

"We get you sir!" Saturn Squad replied with gusto.

"Excellent." Singh glanced at a clipboard. "Cadets Parris, Sugar, Morgana and Ji with me." He marched off towards the first hellijet, followed by the cadets he named.

Disappointment surged through Blue. Singh was one of the few cadets to earn his commission before the official end of the ninth phase of training. The Academy's best pilot and Blue had wanted to go with him.

Ammers beamed, pointing to a second gleaming hellijet parked a short distance away. "Cadets Hermans, Corvus, Veeva and Blue—guess what? You lucky sons of guns are with me."

Hermans bowed formally at Ammers. "This One is most honoured to be chosen. He will endeavour to do his utmost in the forthcoming task, despite his somewhat overactive trepidation."

The red-faced youth glanced up at Hermans and smiled. "You'll be fine...unless you crash the thing and then it's game over. Boom!" Ammers nudged the Ganymedian with a heavy arm and strode away laughing to himself.

"You're nervous as well, huh?" Blue asked Hermans as they chased after him, beads of sweat making funnels down his face.

"This One's piloting skills are limited to crafts of a more waterborne nature. The notion of propelling oneself through the air is somewhat awe-inspiring if not forbidding."

They arrived at the hellijet. This close and in full daylight, the machine mesmerised. A retro Aston Martin or a Jaguar automobile made into aircraft form. Sweeping impossible curves. Glossy metal. Polished chrome and tinted smoky glass. A sexy-cool hunk of living art. Blue ran his long brown fingers over the golden fuselage and whistled.

"She sure is a fast bird," said Ammers suddenly at his side. "You all be careful with her, you dig?"

"We dig you, sir," they answered.

"Good, Hermans you're first up."

The Ganymedian made a sort of high-pitched whine. A whole mess of worry crossing his elongated face.

"Hey," began Ammers, "I know one or two things about nerves. I was Singh's flying partner back in the day. That guy could scare dried cornshit out of a constipated chicken. Not that using the can was a problem after being up with him, that's for sure. Best way to deal with fear is to get it over quickly." He opened the cockpit door and bowed formally, mimicking the Ganymedian.

Hermans took a lungful of air, bowed, and clambered into the pilot seat, Ammers jumping in next to him. "The rest of you in the back."

Despite his trepidation, Hermans showed himself to be more than a competent pilot. Ammers thumped him heavily on the back and whistled when he had finished. "What did I say?"

Hermans winced, but could not hide his peculiar off-world smile.

Pleased for his bunkmate and determined to do better, Blue was disappointed when Ammers called Veeva next. Nerves made her flying jumpy and erratic. She exited the flying seat, pale and shaky. Corvus, a steady unremarkable flier, took the aircraft through the basic set of manoeuvres, although his whites became drenched in sweat. Blue enjoyed watching the cocky youngster struggle.

Blue made the most of waiting to fly. His mind distinguished the different noises of the aircraft and associated them with its construction and controls. With Ammers on the stick, the hellijet had a particular hum. A combination of sounds missing when Corvus or Veeva flew. As soon as Blue took the pilot's seat, he balanced the hellijet's systems and performed the basic manoeuvres without instruction.

Corvus voiced what they all thought. "Way to go, Blue, you're a natural."

"Thanks, Corvus. Look, I'm sorry about yesterday, talking back to Captain Sekhmet like that and um starving everyone."

Corvus ran a hand through his thick raven-like hair. "Forgotten. Putting you Off-Limits was a tad extreme. Shelley gave me a right old ear bashing."

Ammers sat back in his seat. "You fly like a pro, Blue. Perhaps we can try you with a few advanced manoeuvres. She's all yours."

Blue's mind flashed a range of exercises. He flipped the hellijet this way and that.

Ammers whistled. "You sure you've never flown before?"

Singh's voice over the radio, "How you doing, Ammers?"

"I've a sweet one here. Cadet Blue is gonna put you to shame one day."

"Yeah? Cadet Parris made a landing and on his maiden flight.

Saturn is always full of surprises."

Blue pulled back on the stick, throttling the twin engines, taking the hellijet into a quick, steep climb. "We can't let Parris get all the glory. I'm gonna loop-the-loop."

"No, Blue!" Ammers reached for the controls, but was too late. The aircraft stalled and plummeted.

"What the?" Blue struggled to regain control of the hellijet.

"Let me have her."

The jets died. "No, I can handle this," said Blue through gritted teeth.

"I'm giving you a direct order."

"This One advises Cadet Blue to follow his superior officer's most urgent command," said Hermans, his voice an intense reedy warble. Veeva screamed.

Corvus grabbed Blue around the neck, pulling him backwards, forcing Blue to let go of the stick. Ammers took quick control. The prop burst back into life with the reassuring whine of turbines. They were still dropping, Ammers gaining more control, stopping their spin and pointing the jets downwards. The ground rushed towards them. "Here we go. Brace!" The engine whine increased to a deafening roar, and seconds later, they made a heavy, but safe landing atop a sand dune. Ammers, flung the door open. "Out!"

Corvus pushed at Blue. "You nearly killed us."

Veeva came at him, her face full of tears. "What were you thinking, Blue?"

Blue grimaced. "I don't understand? The jets shouldn't have stalled."

"Look." Ammers thrust an enormous hand into Blue's afro and angrily dragged him to the back of the hellijet, roughly pointing his head towards the running boards, a series of mini-wings used for in-flight stabilisation. "The fins are clipped. This is a Mark Two-Point-*Four*, designed for speed, not manoeuvrability. There's no way you can manage a loop-the-loop in a crate like this." Ammers bashed Blue's head against the hollow fuselage and pushed him aside.

"I didn't realise. I'm sorry, okay?"

"Far too late for sorry," spat Corvus.

Ammers took a deep breath. "Okay, cadets. Let's calm it. We're uninjured and the hellijet undamaged." He shook his enormous head at Blue, his face, if possible, even redder. "This is why we train—to learn from these basic mistakes."

"I thought I knew what I was doing. I just didn't—" Blue dried. His legs suddenly wobbly. The after-effects of the adrenaline surge kicking in.

"A natural pilot you may be, but you must never disobey an order. You understand?"

Blue closed his eyes in shame. "Yes, sir."

"You idiot," accused Corvus, also shaking. "You stupid shitcan."

"Enough," said Ammers.

After a tense flight back to the Landing Field, Ammers marched Blue over to Singh who preened irritably at his flimsy moustache. "I hear you're one son of a flier?"

Blue didn't say anything. Over Singh's shoulder, Veeva and Corvus chatted angrily to Parris and the others.

"Disobeying an order almost got you, your friends and Ammers killed. I have wanted to kill him a few times myself, but that is no excuse. Still, I can't ignore your raw talent. And I certainly was guilty of many transgressions in my training. Transgressions I learned from. You, I'm sure will do the same. I don't doubt you are ever going to forget what you did today. So I will let this pass. But be warned, you ignore orders again and I'll bust you so fast your Gote feet won't touch the ground."

Blue opened his mouth to speak. Singh shook his head as if this was a really bad idea. Blue took the hint. The Second Lieutenant marched away, barking out the names of the next cadets to go flying.

Ashamed and humiliated, Blue sauntered over to Saturn Squad.

Corvus raised a finger. "Get lost."

BUSTED

During evening Mess, a soundless affair of disgusted looks and accusing eyes, the incident with the hellijet refused to leave Blue's mind. He wanted to disappear, hide away. Impossible here in the Academy. Corvus was still pale, but whether that was the after-effects of the crash landing, or his continuing anger, there was no way to tell. Occasionally his pale-blue eyes would fall on Blue and his familiar sneer was soon to follow.

If I could only go back in time and change things.

Blue caught his own thoughts and couldn't hide a smile. Going back in time to fix the mess of his life was rapidly becoming the solution to all his problems. But I'll never give up on Annie or on returning home. Never. Popularity, girls and flying stupid hellijets are just distractions, aren't they? Guilt, humiliation, anger and grief spiralled inside his mind. Shards of hot metal burning everything they touched.

Parris sat down next to him. "You okay, Blue?" he asked, prefacing the question with a nervous bite of his lip. His words crashed into the silence around the table like a shout. Some heads shook. Others turned away.

Embarrassed, Blue said nothing.

Parris continued, ignoring the frowns. "You thinking about what I think you're thinking about?" His tone was concerned, his expression as usual pinched and worried.

Blue filled his lungs and let out a guilt-ridden sigh. "Yeah, yeah I am."

"Hey, I'm sure I wouldn't have noticed the clipped running boards either."

Blue lowered his voice. "Ammers ordered me to stand down and I ignored him. Does everybody hate me?"

"Veeva is peeved," replied Parris, whispering conspiratorially. "Morgana is disgusted. Disobeying orders and all that. You scared Corvus. And we all know how that self-important shyster hates to be shown up. As for Hermans? Who can tell? Wurtz thinks it's amusing. The rest?" Parris glanced around the table, his twisted rabbit teeth nibbling at his lip again. "You're not exactly popular."

"Figures."

"Everyone else might be ragging on you. But not me. Okay? It was a silly ass-backwards mistake. Nothing would have happened if I hadn't been showing off. Making a landing to impress Singh."

It was nice of Parris to try to take the blame, but Blue was not convinced, the fault was all his. "I'm the Class-One idiot here, not you."

"We all make the occasional gaffe. It's just that yours are spectacularly stupid. To be honest, Blue, before you came along, I wasn't popular. I was the squad dork. I seem to rub people up the wrong way."

Blue didn't want to admit it, but he knew what Parris meant. He angered a little too quickly, was down on himself, insular and needy. *But he's on my side and that speaks volumes.* "You're the one person who's taken an interest in me since I arrived here. Apart from Morgana and she's a Crazy Amy. That means a lot to me."

"Thanks. We'll talk later. Shelley has summoned me to her rooms."

"Anything serious?"

"More of her 'character building' stuff. She's taken a shine to me."

Soon after, Blue left the Mess and went straight to his quarters. He lay on his bunk, trying to sleep, trying to ignore the events in the hellijet that played on continuous loop in his head. The sound of the hypnotic distant waterfall calmed him, but he remained wide-awake.

Hermans entered, his stretched face full of ill news. "Please forgive This One, Cadet Blue, for he is the bearer of information his bunkmate will find distressing."

Blue swallowed. "Go on."

"Ever since This One heard of the dreadful turn of events he has been saddened, but most of all, perplexed by what has happened."

"Don't string it out, just tell me."

"First Cadet Blue must forgive him for delivering such displeasing news."

Blue sighed. "I forgive you. Now spill the beans."

"This One is thankful for Cadet Blue's forgiveness and he will be more than willing to drop any number of legumes to find favour with his bunkmate, however, he must regretfully announce he is not familiar with this particular ceremony and, unfortunately, he does not have beans in his possession."

"Are you pulling my leg?"

Hermans' face took on a perfect mask of elongated confusion.

"Forget it. Just tell me the news."

The tall boy lowered himself next to Blue. "It would appear Commander Dauntless was informed about Cadet Blue's unfortunate escapade in the hellijet."

The full implication of the Ganymedian's words punched Blue squarely in the chest, knocking him sideways. A sickening wave of fatigue left him momentarily speechless.

"As Second Lieutenant Singh decided to ignore such a blatant disregard of orders, the commander had no choice but to demote him back to private. Commander Dauntless has also placed a black mark against Saturn Squad."

Blue found his tongue, although it was suddenly dry in his

mouth. "But…but Singh wasn't even flying with us."

"Cadet Blue is failing to comprehend that Second Lieutenant Singh was the commanding officer for our lesson Topside. Quite an honour for a cadet at the end of his training. Has Cadet Blue forgotten what is written on the Mess wall? 'Remember: when in command, the buck stops with you'. The Second Lieutenant made the decision to give Cadet Blue a reprieve. This One had assumed the matter was a closed one with those in Saturn Squad closing ranks. However, someone informed, someone from our squad." He shook his extended head, his eyebrows pinching together in a Ganymedian imitation of a frown. "This One, as Cadet Blue might relate to him, is *gob-smacked*. In the normal course of things, the irrational loyalty to one's squad will always outweigh all other considerations. Even when the actions of one of its members are dangerous. This One may not be acquainted with life in the Academy, but he does know the squad always comes first. Always. And Second Lieutenant Singh was from Saturn."

"You're saying someone ratted on me? Who?"

"This One cannot think of a single individual who would bring such disrepute to Saturn Squad."

"What about Morgana?" said Blue, eager to transfer the blame on to anybody else. "She doesn't like cadets who disobey orders."

"This One finds that most unlikely."

"She strangled me half to death and humiliated me in front of everyone because I was fighting Wurtz. You know why? Because it was against the rules. She's a sure bet. Corvus told me himself, 'she loves the rulebook.'"

Hermans placed a long thin palm in front of Blue's face and shook his head determinedly. "No. Cadet Morgana acted to help you. Cadet Blue should be thanking her, not seeking to find blame. If culpability is what you are after—" One long finger broke free from his hand and pointed at Blue accusingly. "This One suggests Cadet Blue search no further than himself."

Between all his lengthy words and his elegant singsong

delivery, the Ganymedian was telling him off. Blue didn't blame him. *I* almost killed him in the hellijet. What a mess. One giant stupid mess.

Hermans pushed himself on to creaking legs and walked to the doorway. "This One believes Cadet Blue has not considered his role in the sorry events of today. He suggests that Saturn Squad's newest member meditates on the concept of humility." He turned and exited.

Blue sighed. What did any of this matter anyway? He lay on his bunk, closed his eyes and let sleep finally take him.

A WARNING

Blue woke with a start to find Captain Shelley standing over him. "Ma'am?"

"Here." She gave him a folded piece of paper. "An Evening Pass. I'm ordering you to visit The Museum of Indulgence."

"The what?" asked Blue, suddenly wide awake and full of remembered dismay.

"This will get you away from the Academy for a few hours. I've included a map. Be back before Lights Out."

"Is this because of Singh, ma'am?"

"Yes. I have spent the last hour with Commander Dauntless. The man was apoplectic with rage. He has put a black mark against Saturn. As punishment, he has ordered you to visit the Museum of Indulgence. He believes you need some perspective. And for once, I am in agreement with him."

Blue had never seen his captain like this. Shelley gave the impression of being terribly let down. Suppressed anger flashed behind her googly eyes.

"I am very saddened by your reckless behaviour. Do you want to get yourself thrown out of the Academy?"

Blue didn't know the answer to the question. A dreadful stillness filled him, ached within him as if his molecules, unable to move, screamed at one another.

"Now take this and go."

His arm jerked into sudden motion, taking the permit from Shelley's flabby hand. "Yes, ma'am."

Captain Shelley stared at him for long seconds, as if trying to understand the workings of his rebellious mind. A disappointed twitch of her jowls and she was gone.

After a quick shower, Blue headed towards the Academy entrance with his kitbag over his shoulder. Here, he was surprised to find Sugar chatting to a handsome, blonde-haired Jupiter Squad cadet on guard duty—his name: Hansen. Blue handed him the pass.

Sugar's brown eyes widened in amazement. "An Evening Pass, after what you did to Singh? Seems like someone thinks he's the golden boy."

Ignoring her, Blue jogged down to the valley bottom, following a route through fields and woods. Like any country walk back home. But he would notice the cavern walls in the distance and the hint of blue passing for sky and be amazed. Ahead, the silver-tinted city he had glimpsed in the R&R room rose from green fields. Enormous towers, spires and impressive buildings glinting in the afternoon-tinged sun.

He passed abandoned farms and houses. Overgrown and forgotten gardens sat untended in an eerie all-consuming quiet. He tried to whistle to fill the empty air with anything other than his own loud footsteps. The sound died on his lips.

Has the rip swallowed everybody?

Following Shelley's map, and quickening his steps, he walked into the deserted city centre, buildings rising above him on all sides, until he reached a vast square. Statues, fine houses and wonderful and abandoned architecture dominated the place. The people who had once lived here had put a huge effort into their surroundings.

But the lure of off-world must have taken them all.

From what Parris and Shelley had told him, Earth was awaiting an ice-age lasting for thousands of years. The Hab, despite the wonderful controlled environment, was in reality a green, welcoming prison. Blue understood the attraction of new worlds, to be free of Earth's depressing future and the oppression of Earth Corps.

He entered an imposing wrought iron gateway leading to a vast central park. Half a mile away stood a construction of gleaming metal, rods and wires shining with colours of the rainbow. Hues shimmered and changed.

The Museum of Indulgence.

The building lurched in strange unbalanced directions. Blue had the impression the slightest breeze could topple the magnificent structure.

The park had once matched the splendour sitting in its centre, but the automatic machinery was failing. Straight manicured hedges crashed into overgrown, tangled verges. Outlandish bushes, seemingly trimmed by the remnants of tormented souls, ran madly across neat and elegant lawns. Order met chaos in an explosion of clipped greenery.

Blue arrived at the rather glish building and ascended beautiful, wide and sweeping steps that illuminated when he stood on them. The museum coming alive at his presence. Fountains burst into sudden life, music playing. A tinny version of *The Blue Danube.*

The Blue Danube. A waltz by the Austrian composer Johann Strauss II. Composed in 1866. One of the most popular pieces of classical music. Famously used in the Stanley Kubrick science fiction film 2001: A Space Odyssey.

Lights inside brightened. Perplexed at all this cheesiness, Blue entered the dusty, immense and gloomy entrance hall. A movable roof opened to let in sunlight from above. He almost fell over in shock. The ancient and majestic circle of Stonehenge, revealed as giant silent sentinels of cold grey threatening stone, surrounded him.

"Bloody hell," Blue whispered, as much in awe at their sudden presence as by the stones themselves.

Stonehenge. A Neolithic and Bronze Age ring of standing stones built between 3000BC to 2000BC. Located in Wiltshire, England.

One of the most famous prehistoric sites in the world.

He ran his hand across one of the four and a half thousand year old trilithons. Even here, in this far-flung and decimated future, the famous monument still had the power to amaze.

But Stonehenge is hardly a symbol of indulgence?

As the light increased, he became aware of the Statue of David standing in a mammoth side hall next to the remnants of the Sistine Chapel's ceiling, its rough, broken fragments held together on a metal frame. The dominating feature of this space was the decapitated head of the Statue of Liberty. He strode over, staring straight into her solemn eyes, at her now abandoned iconic visage. Here also was Admiral Nelson, free from atop his column, the Mother of Russia, her broadsword broken, and the reclining Monywa Buddha, her white painted face cracked and stained, as well as other statues both exotic and formal that Blue didn't recognise.

He found a side hall stuffed with some of the most famous paintings on the planet. He recognised Van Gogh, Rembrandt, Warhol, Picasso, Dali, Cézanne, Monet, Jackson Pollock and Turner. The list went on and on.

Did no-one care about them? The real treasures of civilisation, not those silly posters of Shelley's?

Lights brightened before him, illuminating and guiding him at the same time. He entered a tight corridor to the first gallery. A room the size of a school lecture hall but without seats. The walls came to life, filled with cascading images and videos of a world familiar to Blue.

An immense beach crammed full of humans enjoying the sun as far as the eye could see flickered in front of him. More beaches, airports, crowds on the streets of New York and other cities. Hong Kong. Dubai. Lagos. London. Wembley Stadium packed with people in reds and blues. A huge Chinese rally. Never-ending fields of corn. Supermarkets, warehouses, factories. Thousands of sheep, cows, chickens and pigs. Domestic animals of all kinds. Slaughterhouses. Eating. Restaurants. Piles and piles of waste. Traffic jams, vehicles and many types of aircraft.

Blue experienced a terrible yearning to be back there. The greed, indulgence; the noise, the crowds, the mess and the smells. Even in its ugly pleasure-seeking splendour, the past outshone this awful empty century.

So much has been lost.

He entered the next gallery, this one lit by violent reds and oranges contrasted by enormous swathes of black. Familiar images flashed before him. War. Terrorism. Refugees filling a road stretching to the horizon. Suicide bombings. Executions. Explosions. Rioting. Gunfire. Poverty, starvation and famine.

Too depressing. Too normal.

Blue had lived with these things every day of his life, but transplanted to the future, he saw their true horror and was ashamed.

The next galleries showed him what had happened since he had left Dooleys Wood all those centuries ago. Cities full of sand dunes. Fires raging in Peking. The USA from orbit, its entire land mass covered by a single, immense hurricane. Earthquakes in Northern Europe. Tsunamis. Lava and volcanic activity amidst an unfamiliar city. A nuclear explosion as seen from space. London flooded, bloated bodies floating around once proud towers.

Blue had witnessed the beginnings of the weather changes that would literally take the world by storm, the flooding, the forest fires, the unpredictable squalls and the melting of the glaciers. Like everyone else, he'd felt powerless. He'd lived with climate warnings and scares all his life, never believing humankind would let it happen.

He went through gallery after gallery, each one telling Blue of the fall of civilisation. The first substantial killer—famine. Then disease. Then humans murdering one another to survive. Within fifty years, the planet dropped back into barbarism. Only fragmented government, militia, scientists and their families survived. The last gallery, simply called *Hope,* was all about the building of the Hab and the coming together of the world's remaining dissolute communities.

Blue arrived back at the entranceway. Dusk. The dimming sun outlined the magnificent liths of Stonehenge in blood red. They stood in the near blackness as stark and powerful accusers. Thousands of years of mystery surrounded the once proud stones of Stonehenge. The circle was created, it was believed, to be in balance with the Earth; used to predict the position of the Sun, Moon and stars; marking the beginning of human technology, a technology that had increased at such a fast rate this balance was lost and the world thrown into abject destruction.

Blue now knew why Stonehenge dominated the entrance to this museum. It was a potent symbol of the wonders and the dangers of civilisation and of progress.

A warning.

He walked to the centre of the henge, sat on the Altar Stone and wept. An uncontrollable body-wracking lament. Everything was gone, destroyed. He sobbed for the Earth, for humanity and most of all for their blind stupidity.

Finding these potent relics of humankind and experiencing the images from the end of civilisation changed him somewhere deep inside.

Am I beginning to accept my place here?

Blue didn't know the answer. He'd never give up on Eddi, Newt and Annie, but he couldn't ignore where he was now. He'd been in the twenty-fifth century for just a few days yet had done more in those days than in his entire lifetime. To go back home meant returning to his humdrum existence.

Blue stood up, the great trilithons surrounding him, their shadows immense, powerful. "It's a price I am more than willing to pay," he whispered. It may be a total confuckulated mess, but the past, with all its problems, is where I am from and where I need to be. He wiped his eyes, straightened his whites and, with purpose, strode back to the Academy.

Blue Into The Rip

STORMS

Blue Into The Rip

THE SAND INFRACTION

Saturn received an unexpected R&R period the next morning in preparation for the afternoon's practical flying exam. Blue took a leaf out of Hermans' book and after breakfast went straight back to bed for a full-on snoozathon. He needed a decent kip just to give his mind a chance to reboot.

After a sleep still infected with swamps, flies, slimers and a sense of terrible loss—

Why is that?

—he forced himself to the Mess. Lunch was another awful affair eaten in silence. Their stomachs full, Saturn Squad made the long trek Topside to the landing field again. The cadets a few steps ahead, Blue walking behind. Alone. Ostracised.

Captain Sekhmet, resplendent in her pristine flying whites, her lustrous black hair braided and tied with golden wire, emerged from the Run-To. Blazing light reflected off her skin, as if she and the sun shared a special bond.

Behind her, and a good two heads higher, strode the immense Captain Khan. His blacker than black skin appeared glossy under the harsh rays. As ever, he remained impassive, intractable. A powerhouse of a man unaffected by such trifles as the midday desert sun. He wore a new set of sunglasses wrapped tightly around the cannonball of his head.

A surge of guilt rocked Blue combined with a stab of anger at his own stupidity. *Why did I steal his other sunglasses? What was I thinking? Does Khan know? Does he guess it was me?* But as ever, Khan betrayed no emotion.

They stopped in front of Saturn squad. At Khan's side, the not so diminutive Sekhmet appeared petite. They made a striking couple. Blue was ashamed to see them instead of Ammers and Singh.

"Squad attention!" barked Khan, his voice still booming outside the Academy confines.

Sekhmet took a gulp of water from her bottle, swilling her mouth before swallowing. "Shame what happened to *Private* Singh. A squad should always stick together. You would never find any of my cadets ratting on each other. The commander was not only disappointed by Singh, but by the one sorry ass in Saturn who went running to him. Now I don't know who that was and I don't care." She stepped forward, large brown accusing eyes peering over Blue's shoulder, flitting from one face to the next. "But listen up. You will do yourself and your squad no good. No good at all."

Saturn eyed one another suspiciously. Blue glowered at Morgana. At her side, Corvus hung his head, his disappointment at Saturn seemingly too much to bear.

"You dig?"

"Yes, ma'am,' the cadets replied sullenly.

Captain Khan stepped forward and slowly filled his lungs. His words, when they finally arrived were toneless, but Blue was sure he could detect a hint of displeasure. "I've been told Saturn has many good fliers, a few top-notch fliers and some poor fliers. Forget that. You all start with a blank canvas with me. To earn your wings, you need to convince Captain Sekhmet and myself you deserve them. You get me?"

"Yes, sir! We get you!"

Sekhmet lifted her clipboard. "Cadets Corvus, Morgana, Hermans and Cadet Blue, with me."

Corvus turned to Blue. "You try any of your stupid tricks

and—"

Blue held his hands aloft. "I won't."

Corvus flew first. His take off, according to Captain Sekhmet, was 'textbook cool' and, after a competent few minutes, he navigated the ship to a designated point and landed with a slight bump. Sekhmet smiled. "Satisfactory, Cadet. You are ready for your solo flight."

Corvus smirked.

"A marker is placed at these co-ordinates." Sekhmet passed him a chart. "Take the bird up, get the marker and return. Everybody out."

Ten minutes later, beaming from ear to ear, Corvus landed the hellijet and emerged with a coloured flag.

Sekhmet saluted. "Cadet Pass. Well done, you've earned your wings."

Morgana was next. Shaky at first, she soon found her feet. Stunned and proud, she received a pass and saluted Sekhmet so many times the captain had to grab her hand to make her stop. That left Hermans and Blue. Despite his earlier self-confidence, Blue's nerves were getting the better of him.

Sekhmet turned her attention to them both, her olive-skinned, striking, features twisted into a mischievous smile. "Cadet Hermans."

Blue guessed making him wait was a subtle punishment.

Hermans was again an excellent pilot. Blue couldn't fault him. Sekhmet announced a different route for Hermans' solo flight with more complicated navigation and some extra manoeuvres. Blue realised what the captain was doing. Making it harder for the 'true fliers'. Hermans' prelim flight was nearly over when the tall boy leant forward in the control seat, straining his eyes into the distance.

"You spotted something, Cadet?"

"O-Oasis, ma'am," he stuttered, his elongated head twitching in embarrassment.

Oasis. An area of fertile ground located within a desert usually containing pools of fresh water. Can support vegetation and limited animal life.

"You sure?" asked Sekhmet, examining her maps. "Nothing on any of my charts. Just sand for hundreds of clicks. Although you do possess twenty-twenty plus vision."

"Yes, ma'am, This One is certain," said Hermans with growing confidence and the first hint of excitement to his voice.

Sekhmet sat back in her seat. "Good, let's go take a gander."

Blue didn't care about the oasis. He had been waiting over an hour for his turn to fly and this whole diversion thing was doing his head in. "How long is this going to take, ma'am?"

Corvus scowled at him. Morgana twisted her head from side to side in undisguised disappointment.

"What?" said Blue petulantly.

Sekhmet radioed the Run-To to tell them they were leaving their registered flight co-ordinates to investigate what she called a possible 'sand infraction'.

"Good luck, Captain," came the crackly reply.

A short while later, they flew over the oasis. A fertile circle of land containing a small natural lake surrounded by huge dunes. Vegetation thrived for hundreds of metres, iridescent trees, hardy shrubs and grass-like meadows. It stood in the sand like a large emerald eye with a pupil of pure blue. An explosion of jungle green amongst the featureless coffee-coloured desert.

Morgana cheered. "Well done, Cadet Hermans."

"Well done indeed," intoned Captain Sekhmet. "This will make a fine addition to your record."

Hermans brought the hellijet to a controlled landing on one of the sparse grassy meadows below a large dune and they disembarked.

"Cadet Hermans with me. You three stay here with the Helli'," Sekhmet ordered, much to their disappointment. The Ganymedian smiled in apology before stalking off into the trees and disappearing.

"Where did all this come from? I thought this was supposed to be a desert?" said Blue.

"An interesting question," replied Morgana. "The Amazon is

a dust bowl, but water from underground springs supplied from permeable aquifers sometimes reaches the surface. No one knows how or why. The sand is full of old seeds and insect pods left over from the mother of all rainforests. As soon as moisture arrives, life explodes out. Sounds simple, but the process is vastly more complicated. The eggheads are stumped. This is why Hermans' discovery is so brilliant. They can learn loads from this place. Some think it might be possible to rebirth the jungle."

Blue had forgotten Morgana's voice. She pitched it even higher in the open desert. An irritatingly noisome blurt of over emphasised vowels and sharp consonants. She carried on for a while but Blue's disinterest, meant she soon lapsed into an uncomfortable silence. Corvus stood a few feet away, his arms crossed. Making it very clear he wanted nothing to do with either of them.

A long time passed. Far too long. "Where the hell are they?" Blue asked finally.

Corvus opened his mouth to speak but changed his mind.

"I'm going to investigate," announced Blue, walking off.

"We can't," said Morgana. "We were ordered to stay here."

"He's right," agreed Corvus begrudgingly.

"You think so?"

Corvus grabbed Morgana and dragged her along. "Let's go."

They ascended a grassy dune, disturbing a multitude of fat beetles that lurched clumsily into the air, crashing into their legs, trying to escape. Smaller flies, a cloud of black dots, flew into their eyes and mouths. Bugs crawled and scuttled everywhere. Elongated sandy footsteps led down the other side to a line of thin trees growing in number and size surrounded by a sea of shrubs and vines. Muffled shouts and yells came from further ahead, hidden by tightly packed vegetation.

Hermans and Sekhmet.

They ran towards the voices, trampling plants underfoot, pushing through exotic greenery, disturbing even more and larger chattering insects before entering a tree-shadowed glade that surrounded a deep pool of bluest azure. The sounds of shouting became louder, until, in the distance on a small shore, they spotted Hermans and Captain Sekhmet fighting with what appeared to be an invisible enemy. Blue was a good fifty feet away, yet the fear on Hermans' face, as he swung a heavy branch around him, was obvious.

"Stay back, Morgana!" shouted Captain Sekhmet. "Stay back all of you. That's an ord—" Sekhmet lost her footing and fell to the ground. A wave of sand-coloured writhing shapes engulfed her.

"Crawlers!" Morgana shrieked, running forward under a wide arch of vine-entangled trees.

"Cadet Morgana, no!" shouted Hermans. He tried to fend off even more of the voracious insects. A gigantic snake-like crawler landed on his shoulder, sinking chitinous fangs into his lengthy neck. Hermans wrenched the insect away and, kicking the crawlers aside, bent over Sekhmet, pulling the bugs off her, stamping on them with stilt-like legs.

A crawler reared at Morgana's feet. She kicked it viciously in the head. She ran to the aid of Captain Sekhmet and Hermans.

"Be careful, Morgana," warned Corvus, "they're everywhere."

Corvus and Blue stared at each other and shook their heads in fierce resignation. They jogged forward, the heavy sound of falling crawlers thudding around them. They joined Morgana who had reached Hermans' side and dispatched as many of the creatures as possible.

"This One tried to stop them. Unfortunately, he was somewhat outnumbered by the voracious and rather irritated insects," Hermans rasped, clutching at his wounded neck. "This One should have protected his captain."

Morgana sank to her knees to examine Sekhmet. "That's not important now."

Corvus kicked a still twitching crawler. "How bad is the captain, Morg'?"

"She's unconscious. Covered in bites. We have to get her back to the Run-To. Otherwise—"

::

A blur of shouting, dragging, smashing, swatting and fear. Blue had no memory of how they managed to haul Captain Sekhmet past the crawlers to the hellijet. By the time they arrived at the ship, her golden skin was ashen, her breath short and rasping. Hermans collapsed into a fever soon after and drifted into unconsciousness. Blue jumped into the pilot's seat and cycled the prop.

"No way!" shouted Corvus.

"Huh?"

"Maybe you missed it, Buddy-boy, but I have my wings. There's no way you're gonna fly me again, not after what you did."

"I—"

"No time for argument," said Morgana. "Corvus, get on the radio and tell the Run-To we have an emergency. We'll need serum ready. Blue, come back here and give me a hand."

Corvus pushed Blue aside and took over the control column. "Hab Control, Hab Control," he said, bringing the hellijet to life. "This is an emergency, over."

Static.

Corvus cycled the frequencies. Still no signal. "The damn radio's down."

"Try again in the air," ordered Morgana.

"No probs," replied Corvus.

The hellijet lifted off. Blue clambered into the back to join Morgana. Captain Sekhmet was deathly, whilst the fang marks on Hermans' neck had turned black. Blue shuddered.

"Hab Control, Hab? You dig me?" Corvus continued on the radio. More static. "We have an emergency. Two with crawler bites. We will be at the Run-To in…approx. eighteen minutes. Hab Control, do you read me?" Corvus repeated his message over and over. No reply.

"Anything we can do?" Blue asked Morgana.

"They need serum quick, or we'll lose them both," she replied with tears in her eyes.

Long minutes passed until, with a whine, the hellijet lurched violently sideways.

"What was that?" Morgana shrieked.

"I don't believe it," whispered Corvus. "I don't jazzing believe it."

RACE TO THE RUN-TO

The hellijet rocked. Corvus, struggling with the controls, bounced on his chair like a rag doll. A high-pitched squeal behind the sound of the engines. Cold swirling sand whipped against the cockpit window.

Blue climbed over the seats and sat next to Corvus. "Another sludge-storm?"

They were about five minutes from the landing field, the shrouded shape of the Mound faint in the distance. Wind whipped and snarled at the hellijet.

"We'll have to turn back," barked Corvus.

"Nowhere close enough," said Morgana. "If we don't land in the next few minutes, Hermans and Captain Sekhmet won't make it."

The rapidly growing storm seemed to transfix Blue. "I can fly this."

"Don't be stupid. You'll kill us all," sneered Corvus.

Blue pulled his attention away from the squall and looked straight at the raven-haired boy. "We can't let Sekhmet and Hermans die—*We can't.*"

"But to fly into a sludge-storm is suicide."

"No. I can see inside it," said Blue. The calm certainty of his words surprised him. "I see wind patterns, pressure lines and speed vectors. I can fly within them."

Corvus was adamant. "We'll all die."

"If you were injured instead of Hermans," implored Morgana, "wouldn't you want Blue to try? Ammers said Blue is the best pilot he's ever seen. Better than Singh. Why else did Singh let him off? And I dunno, I trust him, okay? We knew when we signed up there would be danger. If we are going to die, let's at least go out with honour—trying to save lives."

"We're not going to die," insisted Blue. "I can get us there. I'm not making the same mistake twice."

"This is not about skill," said an unconvinced Corvus. "Nothing can fly in a sludge storm." As if to prove his point, a violent updraft slammed into the hellijet knocking him sideways. Blue grabbed the control column and slid into the pilot's seat.

The hellijet immediately stopped bucking.

Corvus stared at Blue as if for the first time. "Hey! How you doing that?"

"Like I said, I can take us home." The golden craft twisted in the volatile winds, yet Blue, somehow kept control. "What do you say? You gonna let me try?"

Corvus leant back in the seat. His hands shook, his normally confident eyes full of anxiety. A quick flick of his head and sudden determination replaced his fear. He set his jaw and smiled. "Why not. Let's give it go at least. But if you can't handle the stick, we turn back. Agreed?"

"Agreed."

"Strap in the passengers," Blue ordered, his mind becoming absorbed with contours and vector lines, eddies and pressure changes.

They spiralled closer to the landing field.

"I think we're gonna make it," said Corvus.

As if in response to Corvus' words, a strong gust upturned the hellijet.

"Hold on," yelled Blue who, rather than wrestling the controls, let the flying machine be carried this way and that. Seconds later, the straining craft righted itself and Blue was again in control.

Wet sand began to block the windows. With a grinding rasp, the prop stopped spinning and the jets spluttered.

"I knew it," growled Corvus. "I damn well knew this was a stupid idea."

"Don't listen to him Blue," said Morgana. The fuse jets screamed in protest. "You can do it."

The sand build-up was disastrous, clogging the hellijet's essential systems, sticking to the outer hull, making the ship heavy and impossible to manoeuvre. With a deep breath, Blue turned off the fuse engines and the hellijet dropped from the sky like a stone.

"What are you doing?" howled Corvus in alarm.

"I vowed to never make the same mistake again. I've learnt my lesson. This time I know the schematics backwards—*and then some.*" Blue pulled the Fuel Dump lever.

"No," protested Corvus. "We'll never restart the prop."

Ignoring him, Blue cycled the fuse engines and the fuel ignited. A massive explosion erupted below the hellijet, bright orange flames searing the cockpit windows, burning away the sand and bathing Blue in arcane red and golden light. To Corvus it seemed Blue was made of fire rather than flesh, blood and bone.

The flames did not engulf the craft. Instead, the flying machine rode on the back of the fuel burn like a cushion. They descended, landing with a controlled thud. The blaze died, replaced by the cruel whip of sand and sludge.

"We're here," whispered Blue as if from a dream.

Corvus sat open-mouthed, too amazed to speak. "How?" he managed.

"Break out the tarps," ordered Morgana. "We must get the casualties to the Run-To now."

"How are they doing?" Blue asked, coming back to himself.

Morgana shook her head. "Not good."

They busied themselves with the tarps: thick plastic-like blankets used as shields against the grating sand. Blue put

Captain Sekhmet on his back, whilst Corvus and Morgana carried Hermans between them. They left the hellijet and, with Blue leading, they struggled blindly through the devastating storm, the grit whipping at their exposed feet. They found one of the many Run-To doors and pounded for all they were worth.

A shocked ground crew let them in. "Where in space did you come from?"

"No time," replied Blue. "These two need serum now. Crawler bites."

A group of medics took Hermans and Captain Sekhmet away, Morgana going with them.

Blue brushed sand from his face and rubbed at his sandblasted feet. As his eyesight recovered from the sludge-storm, he became aware of Saturn Squad and the ground crew staring at them with a mixture of confusion and amazement.

"Blue flew us in," explained Corvus with a dry croak. "He saved Captain Sekhmet and Hermans." He faced Blue and offered him his hand.

Blue took it and they shook. Around them, Saturn Squad and the ground crews erupted into spontaneous applause.

"Well done, Blue," said Parris jogging over.

Blue ignored him. Morgana had returned, her face a mask of grief.

WORMS

The Squads met in the Mess first thing next morning and stood the line. Dauntless appeared, resplendent in his official whites, his breast covered in a showy riot of colour from many bars and medals. The commander did not wear his sunglasses and Blue was shocked to discover outsized blue eyes mirroring his own. They somehow humanised the man.

The twacker is still an unfeeling git, obsessed with orders and rules.

Next to the commander, stood another older man of similar stature with even more medals. Dark-skinned, a hint of American Indian with wiry straight grey hair tied back in a long ponytail. Penetrating brown eyes sparkled with keen intelligence from a weather-beaten pitted face dominated by a powerful nose.

"Who's the stiff?" asked Blue.

"Wow," whispered Parris. "That's Fleet-Admiral Apache, the High Commander of Our Very Earth. Of Earth Corps."

The Apache. Several culturally related tribes of Native Americans originally from the Southwest United States. Fierce warriors and expert strategists.

"I don't like the look of him."

"He's the head-honcho. The big cheese. The boss. Only Admiral Joplin of SEARCH comes a close second. But even she has to yield to the Fleet-Admiral."

"Apache? Dauntless? Sekhmet? Joplin? Shelley? Why does everybody have such self-important and famous names?"

Parris shrugged. "Earth Corps tradition. When you reach the rank of captain, you can pick any name you fancy. Many go for historical names. Others choose cool places. Or even races. Like the High Commander."

"And Dauntless?" asked Blue.

"After some famous British warship I think."

"So, this Apache guy is the high muck-a-muck, huh?"

"As important as you can get."

"I bet the commander loves having him here."

The other Academy captains walked solemnly behind Apache and Dauntless. The sudden appearance of the bear-like Captain Khan made Blue reel. Proud, and without a tear on his cheek, his sprawling black face betrayed such awesome grief to make Blue sway where he stood.

"Khan was Sekhmet's lover," whispered Sugar gravely.

Dauntless ushered the Fleet-Admiral forward and exited to the Wheel, followed by the other captains.

"Jupiter and Mars with me," Khan ordered. His usual booming voice a hoarse, guttural whisper.

Sugar sobbed, tears glistening against her bronze-brown skin. "Shhh," admonished Morgana.

"You don't understand," explained Sugar. "These tears are for Captain Khan, he is too proud to cry. I'm weeping for him." Ji draped a hand over Sugar's shoulder, whilst Coop hugged her.

The other captains called their squads and when assembled, led them from the Academy Column and down onto the valley floor. The reddened sun grew into slow life, marking the start of another day in the underground habitat. This early, before the harsh sunshine blinded him, Blue was able to once again marvel at the sheer engineering genius behind its construction. A vast neon tube stretching across the many kilometres of the cavern. Behind them, the alien skull of the Academy stalactite sat upon the valley side like some weird tombstone highlighted in blood.

Blue shivered.

They walked to a park-like grassy area on the shore of an enormous lake, familiar robotic mowers pausing to let them pass. A simple but extensive wooden seating platform waited for them in front of which lay the body of Captain Sekhmet on a raised table garbed in featureless grey cloth. No attempt had been made to disguise the reality of death from those still living. Sekhmet was a vibrant, powerful woman forcing him to eat slugs and starving everyone. His memory of her and the thing lying on the bier jarred. Her golden skin was ashen, her closed eyes sunken, once full, fleshy lips twisted into a dreadful leering rictus. A lopsided, toothy sneer. Blue had not known Sekhmet for very long, but the expression was not hers.

Why show us death like this? Ugly and unforgiving. Blue knew the answer. Earth Corps is not intentionally callous. No. It suffered from something far worse: rational practicality.

Physician Phelps, wearing her fine Medic's white and red dress uniform, a Venus Squad cadet on either shoulder, strolled over to stand by the pallid body. Dauntless, the Fleet-Admiral, the captains and other Academy people including Cookie and the catering staff ascended the platform. Blue and Saturn Squad joined them.

Blue was confused. "Where's her family?"

"The Corps is her family," answered Morgana, her usually loud voice for once hushed.

"What about her mother and father and brothers and sisters?"

"The body is a vessel for consciousness and nothing else. This is no funeral, but a regulation ceremony to dispose of her remains."

Dauntless coughed and all attention moved to him. "Life is a wonderful journey," he began solemnly. "Everything that has ever lived on the glorious testing ground of Gaia, which is Our Very Earth, shares the same simple immutable fate. *All must one day die.* Yet to live is to learn how magnificent, how normal and how precious life is. And whilst alive, we must embrace existence and its many facets. Captain Sekhmet was no exception to this rule. She lived as she died: as a member of the Academy, as an explorer, as a teacher, as an innovator and as a woman worthy of the life she led. She went into death in the full knowledge of what her existence meant and with a long legacy of all the things she did for others. She has been an outstanding daughter of the Corps and humanity." Dauntless paused and nodded to the physician.

The two Venus Squad cadets, followed by a grave looking Phelps, carried Captain Sekhmet's body towards a peculiar wheeled structure like a giant's overturned bicycle and placed it on a grassy mound. Blue had not noticed the apparatus before, assuming it was a piece of futuristic art. All black-painted wires, cogs and chains.

The commander's tone became, if possible, even more solemn. "It is time for our colleague to return from whence we all came."

Phelps spun a small wheel and the machine launched into sudden thumping life, accompanied by a growing thudding sound from odd-looking spinning paddles striking the ground.

Long seconds passed, the earth vibrating under his feet. Blue noticed a disturbance around Sekhmet. The machine is calling something—something underground.

As if this was a sign, everybody bowed their heads. Blue continued to stare. The soil boiled under the dead captain. Long muscular shapes writhed and twisted in the dirt, reminding him of the awful crawlers that took Sekhmet's life away only hours before. He shuddered in revulsion, fearful that the dreadful creatures might take him from below. But the grass was firm, undisturbed.

Sekhmet became engulfed, slowly sinking, crumpling into the earth. All that remained was a mound of disturbed soil. Phelps returned to the machine and the pounding ceased.

"What the hell just happened?" whispered Blue in revulsion.

"Worms," answered Morgana matter-of-factly. "They take anything that is dead and disperse the remains into the Hab. The natural way. They were one of the first successes of the geneticists. The Hab is a controlled environment; the worms increased in size and altered to keep the soil aerated and fertile. They do lots of other stuff as well."

Blue sighed fitfully. "Why did no one warn me about this?"

"About what?"

He shakily pointed to the peculiar apparatus and the disturbed earth, exasperation finally getting the better of him. "…That was just Whacko-Jacko!"

"Shhh. Do not be so disrespectful."

THE TWO SONS

The ceremony ended with the taking of Sekhmet. Captain Khan came over to thank Corvus, Morgana and Blue. The once proud, powerful man was a shadow of his usual self, bent under the weight of overwhelming grief.

Afterwards, everyone headed home to the Academy Column. With no specific order to return, Blue held back. He wanted to examine the mound of earth that had engulfed Captain Sekhmet. And besides, *I like being out here. Apart from the Crater, the gloomy underground caverns and tunnels are oppressing.*

"—it was a bold choice to bring him to the Academy," observed a distant voice carried on the breeze.

Blue froze. Nothing except the wooden seating platform. Everyone else had gone.

"Yes, yes, you are right, Fleet-Admiral—"

The distinctive tones of Commander Dauntless.

"—I wanted the boy where I can keep an eye on him. You are aware of how important he is. I was in the right place at the right time and I believe in making the most of all my opportunities."

Blue peered through a crack in the timber beams and discovered Commander Dauntless and Fleet-Admiral Apache smoking cigars.

"Yes, the Academy is the best place for him. He should be

safe in your hands. How is he settling in?" Apache asked, his voice rough as if he had been barking orders all his life.

Dauntless took a long drag on his cigar. "He is showing a typical disrespect for authority."

"Well, we did expect that I suppose, considering where he's come from and being forced to adapt to your strict regime."

The two men laughed.

Apache smiled. "Of Course, SEARCH is very interested in the boy and annoyed at your interference."

"You read my report on the assassination attempt in the Academy Sanatorium?"

"Yes, our suspicions are confirmed. The assassin did not rip through any machine of ours. You were always the bold one, Jack. Be careful. SEARCH are not to be messed with."

Dauntless' voice held a sneer. "And Wilhelm's son, Dore? What of him?"

"Dore is as twisted as he is ambitious."

"He would need to be: he poisoned his own father at the banquet held to open the talks. Still, Dore is not particularly bright. I'll warrant SEARCH made a mistake by sponsoring him. They intend to replace Wilhelm with such a fool?"

Apache nodded. "It would appear so. His father, he is not."

"No he isn't. SEARCH does not make many mistakes. I wouldn't be surprised if Dore is merely the first player in a longer game."

"Possibly."

Dauntless grimaced. "How is King Wilhelm? Recovered? Phelps won't tell me anything. Hippocratic Oath and all that."

Hippocratic Oath. A pledge taken by physicians and other healthcare professionals swearing to follow a number of professional ethical standards, including doctor/patient confidentiality.

Apache took a long drag on his cigar, his penetrating brown eyes unblinking. "He is as well as you might expect after a near fatal poisoning."

Poison? Then the noble Berg I saw in the Sanatorium was King Wilhelm. Wow. SEARCH must have had him poisoned in an effort to gain control over the H_3 supply. When they realised that hadn't worked, they sent in an assassin. It all now makes sense.

Admiral Apache lowered his voice and Blue had to strain to hear. "Phelps is the best physician in the Hab and the most discreet. The poison went deep and Wilhelm will suffer for months. The Berg race is a proud one; if the King shows any sign of weakness, the other families and those seeking to overthrow him won't sit idly by. Phelps is giving him drugs to mimic the appearance of strength for the duration of the talks, yet she is not happy. She assures me of a full recovery—given time."

"Why do we need the talks at all?" asked Dauntless with irritation. "I'd give the Bergs rip technology and be done with it. Wilhelm is trustworthy. He has proved that to me time and time again."

"Wilhelm was your friend at the Academy when you were both cadets and those friendships run deep. But things are not that simple when SEARCH are involved. The Council of Our Very Earth needs to be convinced and Admiral Joplin is against such a move."

"Joplin *is* SEARCH. They corrupted and groomed Dore. With Wilhelm dead and Dore in his place they can control the H_3 for their own secret rip machine. You have to admire their audacity."

"Jack, this is a delicate political situation and you are a man of action. Let me and Wilhelm deal with the problem."

Dauntless tapped his impressive array of medals. "I can play the political game when need be."

"I'm sure you can." Both men laughed. "Wilhelm is a strong king, he can control his sons."

"Can you be sure?" Dauntless asked, rubbing one hand over the baldpate of his head as if to flatten imaginary hair long since departed. "With Dore working for SEARCH, it is just a matter of time before another attempt is made on Wilhelm's life."

"The kingdom is safe while he still holds his signet ring. Wilhelm will not willingly give away such a powerful symbol of his kingship and authority to Dore, even if he is his oldest son. He can bestow that gift to any he pleases."

"Yes, Wilhelm is as wily as he is intelligent. I'm sure he has made plans to keep the ring safe."

"True." The Fleet-Admiral took another long puff on his cigar. "I was surprised to see Major Shelley at the Academy. What's the story there?"

"She was demoted, thrown out of SEARCH and posted here. She is now *Captain* Shelley."

Apache's brown glasslike eyes narrowed for a moment. "You don't say?"

"I was intrigued at first," said Dauntless, "if not worried. The coincidence of her arrival is something I cannot ignore. I think she is harmless, apart from her disrespectful mouth. I can guess how she fell out of favour with SEARCH. Still, her cadets love her."

"You have someone watching her and the boy?"

"Of course. A cadet I can trust."

"Better to be safe than sorry when SEARCH are involved."

Dauntless ground the remains of his cigar under his heel and straightened. "Sekhmet was an exemplary officer and a fine friend. I will miss her. I am expected to lead the speeches at the wake. We'd better get on."

"It's been good to catch up, Jack. You make sure to keep in touch and your eye on your special cadet. Be careful."

The two men made their way around the platform.

Blue held back, avoiding their line of sight, his mind a swirl of thoughts.

Were they talking about me then? I'm at the centre of some political intrigue! I must be.

One thing Dauntless said disturbed him the most: another cadet in Saturn is watching me. But who is it?

WINGS

Blue's feat of landing the hellijet during a sludge-storm on the top of a fuel-burn was the stuff of legend and put the incident with Singh well into the past. In fact, all the squads treated him like a hero. Blue had no time to enjoy his new popularity. The intensive hellijet training schedule started with a vengeance. Those who passed the pilot's exams received no ceremony. In Blue's case, he discovered he had earned his wings when Captain Shelley brought Saturn together to give them the next four weeks' itinerary and a new wing-shaped pip for his collar. Swick.

The retro-looking, golden ships were the fastest machines ever designed. Blue soon learned to cope with the extreme gravities when accelerating or decelerating the awesome fuse jets including how, disturbingly, to fix his Grav suit to stop his internal organs 'exploding'. High Gee flying needed strength and stamina. Blue had orders to attend an intensive gym and self-defence schedule. Soon, despite the somewhat horrible Mess food, Blue was no longer the skinny runt of the pack and their duties began in earnest.

Earth Corps had many world bases and for their final week of training Saturn Squad were ordered to perform non-stop cargo and transportation duty. He was glad to escape from the Academy, the Hab and all the staring eyes. Eddi and Newt didn't travel. Blue had never been more than a mile or two from his neglected house. Piloting hellijets across continents and around the world at speeds in excess of Mach 10, he flew to every destination on the globe. He jagged over abandoned cities: enormous empty bone yards in which the once gleaming skyscrapers stood like ancient cracked tombstones. The might of all that money and power now nothing more than submerged masonry, twisted metal and stained, broken glass. Blue could only guess at the millions lying dead below.

During a rare break in training, Blue discussed the overheard conversation with Parris.

The serious boy became agitated. "Dauntless is having you and Shelley watched? What is special about you? Did he say?"

"No. It's something to do with King Wilhelm and his turncoat son, Dore, who is conspiring with SEARCH. Dore poisoned his own father to try to steal the kingship and his signet ring. It's all about control of the H_3 supply. I don't understand how or why, but I'm somehow involved with that."

"You think?"

Hearing his own words, Blue realised just how farfetched that sounded. But the assassin knew my name and spared my life. "There's some connection, there has to be."

The blonde boy nibbled at his lower lip with familiar rabbit teeth. "If you say so."

::

The weeks literally flew by during which Blue grew to love his homeless life, sleeping at the many disparate world bases, including a brief stint at Buckingham Palace. Nothing could replicate the feeling of flying alone, high above the clouds, the magnificent vistas, the blue seas, mountains and plains. From the air, the world was a breath-taking place. He could almost imagine he was far away on a distant planet. But as soon as he descended to land, he met the ruins of civilisation and the illusion was broken. He still dreamt of swamps and flies, yet a growing determination and purpose replaced the awful grief of his earlier nightmares.

Blue clambered into the hellijet for the last time, journeyed back to the Hab and touched down. He ate a late meal in the Mess and returned to the Crater to find Hermans snoring. He undressed and slipped into bed.

RIPWALKING

Blue did not sleep well, stuck back in the damn swamps again, and ate breakfast with considerable irritation and a dull head. Captain Khan sat alone on the Officer's Table, his massive bulk hunched over a simple meal. Saturn Squad, returned from their cargo flying duties, were full of stories of high-speed piloting and near misses. The chatter was deafening. The other squads stared at them with envious eyes. Blue had had a different experience.

"Ever visited another planet, Recruit?" asked Corvus barging into his contemplation. Thick black wavy hair, pale-blue haunting eyes and an ever-present sneer.

"Huh?" said Blue, still half-asleep. *Was Corvus reading my thoughts?*

Coop laughed. "Don't get the Gote over-excited."

"We won't be stopping Off-World. Just a quick rip there-and-back," said a nervous sounding Ji.

How did I forget? Today I'm gonna be ripping the void!

"Commander in the Mess!" barked Captain Khan.

Dauntless entered, a dour expression plastered across his already stern face. Everyone jumped to attention. The commander never joined the cadets for breakfast.

"Good morning Recruits." Dauntless had an annoyed edge to his voice. Instead of the 'be cool' command, he kept them standing. "I address you all with a certain amount of disappointment and a whole chunk of anger." He removed his sunglasses. Large blue eyes. Penetrating. Full of suppressed rage. "We have a thief in our midst."

"No!" erupted the cadets on Saturn table and the other squads.

"He or she is in this hall and listening to these words. You will be caught, punished and thrown out of the Academy. That is all." Dauntless turned and exited.

The Saturn table erupted into more discussion. "Who'd be daft enough to steal from the Academy?" said Parris with incredulity. "What can they hope to achieve? They must be mental."

Blue reached for his kitbag, his constant companion over his time in the future (he would not let Jonesy be stolen again) and remembered the moon rock he had taken on his first day, the solid-silver and gold cutlery from the Mess, Captain Khan's sunglasses as well as a few other bits and bobs he had found lying around. Realisation dawned. *It's me. I'm the thief. How could I have been so stupid to think Dauntless wouldn't find out?*

Parris noticed Blue's distraught expression. "What's bugging you?"

"You don't want to know."

How am I ever gonna get back home if I'm thrown out of the Academy? This place was my one chance and I've blown it.

"You peeved that Dauntless is taking us for rip training?"

"Dauntless?" A long, weary sigh escaped from Blue's lips. "That's all I need."

::

Half an hour later, after an awe-inspiring journey across the Hab's roof on the monorail system, snaking through inverted valleys and ravines and scything into tunnels, they arrived at the Rip Column, an immense upside down cone of rock. Blue hardly noticed; his mind caught up with his own stupidity and guilt.

Thief. A person who steals another person's property usually by stealth and without using force or violence. A cheat, burglar, robber. A pilferer and filcher.

The stalactite stood alone at the far end of the underground cavern. Isolated. The Academy Column lost in the haze of distance.

They disembarked onto a wide rock-hewn platform at its base. The security was super-strict. After what Blue's parents had done to the last rip machine, and the thirty years needed to rebuild the mechanism, he understood why. They were met by fierce military who escorted them down a maze of corridors until they arrived in what Blue guessed was some kind of reception hall. Weapons of many differing types pointed at them from strategically placed alcoves: an ever-present force ready to rain death on any unwanted intruders. Blue baulked.

Finding himself first in line, a rough guard thrust Blue towards an imposing door-sized, metal arch.

"Is this...*is this the rip?*"

Coop chuckled, "You total noob."

Sugar playfully flicked Blue's shoulder. "That's just the weapons detector, Honey. Nothing to worry about. Unless you're packing something extra in that uniform of yours."

Blue walked through, the guffaws of Saturn Squad echoing after him, wondering if the detector would discover the stolen stuff in his bag.

"Don't tell them you're a Gote or you'll be done for," joked Parris.

No one laughed, but Blue's ears burned. He emerged on the other side without incident and waited for the others. They went through numerous checkpoints and arrived at a doughnut-shaped space. An impressive semi-circular chamber carved out of the rock, surrounded by what Blue guessed currently passed as computers: banks of crystal and flashing lights attended by technicians. A single central dome of curved glass gave an unrestricted view to an immense chamber below. The cadets rushed over to stare down at the unimaginatively named Rip-Room. A vast warehouse-like empty space. A bright flash, the lights dimmed and about a hundred men and women appeared from nowhere, accompanied by a range of peculiar vehicles. An unremarkable upright slab of metal, like one of Stonehenge's mighty liths, glowed white-hot and sank back to deep molten red. Blue could not help but be reminded of The Museum of Indulgence and its stark warning.

The commander entered the chamber and Saturn Squad jumped to immediate attention. "Today we will be stepping between planets," he said, as if he had no knowledge of the impact of those simple words. He ushered Saturn Squad down further corridors to another heavily guarded entranceway and finally into the Rip-Room proper.

Blue's mind had conjured any number of fantastic descriptions for the rip, all exotic and amazing. In reality, it was nothing more than a rundown hangar big enough to park a jet or two. The floor stained with oil and faded paint. Ozone and something metallic and nasty irritated his nose.

The commander marched Saturn Squad over to a well-trod white line on the ground. They stood along it, a good fifty feet from the still glowing upright monument sitting at the centre of the hangar. Blue realised his mistake. Even at this distance, the hunk of red hot, fused metal was at least three times larger than anything from Stonehenge. His eyes refused to focus upon it. The thing radiated heat though. Lots of it. And static electricity prickled at his skin.

"That is the Obelisk," began Dauntless. "Where the rip co-ordinates are created and stored.

Obelisk. A tall, four-sided shaft of stone, usually tapered and monolithic, that rises to a pointed pyramidal top.

"Don't judge by appearance, this uninteresting if not oversized lump of fused alloy controls and opens the rip. Sitting somewhere inside is what we call *The Nub.*"

Blue's ears pricked.

"Think of the Nub as a swelling pearl, except that at the

centre of the pearl you will find no grain of sand, but a tiny black hole encased in pure quartz."

Blue glanced at the rest of the cadets. Dauntless was telling them nothing new.

"This gem is irreplaceable, unique. Hence the security." Dauntless stared at Blue. "The Nub from the first rip machine was removed by terrorists. After its taking, we lost our connection to the New Worlds. Twelve planets settled by those willing to leave Earth-hab for better climes. We have rediscovered some of the misplaced colonies, although most are still missing. But—*the search goes on.*"

"How does the rip work, sir?" asked Blue.

"By use of a vast amount of fusion power ripping the fabric of the universe of course," he said with a smile that pulled awkwardly at his facial scar. "Hence our dependence on Helium-3." Dauntless turned his attention to Wurtz who shuffled uncomfortably. "The rip opens and we walk through. Simple."

"And the rip can be opened to the past, sir?"

Dauntless nodded.

"And people are still sent there?" Blue asked hopefully. "Back into time?"

The commander's head gave the barest of shakes. "The resources needed to rip into the past are enormous, Blue. Months of preparation and precise calculation and thousands of man-hours. The energy expenditure alone is prohibitive. No. The desire to bring back those lost in history was a noble one, yet the process is slow, lengthy and, as we find by your unexpected arrival, the return journey is somewhat unpredictable. The last rip through time occurred over seventy years ago, but that doesn't mean you Gotes don't keep on turning up. A regular reminder of how haphazard the process can be. And besides, playing with the timeline is a risky business. Our Very Earth banned time-rips for good reason. As I said to you on your first day here: Technically, we can open the rip and send you back to your time, but in reality, no, that will never happen."

Blue Into The Rip

Blue swallowed. A black wave of desolation sank over him. *I can never go back?* He wanted to scream, shout, to tell Dauntless he was wrong. But where his anger should've been there was a yawning hole of nothingness. *It's over. What do I care anyway? The Academy will kick me for stealing a piece of moon rock and some stupid cutlery. I'm going to tell Dauntless here and now. I have nothing to lose anymore.*

The commander made a sign and the air in the room became suddenly charged. Arcs of lightning erupted from the Obelisk, smashing into the floor and ceiling. Coruscating with raw, unadulterated energy. Beside him, Veeva's heavy dreads sprang forward, caught in a growing electromagnetic field. A flash of blinding light and the rip crashed into sudden, awesome being.

Blue stared aghast, all thoughts of giving himself up forgotten, torn from his mind by the gobsmackingly breathtaking, yet dreadful spectacle before him: the very fabric of space ripped open and hanging like the mouth of some nightmarish, grey, shimmering demon. The rip bleached all colour from the universe.

Blue took a step backwards in fear, overwhelmed. *Here is the thing that has destroyed my life. That snatched me from my home in the past and dumped me in this awful, uncaring future.*

The other cadets also stood back, moving away from where the air crackled and screamed.

"No," commanded Dauntless. "Move closer."

Corvus was excited. Morgana appeared grim but centred. Sugar held hands with Ji and Coop. Veeva frowned, whilst Wurtz seemed hypnotised, his eyes sparkling with the reflected rip field. The other cadets were mesmerised, except Hermans who gave the impression of calm.

Perhaps he was used to this spectacle?

"As you approach the rip, you feel what we call *The Drag*," said Dauntless. "This gets stronger the closer you get, whereupon you experience *The Push;* an understated term for the sudden thrust shoving you into the field. You arrive milliseconds after you leave, thrown against *The Wall*. An invisible force slowing you with a sharp jolt. The art is to become an experienced *ripwalker*. To stride across the void without falling flat on your face." Dauntless raised a hand. "Now, on my mark, I want you to approach the rip—*Mark.*"

Blue took a step forward and was thrown through the air into the rip. The Push was less of a shove and more like an almighty kick. For the barest of milliseconds, he was at one with the universe. Billions of stars and galaxies burned in an immense cosmos of which he was an infinitesimal part. His own light, tiny in comparison, nothing more than an insignificant spark. He landed with a thud, sprawled on the floor on the opposite side of the hangar, Morgana lying on top of him.

Dauntless stepped next to him, as if coming from nowhere, his limbs elongating in the gleaming rip field. He glided to a smooth controlled stop and smiled. "Not to worry, Cadets. Gaining your rip legs can take some practice. To those who managed to stay on their feet, well done. Well done indeed."

Corvus, Veeva, Parris, Wurtz and even Hermans, beamed with pride.

"Do not be dismayed, Cadet Blue." Hermans offered Blue his paddle-like hand. "This One is convinced his esteemed colleague will not take this setback to heart and shall soon be stepping across the void like the most seasoned and disciplined ripwalker."

"Thanks, Hermans, but ripwalking is the least of my worries." Blue stared around him in confusion. "Hey, we've not gone anywhere."

Dauntless smiled again. "Yes, Rip-Rooms are similar. Believe me, we are thousands if not millions of light-years away from the Hab. Notice on this side, there is no Obelisk."

The intimidating slab of fused metal had vanished. "Then how do we get back, sir?"

"Earth Corps guards its rip technology fiercely, Blue. We do not give our secrets away willy-nilly. Worlds must earn the right. The void will be opened from Earth for the return journey, and only from Earth."

"But?"

"Enough. I have things to do. Corvus is in charge." Dauntless Strode off towards the exit.

"But how do we know we went anywhere?" Blue asked.

Corvus grabbed Blue by the shoulders. "Get real, Buddy-boy. Where do you think all the settlers in the Hab disappeared to? You've seen the deserted cities and towns."

Blue frowned, pulling away from his grasp.

Sugar put her hand on her hip. "You ripped over four-hundred years in time, Honey. Ripping light-years is small-beans in comparison. You gotta get real okay? You gotta start making a life here."

"Sugar is right," said Parris.

"I'll never give up on my family." Blue stomped away.

Parris followed him. "We're on your side. You're one of the Ringers now."

"Not for long. I'll be leaving here soon."

"Don't talk like that, Blue. You'll graduate. No probs."

Blue lowered his voice to a whisper. "Remember the Academy thief, the one Dauntless mentioned?"

Parris tilted his head for a moment, like that of an inquisitive bird. "Sure. The sooner that bastard is caught, the better."

"Don't be too sure—*It's me.*"

Parris stared at Blue in a confused way, as if he was looking at a totally different person. "What is wrong with you?" he finally blurted.

"Apparently I'm an A-One prize jackass. Who would've guessed? It's all here in my kitbag."

Parris seemed almost angry. "Why would you do that? You idiot. You stupid idiot. Don't you realise just how lucky you are to be here? Why jeopardise that?"

"I didn't believe Dauntless when he first told me I couldn't get back home. Why should I? So what if I took a few things? How could it possibly matter? That's what I thought anyway. But the last time rip was seventy years ago. *Seventy years.* Even if they wanted to send me home, which they don't, programming the rip takes months and thousands of man-hours. And it's banned. Hopeless. I'm going to the commander when he returns. Tell him everything."

"Don't do that!" Parris' eyebrows knitted in alarm, the threat of Dauntless suddenly cooling his overheated mind. "You'll get kicked for sure."

"I can't sit around waiting for him to catch me. It'll drive me nuts."

"But what about me?" Parris was strangely upset, as if he was also the victim of Blue's thievery. "You can't leave me behind. You're all I've got. My parents died off-world when I was young, Blue. I went from foster family to foster family. The Corps took me in to their 'advancement program' for the dispossessed. I wouldn't recommend that to anyone. No one likes me. But I met you Blue. You changed me. Became my friend. You can't talk to Dauntless. I won't let you."

"I don't have a choice. It's over. Kaput."

"Listen to me, okay." Parris grabbed Blue's arm with both hands, like a child imploring a parent. "Do what I say. You promise? Talk to Captain Shelley."

"Huh?"

Parris grasped more tightly. "She's our captain. Your duty is to inform her first."

Blue filled his chest for a big speech, to tell Parris it was a waste of time, to tell everyone. But the words would not come, the air instead escaped from him in a long relieved sigh. "You're right, Parris. I'd rather admit my guilt to Shelley than that git Dauntless."

Parris released his hold, the rabbit teeth reappearing in a thankful smile. "She'll sort something out. I'm sure."

Blue didn't share his friend's optimism.

Dauntless returned a short while later. "Cadet Blue questioned whether we had travelled to another planet. As a treat for your efforts, follow me."

They went through a series of well-protected doors and long corridors, emerging on to a wide sweeping balcony on the side of an upside down, cone-shaped, burgundy coloured building mimicking the Rip Column back in the Hab. This was secondary to the sight before Blue's eyes. Sunset. Unlike anything on Earth. Twin sinking suns boiled in a mauve sky, revealing at least six moons. A vast city lay across a long sweeping bay. Low white-painted structures, like Cycladic houses on the Greek Islands, stretched into the distance. The air held an exotic, extra-terrestrial fragrance. The suns sank towards the horizon, revealing even more moons and an alien starscape.

Blue whistled. "I really am on a totally different planet."

"Yes," whispered a voice behind him. "To rip the void to a brand new world is a rare experience indeed."

"It truly is."

The voice had a sense of wonder and calm certainty that fitted the moment perfectly. Blue turned around and was shocked to find Commander Dauntless.

COMING CLEAN

Back in the Academy Column, Blue's willpower seemed to lack both determination and purpose. Shelley was more of a friend than a captain. He wanted to run away. Instead, he made his slow way, footfall by footfall, to enter Shelley's cramped and somewhat *girlified* quarters to sit once again on her uncomfortable stool. Heart thumping in his ears. Faint. Wishing it was all over and done with.

Shelley perched upright upon her divan. Her body rigid. Wet eyes assessed him from the confines of her flabby face. "Oh dear, mister. You do seem upset. Now, how can I help?"

Blue's practiced words left him. His long apology lost in the moment of confession. "I'm the thief, ma'am," he blurted. "I did it. It was me—I'm sorry, ma'am."

The eyes narrowed, but other than that, no emotion crossed the captain's face.

"Did you mishear me, ma'am? The Academy thief—is me."

The rigidity left her plump body and Shelley slipped back into the divan. Long seconds passed as she made herself comfortable. "I know," she said finally, her tone suddenly hard. "Cadet Parris came to me earlier. Told me everything."

"Parris?" Blue wasn't sure if he was angry or relieved.

"Yes. I was, to say the least, disappointed. You get me?"

"Yes, ma'am."

A long silence.

"You're angry with me. I know that. I'm angry with myself. With everything. With this stupid future."

"Anger is a tool to be used wisely. Do not waste it in situations where it will do no good."

Blue drew breath to speak, but the barest shake of Shelley's head stilled his tongue.

"Do not waste time on recrimination or apology. What is done is done. The question is: *what shall we do next?* You have the items with you?"

"Yes, ma'am." Blue pulled out the stolen objects from his kitbag and passed them to Shelley, grimacing at the petty collection of golden knives, forks and spoons.

The captain said nothing. She preferred to let the silence do its work. Blue finally produced the lump of Moon rock and sat back.

Shelly's face puckered in disgust. "Quite a haul. But they can be returned with none the wiser."

"Ma'am?"

"I am taking a chance on you, Cadet. Commander Dauntless prefers to see things in black and white, as right and wrong, I perceive the world quite differently. We all make mistakes. I'm a firm believer that learning from our mistakes is a better teacher than punishment."

"You're letting me off?"

"Did you not learn from the incident during hellijet training? Would you have been able to fly a sludge storm without it? No. In vowing to never make the same mistake twice, you became a more proficient pilot, you saved a life. And I cannot ignore the fact that you risked yourself for members of the Academy and your squad."

Blue almost choked on his words. "Thank…thank you, ma'am."

"We all deserve a second chance, Cadet. We all make silly mistakes. No good will be served by throwing you out of the

Corps. I see the bigger picture, even if Dauntless cannot."

Was this all about the commander then? Something personal? "I have some information you might be interested in, ma'am."

An eager expression flashed across Shelley's face.

"With the hellijet flying and rip training, I had no time to tell you what I overheard at Sekhmet's funeral: Dauntless and Fleet-Admiral Apache talking about me, ma'am—and you."

"You sure?"

"They were discussing a cadet under the commander's control, ma'am. A boy SEARCH was interested in."

The captain contemplated the information for a second. "Blue, you are not that cadet."

"Are you sure? They were laughing about him."

"I gave my word not to reveal the cadet's identity. But I can tell you that Dauntless likes to play games with people's lives and will use everyone and anyone to further his ambition. I say this with a certain degree of understanding. I too used to share his type of zeal, his desire for greatness. I have long realised such feelings to be a false cross upon which we are all one day crucified. The cadet is at the centre of a complex political situation; and that is all I will tell you. You must promise to tell no other."

"I promise, ma'am."

"Good. I have done and said enough already. Indeed, my forthrightness brought me here to the Academy. A demotion to some, but no demotion to me. Here I can do good works for the first time in my life and I am starting with you." Shelley set her jaw, jowls quivering ever so slightly. "Now, what did Dauntless and the Fleet-Admiral say about me? Something nice I hope, heh?"

"Dauntless is having you watched. A cadet in Saturn Squad."

"You know who?"

Blue thought of Morgana again, but despite his suspicions, he wasn't sure anymore. Hermans was adamant she would never do such a thing. "No, no I don't."

"Thank you, Mister. I like what I'm seeing in you."

"You do?"

"Yes, but step one millimetre out of line and I will be down on you like Ten Gravs. You get me?"

"Yes, ma'am." Blue saluted. "I get you."

"Good. Only Cadet Parris, you and myself know of this. Keep it that way, understand?" Shelley smiled. "Now get lost."

Blue left the captain's quarters and made his way to the Crater. He was relieved to be let-off, but the feeling was temporary. *I'm still here. Stuck in the future with no chance of getting home, but I'll never give up on Annie, on Eddi and Newt.*

Blue opened the hermetically sealed doors to the Crater and a short while later bumped into Hermans standing at the side of the jungle path, the normal yet exotic greenery a riot of colour. Everything was blooming.

"This One frequently visits the hydroponic rainforest," Hermans warbled with what Blue guessed was Ganymedian enthusiasm. "Indeed, he prefers it to his rather cramped quarters. This place is a living thing, reminiscent of the Amazon under which it sits as a relic of times gone past."

"How come I never noticed?"

Hermans took a step forwards to look directly into Blue's eyes. "It is This One's fervent belief that Cadet Blue is too self-involved, too selfish to think further than himself."

"Hey, that's a bit unfair."

The thin, baseball-like head shook. "This One cannot agree. Since Cadet Blue arrived in this century he has spent most of his time contemplating the passage of Jupiter's red storm when instead, he should have been watching where his own feet were taking him."

"A Ganymedian saying?"

"Those shallows can be treacherous, Cadet Blue."

"You're not still upset that you lived when Sekhmet died are you?"

Hermans' arms waved in the air like a drunken stick insect doing dance moves. "This One thanked Cadet Blue as profusely as etiquette will allow for saving his worthless life. A most outstanding feat," trilled Hermans. "Indeed, his family unit is indebted to Cadet Blue and will-."

"Yes, yes." Blue had had enough of Hermans' heartfelt thanks from him, his family unit and no doubt all of Ganymede to whom he seemed to be related. "But something is bothering you—yes?"

Hermans stooped, placing his head right in front of Blue. "This One may be handicapped by the higher gravity, yet his mental facilities are more than adequate to make a disturbing deduction. Cadet Blue is the Academy thief."

Blue sat down by a gigantic creeper-covered tree, its topmost reaches disappearing into mist. "You're right, Herms. I'm a class one, twenty-four carat cockwad."

"This One is indebted to Blue, but unfortunately he must agree with his friend's accurate and astute self-assessment."

"Thanks." Blue took a deep breath. "I've been to Captain Shelley to admit everything."

"Cadet Blue has done this?" Hermans crouched down next to him, a surprised expression pulling at his elongated face. "This One offers Blue his most sincere apologies for such a serious misjudgement of character. He will sorely miss his roommate and promises to do all he can to send him help to adjust to his new life outside the Academy and the Corps."

"No Hermans, you don't understand. She let me off."

"Captain Shelley did what?"

"She put me on probation. I thought I was done for."

"Cadet Blue is saying our captain is *not* to inform Commander Dauntless of his thieving?"

"I mess up one more time and I'm outta here."

Hermans leaned forward. "This One does not comprehend why Captain Shelley is willingly disobeying orders. If Commander Dauntless were to find out, our squad leader would be given a Court Martial and be thrown out of Earth Corps."

"I don't pretend to understand what is going on between those two, but I get the impression she doesn't like Dauntless. I think she enjoys annoying him. She told me not to tell anyone. Are you gonna squeal on me? If so, give me a chance. Let me go to Dauntless first."

"Cadet Blue insults This One most highly by even suggesting the merest hint of a possibility that—"

"Alright, calm down, big fella."

"Whatever happened between you and Shelley is not This One's business, Cadet Blue, but for a captain to disobey a direct order of the commander, in this case, informing they had found a thief, goes against everything the Corps stands for. This One would be wary of Captain Shelley's motives if he were in a similar position."

"You're wrong Herms, very wrong. She helped me stay here. She is loyal to her squad, not Dauntless. She's a Ringer as well."

Hermans shrugged. "Perhaps Cadet Blue is correct."

"Only you and Parris know what happened, let's keep it that way."

"This One understands." Hermans placed long thin fingers on Blue's forehead, his hand squatting like some exotic spider. "He takes a solemn oath to protect Blue in this matter. He will not speak of the subject again." He put his other hand over his mouth and nodded.

"Um…thanks."

THE PUSH

Next morning, Blue awoke more tired than when he went to bed. His dreams had taken a downward turn. Stuck in the swamps again. *Why is that? Why do I dream of mud and murky water, guilt and anxiety night after night?* But the sense of dread did not follow him into wakefulness. He met Parris outside his quarters and the two boys climbed the steps to the Wheel. "I should be angry, you going behind my back to Shelley like that…But you made a good call. She's been a real friend to me over this."

"Stealing from the Academy? You need as many friends as you can get."

"Keep your voice down, I don't want anyone else to know."

"Sorry."

"Although Hermans knew all along."

Parris stopped in his tracks, his face darkening. "What? Is he going to tell Dauntless?"

"No, of course not."

"He can go to the commander anytime. We'd be sunk."

"We?"

"You and me, Blue. Anybody who knows about this and keeps quiet will be kicked."

"He's a Ringer, Parris, which means he'll never betray the

squad, no matter how much of a twacker I've been. Herms is a good friend."

Parris nodded, but his eyes told a different story.

::

Rip training carried on for another week. Each morning they travelled with Dauntless to spend an hour stepping across the void. Despite his excitement, the experience became mundane and irritating. Blue could not find his rip legs. At first, he treated his failure as a joke, after two or three days of the same, his lack of ability turned serious.

The Push sent Blue sprawling. Everyone had passed by day three, using the rest of the week to practice their technique. For Blue, ripwalking was one humiliating fall after another. On the seventh and last day of training, he got up with a bloodied nose.

Dauntless pulled him to his feet. "I'm afraid I must fail you Cadet," he said, wincing at the blood leaking on to Blue's whites and the floor. "You cannot pass on to Phase Two of training unless you master this basic manoeuvre. Tripping the void in the Corps is a vital everyday function. You can't arrive on a diplomatic mission or in a combat situation flat on your face. You will have to use your R&R time when we get back from *The Charles Darwin* and if you still cannot find those rip legs, you will be kicked from the Academy and the Corps. And failure counts against your squad when I decide which squad is heading for the six week Drop. You get me?"

"Yes, sir," said Blue miserably.

The next day they packed for *The Charles Darwin:* the peculiar star and its satellites Blue had seen on his first dreadful evening in the future. He thought back to the blackest of black nights trapped in Dooleys Wood and the crocodile attack. The rescue seemed like a million years ago.

Blue and Parris were sitting in the Mess tucking into their pre-flight breakfast when Commander Dauntless entered. "Squads attention!" he barked, his rage plain for all to see. "It seems the Academy thief has suffered a change of heart. The stolen items have miraculously returned back to their rightful places. You may think this lets you off. Think again." The commander paused. "I have a message for this criminal: you will be caught and expelled." With a curt nod, he left.

Blue found Hermans staring at him across the table. He didn't doubt the commander would try everything to catch him. *At least I can trust the Ganymedian.*

A while later, they exited Topside into the early morning heat of Desert Amazon. "Convincing you to go see Shelley certainly paid off," whispered Parris. "I did good. I did very good."

Blue didn't say anything. He was too ashamed.

"Not even a *thank you?*" Parris stormed off.

Blue ran after him, grabbing his shoulder and spinning him around. "Of course I'm grateful," he said, keeping his voice low. "I thought that was obvious. I'm just a bit nervous about the flight, okay? I'm flying into space to live on a spacestation. Where I'm from…well…it's kind of a big deal. Bonkers of course, that's why I'm freaking out a little bit."

Parris pulled away, his eyes flashing darkly, as if he was mirroring the rage seen in the commander earlier. "I don't think you realise just how much I'm putting on the line for you. I could lose everything."

"Okay then, Parris," replied Blue, his own anger rising. "Tell me what I'm supposed to do? As far as I can see, saying *thank you* is all I've bloody got. Unless you want me to do a dance for you."

"Huh"

"You want me to?" Blue blurted, stabbing his finger into the blonde boy's chest. "I will. If that is what it bloody well takes."

Parris tried to resist a smile, but it was a losing battle. It erupted uncontrollably over his face. "A dance? Have you gone space crazy?"

The two boys fell into a fit of giggles lasting all the way to the landing field, only silenced by the sight of *Old Dinger.*

Did I fly into orbit in that? She sure is a rusty bucket of bolts. Fins twisted and scored from numerous sand and sludge storms, her tubes blackened and bent from the intense heat of the fusion engines.

"Hey, my favourite Gote."

Blue turned around and found the familiar reddened face of Private Ammers smiling at him from his enormous curly-blonde head. Greenish-blue eyes sparkled in recognition.

He saluted. "How many Gotes do you know, sir?"

"Just the one. A bit of an idiot by all accounts. Got my buddy demoted and transferred."

Blue flushed. "Um...sorry, sir. I—"

Ammers shrugged impressive shoulders. "Hey. Don't beat yourself up. You're not the rat. And don't worry about Singh. Dauntless might have torn a strip off him, demoting him to private again, but he transferred him to Titan Patrol. That's some break."

Coop whistled.

"And landing a helli' in a sludge storm? Stuff of legend."

"Thank you, sir.

Saturn and the other squads gathered for take-off.

"Now, Blue," began Ammers, "you up to piloting this crate with me?"

Blue's eyes widened in shock.

Corvus clapped Blue on the shoulder. "Way to go, you deserve the Second Seat."

The Second Seat. Second in command. Co-pilot.

Veeva saluted. "Well done, sir."

Blue saluted back. *She called me, 'sir'. Cool.* "Thank you, Cadet Veeva. At ease."

Ammers stood on the ladder. "Cadet Blue, with me."

Blue followed Ammers up through the ship to the bridge—a room the size of a cupboard at the top of *Old Dinger*. A circular row of rectangular windows sat above a simple flight console. A joystick, a bank of switches and a few readouts and that was it. Two leather seats, encased in familiar Gee webbing, perched in front. The extended armrests allowed the pilots to operate the controls whilst being cushioned from the Gee forces of take-off.

"Right, get installed and I'll hit the Amber lights. You've five minutes, Bud."

Blue stashed his pack and strapped himself into the seat, placing his arms in the rests and adjusting the webbing. In the five minutes before take-off, Ammers familiarised Blue with the controls and the launch sequence.

"You have the schematics?" Blue asked.

Ammers grinned. "Yeah sure." He opened a gimballed drawer and produced faded plastic sheets, passing them to Blue. "You're like Singh. You do everything up here." He tapped his forehead. So—you wanna launch this baby?"

"You mean?"

"No looping-the-loop. Promise?"

"Bring it on."

"Bring *what?*"

"An old twenty-first century expression. Yes, I'd love to fly her, sir."

"I'll even let you attempt the docking procedure, if you look the part."

"Swick."

Ammers winked. "Best warn the cargo."

Blue found the ship intercom. "This is your…er…pilot, Cadet Blue," he announced and, even through the thick metal walls of *Old Dinger,* he could hear Saturn Squad's cheers. "We will be lighting the fuse very soon."

Ammers pressed the red lights button and Blue powered the engine. A roar exploded under them. *Old Dinger* wobbled, sudden acceleration pushing him back into the creaking leather and webbed seats. A lurch to the left and Blue compensated. A slight twist to the right and Blue corrected. Within a few minutes, the sky turned to a star-studded black. With a nod from Ammers, Blue disengaged the engines and began the complicated navigation procedure to take them to *The Charles Darwin.*

Blue Into The Rip

SPACE

Blue Into The Rip

THE CHARLES DARWIN

Half an hour later, Blue approached the three-ringed bright white wheel that was *The Charles Darwin Spacestation*.

Charles Robert Darwin. An English naturalist who outlined the theory of evolution in his scientific masterpiece 'The Origin of Species'. He proposed that evolution could be explained in part through natural and sexual selection. He contributed not only to the theory of evolution but also to other branches of science including geomorphology and geography. Known as 'the father of biology' and one of the greatest scientists of all time.

Distances were deceptive, Blue soon found out. As he made his approach, the station grew steadily before him, dwarfing the rocket ship.

Ammers kept an eye on his every move, double-checking their position and warning Blue about momentum. "There are no brakes in space, Bud, only forwards, backwards and sideways thrust."

Blue did not need telling twice. He brought the ship in slow, towards the central docking platform. A skyscraper sized protrusion sticking out from the station's hub like an upside down tower festooned with ships of various shapes and sizes. "So many spaceships. Where are they from?"

Ammers stuck out his bottom lip and furrowed his eyebrows

as if the question had never been raised before. "To be honest, I'm not sure. Most are abandoned. Not been used since the rip was discovered."

Blue had little time for contemplation as the massive bulk of the station reared up before them. He hit the reverse thrusters, matching the rotating speed of *The Charles Darwin* exactly and the automatic docking procedure took over.

"If I had a hat, I'd take it off to you, Mister," congratulated Ammers, his face even redder in zero gravity, his head, if possible, even larger. "You're a natural."

"Thanks. That was um…fun."

"Fun? I'm guessing where you came from the chances of piloting a rocket ship into space were abysmal, yeah?" Ammers un-strapped himself from his seat and glided upwards. "That was an experience of a lifetime, Buddy." They waited until everyone had exited the ship—the pilot always the last to leave—and floated down to the hatch in the now deserted spaceship.

Ammers ushered Blue along the spacestation's metal-grey corridors stuffed with pipes, the tangled spaghetti of wires tied into bunches and open panels revealing even more wires and pipes. Every fifty feet they were met by a closed magnetic door.

"If the *Darwin* is breached, holed by a space collision with either a spaceship or a meteorite, these doors magnetically seal shut and are hydraulically clamped. Anybody unlucky enough to be trapped in a non-pressurised section without a spacesuit?" Ammers made a gagging noise whilst miming the majority of his intestines including, Blue guessed, his stomach, spleen and liver erupting from his mouth. "Game over."

"Nice."

Bit by bit, the gravity returned.

Artificial Gravity. The creation of apparent gravity by use of centrifugal force (a rotating wheel) or by acceleration.

There was an awkward moment when Blue wasn't sure if he should walk or float, but soon they were bounding along the corridors at a fast pace, travelling away from the centre to the first rotating wheel.

"This is Loop One," Ammers announced when they arrived. It consisted of a long wide walkway curving upwards in both directions. Like standing on the inside of bicycle wheel. "Grav here is point-five. Science and Medical Decks, habitation for our visitors from Ganymede and *private recreation.*" He winked. "Academy cadets are quartered in Loop Two, where we are now heading."

He led him a short way along the curved walkway, before venturing off through more corridors and doors in the direction of the next loop, travelling further away from the centre of the spacestation, gravity increasing with every passing metre. They arrived in a wider corridor. Military personnel busied past in both directions.

"Welcome to Loop Two. Grav one-point-zero. Just like home. Here you will find the main decks of the station, divided into five distinct sectors." He pointed to a white stripe running along the sides of the walkway. "This is White Sector. Cadets cannot leave White unless an officer accompanies them. Anyone found outside White will be Hung-Out-To-Dry. Do I make myself clear?"

"What's Hung-Out-To-Dry?"

"Nasty."

Ammers guided him through another pressurised hatchway and they were once again in the gunmetal grey corridors. He took him to a hub room from which seven doors led off.

"These are the Cadet Quarters. The far door leads to the Heads. Your door is marked 'Saturn'. You can work the rest out for yourself. And that, Cadet, is the tour. See you later." He spun around and bounded away.

Blue went through the hatchway, to come to yet another door—except this one contained a glass panel. Inside, Blue found Corvus, Hermans, Veeva, Wurtz and the rest of Saturn Squad. The door clanged open to a clamour of voices.

Blue entered the overcrowded room, knocked off his feet by the many pats on his back and attempts to shake his hand. His enjoyment was short-lived. Their new quarters were half the size of the cramped B-Pal dorm, the bunks crammed next to one another and no lockers. A rank smell of stale sweat made Blue's nostrils curl.

Corvus patted the bed next to his. "Here. I've saved you a bunk. The top recruits should stick together. Stash your kitbag and tell me all about the flight."

"*Top recruits?* I can't even ripwalk."

"Yeah, that is a bit of a problem, but you'll find those legs. I'm sure of it. You've a whole week of R&R to practice when we get back. Hey, I might even go with you and give you some tips." Corvus appeared uncharacteristically friendly.

Perhaps being in space had affected his brain? "Thanks for the offer, Corvus, but I promised I'd bunk with Parris."

"Suit yourself," he said, a little crestfallen. But not for long. He turned his attention to Sugar "Hey girl. The bunk next to mine is free."

The amber-skinned beauty smiled, revealing her wide set of perfect teeth. "You know how much I look forward to waking up next to you," she said to hoots and whistles.

Blue joined Parris at the opposite end of the overcrowded dorm.

The blonde boy sat on the edge of his bunk, sneering. "Corvus can be a real creep."

"He's not that bad. In fact, he's a decent sort when he's not showing off."

"You don't believe that—*do you?* I'm your real mate. Not him."

"I'm just saying that despite the constant crapola, he's sort of alright."

"You have no idea what you're talking about. I've known people like Corvus all my life," said Parris, his hands unconsciously curling into angry fists. "I don't see him helping you out like I did."

"Shhh. Keep it down."

Parris flitted his eyes at Hermans perched on a bunk nearby. "You need to be very careful about who you trust."

Blue dumped his kitbag on his bed opposite and sat down. "Mate—I don't know what's wrong with you at the moment, but you need to chill out, okay? Something bugging you?"

The rabbit teeth appeared, chewing at his lower lip. "I suppose I'm a little freaked out. About this whole living in space thing. My first time."

"You too? After what you did for me in *Old Dinger*, I thought you were a seasoned astronaut."

The blonde head shook in the negative. "It's a bit overcrowded. To say the least."

"We're to spend four weeks in this tin can? We'll go ape on one another, sure." On the bunk next to his, Hermans trembled. "You okay, Herms?"

"He's suffering from claustrophobia," said Morgana, the irritating tone of her voice muffled by the many bodies squashed into the tiny quarters. "Common amongst Ganymedians. Four weeks won't seem long. They'll keep us busy. We won't notice the time passing by," she said hopefully.

Captain Shelley appeared in the hatchway and the cadets jumped to attention. "Now squad, let's get you acquainted with the most important piece of kit you will need in space. Follow me."

THE ROYAL BARGE

"Spacesuits?" Blue blurted to Parris.

"Yes, Mister Blue, spacesuits, although in this century they are called *Skins,*" said Shelley as she led them out of the dorm. "In space, your Skin is the single most important item you own. Getting you suited and booted is the first thing on our agenda."

They walked along Loop One for a good twenty minutes. Blue was impressed at the sheer scale of the spacestation. The corridor curved upwards in the far distance, yet where they stood seemed horizontal. More pressurised doors and they entered an impressive functional chamber with seats and lockers. Two officers, standing behind an official looking counter, doled out what looked like wetsuits to each cadet, tailored to their build, race and sex.

Blue took his and was surprised by its weight—or lack of it. "We wear this in space?" he whispered to Parris, fingering the flimsy rubber and felt-like material.

The next hour was spent familiarising himself with the Skin and its controls. A simple design, capped by a helmet attached with a single Velcro strap. Black in colour, each Skin had three thick diagonal white lines across the torso and arms, used, according to Shelley, to locate anyone foolish enough to 'get lost in space'.

"This is your Rookie Skin. A basic model. No computers or thrusters, but more than enough for your present needs. The Skin also has an air reclamation system for short jaunts away from the confines of your space or planetary vehicle." Shelley pointed to her left shoulder and lifted a flap. "Otherwise, you will need a tank or an umbilical. Both attach here. You can remove and insert your air hose without fear of decompression."

Blue gulped. The idea of decompression—the air sucked from his spacesuit replaced with the cold vacuum of space and an instantaneous, horrific, freezing, choking death—was not comforting.

Shelley narrowed her googly eyes. "Waste, unwanted bodily products—faeces, urine, dead skin, etcetera—are all dealt with by inbuilt systems."

Blue was disgusted, but noticed no such reaction from the other cadets, notably Wurtz who seemed at home in his well-fitted suit. He is from Asteroid Belt. Spacesuits are probably everyday wear for the average Berg.

"The Skin can sustain you for six, maybe seven weeks before needing a refresh, but only in extreme circumstances."

The thought of wearing the same clothes for more than a few days appalled Blue, never mind being forced to relieve himself in them as well. He had little time for contemplation.

"Now, as we are on an Earth Corps spacestation, you are required to take part in Orientation. Boys and girls, get ready for your first spacewalk."

Spacewalk. Extra-vehicular activity in space. A period of astronaut activity outside a spacecraft.

Blue swallowed. His mouth suddenly dry. Corvus smiled determinedly, as did Parris and even Morgana. Veeva pulled her familiar *I can do it* face, yet Blue saw her doubt.

Shelley put on her helmet and indicated the cadets do the same. Hermans, frowning, fitted his adapted helmet. Blue fastened his strap and took a deep breath of the peculiar smelling suit air.

Space. A mostly empty expanse in which the Solar System, stars, galaxies and the rest of universe exist. A hostile place due to extreme cold, exposure to dangerous radiation (cosmic rays) and threat from small particles of dust or rock or orbiting debris from spacecraft moving at high speeds.

"I'm in the future, I'm on a spacestation and I'm going to walk in space," Blue said to himself quietly.

"You certainly are," said Shelley over the helmet radio, "A normal day in the Corps."

Within a few minutes, they were staring through an open hatch into a cold unforgiving black emptiness. The Skin tightened reassuringly in the vacuum, like a blood-pressure collar, but not in an uncomfortable way. The material changed, becoming harder. A tough, resilient and flexible plastic.

Blue had read about the universe lots of times in important swanky books with impressive pictures and diagrams. As he was about to venture into the cosmos, he realised space wasn't 'mysterious' or, indeed, 'wonderful' as it was often described. Just terrifying. None of the books mentioned that. If I survive and ever manage to get back home, I'm going to write in to the authors and complain.

"Follow me." Shelley stepped through the airlock. "Pull yourselves along using the handrails."

"No safety cord?" Blue blurted.

"No, Mister. Those who are clumsy enough to find themselves drifting alone in the cold, vastness of space after missing a handhold, tend not to be as clumsy a second time. But do not worry; they are usually rescued within a day or two, heh."

"Right."

Blue pulled himself along haphazardly, blood rushing through his ears, his heart pumping manically. After a few minutes of not dying horribly or being swept off into space, he began to relax, although his heart still thumped heavily.

Ahead of him, Parris pointed at the vast bulk of an oddly designed golden spacecraft. Everything of Academy design had the simplicity of straight lines and smooth uncomplicated surfaces. This ship was organic. Decorated with unnecessary curves and fluting reminding Blue of the Queen's Golden State Coach.

"Whoa!" Corvus blurted over the radio. "That the Royal Mining Barge?"

"Sure is," intoned Sugar.

"Dat Wilhelm's ship. He must be here, on da Darwin." Wurtz's voice held a trace of anger.

Blue thought back to the Sanatorium, to the poisoned king he had unwittingly rescued. *He is one tough customer.*

Sugar's rich tones crackled from the tinny speaker in Blue's helmet. "The old boy has kept peace amongst all those warring families for over fifty years. You have to admire that."

Parris whistled. "She sure is a beautiful bird."

"She may be ostentatious and showy, but these ships are designed for manoeuvrability in the dense asteroid fields," said Veeva. "With those quad-fuse engines, they're fast too."

"You sure know your stuff, Veeva," said Parris.

"Well, propulsion systems and astrophysics are my speciality," Veeva replied with a hint of pride.

"Why isn't the ship docked?" Blue asked, hoping that if he joined in with the conversation, he might forget what he was doing.

Ji answered; her voice reedy over the radio. "You've seen the size of Wurtz? The ship has its own spin to give the crew their preferred Two-Gees."

"That's not the only reason, Ji," said Parris loudly. "It's also because they are way too arrogant to have anything to do with us puny earthlings. Right Wurtz?"

"Enough chatter, Mister," ordered Shelley. "I'm sure you can find plenty of time in R&R to impress your girlfriend. Please concentrate on the task in hand. And to the rest of you: no more radio chatter."

Possibly upset at the rebuke, Parris stopped suddenly. How he managed to check his forward momentum so effectively, Blue had no idea. He piled into the back of him, his helmet banging loudly. And then, like some horrible nightmare, Blue reached for the handrail, missed and spiralled, arse over head, into space. Within seconds he was twenty metres away, thirty. Blue tried to scream, but terror got the better of him. *The Charles Darwin,* a starry blackness and planet Earth span dementedly.

Something grasped his foot, checking his motion.

"No one runs away in my squad, heh," said Captain Shelley.

Blue's uncontrollable spin stopped suddenly and he found himself floating face to face with his captain. She leant in so that their helmets touched. "You okay, Mister?" she asked. Her voice was muffled; she was not speaking over the radio.

"Yes…yes, ma'am," Blue replied, still aware they were both drifting away from the spacestation.

"Good. I won't let you escape that easily, heh."

A puff of gas from Shelley's more advanced Skin and they were flying back to the spacestation. She guided him to the airlock where he waited for the others to return.

Shelley recycled the air and removed her helmet, as did the other cadets.

Blue stood transfixed, unable to process the experience. "I shouldn't be doing stuff like this," he finally whispered. "I'm only fifteen. I should be getting drunk, going to parties and bunking off school."

"You sure are a dork," said Corvus, putting his arm around Blue's shoulder. "But this time, I think I might agree with you. That was intense."

"Well done, Mister," said Shelley, coming over. "You handled yourself admirably. Now listen up," she continued, talking to the rest of the squad. "Losing a handhold can happen to any of you at any time in space. Whilst you are still in your Rookie Skins, do as Mister Blue did. Stay calm and await rescue."

Blue remained numb. The experience had been as far away from 'calm' as anything in his life had ever been.

Hermans was pale. "The helmet, This One does not like the confines of his helmet."

"I'm hungry," said Ji, ignoring everybody. "Is it time for lunch?"

INSIDE THE TIN CAN

The next three weeks passed without incident, like being back in the Academy Column: enclosed depressing corridors and seshrooms, and the same daily routine. Breakfast, lessons, gym, lunch, lessons, tea, R&R (if you called sitting in their cramped bunkroom 'Rest and Relaxation') before Lights-Out and bed.

Astrophysics and Navigation was the best sesh by far, taught by math-loving Captain Lovelace of Titan Squad. A quiet, yet firm woman with unremarkable features, but possessing an analytical brain envied throughout Earth Corps. Under her expert direction, Blue calculated flight-paths, weight loads, solar-wind variances, gravity wells and navigated imaginary spaceships of every shape and size in and around the Solar System, experiencing the three-dimensional universe in all its mathematical glory.

With Blue a far-away second, it was Veeva who excelled. She had an aptitude for maths that surpassed everyone else.

Commander Dauntless took over Captain Sekhmet's role of Survival Specialist for Decompression Training. He loved imparting his never-ending knowledge about accidental death and the drastic effects of the vacuum of space on the human body. He explained about *The Charles Darwin's* 'double shell', protecting the spacestation from even the largest micrometeorites, some of which, he assured, 'were two, maybe three times the size of a grain of sand'. Anything the size of baseball could obliterate an entire section. As a result, Blue learned to be suited and in his helmet in minutes.

"You not able to sleep?" asked Parris one night in their overcrowded quarters

"I dunno," said Blue, his mouth dry from the recycled air. "Ever since we started the decompression training, well, I've found relaxing impossible. I sleep in my Skin just in case."

"Me too."

Morgana rolled over on her bunk and propped herself on one arm. "Captain Khan told me we need a month or two without being sucked into space to properly relax."

"Oi, put a lid on it!" shouted Coop, from a few bunks away.

"You can talk," said Ji. "Your farts are like a twenty-one gun salute every evening after Mess."

"Thank your lucky stars you can only hear them," moaned Corvus.

Coop seemed almost betrayed. "Space is playing havoc with my insides, okay?"

"Yeah, and my nose."

"This One fervently wishes cadets might occasionally consider those around them and be quiet. Night after night This One suffers."

Heads turned to stare at the irate Ganymedian. He had become increasingly vocal over the last few weeks.

"This minuscule dormitory is awful enough without your constant blathering. This One has no problem in admitting the nightly cacophony is driving him quite mad."

The nights were the worst for the tall boy; his claustrophobia was having a serious effect on his cool. All the cadets remarked on this change of character.

"Hermans is right," said Corvus. "Let's cut the cackle and get some kip."

Everyone stopped talking and, a short time later, the room became filled with gentle snoring.

Blue couldn't sleep. He tossed and turned for a few hours and when he was finally nodding off, he noticed Wurtz leave the bunkroom. He didn't think much of his departure at first. The Heads were outside in a room adjoining the corridor. Blue drifted in and out of consciousness, until, with a jolt, he realised Wurtz hadn't returned.

After another twenty minutes, Blue wondered what had happened to him. Unable to sleep and intrigued, he made his way through the cramped bunkroom to the toilets.

"Wurtz?"

Empty stalls. The same thing happened two nights later. Next time, Blue vowed, he would follow him.

In the meantime, Blue acclimatised to spacestation living. The squeaks, groans and clangs of 'The Giant Tin Can' had stopped filling him full of dread. Now they represented a comforting normality. Blue found himself drifting off to sleep when trying to stay awake for Wurtz. Not that his dreams gave him any kind of solace. If anything, the swamps and sense of impending dread were getting stronger.

One night, close to the end of their stint on *The Charles Darwin*, when Blue had all but forgotten about Wurtz's mysterious excursions, he awoke to find the hatch swinging shut and the Berg's bunk empty.

Blue struggled into his whites and followed. He took a step forward and felt a hand on his arm. "Waa-!" he squealed into the quiet, until another hand clamped over his mouth.

"Where do you think he's going?" asked Corvus.

Blue pushed the hand away. "You nearly scared me half to death you idiot."

"Let's follow. C'mon."

With Corvus leading and Blue behind, they trailed Wurtz until he came to a side door. He glanced around and snuck inside.

Blue and Corvus arrived a few seconds later and, shrugging, pulled the hatch open. A cramped service corridor lit by a dim light. Wurtz lumbered ahead and, as nimble-footed as they could manage, they went after him.

"You know where he's going?"

Corvus shrugged. "Nope, but let's find out. And we're no longer in White Section, Buddy-boy. We're officially Off-Limits."

They entered Yellow Section, pursuing the purposeful form of Wurtz who turned into yet another service corridor leading towards the third ring. Blue's weight increased with every step, his knees creaked and his heart thudded.

The superstructure of the spacestation reflected this increase in gravity—thicker pipes, gantries and supports. Metal struts braced the ceiling and floor. The whole character of the engineering had changed. In comparison, Loop Two seemed rather flimsy and unsafe.

"This is what our gravity is like for Hermans?" Corvus wheezed. "I have a new respect for the Minnie."

Wurtz went through more gloomy corridors and port-like doors until he arrived at the outer ring of Loop Three.

"I hope you're remembering how to get back," said Corvus, his chest heaving. "I lost my way a few turns ago."

"You did?"

"I can't walk in this damn gravity and navigate as well."

"Seems like the wonderful Corvus is a janky human after all."

Corvus shrugged, trembling from the simple effort of standing.

Wurtz, on the other hand, seemed to grow in the higher gravity. He turned into a wide corridor leading to the outer rim, Blue and Corvus following, their joints screaming in pain.

In the distance, Blue noticed an airlock next to a viewing porthole. Outside, in the cold blackness of space, a showy Berg ship waited.

A flash of light and the wall behind Wurtz sizzled and blackened as if heated. Exploding outwards in a ball of short-lived flame. The immense boy leapt aside, rolling and jumping along the floor like an overweight, but well-trained gymnast.

"Down." Corvus grabbed Blue and pulled him to the deck.

Two Bergs, weapons raised, jogged towards Wurtz. Another flash and the floor where Wurtz crouched moments before burned.

Blue had never seen the Berg move as fast—he dived along the ground, rolling closer to his attackers, avoiding yet another silent beam.

Pulling away from Corvus, Blue struggled to his feet and half-ran, half-hobbled to the wall, his hand raised to press one of the regularly spaced alarms. He reached for the Panic Button and became aware of an intense heat. The second attacker targeted him with his, for want of a better description, *Heat-Ray.* Blue flung himself backwards—and just in time—the wall exploded into a shower of sparks and short-lived flame. He scrabbled away, bits of his afro and whites scorched and smoking.

Wurtz jabbed a powerful stubby leg at one of his attackers. A sickening snap and the man collapsed like a sack of potatoes, dropping his gun. The Berg made a desperate grab for the weapon, but the second assailant was on him. Instead, Wurtz kicked the dropped firearm towards Blue. "Grab it, Gote!"

Blue lurched forward, his knees complaining with the effort and grasped at the weapon with both hands. He had never touched a gun before, never mind used one; yet the grip fitted into his hand with ease, his thumb finding a stud.

The second attacker wrestled with Wurtz, using his sturdy firearm like a club.

"Shoot da gun!" shouted the Berg.

Blue lifted the barrel, his heart pounding with the effort, and fired. The intense beam hit the second assailant in the shoulder, flinging him backwards, to lie motionless on the deck.

"Whoa! That was a crash-hot shot, Blue," congratulated a relieved Corvus, scrambling over to Wurtz who was still fighting the other attacker.

"Get off him," wheezed Blue, pointing the heavy gun.

"Shoot him," commanded Corvus.

At those words, the man ceased struggling and Wurtz pulled himself free.

Blue, grimaced at the Berg he'd shot. A steaming burnt hole of charred bone and flesh in place of his enormous shoulder. The man groaned in pain.

"Dey try to kill Wurtz. Dey die for this."

Corvus stumbled along the corridor to another alarm panel.

Within minutes, the place was swarming with guards. Commander Dauntless arrived and took Wurtz off to one side to give him a severe telling off—although Blue could not hear his words.

Dauntless had a quick conversation with Corvus, but said nothing to Blue. They were then escorted back to their quarters.

"Well?" barked Blue, as they walked through the spacestation, thankful for the returning lower gravity. "Anyone going to tell me what this is about?"

Corvus shook his head. "'Fraid not Blue. I have a direct order from the commander not to discuss what happened. You are under the same orders. Keep schtum, you understand?"

"Dauntless wants me to keep quiet about this? Why?"

"Wurtz was warned about wandering around the station at night. He's in trouble and not just with the commander. You did well Blue. We both did. Even though we were Off-Limits, Dauntless is pleased, but that's all I can tell you."

LOSING IT

Later on back in the dorm and despite the specific orders of the commander, Blue told Parris what had happened.

"You reckon Wurtz was visiting his family and someone tried to assassinate him?" his friend asked.

"I dunno. Is that likely?"

Parris shrugged. "Berg families are notorious for their infighting. They are always knocking one another off. Their favourite pastime. Other than mining. What I don't understand is why he was let off by Dauntless. You were all Off-Limits."

"Listen to you two," broke in Morgana. "You are like a couple of gossipy old men. Dauntless is a great man. He would never do anything to jeopardise the Academy. He is noble, principled. The Academy and its cadets come first with him and nothing else."

Hunched on his bunk like a collapsed spider, Hermans nodded in vigorous agreement.

Blue raised his voice. "What a load of bullcrap! Something is obviously going on with Wurtz and your mighty commander. Corvus knows, but he won't tell me."

"You what?" Corvus came over from the other end of the dorm, followed by the lumbering Wurtz.

Blue pointed at the Berg. "Why don't you ask your friend?"

Wurtz knocked Blue's hand away with a thickset arm. "You told ta shut it, Gote."

Blue winced. "You see, Morgana? Dauntless ordered them to keep quiet."

"Then the commander must have good reason," she replied.

"Soldier Girl is right for once," said Corvus. "You need to button that flapping lip of yours."

"Well there's a surprise," said Blue. "The oh-so-cool Corvus is as brainwashed as every other gung-ho Space Corps robot. And I was starting to think you were kinda alright. I should've listened to Parris."

"You are wrong, Blue." Morgana pushed back her sandy blonde bob to reveal an impassioned face. "Corvus is following orders. He can't tell, even if he wants to. And we never question orders. A punishable offence."

Blue stared into Morgana's intense green eyes. "Only punishable if someone ratted on me."

Hermans jabbed a long, paddle-like hand in front of Blue's face "This One must inform Cadet Blue that he oversteps the mark," he said, his voice pinched, reedy and containing the first hint of anger Blue had heard from the boy. "He asks him to immediately retract his accusation against Cadet Morgana, or—he may be forced to intervene."

Corvus waved him aside. "Stay out of this, you stupid Minnie. But Blue is right, we have a rat somewhere in Saturn Squad."

The rest of the bunkroom became deathly quiet.

The raven-haired boy shrugged. "Someone blew the whistle on Singh during pilot training and got him demoted. The question is *who?*" Corvus turned towards Morgana. "Blue obviously thinks it's you."

Hermans bounded to his feet, his head banging into the curved metal ceiling, his normal sing-song voice shrill and strained. "This One has already warned Cadet Blue. He suggests that Cadet Corvus also takes his warning seriously!"

"Hey, I was only joking," said Corvus, as disturbed by

Hermans' manic appearance as by his enormous height.

"He's right, Hermie," interjected Sugar. "I think living in this tin can is getting to you. What am I saying? The claustrophobia is getting to us all."

Morgana smiled at the tall Ganymedian. "Ignore Corvus. Sit back down and leave him be."

"No, Cadet Morgana. No. This One has observed time and time again how insulting Cadet Corvus can be, especially to Cadet Morgana. He is an embarrassment to this squad and to his family unit."

"What? I never talk to the girl, although she'd be more than pleased by the attention. And you know me, I like to have a go at everyone."

"I am from Ganymede," said Hermans, shocking everybody by his use of the first person, "and I am warning you."

Corvus bristled. "Hey, warn all you like, you don't frighten me. Maybe you're the rat. Maybe you were so freaked Blue nearly killed us in the hellijet you went running to Dauntless and we all know your showing off was the cause of Captain Sekhmet's death."

With a loud, nasal shriek, Hermans lunged at Corvus, his elongated fingers knotting around the cocky boy's neck.

"Wha—" Corvus tried through strangled gasps.

"Enuff!" Wurtz grabbed Hermans with stubby powerful hands and pulled him off.

"No!" Hermans voice trilled. "Not enough."

"Isn't it?" Corvus stared wide-eyed at the tall Ganymedian.

"Cadet Corvus needs to be taught a lesson." Hermans' eyes bulged in his long face. "Do not think I am still the weakling you made fun of on day one. I am changed and ready."

Blue had never seen his friend this heated. "Herms? You okay?"

"This One is fine, Cadet Blue."

"I'm not sure you are," said Sugar, staring at the Ganymedian. "You need to calm down a little bit."

Morgana put both hands on Hermans' arm. "Sugar is right,

and fighting amongst cadets is against the Academy rules."

Hermans' voice was a thin reedy whisper. "Get out, Corvus."

Corvus rubbed his neck. "What?"

"Out!"

Corvus shrugged, his expression turning to one of resignation. "Fair enough."

Hermans stalked angrily through the hatchway.

"Do something, Blue," said Morgana in alarm.

Blue followed him. "This is a bad idea, Herms. You're not yourself." The tall boy ignored him. "Parris, help me break this up."

Sugar, her hair a riot of unmanageable curls—the dry spacestation air was playing havoc with her blonde mane—put her hand on Morgana's shoulder. "Two cadets fighting over you, huh?"

"It's not like that," protested Morgana, exiting the hatchway in step behind Parris.

"You sure, Honey?"

Morgana couldn't answer. The entire spacestation rocked and shuddered with a terrific bang.

BREACHED

Blue, Parris, Hermans and Morgana found themselves on the floor of the corridor. Blue jumped to his feet first, gobsmacked at the scene in the bunkroom. Most of the hull had buckled inwards, sending everything flying. Cadets lay prone amongst the upturned bunks like crash-test dummies. And above their moans, the dreadful hiss of escaping air.

"We're holed!" shouted Morgana. "A hull breach."

With those words, the hatch to their quarters clanged shut; locked by powerful hydraulic emergency clamps. Lights turned from white to sickly red. The decompression klaxon screamed into life. Blue's ears popped. Deep within the spacestation, other sirens shrieked and wailed.

Blue pulled at the heavy door. "We have to get them out."

Morgana shook her head. "You can't. The hatches seal shut automatically under depressurisation."

"No way."

Tears spilled onto Morgana's face. "Once a compartment is holed, the automatic systems take over. They won't compromise the rest of the ship. Orders."

Parris got up and stared into the bunkroom. "She's right, Blue, we need to leave before we are all sucked into space."

"I'm not going anywhere."

"They're already dead." Morgana cupped a hand over her mouth as if she wanted to stop her own terrible words.

"Not while I'm still here." Blue went over to the intercom and pressed the alarm button.

A few seconds delay. "Report." A cold dispassionate voice. Dauntless. "What's the situation?"

"This is Cadet Blue. Saturn Dorm is holed, sir. Cadets are trapped inside."

"How many?"

"All of Saturn, except me, Hermans, Parris and Morgana."

"Are they wearing their suits?" asked the commander.

Wurtz was pushing a mattress into the breach, whilst behind him Corvus held a cracked spacesuit helmet, his face panicked and turning blue. Sugar had her arms around an unconscious Ji. "No, sir. Open the hatch now."

"You know the drill, Cadet. We cannot endanger the rest of the station. The whole area can decompress at any moment and you'd be trapped as well. Get out."

"We can rescue them, I'm sure."

"That's against hull-breach regulations, vacate the section. We'll send a specialist team in."

"They don't have time." Blue again stared through the round, glass window and into the holed bunkroom beyond and knew he would not abandon his squad. With a flick of his finger, he switched off the intercom. "Hermans, can you by-pass the magnetic lock and clamps?"

The Ganymedian lay dazed on the floor, blinking in the harsh red, flashing lights. "What happened?"

"A breach!" wailed Morgana.

Blue grabbed the Hermans' shoulders. "Can you by-pass the lock?"

Hermans rubbed his head. "This One must fervently apologise for his recent behaviour, he is—"

"Snap out of it, we don't have time. Can you?"

"Yes, but—"

"They're our friends, get going."

Hermans took a deep breath and pried open a control panel the size of a smart phone.

"What are you doing?" yelled Parris. "Listen to Dauntless. To unlock the door is suicide."

"Parris is right," whimpered Morgana. "We've been ordered back."

"No-one is asking you two to stay," said Blue. "And I heard no direct order."

"Do not worry yourself, Cadet Morgana." Hermans' long pencil-like fingers slipped behind the panel and freed a wad of complicated wiring. "Go forthwith and inform Commander Dauntless there is still a chance to rescue everyone."

With tears streaming down her face, Morgana ran to safety.

"I'm not going to let you die, Blue," said Parris. "You're coming with me. Even if I have to drag you myself." He lunged at Blue, grabbing him around the waist, wrestling him to the floor. They fell. Parris' head hit the metallic wall of the corridor with a clang, stunning him.

"Parris?" The dour cadet was unconscious. "Well that's great. Now we've another casualty." Blue gave Hermans a helpless look. "How long?"

"This One regrets to inform Cadet Blue the procedure might take some time. Five to six minutes at least."

"They don't have minutes, they're dying." His friends were asphyxiating. Sugar pulled and kicked at the door. Terror etched across her face. She fell unconscious to the floor.

They're going to die and I can do nothing...

BLACKOUT.

...Blue opened his eyes and found himself inside the Saturn dorm with an amazed Hermans, the door hanging bent and battered but still on its hinges.

What happened?

"Get them out!" shouted Hermans.

No time to think, my friends need help.

Blue grasped at Veeva, her long red dreads blinding him, whilst Hermans, grunting with the effort, put a cadet over his shoulder. Corvus, pale and shocked, helped Sugar with Ji. Wurtz grabbed at three of the prone cadets and dragged them through the hatch. His brute strength had never been so needed. One trip, two, three.

"Where's Coop?" shouted Sugar in sudden panic.

"I'll find him." Blue rushed back inside the dorm. The hissing became louder. Metal groaned and buckled. A freckled arm protruding from under a bunk. Blue found Coop unconscious below, Blue's precious kitbag next to him. He grabbed them both and struggled past the open door, which he slammed shut with a loud clang.

The sound of shearing metal, and the vacuum wrenched the bunkroom and its contents into space.

For an awful few seconds, the corridor buckled. Air rushed out through the mangled hatchway. Some dreadful force had bent it out of shape.

What did I do?

The glass in the hatchway cracked. A black starry void beyond.

"Run!"

With tremendous effort, Hermans dragged the still unconscious Parris over his shoulder. The other cadets, recovered now they were breathing oxygen again, ran along the tight corridors of the Academy section. More decompression klaxons burst into life.

They passed through doors and hatchways, sealing shut with a hisses and clangs behind them. Blue, who had made sure everyone was up and running before escaping himself, took the rear behind Sugar. Ahead, the final hatch stood open, beyond which was Loop Two and safety. Wurtz lumbered through, followed by Hermans, whose stalk-like legs had made a lot of distance, even with the burden of Parris across his shoulders. More cadets escaped.

Sugar stumbled, falling to her knees. Blue helped her back

to her feet. The remaining cadets slipped through the hatch. Corvus paused in the doorway. Their eyes met and both boys knew it was too late for Blue and Sugar. Corvus pulled back and the hatchway slammed shut.

"We're done for, Hon." Sugar shook her head. "You should've left me behind."

"Yeah, you're right. Still a guy would do about anything to get alone with you." The words left his lips before he realised he was saying them.

"Well, aint you the dark horse. And you know what they say, 'If your number's up, try to make the best of it'. Come here." Her lips touched his. The klaxons stopped their incessant wailing. A loud hiss, a clang, a resounding cheer and a few wolf-whistles.

Blue opened his eyes. The hatch was open in front of him. Wurtz reached in and pulled them through into the safety of Loop Two. "That's three times, now, Gote," he said. "Maybe dis time you dint want rescuing. Hah."

"That was a close call," said Sugar.

Blue didn't know if she meant the kiss or their near death experience. Their eyes met for a second and Sugar smiled.

The squads, white faced and shocked, and their captains, crowded on the other side of the door.

Corvus gave Sugar a knowing look. "You were lucky. Enough doors closed behind you for the commander to get you out, otherwise who knows what might have happened."

"Thanks, Blue," gasped Coop. "You rescued us all."

The rest of Saturn, who had suffered a few cuts and bruises, surrounded Blue, clapping him on the back and congratulating him. Blue shook his head. "No. Thank Hermans. He managed to spring the hatch mechanism."

Everyone then hugged the Ganymedian who stared at Blue in a mixture of awe and confusion.

"This One must explain that—" protested Hermans, prevented from speaking by many thankful embraces.

A distraught Morgana stood next to Commander Dauntless. "I'm so happy you're alive, Blue," she croaked.

Parris came over. "I'm sorry," he said, rubbing at a bump on the side of his head.

Before Blue answered, two tough Military Policemen grabbed Blue and Hermans.

"Hey!"

The MPs spun them around to face Dauntless. The commander's expression was a mixture of anger and relief. "Cadets Hermans and Blue. You are under arrest." He nodded to the Military Policeman. "Take them to the brig," he ordered, before turning around and marching away.

HERMS

Blue sat opposite Hermans in *The Charles Darwin* brig. A stark utilitarian metal cell with a single toilet and two uncomfortable bunks and considerably more airy than their cramped quarters.

"What you did, Cadet Blue—This One is advanced in wisdom and experience for one of so few years, but how did you open the bunkroom door?" Hermans' face twisted into a peculiar confused frown, his words trilling in amazement. "It was beyond human."

"One moment the hatch was clamped shut, the next, I was in the dorm. I can't remember the in between—What the hell did I do?"

"This One could not believe his Ganymedian eyes. You grappled the hatchway and wrenched the door free as if the hydraulic clamps were wet cardboard. So much raw unadulterated power and determination. How?"

"I dunno. I'm not like you, remember? I'm a Gote." Knowing he was the result of some mysterious genetic manipulation had sat uneasily at the back of Blue's mind since Shelley told him about his peculiar chromosomal history.

Hermans raised an eyebrow. "The eggheads tampered with the Gote's genome for many, many years, Cadet Blue. We can only guess at their motives, but what you did was way outside the normal range of strength and capability. Beyond human."

"Stop saying that. I don't feel *beyond human.*"

"This One offers Blue his most heartfelt apology."

"Thanks—But you are thinking the eggheads perhaps gave me some new abilities? Yes?"

"Possibly. Instances of humans showing extreme strength in stressful circumstances are well documented. Maybe they isolated that particular gene and gave it to you—Is that your only hidden talent?"

"Well," Blue said, his mouth dry, "back in the past, I sort of sensed people, the ones I was close to. Eddi, Newt and my sister, Annie. Not voices, nothing tangible like words. And… and I somehow experienced the terror of everyone trapped in the holed bunkroom before I blacked out."

"I have heard of parents knowing when their children are in danger, of twins experiencing the same pain hundreds of miles apart. The eggheads possibly gave you that heightened ability as well."

"So I'm not some terrible freak boy?"

"I think we are all unique, Cadet Blue."

"That's a polite way of putting it. Can this be our secret?"

"Everyone already believes Cadet Hermans opened the hatch."

"Do me a favour and pretend just that, yeah?"

"I am still profoundly embarrassed by my recent behaviour back in the bunkroom. This One is not worthy of such heartfelt praise from his respected colleagues."

"Worthy? Everyone in the squad will understand why you lost it, and I bet more than a few of them were pleased you stood up to Corvus. If you hadn't left the dorm when you did, we would all be dead. And that was a great job hauling Parris to safety."

"Pure adrenaline, Cadet Blue."

"I wish I could say the same," Blue laughed darkly. "I guess Ganymede is different from here, yeah?"

"Oh yes." Hermans stared into the distance and beamed

from ear to ear. "Our settlement is one vast ocean. Wide seas, fishing and trade between the many island villages drifting on the natural tidal currents. I am not used to closed rooms. No. I slept on open beaches or on deck when sailing. I will take you there one day."

"Hermans, can I...um...mention something?"

"Of course, Cadet Blue."

"You are not referring to yourself as 'This One.'"

Hermans reddened. "True, Cadet Blue. I do apologise. Formality, despite its importance on my world, is sometimes a wall we fashion against others. It would now be erroneous for me to use the formal third person imperative. We have shared in life-changing events. You are no longer my trusted colleague but my good friend. In the normal course of things, such a change in our relationship would be marked with ceremony and gifts, but as that is impractical, all I can offer you is my hand."

They shook, long fingers curling around his own. "Thank you, Herms."

"From now on that shall be my informal name. I will wear it with the honour of true friendship. I will always be *Herms* to you." He bowed formally.

"You can call me...er...*Blue,* I suppose."

"Thank you, Blue." Hermans lifted his head and smiled. "How do you think Cadet Morgana is doing?"

"As usual, she ran straight to Dauntless, she—"

Hermans uncharacteristically cut him off mid-sentence. "Listen to me, Blue. I have no proof, but Cadet Morgana is not the rat. It is not in her nature. She is a follower of rules, is lawful, but the strongest unwritten rule is loyalty to one's squad. She would not break such a tenet."

Blue had seen the same look in the Ganymedian's eyes back in the dorm and decided to take his words seriously. "Maybe you are right, maybe I shouldn't always be blaming her. But, to be honest, she annoys me. She's constantly there, barging into my conversations, getting in the way."

"As ever, Blue misses the obvious—Cadet Morgana likes

you."

"She does?"

"Every time I look at Morgana, her eyes are fixed on you."

"Oh. You mean—?"

"Yes, I believe so."

"Who would've thought it? The girl turns out to have great taste. But joking aside, no, that could never happen. Not in a month of Sundays."

"I must admit to a certain feeling of relief at Blue's frank statement."

"You don't have the hots for the Academy's most gung-ho girl…do you?"

The Ganymedian's head twitched. "Blue is uncharacteristically correct in this particular instance."

"Well I'm not gonna stand in your way. Go for it, fella."

"If only Blue's permission was all that was needed. I'm afraid Cadet Morgana sees This One as a friend. An honour, but—This One wishes for more."

"Hey, now you're the hero, things might change."

"I fervently hope so. In the meantime, I want you to forgive Cadet Morgana and also Cadet Parris for their actions."

"That's a tall order," said Blue, hoping to raise a smile, but the pun fell on deaf ears.

"Cadets Parris and Morgana were orphans, Blue. Earth Corps is all they have ever had. It means everything to them. You cannot expect them to change overnight."

"I suppose not."

"Forgive her, Blue. Forgive them both."

"Really?"

"Would Blue want me to divulge the reality of the astounding events surrounding the rescue of Saturn Squad?"

"…You push a tough bargain, but okay." The two boys shook hands again.

The hatch opened. Two Military Policemen entered and roughly escorted them to what looked like a courtroom. Benches lined up in front of a dais upon which stood Commander

Dauntless. The room was empty except for a few grave-looking military personnel. They were pushed forwards to stand before the commander. He wore his familiar tinted sunglasses. Blue couldn't fathom what he was thinking.

"Cadet Hermans, Cadet Blue," he said, his dispassionate voice carried on the intercom system and echoing across *The Charles Darwin*. "You both disobeyed a direct order from your Commanding Officer." Dauntless focused on Hermans. "However, one of you re-wired a spacestation hatchway to open a sealed door in total disregard of depressurisation protocols. You not only put yourselves in danger, but you threatened the lives of everybody on this station."

Hermans stood to sudden attention, appearing taller than Blue had seen him before. "I—" he began, causing Commander Dauntless' eyebrows to rise above the rim of his sunglasses, "I did it for my friends, sir, for Saturn Squad. I am solely to blame. I could not sit back and let them die—I would gladly disobey orders again."

A flash of anger crossed Dauntless' face and Blue knew Hermans had gone too far.

Why did he say that?

"Cadet Hermans, I am surprised and disappointed by your reckless words. For disobeying my direct order, for putting *The Charles Darwin* in danger and including Cadet Blue in your disobedience, and for showing a complete lack of deference to your commanding officer, I have no choice but to sentence you to be Hung-Out-To-Dry for a period of no less than seventy-two hours."

An audible gasp filtered back through the ship. Hermans rocked backwards on his long feet. It was as if Dauntless' words had had the power to send him reeling.

"Cadet Blue," Dauntless continued. "I cannot ignore your part in Cadet Hermans' insubordination. By all accounts you acted bravely, if not stupidly. You must also be punished. A Class One Reprimand will be added to your record."

Blue drew breath, but Dauntless did not offer him the chance to speak.

"Take Cadet Hermans away," he barked.

::

Half an hour later, the squads of the Academy stood in a carpeted observation suite big enough to hold all squads. The port doors were open, revealing the triple rings of the spacestation and the beautiful curve of Earth making slow transition. After recent events, such a large expanse of unprotected glass made Blue nervy. He shuffled uncomfortably. But it was more than the threat of micrometeorites that bothered him. By convincing Hermans to take the praise for saving Saturn Squad, he had unwittingly put him in the firing line. Blue couldn't change things, no matter how much he wanted to. Only Herms was dextrous enough to get his fingers inside the door panel. The other alternative, saying I somehow wrenched the hatch halfway off its hinges? No one would believe that. And now Hermans has to take the blame. It should be me.

Dauntless entered with the rest of the captains and some other officers Blue had not seen before. Official personnel sent to view the forthcoming punishment. Everyone stood to attention, including Blue.

I'm like some Pavlovian dog. The master calls and I jump.

Physician Phelps entered, walking side by side with two Military Policemen and a resolute looking Hermans wearing a tight Skin. Phelps said a few private words to the Ganymedian, checked his suit and fitted a visorless helmet.

"He'll be okay," whispered Coop at Blue's side. "He's a survivor."

"He did good, for a Minnie," added Corvus who seemed to have forgotten Hermans tried to strangle him.

Morgana drew breath to speak. Blue glared at her. She covered her face with a hand and sobbed. Blue remembered his promise to the tall boy. "Don't worry, Morg'," he said. If anything, her sobs increased.

They took Hermans through a door and a short while later they heard the muffled klaxon from the airlock. Hermans drifted into view outside, attached to the station by a long umbilical.

Dauntless stood at a podium. "Let this be a warning to you all. For those who need reminding of the seriousness of this crime, disobeying a direct order in Earth Corps is a capital punishment. Cadet Hermans has got off lightly. Dismissed."

"Hermans put his head on the chopping block for us all," said Corvus on the way to their new quarters. "He's a real hero in my book. I read the guy all wrong. He saved my life."

"Not just yours, Honey," said Sugar. Ji and Coop nodded in fierce agreement.

Veeva squeezed Blue's arm. "He'll be fine."

The next morning, a few new notices appeared on the Ship's Board. Although Blue usually ignored the bulletins, he could not ignore the fact Wurtz had been staring for some time. The first message read:

CHARLES DARWIN SURVIVES IMPACT

```
The Charles Darwin was rocked yesterday
by what eggheads are calling a 'sizeable
meteorite'.  The  walnut-sized  rock
struck the Academy Dorms where Saturn
Squad was enjoying a period of R&R. We
are pleased to announce no fatalities
and, apart from two notable exceptions,
the well-drilled Academy cadets acted
efficiently and effectively.



Commendations go to:
Cadet Morgana, Saturn
1st Class
```

Morgana received a commendation for running away when

everyone needed her help? Typical.

Wurtz stared at another, smaller news item:

PRINCE DORE (BERG) DIES

```
We are sad to announce the death of
Prince Dore (the oldest son of King
Wilhelm) who died from what appears to
be natural causes. Spacestation Cmdr
Marconi on behalf of all Earth Corps
will be giving his official condolences
to the King and his family at this time
of grief.
```

A brief addendum below:

```
All helium-3 talks have been suspended
whilst the remains of Berg Prince Dore
are interred, although we believe the
negotiations are close to resolution.
Watch this space.
```

Dore dead? SEARCH's crony who poisoned his father to further his own selfish ambition had died? Blue scanned the other news stories, but found no mention of the attempt on Wurtz's life the previous evening. "You know what any of this is about?" Blue asked Wurtz.

The Berg said nothing. He turned around and tramped away.

"Fair enough."

The next night, a vivid nightmare stunned Blue into sweaty wakefulness. He lurched to his feet in Saturn's new and even more cramped quarters, swaying in shock. He'd been back in the swamps, atop a tree, staring at the clear night sky and *The Charles Darwin* floating in orbit around the North Star.

He felt certain something terrible was about to happen to Hermans. And, as Blue swayed amongst the island treetops of his dream, the air froze around him, sucking the life from his lungs. He fell, choking on icy blood, knowing he was dying, falling into a well of cold, deathly blackness.

Still dizzy from the nightmare, Blue dressed, left the cramped dorm and entered the Loop walkway. He jogged to the observation suite and the port doors, convinced he'd had a dreadful premonition of some kind. He became aware of a group of medics with Physician Phelps standing around a prone figure on the floor. A trail of thick crimson blood led from the airlock.

"Herms!" he screamed. "Hermans!" Blue ran over and found a sight so horrific and gruesome, that the image would haunt him the rest of his life.

"Decompression," croaked Phelps with an audible rasp of grief. "The fool let space into his suit. Hermans removed his helmet."

"What?" shouted Blue. He turned away from the ripped bloodied and half-frozen mess to stare into the impassive face of the Physician. "Why would he do that? Why?"

Commander Dauntless came around the corner followed by a grim Shelley. He pushed Blue aside. "Suicide?"

Phelps saluted. "Yes, sir."

"That was no suicide," spat Blue, unable to contain his anger at the commander. "You killed him."

"Calm down, cadet."

"He was claustrophobic. You knew that." Blue lunged at Dauntless, but a sharp blow to the back of his head sent him sprawling into unconsciousness.

::

Blue came to a short while later lying on the bed in Shelley's ship quarters. The captain rubbing the back of his neck.

"You must forgive me, Blue."

"You hit me? I thought you didn't like Dauntless?"

"I saved you from yourself. Attacking the commander would not help Mister Hermans."

"Herms," yelped Blue, remembering. "Hermans is dead. His

face!"

"Not a pretty sight."

"Why did Dauntless punish Hermans and not me?" he bellowed. "Why not have us both Hung-Out-To-Dry?" Blue wanted to tell her that it should have been him out there. That he convinced Hermans to admit to something he hadn't done. But the words would not come to his lips.

"That *was* your punishment, Blue. To sit idly by whilst your friend paid the price. The commander is as sly as he is harsh. He told me as much."

Blue was unable to speak.

"I share your loss, Blue. Hermans often talked to me. He admired you."

Blue found it hard to think about Hermans. "I'm leaving. I can't stop here any longer," Blue said finally. "I hate this place; I hate Dauntless." I just want to go home.

"When you arrived in the future, Dauntless, as head of the Academy, became your legal guardian. Until you are eighteen, I'm afraid you have to do whatever he says."

"What?"

"This is not unusual in such cases. I don't doubt Dauntless thought he was doing you a favour. The truth is you cannot do anything without his say so."

"I could steal a hellijet and disappear."

"You are not thinking rationally, Blue. Listen to me." Shelley took hold of Blue's hands and squeezed them. "Play the long game, okay?"

"I don't want to."

"Blue, please bite your lip and wait for time to pass. You are angry; don't make any hasty decisions."

"To stay here now—I'd be condoning what Dauntless did."

"Remember your stealing and how I helped you out? I put myself on the line for you, Mister. I'm ordering you to repay the favour."

Blue swallowed hard. "But Dauntless killed Hermans after he risked his own life to save the squad."

"Even though I dislike the commander, he did not intend for Hermans to die."

"You told Dauntless about Herman's claustrophobia and he ignored you."

"Yes he did."

"I don't think I can sit back and do nothing."

"You have another function to perform in all of this."

"I do?"

"This morning I informed Hermans' parents of his untimely death. They will be visiting Earth and the Academy before the End of Phase Fest. I want you to meet them as his friend to talk about their son. Hold back your anger until you perform this important duty. Is that too much to ask?"

"What do I say to them?"

"The truth. How Hermans saved Saturn Squad."

"And the punishment by Dauntless?"

"Leave that to me, Blue. Tell them all the good things about Hermans. His struggle to cope with Earth's heavier gravity, his fortitude and how he risked everything to save his friends. Your duty is to them."

Blue nodded grimly, "Okay, ma'am."

"Now, I suggest you go grieve with the rest of your squad."

Blue returned to the new quarters, walking slowly, hoping to bump into Hermans' murderer. He understood 'the long game', but he wasn't sure what he would do if he came face to face with Dauntless. That didn't happen. And the commander did not appear later on that day when Hermans' body was committed into space. Blue guessed he had run away.

The squads stood as they had done a few hours ago to see Hermans Hung-Out-To-Dry. This time, there was no umbilical cord on the body they jettisoned into space. Hermans' mummy-like tumbling corpse hit the Earth's atmosphere. A white flash leaving a fiery trail and Hermans was gone. In only a few seconds, everything that was the Ganymedian had disappeared. It made no sense to Blue. How could he be so alive one moment, chatting, talking and strangling Corvus and yet in the next be nothing more than motes of charred dust floating in Earth's empty atmosphere? Blue remembered their last conversation. Was it only hours ago? —and turned to Morgana.

"Herms was a good friend to me," Blue said. "I didn't realise until it was too late. I promised him I'd be a good friend to you too, Morgana."

"He made you promise? Why?"

Blue said nothing.

Morgana glanced again at the curve of the Earth where Hermans had disappeared. "Thank you, Blue,"

"But remember this: Hermans was a hero and your precious Commander killed him."

"Oh Blue," whimpered Morgana, burying her head in his shoulder.

ENDINGS & BEGINNINGS

Blue spent the last few days on *The Charles Darwin* in a daze. The only relief from his anger and grief was exams. With Hermans' death hanging over them like a black cloud, everybody threw themselves into revision and without surprise or celebration they all passed, Veeva with a distinction in Astronavigation and Blue a faraway but respectable second.

Blue had no enthusiasm for returning to the Academy and his empty bunkroom. But finally, they boarded *Old Dinger* and made the long journey back to the Crater. Now in charge of his emotions, Shelley's words made more sense.

I will play the long game and exact my revenge when the opportunity arrives. Like it or not, the Academy is all I have.

One thing stood in the way: his rip legs or lack of them. It was R&R week and he had orders to report to the Rip Room every day.

"Hey, how you feeling, Gote?" asked Corvus, the first morning in the Mess.

"It's odd to be all on my lonesome in my quarters. I keep expecting to see Hermans, but I'm okay."

"Way to go, Blue," Sugar purred with respect.

"We miss da Hermans."

Corvus clapped Wurtz on the back. "Well said. I wish I'd not been so hard on the guy."

Blue wanted to be angry with Corvus, but after recent events, that reservoir of emotion was dry. Despite everything, we're all just kids. We're too young to deal with all *this*. He sighed. "Best not to beat ourselves up too much. None of us knew what would happen. I know one thing though, Hermans was damn revved to be a Ringer."

"The Ringers," pronounced Corvus with respect.

"The Ringers," the rest repeated, Blue amongst them.

"Now," said Corvus, "all this R&R might be fun for most people, but I hate twiddling my thumbs. What is it you say, Blue? 'It's doin' my head in'? Do you want some company whilst you sort out those rip legs of yours?"

"Yeah. That'd be swick."

"Wurtz go too."

"You can rely on my cute ass," said Sugar with a wink.

All of Saturn Squad joined in, except Morgana, who gave him a supportive smile, Veeva whose success at Astronavigation had made her somehow more withdrawn and Parris who had taken the death of Hermans to heart—a pale imitation of the cadet Blue had met on his first day at B-Pal.

Blue had tried speaking to him. All Parris said was: "He saved my life, carried me to safety, and he's dead, Blue. He's dead." Blue left him alone with his grief.

The last time Blue travelled the roof monorail to the Rip Column, he'd taken little notice—besieged by his own problems. Wow. I really missed out. What a fantastic feat of engineering. The train hung suspended in mid-air, held in place by powerful magnets preventing the carriages from falling thousands of feet to the Hab floor. The lack of friction gave a smooth, eerily quiet ride. They darted through tunnels to emerge into inverted valleys, skirting stalactites, sweeping into depressions and ruts at amazing speeds giving any twenty-first century rollercoaster a run for its money.

Back in the Rip-Room, it was no real surprise that Blue strode across the rip for the first time. The Drag was not as unexpected and the Push not as hard.

I've found my timing. I'm changed inside somewhere. More solid, hardened. And I need to be. Tomorrow, Hermans' parents are arriving.

That evening, after complimenting Blue on his ripwalking success, Shelley briefed him about tomorrow's itinerary. He was to meet Hermans' parents after breakfast and show them around the Academy Column and the Crater. They would leave him for lunch at the Top Table and an afternoon spent with Dauntless, Shelley and the other captains.

Blue did not envy Shelley, having to make small-talk to the parents of the boy Dauntless murdered whilst the man himself listened, but Blue had sworn to do his bit for his dead friend. Besides, Shelley promised to tell them everything.

::

Hermans' parents, when they arrived the next day, were technically Ganymedians, but not like Hermans. From Earth, they emigrated to the Outer Solar System before he was born. Now back on Earth, they were thin and weak; forced to wear the same Gee-Suits Blue wore when flying at high Mach speeds in the hellijet. They spent most of their time pushed around in wheelchairs unable to even support the weight of their own heads. Blue told them of Hermans' success at the Cubby Hole, of how he asked and received no special favours because of his 'disability' and how he helped rescue Saturn Squad before his punishment. Blue braced himself for the next question about how Hermans died, but it never came.

Later on, back in his quarters, Blue took Jonesy from his kitbag. "I shouldn't have left you, Annie," he said. "I miss you so much." Alone in his empty bunkroom in a survival space under what remained of the Amazon rainforest four-hundred and fifty years in the future, Blue sobbed for Annie and his parents, for Hermans and most of all—for himself. With tears dripping down his face, he let them all go.

::

The End of Phase Fest held no excitement for Blue. After dinner on the day of the Fest, Blue returned to his quarters to find a set of dress whites laid on his bunk. Showy. Embroidered. Not the simple everyday one-piece uniform. Trousers, shirt, bow tie and jacket. Blue stared at the tie and grimaced.

Over four-hundred years in the future and they still have bloody ties.

A short while later, Corvus, magnificent in his dress uniform, breezed into his bunkroom. "Don't stare, Bucko, I'll drive you crazy," he said with a flash of his pale-blue eyes. "You not dressed yet? Frightened of the competition, huh? C'mon, we're meeting up in R&R."

Blue dressed and went over to his mirror. Even with his afro cut back after his trip to *The Charles Darwin,* the skinny runt was gone. In his place: an assured young man.

"Hey, I'm all growed up."

"You sure are, Buddy," laughed Corvus.

A short time later, Blue joined the rest of the squads in R&R, his eyes roving over the girls. He'd seen them in the showers plenty of times and, although that had its attractions, their flowing academy gowns made his heart beat faster. The girls too, were similarly impressed.

Sugar and Ji stood next to each other chatting, eyeing the boys, Veeva with them, talking to Coop. She had her hair down, her long thick red dreads hanging in a most alluring fashion. Veeva caught Blue staring at her. She smiled and Blue went funny inside.

Morgana appeared and Blue did not know what to think. All the girls wore make-up for the first time. For some reason, the blusher and eyeshade did not sit well on Morgana. The other cadets gave her a spontaneous round of applause.

What?

"Space." Sugar leant backwards, putting one hand on her

hip. "You sure scrubbed up well, Morgana."

"Didn't she just," added Corvus.

"Captain Shelley helped me get ready." Morgana's fingers played with a silver chain hung around her neck, its pendant seductively hidden under the low-cut dress.

Wurtz lunged forward and offered her his arm. Morgana smiled and accepted.

"You Bergs have strange likes," mocked Blue to confused looks from Corvus and Parris. Corvus stared at Wurtz with—

Was it a hint of jealously?

"You like my dress?" said Morgana, catching Corvus' eye. "A different style to the other girls—a simple one piece. One of Captain Shelley's. She showed me a picture of herself as a younger woman wearing it. She had a stunning figure."

Sugar whistled, "She aint the only one."

"Shelley did a top job, didn't she?" said Morgana.

Coop came over and fingered the material. "Lovely. And so light."

"A design from before the Big Meltdown. She's given the dress to me as she's…er…outgrown it. She insisted I wear my necklace. An heirloom."

Corvus took Blue aside. "What was the story about *The Ugly Duckling?*"

Blue frowned, "I don't see it."

::

Despite the glamour, the End of Phase Fest was a dreary affair set in an imposing chamber of bare rock with a high ceiling.

Like a school hall back home, but over-sized and unfriendly.

The future did not seem to understand 'mood lighting'. The space was lit like all other rooms in the Academy. Harsh beams shone from above, bleaching the colour out of everything. A series of wall-hangings, a makeshift stage decorated with cheesy tinsel and an old sign saying 'End-of-Phase Fest' and that was it.

The music came from a band of cadets playing a mixture of

instruments: a beat-up piano, a drum, an ancient out-of-tune double bass and bagpipes. Blue wished for pumping dance or crashing guitars. He had always taken music for granted. Here, four-hundred and fifty years in the future, the past world with all its wonderful death-metal, drum n' bass and middle-of-the-road light entertainment muzak was gone forever.

Shelley and the other captains left early. He guessed they found the event as tiresome as he did.

Parris appeared at his side wearing a sad smile. "Can we chat about Veeva? We both like her. Don't we?"

Blue stared at the ginger-dreadlocked girl again. "Yeah, we do, although I doubt she even knows I exist. And if she does, I bet she thinks I'm some sort of prize twacker. Why you asking?"

"I'm bowing out. She's all yours."

"Really? I don't think it's that easy, Parris. If I'm honest, she hasn't shown much interest in either of us."

Parris didn't seem to listen. "I'm giving you the green light. Okay? A gift. Take it or leave it."

Blue wasn't sure what to say. Parris had not been himself since Hermans' death. "Um…er…thanks. I suppose—You okay?"

A stillness came over the blonde boy, the same stillness Blue had observed before. Like he was listening to some internal monologue that required all his attention. "Hermans' death has made me think," he said finally, as if this was the only explanation required.

"Me too," replied Blue, surprised at how strongly Parris' words resonated within him. "I'm never gonna get home," he said, vocalising the words for the first time. And when those words left his lips, a great weight lifted from him. "I'm concentrating on making a life for myself here in the Academy. I'm gonna become a pilot, flying is all I'm good at anyway. I…I belong here now, with my friends."

Parris opened his mouth to say something, but instead nodded towards Veeva and disappeared.

Blue gulped. I've walked in space, flown a hellijet faster than the speed of sound, ripped the void and docked a rocketship.

That's nothing compared to asking a girl out. Where can we go anyway? The closest this place has to entertainment is the broken Ping-Pong table in R&R or a walk through The Museum of Indulgence. Hardly romantic.

"Hey Veeva," said Blue, after a good half hour of mustering his courage. "Um...nice dress."

"Well thank you, Blue. You're looking fine yourself."

"You enjoying the fest?"

Veeva shrugged.

"I was thinking...um...would you like to...er," Blue's nerve faltered.

"Yes?"

"—To go out with me sometime?"

"You want to court me?"

"If that's what you call it, yeah. I do."

Veeva shook her head. "I'm sorry, but that can't happen, Blue."

Blue's face sagged. He knew that she might say no, but her tone was adamant. Like she never even considered the possibility. "Oh, right, fair enough. I'd better go."

Veeva grabbed his shoulder and whispered into his ear. "I need to tell you something, but you must promise to keep it a secret. Okay?"

"Sure. You can tell me anything. Is it Parris? Is it...him you like?"

"Parris? Don't be silly. No Blue, I'm leaving the Academy."

"What?"

Veeva dragged Blue to a quiet corner. "I don't fit in here. Working with Captain Lovelace, working on all that pure math made me realise this place isn't for me. I'm a bad fit...so I'm going."

"But you're doing brilliant, loads better than me. You can't go."

"The Academy is not for me, Blue. The constant pressure to perform, to achieve. I'm not up to it. I'm stressed all the time. And after poor Hermans...Everything is arranged with Shelley and Dauntless, I'm ripping back home tomorrow."

"Home?"

"You remember the first ripwalking sesh when Dauntless showed us the planet with the two suns and low white houses?"

"That's your world?"

"Please don't tell anyone else. This is my last night. I want to enjoy it and leave my goodbyes till tomorrow at Mess."

"If you were staying, would you have…um…*courted* me?"

Veeva smiled. "I don't know, Blue. This experience has been so full on, I haven't had time to think about anything else. But—you sure are cute." She kissed him on the cheek and walked away.

Blue snuck off back to the Crater soon after. He had lost his appetite for the Fest. He lay on his bed and immediately fell into welcome unconsciousness.

He awoke the next morning to the sensation of being watched. "Herms?" He glanced over at the empty bunk and frowned. He rubbed the sleep from his eyes and was surprised to find a note on his pillow. His eyes gobbled up the words in an instant. "No way—No jazzing way."

NUB

Blue Into The Rip

THE OTHER RIP

```
If you want to get home, meet me in the
Survival Seshroom before Lights-Up.

A friend.
```

Blue grabbed his kitbag and left his quarters.

If this is someone's idea of a joke then—

The possibility didn't bear thinking about.

Walking around the Wheel, lost in his thoughts, Blue passed the corridor leading to the Entrance Hall. Here, he caught Dauntless in heated discussion with a dishevelled figure in a long dirty coat and a rough hood.

Blue stopped and stared.

The stranger was odd in a way that both fascinated and freaked him out. The hooded boy glared right at him—a sunburnt face streaked with dirt. A full-on shiver ran along his spine. He continued quickly on his way, deciding he no longer cared about Dauntless and his many intrigues. He arrived at Sekhmet's old seshroom and entered the unlit chamber. "Anyone here?" He waited for a few moments. "You better not be pulling my leg, otherwise—" A familiar figure stepped into view from the shadows. "You?"

"Yes indeed, heh."

"Captain Shelley?"

She leant forward and smiled, her eyes sparkling. "You still want to go back home, Mister?"

"More than anything, but—"

"No buts this time. Remember, I put myself on thin ice for you, covering for your thieving."

Blue frowned.

"I want your word of honour as a cadet and as a friend not to repeat what I am about to say to anyone, agreed?"

"Yes, ma'am."

A troubled expression creased her features. "I lied to you, Blue. When you overheard Dauntless speaking to the Fleet-Admiral about that cadet—"

"They *were* talking about me?"

"Yes. Dauntless knew you were important, why else would he become your guardian? Why else put you in the Academy? Why else was Hermans punished and you let off? You are no ordinary Gote, Blue. You are more special than you imagine."

Blue braced himself. *This is it. The reason behind my peculiar blackouts and abilities. Have Shelley and Dauntless known all along?*

"You are the Gote whose parents are Commander Edison and Captain Newton."

"Eddi and Newt?" Blue did a double take. *Edison and Newton,* of course.

"SEARCH will do anything to catch those two."

"Oh." Blue was taken aback and, if he was honest, a tad disappointed. "But why are Eddi and Newt any more significant than the other terrorists?"

"They are not terrorists, Blue. Please do not use the vernacular of the commander and Earth Corps."

"Why though?"

"They motivated the Underground to make a stand and planned to enter the eggheads' labs to end their experiments; they made the decision to destroy the rip when they became trapped. They were the ringleaders, Blue, SEARCH wants to bring them back to the Hab for a Court Martial and—*a public execution."*

"No."

"Your being here is jeopardising their safety. That is why I helped you. I am part of the same secret organisation."

"The Underground? That was over a hundred years ago."

"Not everyone thought their actions wrong, Blue. Indeed, to many they are still heroes. Earth Corps vilifies them, but their supporters live on in secret. Your parents are to be applauded, not hunted like animals."

"I never guessed."

"And well you shouldn't. SEARCH recruited me to befriend you and to keep a watchful eye on Dauntless."

"But you told me SEARCH are the number one bad guys and *you're working for them?"*

Shelley gave Blue a patient smile. "I am what you call a 'turncoat,' I no more believe in their ethos, as does Commander Dauntless believe in his much vaunted honour. SEARCH has waited for a chance to capture Edison and Newton for a long, long time, Blue. What a piece of dark luck you arrived when you did. Far too easy for Dauntless to snatch you and make you part of his Academy. He is using you as a bargaining chip to gain more influence. His eyes are on SEARCH, where the real power lies."

"'Dark luck'? What do you mean?"

"His intervention gave me and my friends the opportunity to rescue you. If SEARCH found you instead of Dauntless, things would have gone badly, very quickly. SEARCH sent me to befriend you, to gain your trust and to steal you away. A difficult balancing act to keep you safe."

"You're a double agent?"

"I came to the Academy and Saturn Squad to protect you Blue. Not to help SEARCH or Dauntless, but to aid you and your parents. Earth Corps is an organisation I despise. Not at first though. At first, I respected them, but when I discovered what SEARCH was capable of doing, their inhumanity, I turned against them. And these days Earth Corps is SEARCH."

Blue nodded, trying to take everything in.

"My friends and I work within that organisation. Sometimes it is best to get close to what you hate. Edison and Newton are in danger Blue. Dauntless will trade you for a powerful position in SEARCH and they will use you to go back in time to capture them."

"But ripping in time is forbidden, isn't it?"

"Who told you that?"

"You mean Dauntless lied? Even so, you can't just waltz through all the security into the Rip-Room." Blue's mind made the obvious connection. "Of course, another rip. I heard Admiral Apache talking to Dauntless about SEARCH's secret rip machine."

"Wilhelm knows of its existence. Hence his embargo. He is no fool."

Blue swallowed hard. "Then—I can get back home."

"Yes, Blue."

"So I've been lied to since I arrived here? Even by you?"

Shelley gave Blue a pained look. "For your protection. I had no choice."

"But I can trust you, yes?"

"Of course, but we will need to move quickly. Dauntless has had me transferred."

"You mean you're no longer captain of Saturn Squad?" This was all so suddenly real. Happening. "Why?"

"He is right to be suspicious of me and my friendship with the Academy's most important cadet. I was sent by SEARCH after all, but he never guessed my true motives. Standing up against him over Mister Hermans was the last straw. Dauntless thinks by neutralising me he will be sending a strong message to 'my masters' in SEARCH. And maybe he is. But no matter. We are going back in time to rescue your parents, to take them further back in history. We will be lost to Earth Corps and the future forever."

"I can go back home? Really?"

Shelley nodded.

"But doesn't it take months to program a time rip or did Dauntless lie about that as well?"

"No. Time ripping is a time-consuming activity, but we were already planning an escape back to the past, using a time rip for ourselves. Since your unexpected appearance, we have been recalibrating and reprogramming; why else did I treat you as just another Gote? Although your thieving caused me quite a few problems."

Blue hung his head in shame.

"Dauntless may have forced us to act earlier than anticipated, but we are ready. Your coming changed everything, Blue. *Everything.* Return to the Crater and act normally."

"Go...*back?*"

"Blue, I am leaving the Academy Column for good. This is my last chance to speak to you here. To go missing now will alert Dauntless and SEARCH. We cannot jeopardise the time rip. Meet me in the Nest after Morning Mess."

"I thought the Nest was abandoned?"

"Do you need anything for the journey?"

"Everything is in my kitbag. Will you take care of it for me?"

Shelley nodded and Blue handed over his pack.

"Speak nothing of this to anyone."

"I'll try my best."

"No-one tries in Saturn Squad, Mister." Shelley took his hands and squeezed them. "This is a dangerous time for all of those of noble heart. Wish me luck Blue. Wish us all good luck."

"Good luck, ma'am."

Shelley let him go and waddled away.

BEST OF FRIENDS

Blue picked his way along the side of the Crater towards his quarters, his mind abuzz with thoughts of returning home. The Crater's self-contained artificial sun had not yet awoken from its nightly slumber.

The more he replayed Shelley's words, the more everything made sense. Hermans had been convinced there was a reason why Shelley let him off for his thieving, and he was right.

She's been secretly helping me all along.

The underground hydroponic jungle creaked and rattled, whilst the waterfall crashed into the wide pool below. All the holes were in darkness, except one.

Blue entered his friend's quarters. "Parris? You awake?"

"Blue?"

"Yeah. How was the Fest?" he asked. He didn't care about the answer. All he wanted was to tell Parris his amazing news.

"Awful. Everybody in their dress whites and Hermans dead. We tried to enjoy ourselves but—" Parris stopped in mid-sentence, his eyes widening when he saw the expression on Blue's face. "You've found a way back, haven't you?"

Is it that obvious? But I can trust Parris. He knew about my thieving and said nothing. Of course he did. I can tell him anything. "Yes Parris! Yes! I have…I can't believe it. I'm still in shock."

The blonde boy said nothing, frozen where he sat.

"Didn't you hear me? I'm going home."

When Parris did speak, his voice held no emotion. "Well done, Blue."

"It's Captain Shelley. She has been working on my side for months. She told me not to tell anyone. But I can rely on you to keep schtum, yeah?"

"I think you should be careful who you trust, Blue."

"What? You're not going to rat on me, are you?"

"You shouldn't go blurting this to anyone. You have no idea what might happen."

"Not anyone. You're my mate."

"Yeah. Right."

"I thought you'd be pleased for me."

"But how? Time ripping is impossible. Banned."

"I can't tell you exactly, but soon, sometime this morning after Mess. I have some other news: Dauntless transferred Captain Shelley out of the Academy. The reason why she moved her plans forward."

"Dauntless knows?"

"No, but he's never trusted her. She's from SEARCH."

"'She told you that?"

"There's a helluva a lot more to it."

"And you still trust her?"

"Of course I do. And I was right about Dauntless all along; he's one bad dad, through and through."

"You can't blame him for everything."

"Can't I, Parris? Why is it such a mental leap to believe he and the Academy are corrupt? Everybody is brainwashed. Dauntless can do as he pleases with no one asking any questions."

"I'm not sure I agree with that anymore."

"Well, chew on this. He's keeping me here in the Academy as a bargaining chip. He was going to sell me to SEARCH, but he's been waiting for the right price. The man is nothing more than a cold and calculating bully, a total heartless git."

Parris leaned forward on his bunk. "Are you one hundred

per cent sure you are doing the right thing?"

"Of course I am."

"But what about Veeva? I gave you the green light. I thought you'd be happy."

"She's leaving as well."

"With you?"

"No, of course not. She knows nothing about this. She's going back home because she can't hack it here anymore, okay? And I don't blame her."

"Maybe if I have a word with her, she'll stay?"

"Listen to me Parris. I'm not thinking of girls anymore. I'm going home, to Eddi and Newt, to Annie."

Parris grabbed Blue's arm with a needy hand. "Don't go, Blue. Stay here. It's not so bad."

Blue took a deep breath, forcing his voice to a whisper. "I'm sorry you're upset, but I can't stay here even if I wanted to. I'm in a whole load of danger and no matter how important friendship is, family comes first, always. If you had a family, you'd know how I feel."

A flash of anger crossed Parris' face.

"I know that hurts you. But you'll never understand. I'm sorry."

Parris turned away. "I've nothing more to say, but remember: *I wanted you to stay.*"

"What does that mean?"

"Just go, Blue. Go!"

Parris, who had spent most of his life alone, could not help but feel betrayed at Blue's going. Blue understood that now. It was up to him to say what needed to be said. "You helped me out, Parris. You fought my corner for me time and time again. I don't think I would've survived those first few days without you. I'll never forget what you did for me. I am going to miss you, Buddy. You are a real friend."

"Leave me alone."

"Okay, Parris, but remember what I said." Sighing, Blue headed for the doorway and left.

HUNG OUT TO DRY

After morning showers, Blue dressed in his whites, left his fascinating, fish-filled quarters and headed to the rim of the Crater.

Whatever human horrors made the future such a hellacious place, Blue would never forget the sublime beauty of the jungle. After a long slow walk, taking in the fantastic spectacle for the last time, the hermetically sealed doors closed behind him with a wet hiss. He ascended the winding steps to the Wheel and walked into the Mess.

Blue stood the line with the others, his stomach buzzing with excitement, aware of a commotion caused by the missing Veeva. He didn't say anything; soon breakfast would be over and he, like Veeva, would be ripping the void back home.

Home. Beyond imagining.

Saturn and the rest of the squads waited patiently. The hatches did not open. Instead, Military Policemen appeared at all the exits and in walked Dauntless. He strode over to the Saturn line and removed his glasses. "All squads apart from Saturn are dismissed. Return to the Crater. Breakfast is cancelled."

The other squads left, glancing at Saturn Squad with worry and confusion.

The commander's blue eyes found his. "Cadet Blue?"

Dauntless knows. He bloody well knows. "Yes sir."

"You are under arrest on the charge of murder."

The words hit Blue like a blow to the stomach. "What?"

A wave of consternation passed through Saturn Squad.

"It's over, Blue."

All the exits were blocked. Nowhere to run. "But I can't stay here."

"You will be leaving soon enough, don't you worry."

Corvus stepped forward, Morgana with him, grabbing his arm in support. "Who is the victim, sir? Who has Blue killed?"

"Blue is under arrest for the murder of Cadet Veeva."

"That can't be true!" shouted Morgana amongst other sounds of shocked disbelief. "I don't believe it."

"She was found strangled in the Crater jungle."

Blue met the cold glare of the commander. Impassive, granite-like. Cruel. Veeva wasn't dead. She wasn't. "No way, sir. No way."

"You harboured a well-known affection for her. She did not return the feeling. You left the Fest, waited for her in the jungle and strangled her."

"That's not true, sir."

"Blue would never do anything like that!" shouted Corvus.

"He can be a jerk, sir," said Sugar, tears in her eyes. "But he is no murderer."

"Be quiet, or you shall all join Cadet Blue on *The Charles Darwin.*"

"They're right!" shouted Morgana. "Blue is not a killer, he's just not."

"Silence."

Did Dauntless kill Veeva to trap me like this? Is this his move then? Has he made his bargain with SEARCH? It doesn't matter either way.

Wurtz, Corvus, Sugar, Coop and Ji gazed at him with shocked disbelief. Morgana was distraught whilst Parris stared at the ground.

Did Parris rat me out? Can he be that selfish? Blue hung his head. Nothing mattered now. *I'm finished.*

"With respect, Commander," said Morgana "You cannot accuse Cadet Blue without any proof. How can you be sure?"

Dauntless took a step forward to stare face-to-face into Blue's red-lined blue eyes and whispered, "Did you think you and Captain Shelley could outsmart me, Boy? There's only one way you will escape me and it's not by using the rip."

Blue could not cope with these words and the awful vile proximity of the man he hated more than any other. With a resounding and satisfying thwack, and an audible gasp from all those present, Blue head-butted the commander in his ruined nose.

Dauntless yelped like a dog and crumpled.

"That's for Hermans!" Blue shouted. Two Military Policemen wrestled him to the ground.

The Saturn cadets lurched forward as one, but more MPs pulled them back.

Dauntless staggered for a few moments and regained his composure, wiping a trickle of blood from his nose. "Take Cadet Blue to *The Charles Darwin* where he will be Hung-Out-To-Dry until I decide how he is to be dealt with."

The Military Policemen pulled Blue to his feet and frog-marched him to the exit.

"I'm innocent."

Blue was cuffed and dragged away.

"On the honour of Saturn, I didn't kill Veeva. Dauntless is the murderer. Him!"

As soon as they lit the fuse on the rocket taking them to *The Charles Darwin,* Blue knew it was all over. He would never get to the meeting with Captain Shelley. He didn't even resist when they asked him to climb into the Skin. *What was the point?*

The death of Hermans had had one positive effect on the brutal Academy regime—his suit had a visor.

At least I can have a view.

They connected him to an umbilical, the airlock opened and closed, and with no ceremony whatsoever, they left Blue outside in the cold emptiness of space.

Blue's heart was heavy, his mind full of Eddi and Newt, of Annie, Captain Shelley, SEARCH and the evil Dauntless—and most of all, poor Veeva.

How on earth had she gotten involved in this?

His vision was restricted to the airlock doors and the slight curve of the spacestation and nothing else. Blue lost all concept of time.

Have I been here for minutes or hours?

He could not imagine hanging alone in space with no visor.

No wonder Hermans did what he did.

With that thought, everything stopped as Blue's rationality head-butted him as effectively as he had head-butted the commander earlier. Dauntless had played his hand. He would soon give Blue over to SEARCH and they would use him—and this is where his over-developed rationality kicked in—*to get at his parents*. Blue would not let that happen.

No way.

That knowledge stabbed into his mind like the thrust of an ice-cold knife. Just a few hours ago, everything was aw-wonder-sum—he was going home. Now? The words of Commander Dauntless replayed themselves again in his mind: 'There's only one way you will escape me and not by using the rip'.

I must protect my family above everything. Nothing else matters.

This made what he was about to do so much easier than he had expected. He was thinking of Newt and Eddi, his mum and dad, and of Annie, his beautiful and kind sister, when his hands found the strap to his helmet.

He readied himself to pull free the fastening. He took a deep breath and began to count. He wasn't sure why his imminent and somewhat gruesome suicide needed a count in, yet he did one anyway.

One—Two—Thr—

THE PRINCE & THE STARSHIP

"Hey, wad you doin', Gote?"

The words so startled Blue that his hand floated away from his helmet. A vast golden spaceship drifted next to him. "Wurtz?"

The Berg's voice grumbled over his radio. "Wurtz ask you question an' Blue answer wid da truth. Did you kill Veeva?"

Blue stared in awe at the magnificent Berg starship. "What are you doing here?"

"Answer question."

"On the honour of Saturn Squad, I did not kill her. Of course not."

"Den dat good enough for Wurtz."

A grappling arm clamped and cut Blue's air hose before pulling him towards the golden craft. A few minutes later, he was in a bear hug with the enormous Berg. Behind him stood Corvus, Sugar, Parris and even Morgana.

Corvus spoke for them all. "Don't tell me how Captain Shelley managed the impossible, but Parris convinced us she has found you a way back home and well, after you and Hermans saved us on *The Charles Darwin,* we were honour-bound to help."

"Parris?" Blue turned towards the blonde boy. "So you didn't rat on me to Dauntless."

Corvus raised a warning hand. "Hey, no-one in Saturn Squad rats on anybody okay?"

"Thanks, Parris. You're a star."

Parris stared back at Blue and said nothing.

"Parris told us the whole story," continued Corvus. "We were not about to let Dauntless hand you over to SEARCH. Not after what happened to Veeva. Do you think he had her killed just to arrest you?"

"He's ruthless and won't let anything get in the way of his ambition. Veeva must have stumbled on to something. Why else would he do such a thing?"

"Dauntless has gone too far," Corvus continued. "Besides, we are the Ringers, we help each other or hadn't you noticed?"

"If you have found a way back to the past," said Sugar, "we should at least try and help out. With Captain Shelley transferred as well…a horror story."

Blue smiled at Sugar. He would miss her relaxed beauty. "You all know about Shelley?"

"After what Dauntless pulled on you," Parris explained grimly, "I couldn't sit on my hands. You have to get back to your family, I realise that now."

"Dauntless showed himself to be one despicable S.O.B. today," added Sugar. "Hermie would be alive if Dauntless hadn't punished him. Now poor Veeva. None of us are staying in the Academy after this."

"Rescuing me is going to get you into loads of trouble."

Sugar planted her familiar hand on her hip. "There was no turning back once we stole *Old Dinger*, Honey."

"You nicked her?"

"Hey, you're not the only one who's greasy sweet in the pilot's chair." Corvus blew on to his fingertips with pride. "Sure was the kicks. I parked her on the other side of the station."

"Okay, but that doesn't explain where you found this cramazing ship?"

Wurtz stomped forward and saluted. "Is mine. Dauntless won't dare interfere wid me."

"Yours? Don't be daft. You don't own a starship."

"Ah yes, about that," said Corvus. "This *is* his ship."

"What?"

Corvus frowned. "I have been keeping a few secrets as well. One of those secrets is a sort of biggie. Wurtz is no normal Berg. He happens to be Prince Arnulf Otto Leopold Frederick Wurtz Wilhelm—the son and heir to the Berg Empire."

Wurtz stood tall, pulling his shoulders back. "Dis Prince Wurtz's ship. One of many."

"You mean?"

Corvus flashed a mischievous smile. "Yes, King Wilhelm is Wurtz's father. I have been in on the secret all along. Dauntless swore me to confidentiality after the King placed his son under his care to protect him from SEARCH and his ambitious brother, Dore. Not that Wurtz was happy about his sudden change in circumstances. Hence, his rather bad attitude back at B-Pal. He was trying to visit his family the night we followed him on *The Charles Darwin,* hoping to speak with his sick dad—despite being told to stay in the dorm. Dore set an ambush for him. The accident in our quarters was Dore's doing."

Wurtz frowned. "Dore paid for dat with his life."

"Came as a bit of a shock to us all," said Sugar with admiration. "Kinda swell knowing a prince, though, don't you think?"

"We are taking you straight to *Old Dinger,* Blue. You can fly her down, yes?" asked Corvus.

"Yes, yes I can." Moments before, he was ready to let space into his suit, now Wurtz was a prince, Morgana was disobeying orders and they were taking him to *Old Dinger* and his rendezvous with Captain Shelley. Mental.

"We arrive," said Wurtz.

Old Dinger swung into view outside the Berg ship's enormous portals. They marched along wide squat corridors and arrived at an airlock.

"Here we are, then." Blue's voice croaked, aware this was the last time he would be with his future friends and Saturn Squad. I can't afford too much emotion. I'm saving that for my return home. "Will you all be okay?"

"Wurtz is taking us to the King's Barge. His father will give us sanctuary," Parris said. "We can start a new life."

"Good, as long as Dauntless doesn't get his hands on you."

The Berg grabbed Blue by the shoulders, his beady eyes intense. "Where your pack?"

"My kitbag?"

"No time for discussion," said Corvus seriously. "Where is it?"

"I gave my pack to Captain Shelley to keep safe. Why?"

Wurtz shrank. "Den farewell my friend." He thumped Blue hard on the back. Corvus shook his hand. Sugar had no reservations and kissed him on the lips. "Good luck, Honey," she purred and hugged him for such a long time Blue received the impression she kinda liked him, but it was way too late to be flattered. Then, he was facing Morgana. "Why did *you* come?" he asked. "Isn't this against the rules?"

"I shouldn't have left you and Hermans on *The Charles Darwin* after we were holed. I should have stayed and tried to help. I am too used to following orders, I forgot what was important. I am sorry, Blue. After what happened to Veeva I—"

"Hey, we've all done things we regret. If there were a prize for being the most stupidest, dimwitted num-nut, I would've won the gold cup a long time ago. Don't give yourself such a hard time. Take a leaf out of my book and try and chill out. You get me?" Blue saluted her.

"Yes, I get you," she replied and instead of saluting him back, she leant forward and kissed him on the cheek.

"Thanks for all your help and advice, Morgana. Not that I listened of course," he said.

"I will miss you, Blue." Morgana burst into tears.

Blue went over to Parris, who hung back. "And thank you mate." Blue offered his hand. "You did brilliant."

Parris seemed unable to respond. He did nothing except stare at the floor.

Blue, sensing his discomfort, hugged him.

"C'mon, break it up, people will start talking," laughed Corvus.

Blue pulled away from Parris and entered the airlock. "Goodbye and good luck."

"Be careful, Blue," said Parris at the last moment.

"Hey, I'm Blue. I'll be fine. I'm going home." He stood in the airlock and smiled. "Bye guys. You've been awe-wonder-sum."

The airlock door closed. With a mixture of excitement and sadness, he put on his helmet, infused his suit, opened the outer hatch and propelled himself into space.

THE NEST

After a hair-raising re-entry, Blue brought the old rocketship into land. He overshot the Landing Field and set down atop the Mound.

I'm taking no chances.

If they didn't know he had escaped and stolen *Old Dinger* by now, they would soon.

He jogged into the cave entrance, walked down the enormous ramp, found a golf cart-like transport and gunned the engine down the tunnel at breakneck speed. A short while later, he entered the confusing mass of buildings and shacks of the abandoned shantytown of the Nest, his heart racing.

"Ma'am? Are you here? Ma'am?"

"You made it, heh." Captain Shelley emerged from the shadows. "I was about to go without you."

Her face lined with stress, her eyes red, Blue guessed how much she and her friends were risking.

If this goes wrong, I'm sure they would be executed and me along with them.

Captain Shelley glanced at Blue's spacesuit with confusion. "What happened to delay you?"

"A long story, but I have some good friends in this century."

"Tell me all about your adventures later. We must make

our way to the Rip-Room." Passing him his kitbag, which Blue fastened to his back, the Captain led Blue through the abandoned shantytown of tiny alleyways and close-knit fallen down houses.

He was lost by the time they reached an old and battered gantry leading to a rusty door. Shelley pushed it aside to reveal a spiral staircase dropping into the thick rock roof of the Hab. "This is the Back Door. No guards. Everything was planned to the last detail, but this delay means we must be quick."

At the bottom of the stairwell, they made their way along a series of unlit corridors leading to an enormous doughnut shaped room similar to the one in the Rip Stack. Blue's heart raced.

It's really happening, I'm going back home.

They entered to find two men. They jumped up with relief glancing at Blue with excited eyes and a keen interest. Shelley went over to them. They saluted, shook hands and took part in a brief discussion before giving her a backpack and handgun.

"To be on the safe side," Shelley explained, before taking Blue down to the Rip-Room. The hangar was huge, but not on the same scale as the one in the Rip Column. The Obelisk here was less melted in appearance, but still glowed white-hot. The rip field crackled and screamed into being. Blue had ripped many times and was used to the raw energy and the spectacle. Where all colour bleached from the universe, the time-rip generated a mad splat of ever-changing flashing colours that twirled and intertwined hypnotically, casting arcane and somewhat scary shadows over the room.

A flash of white light and the fabric of time unravelled like a snag in multi-coloured silk; an inviting mouth with lips all the colours of creation opened before them. The rip consumed a massive amount of energy. He stood before a door ripping a hole into history and the closeness to such raw unadulterated power was breath taking.

Shelley stared with awe into the void. "I'm glad you earned your rip legs. I've been told a trip through time is like nothing else. Be prepared." She saluted the glass dome above. "I'm sorry we were too late to introduce you to my co-conspirators. Two of the bravest men I know."

"They are not coming with us?"

"No, they are to play a more important role. My comrades will open a new rip to your parents' time and after we have rescued Commander Edison and Captain Newton, we shall use the portal to go even further into the past. My comrades then will remove the Nub and take their own chances with time."

"You mean?"

"Yes. The same deed as your parents. If it were possible, we would all be going together. Our escape was always to be one of self-sacrifice—one of us doomed to stay behind to destroy the rip. At least now, with your arrival, they won't be alone. But the Nub must be taken or they will find us."

Blue drew breath to speak. The raised hand of Shelley stopped his tongue. "We need to be quick. When we arrive on the other side, back in your time, we must escape the rip field as fast as we can. The initial energy will dissipate and the void will seek to suck us back to the future. Time wants to right itself, wants to put us back to where we came from. We must make sure to escape its pull, heh." Holding his hand, Shelley led him into the rip field.

Blue was slammed hard in the back by the Push. He flew head first, aware of Shelley tumbling next to him. Bright twisting multi-coloured light surrounded him, sucking at him; flinging him backwards and throwing him over and over and over. With an almighty bang, he was sliding through thick undergrowth.

He rubbed mud and grass from his face and hair, and found himself staring at the familiar hill of Dooleys Wood.

the past...
YESTERDAY

"**N**OW that's what I call a rip, heh." Shelley laughed aloud, her hair all over her face. "Run."

They jumped to their feet and put quick distance between themselves and the still glowing rip.

Blue, punched the air in jubilation, unable to contain himself. "I'm home. We're actually here. *Wahoo!* But *when* are we?"

"If we have arrived as calculated, today should be the day of your disappearance."

Blue's heart raced whilst his skin tingled like someone had plugged him into the mains. "I'll lead you to my house. This way."

The air, which Shelley seemed to find disgusting, had a delicious welcoming aw-wonder-sum smell. They descended and Blue began to relax. His heart stopped doing its mad thing and someone turned down the dimmer switch on his full on buzz—although nothing could quell the relief and excitement flooding his being.

Somewhere below, he heard the drone of car engines, whilst jets thundered and air-braked above. Police sirens wailed and people shouted and shrieked in the distance. Blue hadn't realised how much he had missed this everyday noise; sounds he had been blissfully unaware of until they had disappeared forever.

"Please forgive me if I don't share your sense of excitement, Blue," said Shelley. "This past you are familiar with is an alien world to me. The thought of all those billions of people out there gives me the willies."

"The Hab and the Academy had its moments; I'd never have flown a hellijet, docked a rocket or lived in space, but here is where I'm meant to be. I belong amongst the noise, the mess and all this annoying, carefree humanity. I never realised how wonderful *here* was before. I was so obsessed with my own problems that I took everything for granted."

Shelley glanced at the sun in fear, as if she was unable to believe Sol was still a source of pleasure and not the terror it had become over four-hundred years in the future.

Smiling, Blue led her to his poorly maintained house and hid across the road. Never had the potato-smelling hovel looked so good. Every fibre of his being screamed at him to go inside, to see Annie and his parents again.

Shelley put a hand on his shoulder. "You will be with them soon enough, Blue."

A short while later, the previous Blue stormed through the door and into the lane.

"Was I really that skinny?" he whispered, lost in one of the most peculiar moments of his life. He had little time to ponder. A crack of light in the doorway and Annie appeared, carrying her coat and Jonesy.

"Boo-Boo?"

Blue ran over and hugged her. "Oh Annie, I'm sorry I left you behind. I love you."

"You different now."

Shelley joined them. "Let us go to Dooleys Wood and wait for the commander and the captain."

Annie pointed at the smiling face of Captain Shelley. "Who dat?"

"She's my friend. Here to help us."

"You going to Dooleys Wood?"

"Yes, we are. Eddi and Newt will be coming too. Later.

Okay?"

"Yes, Boo-Boo."

"Now," said Shelley, "when you returned, you found Annie gone and you all went into the wood to search for her. We have to make sure the timeline isn't altered. We must wait before we reveal ourselves."

Blue nodded. He had Annie again and everything was going to be all right.

THE BLUE EYES

Parris, Corvus, Sugar, Morgana and Wurtz waited outside Commander Dauntless' office high in the Academy Column. They had never reached the King's Barge. Soon after Blue had made re-entry in *Old Dinger,* Wurtz's ship had been surrounded by Earth Corps' cruisers and boarded.

Corvus had not stopped pacing since five Military Policemen escorted them to the commander's rooms. "I thought you said we wouldn't get caught?"

"He know nudding," blurted Wurtz.

"I doubt that," argued Sugar, who was ashen-faced. "He's gonna be peeved. We are in one heap of trouble."

Corvus rounded on the Berg. "You said the King would protect us."

"Wurtz thought so too." Wurtz's face showed real shock at the betrayal.

Sugar draped her arm over Corvus' shoulder and hung there. "We wanted to help Blue and, after Parris told us his story, what else could we do? But why didn't we just send Wurtz? I mean, Dauntless can't do anything to him, can he? Not the important prince."

"Be quiet, all of you," Morgana hissed in annoyance. "We did what we thought was right. Too late to moan now, anyway."

"It certainly is, Cadet," said a familiar voice. They turned and found Commander Dauntless standing in the doorway. "Get inside."

They walked despondently into the commander's office. The room, like the man, was austere. Empty walls, a single desk and a row of uncomfortable looking chairs. Dauntless sat and produced a thin cigar, the scar across his face twisting with a smile. "Be seated." All the cadets, except Morgana, sat down. "Sit, Cadet. That's an order."

Morgana hesitated for a second until Corvus pulled her down.

Dauntless lit the cigar with a petrol smelling Zippo and sat back. "Did you think I would not find out who freed Blue from *The Charles Darwin* and stole Old Dinger?"

Morgana drew breath to speak. Dauntless narrowed his eyes and Morgana remained silent.

"I must say I admire the loyalty shown to your friend. What you did, should under any other circumstances, get you kicked from the Academy and imprisoned for many years. That goes the same for you, Cadet Wurtz. Do not think for one moment your royalty means anything to me. In the Academy you are treated as equal. I told your father as much when I agreed to take you on. I have spoken to him and he is apoplectic with rage."

Wurtz turned pale.

"However, I was aware of your plans. I allowed you to 'rescue' Blue."

"What?" shouted Corvus. "You knew? But why have him arrested in the first place?"

"Be quiet. I'm doing the talking, you understand?"

Corvus nodded.

"No. Blue didn't kill Veeva," said the commander. "It was just an excuse to arrest him."

"It's all true?" shrieked Morgana jumping to her feet. "How dare you lie to me, to us, to the Academy. I'm disgusted with you and with this place. You are supposed to put the Academy first, not your own selfish ambition. You are a nasty evil man."

Corvus and the others stared at Morgana with a new respect. She had the courage to say what they all thought.

Dauntless smiled. "Thank you, Morgana. Even though Blue didn't murder Veeva, I had no choice to arrest and punish him—my hands were, shall we say, 'tied' in that respect. However, I invited you all here to discover whom I can and cannot trust."

"You want us to keep quiet, to keep your awful secrets?" Morgana blurted. "Well, no way."

"Sit Morgana," Dauntless ordered. "I have someone I want you all to meet. Everything will be made clear."

"Don't sit down, Morgana," said Corvus, jumping up and putting his arm around her shoulder. "We stand together. For Blue."

Morgana nodded to Corvus who smiled with determination.

Sugar stood, as did Wurtz and Parris.

"The Ringers!" shouted Corvus.

"The Ringers!" they all shouted as one.

Dauntless, instead of being angry, was, if anything, rather impressed. "Again, I am in awe of your loyalty, especially you, Cadet Corvus. Bring him in." The door opened and two Military Policemen brought in a stumbling dishevelled, bent figure wearing rags and a mud-covered hood. Dauntless nodded for the two policemen to leave. "I think this will explain everything."

The figure removed its hood to reveal a bruised, dirtied, sore-covered face, from which shone two unmistakable blue eyes.

the past...
EDDIE AND NEWT

ANNIE held tightly on to Blue. They waited in the lower reaches of Dooleys Wood. Soon, they heard Eddi, Newt, and most eerily of all, his own voice calling for his 'missing' sister.

"Dey shoutin' for me."

"Just a game. Eddi and Newt are joining us soon and we are going on a special journey. We need to be quiet though. Surprise."

"Okay, Boo-Boo."

After an age of nervous waiting, Eddi and Newt stumbled into view. Blue called out, unable to contain himself. "Eddi! Newt! We're here!" Blue let go of Annie's hand and raced over to them.

Eddi stood back in confusion. "Blue?" he said, giving Blue a double-take, "but—"

Blue grabbed his parents, hugging them both and shaking. "I thought I'd never see you again." He pulled away, wiping tears from the corner of his eyes.

Eddi's face betrayed a mixture of confusion and wonder. "You're not Blue, *but you are.*"

"A long story, Dad. I'm sorry for leaving Annie okay. I'm back and I promise to never do anything to disappoint you again."

"Annie!" shouted Newt in relief.

"Boo-Boo all big now."

Newt hugged her.

Eddi, relieved to find Annie, but still cautious, stared coldly. "What's the story, Blue?"

"I fell into the rip, Dad. Months ago. But I've brought a friend from the future who's going to help you. Help all of us."

"You mean they found us?"

"Huh?"

"You mentioned *a friend?*"

"Yes. Come to rescue you, come to rescue us all."

Eddi grabbed Blue's forearm. "You led them here to us?"

Shelley stepped from the shadows, holding her gun aloft. "He's right. You made this easy, Blue. SEARCH guessed you would lose all rationality in the hope of getting home."

A cold shiver shot along Blue's spine, dizzying him. "No way."

"No? Well believe this." Shelley snatched at Annie's arm, wrenching her away from Newt. She pointed the gun to her blonde head.

"Mommy."

Eddi's voice was icy cold. "Let her go."

"Commander Edison, how pleasant to finally meet you."

Eddi stepped forward with menace. "I said, let her go."

"You may think me overweight, you may think me slow, you may even be thinking you can take me. Believe me, I am combat-trained and rated 'deadly'. Make one move and I will scorch out your heart. Understand?"

Tears spilled from Blue's eyes. "I trusted you."

"Well I am 'your captain, and your friend', heh."

The laugh at the end of her sentence made Blue sick to his stomach. "You've been lying to me, stringing me along since B-Pal?"

"No. When I first met you, Blue, I did not realise your importance. Just another misplaced Gote. SEARCH sent me to Saturn Squad after the unfortunate *accident* to Captain Lorenzo for the explicit reason of spying on the King's favourite son and his chosen heir."

The truth of these words exploded within Blue's mind. With Wurtz revealed as Wilhelm's son, everything became obvious. "Commander Dauntless and the Fleet-Admiral were discussing Wurtz on the day of Sekhmet's funeral?"

"Yes, Blue. King Wilhelm plays a dangerous game with his Helium-3 embargo," Shelley continued, as if she was briefing Saturn Squad at morning Mess. "Once SEARCH eliminated Wilhelm and Wurtz, and placed his older brother, Dore, on the throne, the Berg Empire and its Helium-3 would be ours. Our singular objective until—I heard your parents' names."

"But I never told you?"

"Don't you remember? Back in my rooms on your first day in the Crater, the last thing you said before collapsing from sunstroke?"

Blue pulled a confused face.

"You notice how we officers choose famous names from history? It required no intuitive leap of intelligence to realise 'Eddi and Newt' were in fact the infamous Commander Edison and Captain Newton. In that moment, everything changed. The Helium-3 embargo became unimportant compared to the prize the two most-wanted terrorists could deliver to SEARCH."

"What prize?" asked Blue.

"We will get to that soon enough. I had to play a clever game to stay one step ahead of Dauntless and keep you on my side. The commander dislikes SEARCH with a rare passion. He was wary of my cover story, guessing my mission was to spy on Wurtz. Dauntless had no idea of your importance. I was more than perplexed when he had you arrested and Hung-Out-To-Dry on *The Charles Darwin*. That threw me. But if I am anything, I am resourceful and there were others willing to help."

As those words left her lips, Blue realised how full-on stupid he had been. *I wanted to get home so much that I swallowed every lie, every half-truth.* Captain Shelley's words allowed for another worrying possibility. "You didn't tell Dauntless about Hermans' claustrophobia, did you?"

"Oh, I did more than that, Blue; as you now suspect."

"You killed him?"

"The Ganymedian discovered I had let you off for your thieving. I could not risk him going to Dauntless. The fool commander made his murder easy for me—having the boy Hung-Out-To-Dry. Simple to sneak through an airlock and remove his helmet. He tried to struggle, but a Ganymedian is no match for someone combat trained."

"No," croaked Blue. "No."

Shelley shrugged. "Regrettable, yes. But necessary."

Hermans murdered. She will to do the same to my family. I must stop her.

"And now, Blue, your usefulness is at an end." She stroked the gun across Annie's head and smiled. "Commander Edison, let me explain how this is going to work. Give me the Nub. Give it to me now or I will first kill your natural daughter, your wife and then Blue. Simple enough to understand?"

Blue sagged at these words. "You're after the Nub?"

Eddi balled his hands into tight fists. "She and her kind will commit any number of atrocities to secure its return."

"Maybe I didn't make myself clear enough." Shelley lifted the gun and pressed the stud. A beam of intense, silent and invisible heat burst through the undergrowth, exploding into orange flames. She pointed the still hot nozzle back at Annie's head. His sister's hair curled and smoked. "Give the Nub to me now."

"Mommy!"

"It's alright, Sweetie." Newt unfastened her jacket.

Eddi lunged at Captain Shelley. "No!"

Another burst of silent heat and Blue's father fell backwards on to the ground, a smoking hole the size of a basketball in his chest.

"Let that be a warning to you, Newton," said Shelley without emotion. "Now give me the Nub and I might let you live," she demanded. "I'm not evil, just practical and ambitious."

Blue went into himself, trying to find the same power he had used before at the playground and on *The Charles Darwin*. He found instead an empty impotent useless hole. His father was dead, lying on the ground before him. "I'm sorry, Mum."

Newt finished unbuttoning her jacket, tears streaming down her face. "Don't blame yourself, Blue. You acted with the best intentions."

"Enough talk. Give me the Nub, now," spat Shelley.

Newt revealed her old silver necklace and held aloft its unremarkable purple-black stone.

"What?" Shelley's eyes stared at the chain in shock. "That's impossible."

With Shelley momentarily distracted, Blue barrelled forward, knocking the captain off balance. A burst of heat, Newt screamed and Shelley landed on the ground, her gun flying from her grasp to land a way off in the undergrowth.

The weapon's hot beam had scorched Newt's neck and face. She struggled to breathe, falling to her knees. She offered Blue the necklace. "Here. Take the Nub. Get away," she rasped

"No, I can't leave you. I won't."

"You must. Don't let her get the Nub, Blue. Do anything to prevent that. The Nub is more important than me and Eddi *or even you and Annie*. More important than anything."

There was a joyful cry behind him. Shelley found her gun.

"Take care of Annie. Go."

Blue had no choice. He took hold of the blue-black stone, its chain hanging between his fingers, grabbed Annie and ran.

"I love you, An—" Newt shouted before her voice was silenced by the heat of Shelley's gun.

Blue was now part of the cause Eddi and Newt had been prepared to die for. Whatever the importance of the Nub, he would not let it fall into SEARCH's hands.

Shelley would have to kill me first. Perhaps that is how I will redeem myself.

He zigzagged across the rising ground, his arm tight around his sobbing sister. He spotted something familiar in the undergrowth. *The Cat*. His other self must have dropped the catapult.

He thrust the lethal slingshot into his back pocket. Sudden warmth and a bush next to him exploded in flames. Shelley sniping at them from below. A tree exploded in flame to his left, grass ignited a few feet away. The captain was close on their heels. Blue placed the necklace around Annie's neck; Shelley would not dare shoot her whilst she wore the Nub.

"Annie!" The previous Blue, not far away, shouting for his missing sister. "Where are you?"

Grabbing Annie, Blue ran and sank behind a line of bushes.

"Annie dropped Jonesy."

"Shhh. We'll get him later."

The younger Blue entered the clearing. He crouched to grab at Jonesy and found what must have been Annie's and his own glowing footprints. "Annie!"

"Boo-Boo, I'm scared!"

The previous Blue turned to stare straight at their hiding place.

I'm sorry, but this is for your—for my own good.

Blue loaded a stone into the Cat, pulled back the drawstring and let fly, catching the earlier Blue across the temple. He crumpled and did not move.

Shelley arrived seconds later, going over to the prone figure, pushing at him with her foot. "What a skinny runt." She turned, waving her gun around and firing indiscriminately into the foliage. "You are here somewhere, Blue. You might as well surrender. You won't get away."

"Stay down, Annie." Blue searched for another stone, but as he turned to their hiding place, his little sister was already walking towards his earlier self and Captain Shelley.

"Boo-Boo hurt?" Annie held the necklace in her hand.

With a slow, knowing smile, Shelley turned the gun on her. "Show yourself now, Blue, or she dies."

Blue stood, trembling.

"I'm sorry about this, Blue. I did like you, but duty must always come first, no matter how unfortunate the consequences."

She pointed the gun at Blue's chest. "Oh and one last thing—the assassin in the Sanatorium?" She curtsied. "Me. Of course, I couldn't kill you when you put yourself in the way of Wilhelm. Not after I knew about Eddi and Newt. The Berg King was lucky that night, heh."

The air behind Annie crackled and popped—a time rip opening. A rainbow of colours sprayed into the glade. The rip bursting into awesome being. Annie wobbled for a second on her unsteady legs before the Drag pulled her reeling backwards.

"No!" shouted Shelley and Blue.

The Push slammed his sister into the rip, her arms and legs flailing in the undulating field. Shelley fired at Annie. The heat of the captain's gun somehow reflected back on her; she screamed, unable to drop or turn off her weapon.

For the briefest of seconds, Annie hung in the rip field, her face twisted in pain, whilst Shelley's clothes began to smoulder and burn. In a blinding flash, Captain Shelley exploded into flame, her bulky frame thrown backwards high into the air to land in a crumpled fiery mass.

Blue was alive, but Annie was gone.

the past...
FIRE

BLUE stood transfixed, the rip field still buzzing, pulling at him. He went over to Shelley. Dead. Killed by her own weapon. Her face a burnt, scorched mess.

Blue spotted a folded picture of himself lying on the ground next to her still smouldering body. The one taken in the playground. A ripped and half-burnt newspaper page, yellowed and discoloured by time and laminated in scuffed plastic. Blue read the story with dismay—the date, *tomorrow:*

FEARS FOR MISSING FAMILY

Fears are growing for a local family after a mysterious blaze in Dooleys Wood on Friday night. The fire, thought to have been started deliberately, broke out in the early evening and engulfed the entire wood. Flames were seen from over twenty-five miles away.

Concerns Raised
A local family, believed to be a Mr & Mrs Smith (first names unknown), and their two children, Annie (2) and John (15), entered the wood shortly before the fire broke out. Further concerns were raised when packed suitcases were discovered inside the family's abandoned home. Police are sifting through

the burnt remains of the wood in the gruesome task of finding possible bodies.

Quiet Eccentrics
The Smiths, known locally as an eccentric, quiet family keen on self-sufficiency, kept much to themselves. "They seemed a happy family, although something was not right about them," said a concerned neighbour.

Troubled Boy
John Smith (pictured above), nicknamed 'Blue' by his friends because of his striking blue eyes, was recently identified as the mystery boy who, in what Police described as 'peculiar circumstances', rescued a young family from a burning car earlier that day. Police are unsure if the two events are connected. A school teacher, who wanted to remain anonymous, commented: "He was an extremely gifted child, but troubled."

Police are keeping an open mind about what happened on that fateful night, as yet—

The evidence leading SEARCH to Dooleys Wood! A family of eccentrics. My weird blue eyes. Obvious. And the police thought I had something to do with the death of my parents—or were, at least, hinting at the possibility...But I did kill them.

A fit of sobs overcame him but he had little time for grief. Dooleys Wood was starting to blaze as the news story predicted. With a roar, fire took quick hold, sweeping across the hill with a powerful updraft.

I can't stay here. I'll be burnt alive.

For a brief moment, he contemplated letting the flames engulf him, but he could not abandon Annie.

His lip quivering, Blue tightened his kitbag, slung the unconscious younger Blue over his shoulder and stepped into the rip. Long seconds later he crashed into the hot and insect-ridden Dooleys Wood of four-hundred and fifty years in the future.

He struggled to his feet. "Annie!" he screamed. "Annie!"

Nothing.

She had to be here. "Annie! Where are you? It's Boo-Boo!"

They had travelled through the same rip hadn't they?

There was no sign of her. Blue remembered the gun. Shelley's heat weapon fired into the void.

The energy discharge could have caused any number of unpredictable effects.

He thrust his fist into his mouth and bit so hard his knuckles bled. He had no idea how long he sat like that. Only the stirring of his former self broke into his reverie. He fell backwards into the underbrush; hiding, ashamed of himself, ashamed of what he'd done to Eddi and Newt.

"Annie!" his earlier self shouted.

Blue died somewhere inside.

"Eddi! Annie! Newt!"

He stood on a branch that cracked loudly. The previous Blue whirled around. He slunk behind a tree trunk.

"Eddi?" said the earlier Blue, the fear in his voice palpable.

A few seconds later, the previous Blue ran away, calling for a mother and father Blue knew were already dead.

SWAMPS & SPIES

A Dishevelled, muddy and sore covered Blue stared at the dismayed faces of his friends in Dauntless' office and began to speak.

"I have no idea how long I spent on the island of Dooleys Wood. Madness and grief overwhelmed me. Lost, disorientated I wandered for days on end. I would catch myself screaming, my head full of wild visions and desolate thoughts. I don't know how much time passed before I started to make sense of things. Of where I was. Of what had happened. With two Blues sharing the same timeline, we were inextricably connected and the reason for all my whacked-out dreams trapped in the swamplands. In the end, I realised I had to leave Dooleys Wood and return to the Academy. I had been such a num-nut to let my former self be rescued. I should have done something, left him a message, warned him somehow. Why shouldn't I alter the timeline?"

He turned to glare at Dauntless. The commander remained impassive.

"Having something to aim for drove me forward—kept my mind off—" Blue's voice dried.

Dauntless sat back in his chair. "Go on, Blue. Tell them everything."

"My Skin saved me, protecting me from the heat, keeping

me cool, although it's pretty knackered after my many weeks Topside. Captain Sekhmet's training helped, but the swamplands are a death sentence if you overstay your welcome. I had to leave and soon. I'd be no good to Annie dead. Having no other choice, I put together a shaky raft, left Dooleys Wood and headed south. What I learned from Captain Sekhmet kept me alive. Those hellacious slimers were already a regular part of my diet and, I think, the reason why I had no trouble eating them back in Sekhmet's seshroom. Remember? Sekhmet would have been proud of me. I hunted with the Cat." He produced his tarnished catapult and squeezed the metal haft with affection. "I had little to guide me, except the rising and setting sun. I paddled my tatty raft in the daylight and slept high and safe in tall trees at night. I was lonely and a bit bonkers mad, yet I had time to think things through. I followed the phases of the Moon to keep track of the days." He paused, swallowing hard. "The night Hermans died I stared at *The Charles Darwin* knowing he suffered. I think I even awoke my other self. He was too late to save him from…*Captain Shelley.*"

Corvus, Wurtz, Sugar and Parris shouted in shock and dismay.

Morgana put her hand to her mouth, sudden tears in her eyes. "That's terrible, Blue. We all thought we were helping you, helping our captain. She really murdered Hermans?"

"Don't blame yourselves. She took me in, hook, line and sinker. Worst of all? I wanted to believe her."

"She fooled everyone, Blue," said Morgana. "She was kind to me, I would have never guessed."

"If we'd realised what a full-on nutta she was, things would be different, but—" Blue staggered, the emotion getting the better of him.

"Sit down," said Parris, "you're exhausted."

"No. I haven't even half finished."

"Go on, Honey," encouraged Sugar. "Tell us what happened, everything."

"Yes, Blue," added Corvus, holding Morgana's hand.

"By sheer dumb luck, I arrived in London and made my way through the choked streets of Piccadilly to Buckingham Palace. I found a wrecked hellijet, some old model scavenged for parts. Its communication system wasn't intact, but I managed to jury-rig a transmitter of sorts. I sent a message to Dauntless. He came to get me."

Commander Dauntless took a drag from his cigar, blowing smoke through his ruined nose. "Yes. Perplexing to say the least. I realised then just how I had underestimated Captain Shelley and her masters." He turned towards Wurtz and nodded. "The King left Wurtz to my care, hoping he would be safe in the Academy. But not as secure as we had thought. Wurtz's brother, Dore, impatient at the inability of SEARCH to neutralise the threat he posed to the throne, planned the attack on Saturn's quarters, puncturing the hull of *The Charles Darwin* and endangering SEARCH's more important goal, the Gote called 'Blue'. That proved to be a fatal error. Dore died from 'natural causes' a few hours later. SEARCH do not suffer fools. The business took all of my attention. I suspected Shelley of spying on the King's son, but after she discovered the identity of Blue's parents, the whole of SEARCH's efforts went into sending Shelley and Blue back in time to capture them."

He sighed.

"I had no way to foresee that. My concern was for Wurtz and, although I'd had Shelley under supervision, she showed zero interest in the Berg. I assumed her cover story to be the truth, that she had fallen out of favour with SEARCH and been demoted."

"Why does SEARCH want the Nub?" asked Morgana.

Dauntless smiled. "That information is classified."

Corvus made the obvious connection. "You knew Blue was headed towards a trap when we rescued him from *The Charles Darwin?*"

"Correct, Cadet. I was astounded to find Blue's double in B-Pal, knowing his doppelganger was here in the Academy. When he told me I'd had him arrested and Hung-Out-To-Dry for Veeva's murder, I had to do the same. We cannot mess with the timeline."

"Poor Veeva," said Sugar. "Did Shelley kill her as well?"

"At last I have some good news to report. Cadet Veeva is alive and well. Veeva was leaving the Academy and had already arranged her departure with me. After talking to the returned Blue, I was forced to accuse him of her murder. I intercepted Veeva before breakfast and sent her back home through the rip. No, she is not dead, Cadet Sugar. Be thankful for that. I would never alter the timeline, not willingly. I even pretended to be the character portrayed by Captain Shelley in her lies. Although Blue forgot to inform me of his rather effective head-butt."

Blue grimaced. "Sorry, sir, but at that time, I hated you."

Dauntless fingered the bruise on his face. "I'm sure you did. Now that all events have played themselves out, I think we have come to an understanding of sorts. Right Blue?"

"Yes, sir."

"That is not everything, is it Blue?" guessed Corvus.

"No." Blue's voice contained so much anger and controlled venom that the cadets jumped. "Captain Shelley told me one more thing before she died; something I had plenty of time to think about as I made my slow way back to B-Pal. Drove me crazy." He took a deep breath. "She said there were 'others willing to help'. Her spy on the inside. A cadet in Saturn Squad." Blue paused as realisation passed across the faces of the five cadets. "Somebody worked with her, a sneak recruited early on to betray me. That someone is in this room."

Everyone turned to stare at Corvus.

"No way," he said. "I worked for Dauntless. I had no choice. He ordered me to protect Prince Wurtz and to report any strange goings-on from Captain Shelley. I'm one of the good guys, honest."

Wurtz, nodded. "Dat is da truth."

"No," said Blue, "I'm talking about…Parris."

THE RIPPED BADGES

Sugar's brown eyes widened in shock. "You're kidding?"

Morgana turned to the blonde-haired boy. "Tell me this is a mistake?"

Blue continued, his voice quiet, subdued but full of suppressed fury. "Parris befriended me on Captain Shelley's orders as soon as she discovered the names of my parents. He ratted on Singh and informed on Hermans. The Ganymedian was perplexed at how easily Shelley had let me off after I admitted my thieving to her. I was too relieved to realise how out of character this was for an officer. For any officer in Earth Corps or even SEARCH. Shelley could not risk Hermans going to the commander with this information and killed him at the first opportunity."

The commander nodded in agreement. "If I had discovered how she helped you, Blue, Captain Shelley would have been demoted, expelled and her ambitious plans ruined. She took a considerable risk."

"I told Parris about Hermans. No-one else. He went straight to Shelley and sealed Hermans' fate. You are the rat, Parris. You all along."

Corvus jumped onto Parris, pushing him to the floor, his fists raised.

"Don't, Corvus. Don't," said Morgana, tears streaming.

"You're better than him and besides fighting is against the rules."

Corvus pulled a wry smile. "I suppose it is. I can't believe Parris would do such—" Anger got the better of him.

"Leave him Cadet," ordered Dauntless. "Parris will need all his faculties to explain himself."

Parris regained his feet. "W-what?"

Dauntless' voice was a cold as stone. "Cadet Blue is accusing you of betraying your squad, his friendship and of being complicit in the murder of Cadet Hermans. What do you say?"

Parris remained silent.

"Speak!"

Parris turned and faced his accuser. "Before Shelley became involved, I was your friend, Blue. Back in B-Pal. Back at the beginning. That's all I wanted." Parris' head dropped and he closed his eyes. "Captain Shelley recruited me when she noticed our friendship. Promised me a career in SEARCH if I helped her. All I had to do? Continue being Blue's friend. Easy." He opened his eyes. "A no-brainer. Surely you must understand, Blue? She fooled me as she fooled the rest of you. At first, she asked me to keep an eye on you. Just to make sure you didn't get into trouble. Why shouldn't I help you? You were my friend. She wanted me to report everything back to her. Like you being put Off-Limits and getting let off by Singh. Yes. I told her about Hermans, but I didn't know she would kill him."

Morgana's face twisted into an ugly mask of revulsion. "But you are a Ringer."

"I came to you in your quarters," said Blue. "I told you I was returning home and you said nothing."

Parris sighed. "I tried to convince you to stay. But you were set on going. Remember?"

"You let me walk into a trap. What have I done to you to deserve that?"

"Don't you get it?" snapped Parris. "You arrived here in the future as an angry selfish Gote. And nothing changed. No matter what you did or said, you always got off. You crash a hellijet showing off and you get off. You steal from the Academy and you get off. You disobey orders and Hermans gets Hung-Out-To-Dry. And despite all this, everybody likes you. Morgana, Hermans, Sugar, Captain Sekhmet, Wurtz. Even Corvus who despises everybody. No-one likes me. I thought you different. But you are like all those families I was forced to live with as a child. In the end, they never gave one jot about me. No Blue. You've had everything given to you on a plate all your life. And what did I do? Made everything even easier for you. I started to hate you for it."

"Easy!" shouted Blue. "You killed my parents, Annie and Hermans."

"No. Your arrogance killed them."

"Don't say that! Don't ever say that!"

"Let me tell you something, Blue. I was ready to tell you everything. I couldn't think about anything else after Hermans died. But you had to brag about going home, didn't you? About having a family. About how I could never understand what that was like. Here you had everything I wanted. And it still wasn't good enough for you. Even after I had given you Veeva."

Commander Dauntless raised his hand. "Enough. Cadet Parris, the only person you are trying to fool with such twisted logic, is yourself. You had your chance a hundred times over, to come tell me what you knew. You betrayed the Academy, your squad and most of all, your best friend."

Parris wasn't Parris anymore, in his place was a white-faced ghoul.

Dauntless took a deep breath. "You have admitted complicity in the murder of another cadet. That alone is worthy of capital punishment."

Capital Punishment. The death penalty. The execution of a person as punishment for a crime.

All heads turned to Parris who trembled and shook.

"No," whispered Morgana. "He's a traitor, but he shouldn't die for it."

"He is too young, anyway," Dauntless continued. "And besides, Blue convinced me otherwise. Instead…Parris is to be let go."

"What?" shouted Corvus. "I don't want the rat to hang for this, but you can't let him off."

"No jazzing way," added Sugar.

"Silence! Parris has another part to play." Dauntless turned his attention back to the quivering blonde boy. "Go back to your much vaunted SEARCH, tell them what you have learnt, let them know Blue is returned, that Captain Shelley, Commander Edison and Captain Newton are dead and the Nub lost. Tell them Blue is of no further interest to them and he and his friends are under my personal protection. Inform them that the second rip machine is an open secret." He paused. "One more thing. Do not ever cross my path again, for it will go the worse for you. Do you understand?"

Parris did nothing. He stood still in shock.

"Didn't you hear me?"

Parris nodded.

Dauntless ripped the Saturn badges from Parris' collar, opened the door and pushed him outside. "Escort him to SEARCH," he ordered the two waiting MPs. "Don't go soft on him."

The commander returned and shut the door. "Blue has suffered more in the last few months than most people suffer in a lifetime. I want you to take him back to the Crater. The Academy is his family now."

"No," said Blue. "Before I do anything, I need more answers."

The commander eyed Blue for long seconds. "Okay Blue," he said finally. "You have earned the right. I will tell you what I can, but not everything."

As Blue took the weight off his feet, Dauntless turned his attention once again to the remaining Cadets. "You four, by rescuing Blue, disregarded many rules of the Academy. And despite the unusual situation, I cannot ignore such flagrant disobedience. As punishment, Saturn Squad will take the Drop this Phase."

"That's not fair," said Morgana.

Dauntless then did a strange thing. He laughed out loud. "You dare speak back after getting off lightly? I admire your spirit young lady. The Drop this end of Phase is to patrol between the orbits of Saturn and Jupiter as well as...*the Asteroid Belt*. I'm sure Wurtz's father will make you more than welcome. Now go. There are things I must discuss with your comrade."

HONOUR

Dauntless sat down and faced Blue. "What can I tell you?"

"I trusted Shelley and she turned out to be a top of the class Crazy Amy. So, Commander, what's your agenda?"

"A fair question." Dauntless lit another of his miniature cigars. "I am what I seem: an overbearing authoritarian, honour obsessed career officer. The Academy, and nothing else, comes first, always. Life is sometimes hard and cruel, sometimes beautiful and rewarding; but we can keep one thing constant throughout all life's trials and tribulations, and that is *our honour.*"

For Blue, honour meant something more than blind duty. I will always be honourable to my friends, regardless of how many stupid orders I disobey, sure.

"Before I continue, there is one outstanding issue: your thieving."

Blue stared at the floor in shame.

Dauntless smiled. "I am letting the matter rest. You owned up, Blue—to the wrong person—but you did the right thing."

"I've wondered about that, sir, about why Shelley helped me stay in the Academy. If you expelled me, wouldn't it have been easier for SEARCH to get to me, to use me?"

"You are forgetting her ambition. Captain Shelley wanted you all to herself and the prestige and glory of returning the

Nub. While she kept you at the Academy, you were all hers."

With the mention of the Nub, a wave of anger and grief washed over him. "Are you going to tell me what this is about? I need to know what my parents died protecting. They seemed to think the Nub was more important than anything."

"This cannot go any further than my office, you understand?" Blue nodded.

"The Nub, Blue. Everything that happened to you was because of the Nub." He took a deep drag from his cigar and expelled a plume of rich-smelling smoke. "It contains the co-ordinates of a particular planet, a world discovered over one hundred years ago—where Earth Corps found the remains of an extinct alien civilisation."

"Aliens?"

Dauntless nodded. "It was named 'Vanir', for at first, it seemed a friendly, fertile planet of plenty. Now we know it as 'Darkworld'. A melodramatic name, granted, yet accurate all the same. Darkworld represents a terrible danger to all humankind, to all off-world civilisations and planets. I will not reveal the nature of that menace, but your parents stole the Nub to protect the Earth and the other worlds. The Nub contains the co-ordinates of Darkworld and it must never be found again."

"I thought all this was about zygotes and genetic experimentation?"

"Blue, I would be lying to you if I said the two are not connected. I cannot and will not divulge any more."

Blue wanted to tell Dauntless about his strange abilities, about what had happened in the playground and on *The Charles Darwin*. He was sure his odd powers were connected to the commander's revelations, but recent events made him suspicious. Dauntless might still be playing the game Shelley accused him of. *I can't trust anybody.*

"Despite calling your parents 'terrorists', Captain Newt and Commander Edison shared the same mind-set as myself," said Dauntless. "Earth Corps thinks them fanatics and extremists. I am obliged to refer to them likewise. But know this: they acted with honour and other people of honour cannot ignore their sacrifice."

"And my sister?"

"We must accept she is gone, Blue. Understand that all eyes are now on Dooleys Wood should she reappear. We will have to hope we can rescue her and the Nub before SEARCH finds her."

"I can't leave things at that, sir. She needs me."

"My attitude to you when you arrived was a harsh one. At the time, I thought it the best way to introduce you to your new life. And yet the message is still the same: you must put what has happened in the past behind you and concentrate on where you are now. Go, relax and heal yourself."

"Easier said than done, sir."

"You are tough, stronger than both of us realised." Dauntless stood and saluted. "Dismissed, Cadet."

Blue stood and saluted back. "I will try—I mean I *will* do my best, sir."

JONESY

Blue returned to the welcoming jungle of the Crater to find the cadets from all squads waiting for him. They stood in formal attention around the rim and, at a command from Corvus, they saluted as one.

Blue saluted back and smiled. *I suppose I'm home.* He stared at the pool far below and let himself fall headfirst into the cooling waters, emerging seconds later to float on the undulating surface. After the sticky, cloying, insect ridden heat of the swamps, the water was aw-wonder-sum.

He swam to the side, peeled off his torn spacesuit and showered, grimacing at the many sores and dark marks left by the voracious leeches using him for breakfast, lunch, dinner and supper. He dried himself, made his way to his bunkroom and dressed. His quarters were as he had left them, except his muddied and ripped kitbag—his ever-present companion throughout his time in the future—was laid on his bed. The muffled sound of the waterfall was music to his ears.

I didn't think I'd say this but—

"It's good to be back." Even though everything had ended in disaster, he did not blame himself anymore.

The guilt left me somewhere in the swamps, sure.

He'd had time to grieve, time to think through what had

happened. But he was still filled with a dreadful emptiness.

I am the shell within which now lives the pale ghost of the Blue who existed before.

Annie occupied all his thoughts. A part of him hoped Shelley's gun had killed her. The possibility of Annie dying alone and lost somewhere in time was too awful to contemplate. He sat down, reached into his dirtied pack and produced Jonesy. The miserable rag doll was all he had left of his sister. "Oh, Annie."

A cough from outside. Wurtz. "Cadet Blue, we come in now."

The prince entered with Corvus and a grey-haired Berg, his hair held back by a thick golden band. Blue did a double-take—the Berg from the Sanatorium—*King Wilhelm*. Blue jumped to his feet. "Hello, sir."

Corvus winked knowingly.

"I come to thank you, Cadet Blue," spoke the king, his voice thick and heavy with the Berg accent, his English far superior to his son and heir. "You saved my life. I, the royal family and the entire Berg nation are forever grateful."

Blue thought back to the Sanatorium and the assassin. "I didn't do much, other than get in the way."

"For your immense service," continued Wilhelm, "I bestow on you the highest Berg honour. I name you, *Baron Blue Wilhelm.*"

Blue stared unbelievingly at the Kings, tattooed and scarred face. "Baron?"

"All members of the royal line are ennobled. Tradition. Prince Wurtz told me of your loss and of your bravery. I have spoken with Commander Dauntless and the adoption is legally binding. Blue Wilhelm, you are now a full member of my family and forty-second in line to the throne."

Wurtz chuckled. "You will have ta answer ta me, Gote."

"Quiet," commanded the king and Wurtz shrank at his side.

"Thank you," said Blue again. "I don't know what to say."

"You not need say anything. You area a *Wilhelm* and welcome amongst the Bergs as long as you live. *Kin.*" He grabbed Blue in a tight bear hug and slapped him on the back. He pulled away, his eyes returning once again to Blue's.

"There's something else?" asked Blue. "I don't have to get tattooed do I?"

The King shook his head. "I am here for a second reason. To reclaim an item important to all Bergs."

Blue shrugged. "I don't have anything of yours."

"Let me explain, sir," said Corvus nodding towards the king for permission.

Wilhelm waved him to speak with a stubby finger.

"Do you remember your first day back at B-Pal when Wurtz stole that raggedy dolly, Jonesy?" Corvus asked.

"Yes, of course I do. Although I'm not sure if I've forgiven him yet." His attempt to lighten the tone of the conversation fell on deaf ears. This was important.

"Well, it was for a reason," continued Corvus. "The arrival of Captain Shelley put the wind up Wurtz good and proper. When you mentioned her impending inspection, we were worried she might find something important to Wurtz and his father and the entire Berg Empire. Something he was hiding. You were exempt from inspection, remember?"

"The most potent symbol of my rule," broke in King Wilhelm. "I gave that symbol to my chosen heir—to Prince Wurtz for safekeeping—should I not survive the talks. If my other son, Dore had gotten hold of it, he would've claimed the kingship on my death and no one would have been able to stand in the way of his greedy ambition."

"You mean—*the signet ring?*" Blue had read about it on the Board weeks before and heard Dauntless and the Fleet-Admiral discussing the Berg heirloom's importance at Sekhmet's funeral. His mind made the obvious connection. "Wurtz hid the ring *in Jonesy?*"

"Yes, a top-notch idea at the time," continued Corvus with a grin, "But you put Jonesy in your kitbag and never went anywhere without the damn thing. How would we get our hands on it again? When you disappeared back in time, Wurtz thought the heirloom lost forever. Now you have returned and the king has come to claim what is his by right."

"Oh." Blue handed Jonesy to Wurtz.

The Berg examined the dolly for a few moments, found an invisible rip and produced a golden ring, its single sapphire sparkling. He gave the priceless heirloom to King Wilhelm who slipped it back on his fattened little finger.

"Again, Baron Blue Wilhelm, you do me the highest service. I can reward you no more than I have already. We will meet again and soon." He stared at Blue in expectation.

Wurtz slapped Blue across the shoulder. "Bow to your king."

"Oh, right," said Blue, bowing once, twice, three times as Corvus smirked.

Wilhelm nodded and turned to leave.

"You did good, Gote." Wurtz handed Jonesy back to Blue and exited with his father. "You did good."

Corvus winked again and followed them out. "See you soon, Baron Blue Wilhelm."

Blue sat on his bunk and scratched his head.

The ring had been in Jonesy all this time and I never noticed? Now I'm a Baron with a brand new family? Mental-lentil. Still, being forty-second in line to the throne of the Berg Empire cannot replace Annie. Nothing can. I'm alone. My sudden royalty is no cure and never will be.

"Blue?" Morgana's voice outside his quarters. "Can I come in?"

"Yeah, sure."

Morgana entered. "I wanted to check in on you. I could not sit in my room with you all alone."

"Of course you couldn't. To be honest, I can do with some company."

"Really?"

"Spend months alone in a swampy wilderness and you'll talk to anyone."

"Oh."

"I'm joking, Morg'. I want to thank you for everything you

did."

"That means everything to me."

"Don't go mushy on me now."

"What was Wilhelm doing here? We are all intrigued."

"Ask Corvus."

After an awkward pause, Morgana said, "I wanted to say I am sorry about your parents, Blue, and for Parris. None of us would have guessed. How terrible to be let down by those you trust the most."

"You're wrong. I wasn't let down by Eddi or by Newt, nor Annie. If I'm honest, I think my love for them blinded me to Captain Shelley."

"And I should've stayed and helped you and Hermans on *The Charles Darwin*. If I went back in time and changed one thing, I'd change that," said Morgana staring at Jonesy lying atop Blue's bunk.

"Hey, we all make stupid mistakes. Some are bigger than others. I killed my family."

"Oh Blue, don't say that. *Don't.* Everything will be easier with time, Blue."

"Dauntless said the same thing."

Morgana grabbed Jonesy. A confused expression spread across her face.

"What's wrong, Morg? That's just Jonesy. Wait till I tell you what Wurtz hid in him."

"'Jonesy'?" Morgana repeated, turning away.

"He belonged to my sister."

Morgana stared at the rag doll in confused wonder. *"Boo-Boo?"*

"What did you say?"

"Boo-Boo? *Is it you?*" Morgana asked, turning around to stare right at him, her emerald eyes wet with tears.

"Annie?" gasped Blue in shock, and in those few seconds, everything changed. "You're Annie? You can't be—*can you?*"

"Oh Boo-Boo."

They hugged, separated, gazed at each other as if for the first time and hugged again. Blue had never experienced such an intensity of jubilation. Of total and utter relief. Annie was alive; was well and living with him in the future.

My little Annie.

He didn't want to let her go. After a long time, they parted. He squeezed Morgana's hands in relief. A terrific surge of love overwhelmed him. "How are you here? I don't understand," he managed to croak through trembling lips.

Morgana wiped away her tears, struggling to speak. "I remember Jonesy well enough, although I had somehow forgotten about him till now."

"The rip must have dumped you here over ten years ago, and not in Dooleys Wood. Just another unwanted, useless Gote. Oh Annie."

"I can't remember, although I *was* adopted. My stepfather left when I was young and my stepmother brought me up in the Hab. I don't think she liked me much. I had an unhappy childhood. She sent me away as soon as she could. I used to talk to her about my brother, 'Boo-Boo'. She said he was make-believe, but…*he was you, Blue.*"

Blue wasn't listening. His mind had made the obvious connection. "Do you remember me giving you anything?"

"I sort of remember you. Vague memories. I can recall Jonesy, of course, but I do have one possession." Morgana eyes widened with excitement.

"Newt's necklace."

"My stepmother called it my family heirloom. I found the necklace in her possessions when she died. Space, Blue. It's *the Nub!*" Morgana reached inside her whites and produced the silver necklace, hung with the familiar purple-black stone Blue had seen worn around his mother's neck all his life. "I wear this whenever possible."

"You wore your necklace at the end of sesh fest, didn't you?"

"Yes. Is that important?"

"Very. Captain Shelley helped you get ready."

Morgana clasped her hand to her mouth. "She told me to

wear it. Oh my."

"She must have recognised it back in Dooleys Wood, no wonder she was distracted. She guessed who you were. Quite some shock. The Nub saved our lives."

"This is like a dream. To think I have been wearing a black hole around my neck all this time."

"All I wanted was to go back to Dooleys Wood and rescue you, and you were right here as one of my friends," said Blue.

"But I was not your friend. Even though you pretended after Hermans died."

"No. I'm sorry for that. I think at some subconscious level you knew who I was, didn't you?"

Morgana smiled, grabbing his arm and squeezing it, as if she never wanted to let him go. "Yes, I suppose I did. I needed you to like me, Blue."

"Know this and never forget it: I love you Annie. I love you Morgana, my sister and I will never lose you again. I promise."

They hugged. Emotion overwhelmed them.

"We must tell Dauntless," said Morgana when they let go of each other.

"No, we can't. No one can discover you are my sister or all hell will break loose." He held the Nub in his hand and gazed into its inky depths. "We must get rid of it and tell no-one."

"Not even the commander?"

Blue frowned. "I think I trust him," he admitted, "don't tell him that though. The less people who know about this, the safer we will be, okay?"

"Okay, Boo-Boo, I trust you, but where will we hide it?

"Dauntless has given us the answer to that question."

"He has?"

"Yes, Annie," he said and explained his plan.

Blue Into The Rip

EPILOGUE: THE DROP

Blue floated above Saturn's huge rings. The six weeks of the Drop as part of the Patrol were now over, but Saturn Squad could not come to this part of the Solar System and fail to visit their namesake.

The Rings of Saturn. The most extensive planetary ring system of any other planet. Consisting of countless particles, ranging in size from micrometres to metres. Made from water ice and trace rocky material.

And beautiful. Never forget 'beautiful'. Other than Earth, Saturn is the most awe-wonder-sum planet in the entire Solar System.

The Patrol, headed by Second-Lieutenant Singh (who had regained his stripes), were fêted by King Wilhelm during their tour of the Asteroid Belt. Here, the King lent the Patrol his fastest light-ship—an enormous solar yacht—and treated Saturn Squad like heroes. The King's yacht, christened 'The Warrior', was plush to the extreme and Wurtz a master of sailing close to the solar wind.

The tour was the most exciting time of Blue's life and nothing at all like punishment. He had lost Eddi and Newt, but found Annie. Tongues wagged at how close Blue and Morgana had become—and to both their surprise—Corvus became quite jealous.

Blue had made a special request to Wurtz, and he flew Blue to the largest of Saturn's planetary rings and left him to float alone in space. The reason? He needed 'time to himself to think about family'. He was uncomfortable about lying to his friends, but it had to be done to keep Morgana safe. He held out the Nub on its long silver chain, his thoughts full of Eddi and Newt and their run down little house.

How many people died for such a tiny dull thing?

Blue knew it must never be found, even if Dauntless wouldn't tell him why. In a single motion, he launched the pendant towards the ring below him, where it became yet another shining iridescent facet of the billions of ice and rock particles floating in silence high above the Sixth Planet. If its whereabouts were ever discovered, it would be like trying to find a single and special grain of sand in the whole of Desert Amazon.

Sometimes, I even amaze myself, sure.

Smiling, Blue remembered his mother's last words: 'Take care of Annie for me'.

"I promise," he said into the silence of his Skin.

A short while later, the beautiful golden sail of 'The Warrior' came into view, shining in Saturn's reflected light.

"Hey, Bucko," came Corvus' voice over the Skin's radio. "You finished?"

"Yes," replied Blue. "All finished."

"Good, let's fly this crate back home."

"Yeah, I can't wait." He gazed at the awe-inspiring planet below him. "The Ringers!" he shouted, the words coming unexpectedly to his lips.

"The Ringers!" yelled Corvus, Sugar, Wurtz and, best of all, his sister Annie.

~

A Note From the Author

Many thanks for reading *Blue Into The Rip*.

If you liked Blue's story, please leave a review. Reviews are not only important for helping a potential reader make a purchasing decision, they're absolutely critical in bringing a book to that reader's attention in the first place. Quite simply, a book with more reviews (and more positive reviews) is more likely to show up in a search, in a 'Customers Who Bought This Item Also Bought' list, and are more likely to be featured or highlighted by booksellers.

A review doesn't have to be detailed or eloquent. Ten minutes of your time is all. That would be awe-wonder-sum. On the flip side, it is very rewarding to hear from readers who've enjoyed my work. It certainly helps with my motivation and might possibly stop me staring out of the window or doing any of the hundred or so things I like to do instead of writing. But seriously, I'd love to get your feedback.

K.J.Heritage

About K.J.Heritage

K.J.Heritage is a UK author of mystery/crime sci-fi and epic fantasy—all with a strong emphasis on action and adventure and occasionally a little humour.

He was born in the UK in one of the more interesting previous centuries. Originally from Derbyshire, he now lives in the seaside town of Brighton.

He is a tea drinker, Asperger's warrior, and Twitter aficionado.

Acknowledgements

Many thanks for the editing skills of *Suzanne Buist*.

Also by K.J.Heritage

SCIENCE FICTION

Vatic - a science fiction whodunit

Into The Rip Series - YA military science fiction
  Blue Into The Rip
  Blue Into The Moon (2018)

Quick-Kill and the Galactic Secret Service

The Lady In The Glass - 12 Tales Of Death & Dying

Compilations
  Once Upon A Time In Gravity City (Editor: Artie Cabrera)
  Chronicle Worlds: Legacy Fleet (Editor: Samuel Peralta)
  From The Indie Side (Editor: Michael Gatewood)

FANTASY

The Scowl (IronScythe Sagas Book 1) - epic fantasy

NON-FICTION

**THE COMPLETE INDIE EDITOR:
55 Essential Copy-edits for the Professional Independent Author.**

Get to know me!

BookBub
Check out the latest cool book deals and get an alert when I publish my next books
https://www.bookbub.com/authors/k-j-heritage

Twitter:
Now over with over 100K followers… mostly
@MostlyWriting

Facebook Group:
Mostly K.J.Heritage
Join my closed group for giveaways, first-sees, and fun discussions
https://www.facebook.com/groups/mostlykjheritage

Facebook Page:
Mostly Writing
News and book releases
https://www.facebook.com/mostlywriting/

Goodreads:
Plenty of reviews and news
https://www.goodreads.com/kjheritage

Instagram:
https://www.instagram.com/k.j.heritage/

Website:
http://kjheritage.com

News & free stuff:
No spam, I promise!
http://kjheritage.com/join/

Email:
Want to get in touch? Well here's your chance
mostlywriting@kjheritage.com

Printed in Great Britain
by Amazon